To: Jan
Merry Christmus
1986

Love,
Rob

New Fiction *from* New England

A distinctive collection of short fiction by nationally known writers, published in YANKEE *Magazine.*

Edited by Deborah Navas

YANKEE BOOKS

A DIVISION OF YANKEE PUBLISHING INCORPORATED
DUBLIN, NEW HAMPSHIRE

ACKNOWLEDGMENTS:
"In the Surprise of Life" and "The Appaloosa
House" by Sharon Sheehe Stark are excerpted
from *The Dealer's Yard and Other Stories,* © 1985
by Sharon Sheehe Stark, reprinted by permission
of William Morrow and Co. "Willow's Mysterious
Sense of Humor" by Ernest Hebert is excerpted
from *A Little More than Kin,* © 1981 by Ernest
Hebert, reprinted by permission of Viking Penguin
Inc. "Upland Game" © 1985 by Howard Frank
Mosher and "Something Might Be Gaining" ©
1983 by Howard Frank Mosher are reprinted with
permission of Don Congdon Associates Inc.
"Rue" by Susan M. Dodd is reprinted from *Old
Wives' Tales,* with permission of the University of
Iowa Press.

First Edition
Copyright 1986 by Yankee Publishing Incorporated
Printed in the United States of America

Library of Congress Catalog number: 85-51875
ISBN: 0-89909-087-7

Table of Contents

Foreword

•

BY THOMAS WILLIAMS

I S THERE A MODE, or flavor, or a set of peculiarities common to contemporary New England fiction? My first thought is that all serious writing, from anywhere, so deeply and importantly transcends the regional that the question seems a little frivolous. The difference between serious and slick fiction, however, is so vast, and so little understood, that I always find myself attending to that problem, and so I hardly ever think about fiction from New England being different from midwestern fiction or southwestern fiction or whatever fiction. Real writers use the images at their fingertips, whatever they are, to give us experience, and after that, hopefully, some truth.

Thirty years ago Henry Steele Commager, in an essay, *The Nature of American Nationalism,* said that American love of country has always been ". . . a curiously general affair, almost an abstract one. Few Ameri-

---

One of New England's most noted writers, Thomas Williams has written poetry, stories, and articles for Esquire, The New Yorker, Harper's, New American Review, *and numerous journals and anthologies. His novels are:* Ceremony of Love, Town Burning, The Night of Trees, Whipple's Castle, The Hair of Harold Roux, Tsuga's Children, *and* The Followed Man. *A new novel,* The Moon Pinnace, *will be published by Doubleday this spring.* Town Burning *was a National Book Award nominee in 1960, and* The Hair of Harold Roux *won the National Book Award in 1975. Williams is a professor of English at the University of New Hampshire.*

cans have [a] passionate attachment to a particular soil, a particular county or region. . . ." He went on to say, "We have a regional literature, but it is rather a tribute to the passing of genuine regionalism than an expression of it."

We can all spot the sentimental or patronizing local colorist, but is a "genuine expression" of regionalism actually regionalism at all? Does the serious writer ever feel regional? And I have to add that in the past 30 years, I've seen the very speech of my own state, New Hampshire, change gradually toward something like midwestern standard, as though the last generation learned as much of its tongue from Captain Kangaroo and Johnny Carson as it did from its parents and grandparents.

But having said all that, as if to declare some sort of basic critical stance, I have to admit that there is more to say. Like several of the writers in this volume, I came to New England from somewhere else, and I remember very well my Currier and Ives expectations, and the shock of a different reality. I was a child, therefore as much a prisoner as if Mohawks, those legendary raiders, had come down from the North and taken me away from an essentially egalitarian and democratic childhood to what seemed to me a dark place of social, religious, and historical demarcations and taboos. I learned about the town I've come to call, in my own fiction, Leah, in the way of wounds and small victories, and it was the first place I'd lived in that I consciously disliked. When I was old enough, I joined the Army, glad to get away. After the murky and dangerous social and familial currents of Leah, the Army with its uniforms, all insignia in plain sight, was a relief.

And yet I came back after the war, and I'm still here trying to figure this place out. New England is different; its literature is different. For instance, it is an American trait *not* to be as sensitive, socially and culturally, as New England is. Yankees are terrified of being snubbed or, worse, patronized. Sincerity is not merely appreciated, it is demanded. In a famous example given I think by Bernard DeVoto, the lost tourist leans from his car window and says, with the gruffness, possibly, of embarrassment, "I want to get to St. Johnsbury!"

After a pause, one of the men sitting on the store steps says, mildly, "We've no objection."

Which means that in this case, the "moral" transcends what could be called common human decency; sometimes the Yankee style is an incentive to cruelty. Of course, a possible reason for all this nervousness is that human relationships are considered to be of more value here than they are elsewhere. I still feel a general resistance to the "Have a nice day!" sort of vapidity, to its glib summary of existence. There *is* less of that sort of thing here than elsewhere.

But here's a slightly more subtle case, this from Robert Bryan's and Marshall Dodge's collection of Maine vignettes called *Bert and I.* It goes something like this:

> "Why're you so het up, Tom?"
> "Oh, I had to shoot my dog."
> "Was he mad?"
> "Guess he weren't so damn pleased."

It's a question of how one interprets this exchange. Do you think Tom misunderstands the question or is ignorant of the fact that "mad" means rabies? It's funny enough that way. But consider the possibility that Tom deliberately mis-answers the question. In considering what his answer will be, he rejects the comforting ordinary for a dark humor that will do better justice to his real emotion. The question, "Was he mad?" is perhaps not insincere, but it is standard, and Tom rejects the standard. He makes the exchange something of a confrontation, with its own dramatic tension (the questioner has been somewhat put down), and the dog, for whom he really grieves, has been made a twinge more real, a force of personality. Again, it's a little cruel, but harder, better.

I see the above examples as a tendency, a prickliness, a moral nudge of some kind, but especially as an attitude toward language. The stories in this volume are quite different from one another, but they are united in the quality of their language, and each acknowledges, tacitly or directly, our common mortality.

One of my favorite short stories is included here — "Walking the Trapline" by Rebecca Rule, in which cold honesty gleams from every careful sentence. It is told by a young girl who is allowed to go with her father and younger brother to check the father's trapline, and the revelation of character, of expectation, of roles chosen and not chosen, of love, casual sadism, selfishness, understanding — whatever felt complications of life there are, are here. The girl tells of her father:

> "But he was a young father just the same, with a hard jaw, all his front teeth, and blue eyes that made you feel dirty when he stared at you. Mother said I had eyes like my father and asked me what I was staring at all the time. She never asked him."

In the story is an absolute authority of *fact*. You have to believe the traps, the cold, the animals, the scent, the economics of it all; the story never patronizes its readers and is never in collusion with its readers against its characters. It is beyond all that sort of posturing.

As for *Yankee,* in which these stories first appeared, I wonder if an equivalent magazine, published somewhere else in the country, would print fiction at all these days, much less fiction that, without apology, takes us where we might not want at first to go. Maybe there is something of the aura of New England about this stubbornness, too.

Introduction

C HOOSING THE STORIES for this collection was an even more difficult job than the original selection of fiction for *Yankee.* That merely involved reading through vast piles of manuscripts, while this chore required eliminating more than half of the fine stories we've published over the past several years. Here is the result — some of the best regional fiction written today, by some of the best writers.

Peter Meinke has published seven short stories in *Yankee* — and if we had the space, we'd gladly reprint them all. The three here are excellent examples of Peter's cogent narrative style: "The Bracelet" is a favorite of ours because it was a risk (could our readers accept a geek?) and a turning point, setting a new standard by which we measured our fiction from then on. Peter's fiction and poetry have also appeared in the *Atlantic, The New Yorker,* and the *Virginia Quarterly Review,* among other noted magazines, and his most recent literary honor was a 1985 Best American Short Stories award. "Getting Rid of the Ponoes" (*Yankee,* 1982) was selected for the O. Henry Prize Stories collection for that year.

Readers of *The New Yorker* have long been familiar with Arturo Vivante's delicately turned stories, which have appeared there over the past 30 years. But he is a New Englander by territorial imperative (a resident of Wellfleet, Massachusetts) and also a longtime contributor to *Yankee.* He has had two novels and three collections of short stories published by Little, Brown and Scribner's.

Rebecca Rule teaches writing at the University of New Hampshire, and her first published story was "Walking the Trapline" with us in 1978. It is so powerful and memorable that we still talk about it in editorial meetings as a reference point for a certain type of rural survival story; you'll see why. She has since published both fiction and nonfiction in a number of literary reviews — *Boston Monthly, Penumbra,* and the *Bradford Review* among them — and *Yankee.*

Diane Coplin Hammond has had a lifelong attachment to New England, nurtured during her undergraduate years at Middlebury College, in Middlebury, Vermont. "Timepiece" reflects that attachment — conveying tremendous emotional power through restrained and understated expression that is a hallmark of our repressed New England sensibility. Her work has also appeared in the *Washington Review, Virginia Country,* and *Woman's World,* and she's currently working on a novel, *Bailing Out.*

A teacher of literature and writing at SUNY Binghamton, Barry Targan has received a panoply of awards for his writing — among them the Iowa School of Letters Award in Short Fiction, the Associated Writing Programs Award in the Novel, and inclusion in the O. Henry Prize Stories collection, 1980, for "Old Light," published in *Yankee* that year.

Sharon Sheehe Stark's originality of language knocked us over from the first story she submitted. We were the first commercial magazine (i.e., pays real money) to publish her work, which has also appeared in about 15 literary magazines and quarterlies over the past three years. Two stories were chosen for the Best American Short Stories collection, 1983 and 1985; and William Morrow brought out her first collection, *The Dealer's Yard and Other Stories* (including the two here, published in *Yankee*), in 1985. She is now finishing her first novel, *A Wrestling Season.*

Edward Gale is a Vermonter whose stories reflect an intimate knowledge of rural life in the shadow of the Green Mountains. But "The Sound from Inside" is not a pastoral rural story by any means. Besides *Yankee,* Gale's work has also been published in the *Burlington Review.*

Kim Yong Ik was born in a small southern Korean seaport and educated there as well as in Japan and the United States. In "The Sheep, Jimmy and I" he observes upper-middle-class New Englanders from the perspective of a cultural outsider, with refreshing innocence and telling candor. His fiction has appeared in the *Atlantic, The New Yorker, The Hudson Review, Harper's Bazaar,* and other noteworthy magazines.

Marcia Yudkin writes both fiction and nonfiction, and her work has been published in *The New York Times, The Boston Globe, Psychology*

Today, and *Ms.* A resident of Northampton, Massachusetts, she drew from her musical knowledge as an amateur flutist in writing "Doors Made to Order."

Howard Frank Mosher is the voice and interpreter of the Northeast Kingdom by way of his mythical Kingdom County, Vermont. His characters are larger than life, as is the wild region he describes in works from Viking such as *Disappearances* (1977), *Where the Rivers Flow North* (1978), and *Marie Blythe* (1983).

Elinor Lipman grew up in Lowell, Massachusetts, and teaches in the Communications Department of Simmons College. "Catering" and "The Fling" were the first stories she published, quickly followed by other publications in *Ascent, Cosmopolitan, The Ladies' Home Journal, Playgirl,* and several magazines in England and Australia. "The Fling" was listed in the Distinguished Story citations in the Best American Short Stories collection, 1984.

Ernest Hebert is a native of Keene, New Hampshire, where he "never did well in English." He has made a living with words nonetheless, as a newspaper reporter, columnist for *The Boston Sunday Globe,* and novelist: *The Dogs of March* (1979), *A Little More than Kin* (1982), and *Whisper My Name* (1984), all from Viking. Ernie's beat is rural New England, more specifically, the mythical town of Darby, New Hampshire, somewhere in the vicinity of Keene. His characters, though inexorably bound to their landscape of tar-paper shacks with decomposing auto bodies in the yard, transcend their worldly constraints in moving, funny, and original ways.

Daniel Asa Rose lives in Rehoboth, Massachusetts, with his two young sons. He writes distinguished fiction for us as well as for *The New Yorker, Partisan Review, Southern Review,* and *North American Review,* among other magazines. One of his stories appeared in the O. Henry Prize Stories collection, 1980.

A University of New Hampshire graduate, Carrie Sherman went out to the University of Iowa's Writer's Workshop for her MFA and then returned to her home state to teach at UNH. "Elmo's Fire" is true to New England, too, to our language and to our closet class distinctions such as natives vs. summer people.

Alan Sternberg is a fiction writer and journalist who has held a wide variety of newspaper jobs, most recently at the *Hartford Courant.* He has had two stories published by us and also fiction and nonfiction in *Northeast Magazine.*

Annette Sanford taught high-school English for 25 years and then turned to writing, with a vengeance. Her stories have appeared in numerous national magazines such as *Yankee, Redbook,* and *McCall's,* and in literary magazines — among them the *Ohio Review, Prairie Schooner,* and *North American Review.* A story of hers appeared in the *Best American Short Stories,* 1979. She also writes original paperbacks under another name.

M. Garrett Bauman has published several dozen stories and essays, and he's won two national awards for his writing. He teaches literature and writing at Monroe Community College in Rochester, New York, and summers on the Maine coast and on Cape Cod, where he and his wife plan to build a home soon.

Susan M. Dodd teaches for the graduate writing programs at Vermont College and the University of Iowa and has had a number of stories published in literary magazines, including *Ascent, Epoch,* and *Northeast.* "Rue" is included in a collection of stories that won the 1984 Iowa School of Letters Short Fiction Award and was published under the title *Old Wives' Tales* by the Iowa Press. A novel will be coming out with Viking Penguin this spring.

"The Odor of Fish" was William Evans's first published story and is so true to small coastal Maine communities that we felt it must surely be autobiographical. It wasn't, Will mentioned to me a year or two later — but he had carefully researched it. Carefully indeed.

Ian MacMillan teaches fiction writing at the University of Hawaii and is a prolific writer of short fiction. He's had some 30 stories in print and has received numerous awards, one of which was the 1979 Associated Writing Programs Award for Short Fiction for a collection entitled *Light and Power: Stories,* published in 1978 by The University of Missouri Press. He has also had short fiction in *Best American Short Stories,* 1982, and *Best of Triquarterly.*

Kathleen Leverich is the editor in chief of the Children's Book Department for Addison-Wesley and is a regular contributor to the book review sections of *The New York Times* and the *Christian Science Monitor.* Her stories have been in *Yankee, Cosmopolitan,* and the *Christian Science Monitor,* among other places.

Deborah Navas
Fiction Editor, *Yankee*

The Bracelet

•

BY PETER MEINKE

A T FIRST SHE HAD felt like a white fleck of foam in a black sea. She would bob along the crowded streets of the old cloth market in Ibadan, looking at the bolts of bright fabrics piled higher than her head in front of the open shops lining the narrow dirt thoroughfares. She had been afraid to buy any of the beautiful material with the mysterious names — *adire, adinkra, kente, kyemfre* — because she didn't know how to haggle over prices and didn't want to pay too much. So she would just flow along with the crowd, small and wide-eyed, the lanes sometimes so jammed that her feet would be lifted from the ground and she'd be carried like a piece of driftwood with the tide.

But that was 10 years ago. She had come to Nigeria as an archaeologist working on her Ph.D. from Harvard. She had done some reading on the Old Kingdoms of the Yoruba and wanted to study them firsthand, particularly the Kingdom of Oyo, one of the traditional centers of Nigerian culture. Ibadan had seemed the natural place to go, an important market city with a new university; and it was less than 20 miles from Oyo, where slaves and eunuchs were still reputed to guard the Oba's palace.

When she arrived, Sally Warren was 24 years old. She was shy and quiet; at the same time, nothing much frightened her. She had clear, brown eyes in a no-nonsense face that she didn't waste time gazing at.

Her plan had been to spend a year or two researching the Kingdom of Oyo and then return to Cambridge and write her thesis. And then she

13

supposed she'd get married. Her fiance Jim was opposed to the trip entirely; he had wanted to get married right away. There was nothing wrong with Jim: he was fine, he was ambitious, he played a decent game of tennis. He was the type of young faculty member who was sure to advance, get tenure, and become chairman of his department. He had it all planned. Eventually they would have two baby archaeologists, a boy and a girl.

Sally was a reflective woman, but not a complaining one, even to herself, so the first time she realized that Jim bored her was when she was flying to Africa. They were flying over the vast expanse of the Sahara Desert; for an hour she looked at the unchanging, almost colorless sand. *Why, that's just like Jim,* she thought, and crossed him off.

Perhaps that was why Africa had given her such an enormous sense of freedom. She had no sooner taken a room at the University than her past years washed away like so many ridges of sand at high tide. Her room, on the second floor of the dormitory, was tiny: a bed, a desk, a wardrobe. An open passageway ran in front of it; she could bring a chair out there and look into the white flowers of a large frangipani tree growing in the courtyard next to the building. In the evening its jasmine-like fragrance flooded her room and she could think of nothing but the fragrance itself. That was what Africa was like to her: it demanded attention to the texture of her life.

For some time she pursued her studies at the University, with occasional field trips to Oyo, always made with great difficulty because of the irregularity of the bus system. To stay overnight in one of the cheap hotels was uncomfortable; she would be the only woman there, a white woman walking through a maze of small rooms where men sat silently drinking palm wine or chewing on kola nuts. At least they were always silent as she walked by, and even when she lay alone in her bed, she seemed to feel them staring at her, their gazes a positive weight on her skin.

So her studies became diffused. As she got to know people at the University, some of whom had cars, she began visiting whatever places they were driving to. If they were going to Oyo, good; if they were going somewhere else, like Abeokuta or Oshogbo, that was good too: off she went. She was learning a great deal about the Yoruba in general but not making much progress on the research for her thesis.

She made one marvelous find, by accident. She had been taken by one of the professors in the Institute of African Studies to visit an old shrine for Shango, the God of Thunder, which had been destroyed in a war but was still regarded as a holy place. It was outside of Meko, and the

14

jungle had almost reclaimed it. On the way back from the shrine, she had gone off the overgrown trail to look at a small crimson flower she saw glowing in the shadows. As she knelt down by the flower, her eye was caught by what seemed to be a tin can buried in the ground. When she pulled it up and brushed off the dirt and leaf-mold, she found it was a brass bracelet about six inches high, with intricately wrought figures and a series of small bells attached to either end.

Her companion was greatly excited. At first he thought it was ancient, but as they cleaned it he decided the bracelet must be between 50 and 75 years old, one of the ornate decorations worn by the priestesses of Shango or some related deity. He wanted Sally to bring it to the Institute for appraisal.

"This is a fine discovery, Miss Warren, you're very lucky."

"I'll polish it up," she said, "and bring it over later."

But when she took it back to her room and worked on it for several hours, using a bottle cleaner, brass polish, and finally her toothbrush, she found she didn't want to give it up or even let it out of her hands. The bracelet was a perfect fit, feeling heavy and snug on her sturdy arm. There was a long mirror on the inside of her wardrobe door; she stood in front of it with the bracelet on, and then slowly took off her clothes and looked at herself for a long time. *Maybe I'm going off my rocker,* she thought, and smiled. But she began doing this every night, sleeping naked under the mosquito netting, wearing only the bracelet.

The months were sliding by. She made two good friends, both of them dancers, with whom she would take her meals in the University dining hall. Andrew Cage was a 30-year-old Englishman who had studied medicine at Oxford and switched to dance late in his student career. He had danced with several of the major companies in England and America and had come to Ibadan two years ago to study African dance. Like Sally, he found much that fascinated him, but his specific studies went slowly. Unlike Sally, however, whose money was running out, Andrew seemed to have a decent independent income, and indeed he often paid for all three of them when they went out together.

The other dancer was Manu Uchendu. Manu was the son of a chief of one of the larger villages in northern Nigeria. Despite his small stature, he was a commanding presence: slow and oracular in talk, dignified and erect in carriage, he looked the part of a chief. His eyes were deep set and yet prominent, almost popeyed. *High blood pressure,* said Andrew. But he inspired confidence; when Manu spoke in his measured, musical tones, people edged forward to listen.

15

When Andrew spoke, people tended to laugh. He was cynical and worldly, and often drunk. Sally thought he might be homosexual. Once she asked him why he had never married.

"It's the old story," he told Sally. "I loved her. She loved her." And that was all she could get out of him on the subject. But he was careful not to be alone with her at night. One evening Sally brought him to her room to see the bracelet; he was edgy and uncomfortable.

"Yes," he said, when she put it on. "You're a natural priestess. I wish you'd put a curse on old Millers." Millers was the stuffy director of Andrew's dance project. "May his tongue swell and his genitals wither." But he wouldn't sit down in those close quarters. He went out on the passageway and stared at the frangipani tree trembling in the moonlight.

One Sunday Manu told them that the fetish priest of a small village near Oshogbo was going to perform, that this was "the real thing" and they should try to see it. "We'll have to bring him some sort of gift, like a bottle of schnapps, that's customary."

"I've got a bottle of Gilbey's gin," said Andrew. "I can teach him how to make a martini."

"Gin will be all right; just let me handle it."

They drove in Andrew's car. The village consisted of several clusters of mud-brick huts with rusted corrugated tin roofs sprawled around an open market. One cluster enclosed a small courtyard where a crowd of villagers, mostly women, were already assembled. Manu spoke to one of the elders, who placed the gin by a large handcarved chair with wooden snakes forming the legs and arms. The three visitors sat down at the edge of the circle of people.

Four drummers had been playing softly in the background; now their beat became faster and more insistent. The crowd stirred as the priest entered the compound. He was a little old man completely covered with a gray claylike substance, snakes wrapped around his neck, wrists, ankles. There was something wrong with his face: eyes and mouth twitching, limbs trembling. "Parkinson's disease," murmured Andrew. The priest sat in the chair, one gray leg still shaking violently, and received gifts from the village women: yams, cloth, pineapples, a large white chicken. He brandished a pair of brushes, made of cowtails; beside him a young man held a basin of white powder. As each woman presented her gift, she would touch the ground in front of the priest, and he would chant to her, dipping the cowtails in the powder and brushing her shoulders.

"He is curing sickness," Manu whispered. "And barrenness and bad luck. He can do it only when he's possessed."

16

"I don't feel well myself," said Andrew. "I could use some of that gin."

Sally was spellbound. She was trying to commit every detail to memory. She wondered if she would be frightened if this were at night.

The drums became more and more excited. Suddenly the priest stood up and began to dance, stamping and shuffling in a circular motion. He took a banana and rubbed it over his face and body, then did the same thing with several eggs. Now his young helper handed him the fluttering chicken. The drummers leaped up and began playing in a frenzy; the priest whirled around, swinging the chicken over his head. He stretched the chicken to its full length and sank his teeth into its neck, tearing at it until he put the chicken's head into his mouth and bit it off. Blood streamed down his neck and torso. Still dancing wildly, he again swung the chicken around, ripping off its wings and legs, blood spattering the spectators.

As the tempo of the drummers slowed, he turned and stopped in front of Sally. Without hesitation she stood up, then touched the ground with both hands as she had seen the women do. He brushed her shoulders with the white powder, chanted for a minute, and it was over.

Back in the car, they were silent for a long time. After a while Sally asked, "What did he say to me?"

"He wished you good health and asked the gods to watch over you here in Nigeria," said Manu.

"It turned my stomach," said Andrew. "I've read about geeks in American carnivals, old winos who bite the heads off chickens for a few drinks. I don't know how you stood up when he came to you."

But Sally was elated. She felt that she had done the right thing, that something significant had happened.

Not long after, Manu became Sally's lover. He seemed to expect it; he didn't press her. They were in her room, talking about her plans, about the experience with the fetish priest; she was wearing the bracelet. When he held out his hands, she went to him, her body pushing at him of its own volition while her mind thought *Why not?*

It didn't seem to make any difference in her life. They were careful; she wasn't swept away by passion. Sally had learned long ago to dismiss all generalizations: they were fine, you needed them to hold a decent conversation, but they never applied to a particular case, to her case (even this generalization, she realized, was suspect: perhaps some did apply to her case). Jim had been a great generalizer; he had theories about everything. But she had never understood theories. As soon as she uttered or wrote

17

one, the exceptions would crowd into her mind like a mob of unruly children clamoring for attention. This trait wasn't helping her write her thesis.

Soon, one day at a time, the year disappeared. Harvard renewed her scholarship for a year, but even so she was hard-pressed for money. Jim's letters, frequent at first, slowed down to a trickle, though he threatened to fly to Ibadan to find out what was wrong with her. But Sally was sure he would never do such an extravagant thing, even for love.

After about a year and a half at the University, she began looking for a job. She worked for a while as a cataloguer in the University Museum: this wasn't bad work, but consumed a lot of time. Work on her thesis had virtually stopped.

Then one afternoon Andrew came in with a great announcement. He had discovered a large abandoned house outside of Oshogbo, near the Oshun River. Years ago many people in the house had died of the plague, and the natives believed it to be inhabited by evil spirits. But the chief of that district paid a man and his wife to guard the house, and they lived in a little hut on the same property. Andrew was sure that if Manu would speak to the chief, Sally could live in the house for nothing; they could fix it up for her. It was the perfect place for an archaeologist as there were many shrines, both active and abandoned, in the area around the river.

Gradually, it was all arranged. Near the end of the second year of her stay, Sally moved into the Oshogbo house. It was a three-story affair, with an ornately carved roof and a porch on the second floor as well as the first. A dirt road around three miles long joined it to the main highway leading into Oshogbo, and it was less than an hour's drive from Ibadan and Oyo. The three friends painted it, fixed the windows, and chased away the family of monkeys living on the third floor. They stocked it with food from the University commissary, and Andrew brought over what looked like a five-year supply of bandages and other medical provisions, and a ten-year supply of candles.

For a short while Andrew and Manu stayed with Sally, Andrew sleeping in a room on the first floor, and Manu and Sally sharing the master bedroom on the second. They swam (and washed) in the slow-flowing river, explored the territory and the neighboring shrines, and in the evening danced by candlelight in the large and empty main room on the ground floor.

It was a good time, but when the men left to return to their studies, Sally looked around at her house and felt strangely exultant. She thought that she always knew that people were essentially alone, and she liked it that way. She remembered being puzzled by movies and books in which men were punished by being placed in solitary confinement.

"That wouldn't be me at all," she said to a large green and orange lizard. "I'd prefer it." And she raised her arms and whirled around the room, the bracelet picking up the candlelight and refracting it on the ceiling and walls as she danced.

A few days after Manu and Andrew left, Sally heard activity in the courtyard. A man and woman were erecting a series of bamboo poles near the native hut. These must be the caretakers who were not in evidence when she moved in; Sally hurried down to greet them. The woman turned slowly around and bowed her head. She was a large woman, a head taller than Sally, and her hands and feet were stained a dark blue. Her name was Vida; she and her husband Ayi had gone into Oshogbo when Andrew's car appeared and had just today decided it was safe to return.

By now Sally could speak some Yoruba, and Vida knew a little English from three years in a government school, so they were able to communicate without difficulty. Ayi was a farmer who worked a small plot of land about two miles from the house. He planted mostly yams, but also grew corn and beans and sometimes melons. Ayi even owned several kola trees and sold kola nuts as his main cash crop.

Vida brought in some money by making the traditional Yoruba cloth called *adire*, which accounted for her blue hands and feet. One reason she and Ayi stayed on a place thought by most to be haunted was the great profusion of the *elu* plant on the property. Vida would take the fresh green leaves of the plant and pound them into a blackish pulp, making a high pile of dye balls about the size of tennis balls. Sally was fascinated by the whole process of dyeing and soon was helping Vida regularly with her work. Andrew or Manu would arrive for a visit and find her tying or folding the lengths of white cotton that Vida would then dip in the large dye pots half buried in the ground. Around the courtyard, strips of the beautiful indigo blue fabric with their intricate designs were drying on the bamboo poles.

"I love doing this," she told Andrew. "I could do this forever. I can already tie the osubamba design." She pointed to some drying panels with large white circles surrounded by many small ones. "Big moons and little moons."

"That's all very well," said Andrew, "but I'm not sure how I'll like you with blue hands and feet." The *adire* dye was very hard to get off; the ground by Vida's hut was stained a permanent blue.

Sally tried to get Ayi and Vida to move into the house with her, but

19

they would have none of it. They thought Sally especially blessed by the gods to be able to live in the house unscathed. In fact, it was clear they saw their roles as handservants to her: Ayi brought her food from the farm, Vida cooked it; once every four days they would clean the first floor of the house for her, though it scarcely needed it. They wouldn't go upstairs, and they wouldn't enter the house if Sally weren't in it. They had set ideas as to what kind of work was appropriate for her. It was fine for Sally to work hard tying and folding the *adire* designs and helping with the dyeing process in general, but they didn't like her to carry things, to cook, to sweep, to pound the yams and cassava for the *foofoo* that was their staple meal. In a very short time a peaceable and efficient routine was established.

Sally liked walking to the cloth market outside of Oshogbo, where Vida would sell their work and buy the raffia string and the white cotton they used. One afternoon on the way back from the market, she met a woman with a sick child.

"She's burning up with fever," Sally said, her hand on the child's dry forehead. She brought them home with her and treated the child as best she could — she had learned a lot from Andrew — giving clear directions to the mother for continued treatment. A few weeks later the woman returned and left two large water pots on the porch. As the year progressed, there were more of these incidents; sometimes women from the small neighboring village would bring their children to the house. They were afraid of the large hospital in Oshogbo, though they would go there if Sally told them to; and they would never stay in her house.

"They think you're a priestess of Oshun," Manu told her, looking at the pots, carvings, little brass figures, and river-worn stones that were collecting on her porch. "Oshun is the Venus of Yoruba, almost as light-skinned as you; if she feels like it she can cause dysentery, stomachache, stuff like that. She was one of the wives of Shango, you know, very famous for her lovemaking."

Sally smiled. "Well let's see if I qualify," and they went upstairs.

Manu had studied the art of divination and he taught the rudiments of it to Sally, using 16 kola nuts, which could be thrown or arranged in any number of combinations. In college, Sally had learned to do the *I Ching,* and this was similar; she memorized the verses and chants for the different combinations with great ease. "You're a born diviner, a *babalawo*," he told her. "It's in your bones."

Sally believed in it, in her own way. She thought it as good a way of regulating one's life as any other. She remembered reading about one of those English archaeologists with the hyphenated names like Pritchard-Evans or Evans-Pritchard, who lived with a tribe somewhere that made its decisions by poisoning chickens with a poison called *benje* and then deciphering the circular patterns in which the chickens ran as they died. The Englishman had lived this way himself for a year and claimed it was about as efficient as trying to reason things out. (Shall I go to market today? Shall I plant my vegetables? Should I marry Alice when I return?)

In this way, time had gone placidly by, like the Oshun River flowing by her house. Tonight, holding Jim's letter in her hand and looking back on her 10 years in Africa, Sally had difficulty remembering what had happened when. Andrew was dead, she knew that; he had gone back to England and then died. And she hadn't seen Manu for a long time: he had returned to his village in the North to become chief. He told Sally she could be one of his wives anytime she wanted. She thanked him and thought she'd rather not.

"You could be one of my husbands, though."

"Yes, I'd like that." But it had been several years since she had a visit from Manu. Now her house was truly like a shrine, surrounded on all sides with the artifacts of Yoruba life and religion. The monkeys had moved back in to the third floor and were her pets. At night they would look out the windows when the young men stood before the house, silent in the moonlight; occasionally, the door would open, and one would enter.

The University had long since severed its connection with Sally, so she had been totally surprised a month ago when its mail truck came bouncing down their road with a thick letter from Jim and one from her father. Sally's mother had died, and they wanted Sally to come home; her mother had left her $10,000. It seemed strange to her that she had parents; they had never captured her imagination, one way or the other. Jim hadn't married; he had been engaged (*engaged?* Sally could barely understand the word) several times, but it had never worked out: he was a disappointed man. He wanted to see Sally again. When she opened the mail her hand trembled; she didn't know how she felt. After reading the letters, she took out her 16 cowry shells and began to arrange them, searching for an attitude. She loved the small, brightly colored shells that someone had left for her to do her divinations with. She would hold them in her hands for hours, their smooth, highly polished surfaces somehow comforting her, joining her with the hypnotic rhythms of the sea. But the shells had said nothing but "Wait," and so she hadn't answered the letters.

And now Jim's second letter had arrived today. He and her father were at the University and would be coming to get her tomorrow. They were terribly worried, they had heard awful stories, and they feared for her very life. Sally smiled as she read this.

The moon was caught in the branches of the God-tree, the three-forked tree leaning over the river, which flowed silently and irresistibly toward the great ocean. She walked upstairs to her room and stood for some time looking at her face in the mirror. She piled her long hair on top of her head. She was wearing one of her *osubamba* cloths around her waist; multicolored beads that the women had left for her hung between her naked breasts, and the bracelet felt cool and solid on her arm. Then she took out the narrow file she had borrowed from Vida and began filing her front teeth into the traditional M-shaped gap of Yoruba women.

Conversation with a Pole

•

BY PETER MEINKE

I HAVE ALWAYS BEEN an excellent drinker, proud of my capacity for downing large quantities of the old elixir without getting a slur in my voice, like Shcott Wilshon of Panasonix, or knocking over ashtray stands like Pete Weaver did regularly when we left the club (he always pretended not to notice, though sometimes he positively limped out the door: must have been somebody else. Maybe Old Man Hotchkiss over there on the other side of the room!). Of course, most men nowadays are proud of their capacities; it's one of the New Frontiers. The action today isn't in the Wild West, but in the Business Lunch, and instead of shoot-outs, we have drink-outs: may the best man win. It's no accident that those short lethal drinks are called *shots,* that we get *bombed* and *blasted;* even the later *stoned* and *paralyzed* imply a violent metaphor. It also works the other way: *Molotov cocktails.* At any rate, you can see the relationship — drinks are like weapons, weapons are like drinks. I have come out of many a lunch drink-out with a fat contract in my pocket, leaving the victim pale and perspiring, or staggering foolishly through a parking lot, looking for the company car, which may or may not be a black Chrysler.

Alcohol has always been a friend I could count on, unlike most of my other friends. Life in the business world is no picnic, and just when you need someone is the time he generally picks to disappear. They transfer, and you have to work with someone new, who has his own friends. They

23

get promoted or demoted. They become unavailable. But alcohol is always available, and adjustable to your needs. What could be better than a cold beer after a set of tennis? Or a good cognac by the fireplace? It's raining outside and you look at your lady and she smiles that special smile and comes to sit next to you, leaning in your arms, sipping from your glass. Or an ice-cold martini while the smell of steak is coming from the kitchen — no, from your outside grill — and the martini and the liver pâté and stuffed mushrooms and shrimp cocktail all go to the back of your neck and untie that knot that seemed permanent until this very moment and you smile thankfully and look at your guests and realize what wonderful people they really are, and you tell them so. Or a Bloody Mary on hung-over Sunday mornings, followed by eggs Benedict and a dry Chablis. I mean, isn't that what life's all about?

When I was in business, I was famous for my lunches and dinner parties, and the purchasing agents fell over themselves trying to get invitations. They would give orders for things they didn't want or wouldn't need for a year, just to visit the club or get a shot at my wife's onion soup and the good Bordeaux that went with it. My two kids, bless them, were just growing up then, and they would hang around, looking like angels, emptying ashtrays and bringing out the hors d'oeuvres. I remember particularly one night, old Bill McShane, the head buyer for McClintock's, and a hard man, a real hard man to please, just sat back around midnight and said, Charlie, you win. I already told Gustafson I'd buy his stuff instead of yours, but I'll cancel the order tomorrow. This has been something else. He had downed about seven manhattans, a bottle of Burgundy with dinner, and was now tapering off with brandy. Lots of people reacted that way; my wife and I would glance at each other then, surreptitiously, and practically wink. It made it all worthwhile. I don't think McShane ever changed that order though. He was one of the toughest men in the business.

I worked for Prince and Co., mainly in adhesives. It's a good field, still expanding, and Prince is the best in the field, if I do say so myself. We make compounds that will hold anything together, any combination: rubber-to-wood, paper-to-metal, plastic-to-rubber, even metal-to-metal. You wouldn't believe it would hold, but it does. Think of everything that needs some sort of adhesive compound. From one point of view, without them our entire modern world would fall apart: houses, furniture, cars, airplanes, telephones, not to mention your ordinary boxes of food and other goods. My wife has literary pretensions; she reads a lot, Book-of-the-Month and all that — she used to sneak some of the professors from our hick local college into our dinner parties, for social uplift she said, but the poor buggers would gulp down the free drinks and puff on my cigars and pass out before dinner, so she stopped doing it. Anyway, sometimes we'd be having a little spat, and I'd be sitting there, swirling a snifter of Armagnac, and she'd shout Charlie, stop that! You're just a goddamn *glue* salesman! And I would say, Patricia — never call her Pat if you value your life — Patricia, without glue all your goddamn books would fall apart tomorrow, what do you think of that?

But then we'd make up, and that was always fun. Patricia is a remarkable person. Like most men, I married out of a sheer lack of confidence, but I was lucky. When it was time for me to marry, I married the one who was in love with me at that time, and that was Patricia; the thought that someone else would ever fall in love with me never entered my mind. She was a lit major from Goucher College, but she still looked like the curvy blonde cheerleader she had been in high school. Her skin was so pale and smooth it was a pleasure just to run my finger over her cheekbone or down the smooth curve of her calf just above the ankle. I was nothing but a glorified stock boy in those days. I knew I wanted to sell and also knew I needed experience and not college to do it; but we had no idea in those goodbad old days of hamburger and cheap beer in returnable bottles that I would rise so fast in the company. In six years I had the largest territory in Connecticut and a lovely old home in Hartford; in 10 years we had an elegant sloop named Asharah that we kept at Watch Point on which we'd entertain during long, sunburned weekends. Those were the days! The sloop was named after some Phoenician sea goddess Patricia had read about, but when I painted it on, I misspelled it — it should have been Asherah — and for a few weeks she was mad and after me to repaint it. But after a while we got to like it: it seemed more original somehow. That's what it was like in those days: even our mistakes turned out right.

Right now the snow is coming down hard outside my window, almost like hail, and I feel a long way from Watch Point. In general, snow has a softening effect on this city, covering the dirty sidewalks, rounding the harsh corners of the apartment buildings. It brings out the kids on their sleds in a nearby vacant lot, and I like to go out and watch them, but my legs aren't what they used to be so I don't go out as much anymore. I can watch the people hurrying into Mac's grocery story or ducking into the Cloverleaf Bar for a quick beer or a game on the bowling machine. I like to lie here and smoke and think. It's comfortable. Did you ever notice how smoke rises in the air but sinks in a bottle? That's right; if you hold a cigarette in your hand, the smoke rises and disperses into the upper regions (except maybe at the Cloverleaf, where the air is thicker than chowder), but if you hold a cigarette down in a bottle, the smoke sinks and curls to the bottom like a net in water. Strange.

But what I wanted to tell you about was this conversation I had with a Polish engineer. It was an important conversation for me; in fact, it led to everything else that happened. I can not only remember every word of it, I can remember, word for word, various variations that might have occurred and led to completely different conclusions. Over the past five years, I have put together a series of possible conversations and followed the implications out to places far, far away from Mac's grocery and the Cloverleaf Bar. One even took me to Warsaw, where I lived in the Old Town in the shadow of the castle Gorska told me about and gave advice to the Party leaders on what adhesives to use: Gorska said they need men like me in Poland. But unfortunately, the conversation didn't go that way, and I've spent a lot of time thinking about why. That's one of the pleasures of retirement: time to think. I wish to God I had studied philosophy somewhere along the line. I often feel I'm on the verge of something really important, something about the way our lives go one way and our thoughts go another, and we're caught barefoot in a no-man's land, where the ground is covered by broken stained-glass windows from old bombed-out cathedrals. That was an actual dream I had once. What it means, I wish I knew.

His name was Zbigniew Gorska — I still have his card. Despite the fact that our national security adviser has the same first name, Zbigniew is tough to pronounce, so everyone called him Bishek, which was funny enough. He was something less than medium height, neat, almost dapper, and curiously young-looking. I had been told he had fought with a troop of boy scouts in the Warsaw Uprising, so I figured the youngest he could be was 45, a year younger than me. But I've always looked mature for my age: I was six foot two when I was 14, and my hair was gray by 35. I think it helped me make sales, and even when I was 15 the older boys would send me in to buy their six-packs: I had a better chance of getting served. Now I was sitting at the Blue Horse Inn with a foreigner who was my age but looked like my son.

Also, I was nervous. I usually take directors or purchasing agents out to dinner, not engineers, but this was a special case, and a big order crucial to the company hinged on the outcome. Frankly, things had not been going too well for me for a year or so, and I'd been called into the office a few times to explain my decreasing sales. But the adhesive business is simply getting more competitive each year, as I explained to Roland

Prince, Jr., a short, stocky man with about half the brains of his father despite having graduated from Wharton Business School. The father and I had been very close, and when he kicked over — out on the golf course, not a bad way to go, except he fell in the water hole: for old time's sake everyone said — I knew Prince & Co. would never be the same for me again. At any rate, at this time I wasn't the only one having trouble, because sales were down all across the country, so when Bill Bishop made a huge sale to ATX Electronics involving the aircraft business and a government contract, everyone was happy because it eased the pressure across the board. But something went wrong, and their engineers told their purchasing department that our product wasn't the best one for the job. I knew it was — I had made a sale, on a much smaller scale, and it worked perfectly. That was why Prince told me to take out the engineer. — You've done it before, Charlie, he told me. Take him to the best place in town. Snow him. Take it easy on the booze, but snow him. This is important, Charlie. You know how to do it.

I won't say that Prince exactly threatened me, but as I said, I was nervous. The Blue Horse is the poshest restaurant in Hartford — you practically have to wade through the carpet — and I got there a half hour early to make sure of a good table. I told them to put a couple of bottles of vodka on ice and was on my third martini by the time Gorska came in. We hit it off right away, though he was a serious type; and I was feeling pretty good. You're not the engineer who invented the Polish parachute? I asked him.

— The one that opens on impact? No. He smiled slightly. I guess he had heard all the Polish jokes.

We were drinking vodka straight because that's what he had ordered: I had guessed right. Anyway, toss an olive in an ice-cold glass of vodka and what do you have? A Polish martini, and not bad either. The Blue Horse featured a Czechoslovakian beer called Pilsner Urquell, and when I suggested that as a chaser, Gorska said that was a good idea. I liked him, a man after my own heart. We got to talking about drinking habits. He always drank vodka straight, but usually here in the States the vodka wasn't served cold enough. In Poland the vodka was better, too; he drank a brand called Zytnia: I had him write it on his card because I'm interested in that sort of thing.

— You Poles are supposed to be real drinkers, I told him. Everyone says, Never try to drink with a Pole.

— We drink too much, he agreed, but not like you Americans. We usually drink only when we eat. What did your Hemingway say? It's a way of ending the day?

— Yes. Well, my wife would know about that. She's a great reader. I think it's a pretty good way of starting the day, too. I raised my glass and smiled at Gorska, and he smiled back. Maybe he had a sense of humor after all. But he really was stuffing in the food, skinny as he was. I wasn't too hungry myself. I was feeling lightheaded, with that wonderful sense of clarity that drink can sometimes give you. Even my vision seemed sharper, and the face of the waiter as he brought us the bottles was like some old portrait where every line, every shadow, had a life and story of its own. His cheekbones alone told me he had spent a miserable childhood.

— Seriously, Gorska said, you Americans must drink every day. You wait all day for the cocktail hour. When it comes close to that time, your face lights up and you make your martini and you sit down and say Aah! Doesn't that mean you're alcoholics?

— We don't *have* to drink every day. We *like* to drink. It's practically a health food. We relax. It's fun.

— But you *do* drink every day! He was beginning to get a little irritating, and I was glad to detect a slight slur in his voice. What's the difference between having to and wanting to, as long as you do it? When was the last day you *didn't* have a drink? he asked, and sat back like some goddamn prosecuting attorney.

I tried to think, but who keeps track of things that you *don't* do? He smiled broadly, exposing a set of discolored teeth.

— If you drank more, I said, your teeth wouldn't be so bad.

He covered them up. — You still haven't answered my question.

— I could stop any time I wanted to, I said firmly. In fact, I probably won't have a thing tomorrow. As I said this, I remembered we were supposed to go to the Martins' for cocktails, and for some reason this infuriated me. Suddenly it seemed hard to breathe, and Gorska's complacent face appeared to float across the table like some obscene Halloween balloon.

— You still haven't answered my question, he repeated. When was the last day that you didn't have any drink at all?

I suppose at that time I had been hanging by a thin emotional thread. I was tired — I hadn't slept well in weeks — and nervous, and the combination of these things with this infuriating cross-examination as if I were back in Townsend High School with its collection of vicious and sadistic teachers, all of this, simply, caused that thread to snap. Even so, I reacted reasonably calmly. I reached out, slowly — in actual slow motion, it seemed to me — and grabbed his tie. I pulled his head toward me, dragging his tie through the unspeakable goulash he had chosen to eat.

— Listen, you stupid Polack, I said in a low voice, get off my back and stay off. I meant to say, I'll drink when I want and *not* drink when I want, but I never got it out. Gorska jerked back, and somehow, as I released his tie, my chair fell over backward, and I was lying on my back in the deep-piled carpet of the Blue Horse.

It was a disaster, of course. The waiter helped me up, everyone staring, and mumbled something I couldn't understand. I brushed him away, walked directly to the cloakroom, got my coat, and left the restaurant. Only when I got out in the fresh air I remembered I hadn't paid the bill, which I knew would be a whopper: the Blue Horse had fancy prices, especially on its liquor. Well, that was Gorska's problem; my problem was, we hadn't even begun to talk about adhesives.

Patricia didn't seem surprised to see me home early. She was working in the yard, which she loved to do. I poured me a whiskey, then changed my mind and dumped it in the sink. I sat by the window, looking out at our beautiful azaleas, and as usual I was disappointed. Their bloom lasts so short a time, we wait for it so long, we build up in our minds such an image of impossible beauty and fragrance that the actual imperfect presence of these fragile flowers is always anticlimactic. It's similar to what we do with our children: such energy, effort, and emotion are invested in them that we take it as a personal affront when they don't measure up to our totally imaginary and ridiculous expectations.

I was already replaying the conversation with the Pole and worrying how I would explain it to Prince. But mainly I was thinking, maybe Gorska was right; I shouldn't drink so much, I should get some exercise, golf or something. I really wasn't in good shape. In fact, my doctor — old Benbow, who never said you actually *had* to do anything, he was of the permissive school — had recently suggested that I cut down on drinking and smoking.

— On both of them? I asked, winking at him. What will you want me to cut out next?

He didn't wink back. — I'll let you know, he said. That'll be twenty dollars.

And I still might do it, but every time I think of starting (of stopping, rather), I think of my grandfather, old Grandpa who grew up on beer and cigars in Schweinfurt, Germany, and sustained himself on American whiskey until he was 88, working right to the end (illegally, I'm sure) as a night watchman in Bridgeport. Of course, he didn't like cigarettes. Put out them stinkaroos, he'd tell me, passing a cigar. Have a real smoke. He even said that to Patricia, who had innocently lit up her mentholated filter tip — the kind Grandpa hated the most — at the dinner table.

She stared at him. He stared back. Then she took the cigar, jabbed her fork through it, and proceeded to light it up in a positively Olympian cloud of smoke. There was silence around the table (except for the sucking puffing sounds Patricia was making). Everyone was afraid of Grandpa. After what seemed like an hour but must have been just a minute or so, Grandpa turned to me and said, She's all right, and everybody laughed and dinner started again and Patricia and I got married.

Gorska had got to me, all right. I went upstairs to bed without another drink (without supper, either). In the morning I told Patricia I was going to the club to play golf.

— You don't know how to play golf, she said.

— No problem, I said. Gene Martin has played for 20 years and has never broken 100. And that reminds me, I don't feel like going to their cocktail party tonight.

She looked at me. It occurred to me that she didn't look at me very much these days. — Suit yourself, she said.

But the club was packed and I had only a vague idea of where to rent or borrow golf clubs. I soon found myself at the 19th Hole with Archie Miller and Hank Leone. I said no to the beers, but they came anyway. I felt sad, positively sinful, as I took my first sips, but as the day wore on I gradually became angry again, just like at the Blue Horse. I could see the Pole's face leaning toward me. It was only poor, overweight Archie Miller, asking what I wanted for lunch, but I felt like strangling him.

— Your trouble, Archie, is that you only think about food. That's why you look like a goddamn beach ball.

I stayed angry while I drove with Hank Leone, who had been recently divorced and was in no happy frame of mind either, to the Martins' cocktail party. I was still in good control of myself, but when I get angry I drink faster. I was worried about the lost contract, and I was worried about Patricia, back at the house. Sometimes I think I have a positive genius for suffering. I've noticed some people never seem to suffer at all, no matter what they do. Some people, even very tenderhearted ones, are entirely without conscience. I've known men and women who help strangers, love animals, cry at tragedies on TV, who think nothing of ripping off a supermarket, cheating on their income taxes or spouses, exceeding speed limits. They seem to possess no sense of guilt: these are the lucky ones. But we can't have too many of these people or our society,

30

which is constructed almost entirely on guilt, would collapse. When the deep inner voice stops crying Thou shalt not, the stones will crack, and grass and weeds will reclaim the streets.

In the middle of the party, Roland Prince, Jr. arrived with his long-nosed wife. I saw right away that he had heard about my lunch with Bishek Gorska. He avoided me for a while, but when I went up to him, he said he would like to see me in his office on Monday.

— You can talk to me now, I said, if you're not afraid to speak (I nodded at his wife) in front of Cyrano here.

— You're fired, Charlie, he said.

— Listen, shrimpboat, I said, let's step outside and see who can fire whom. I knew as I said this it didn't make much sense, but I was past caring by now. Hank Leone somehow steered us apart, and later on in the evening Patricia came to pick me up. I was lying on a big pile of coats in the guest room. The next morning I got up, hitchhiked to the club, picked up my car, and started driving west.

That was five years ago. I had the vague idea of going away, drying up, starting over. I kept going till I came to this sleepy midwestern city with its pink motels and cheap flophouses and free lunches. Small checks follow me, and I'm reasonably contented. Now that I'm over 50, I don't have the energy I used to have. I could write the kids but somehow even that seems too hard to do. Once in a while, when a check comes, I splurge on a bottle of Martell's Cordon Bleu and share it with the gang here. They don't even know what it is. We sit around on our bunks drinking it out of paper cups, hiding them when Mrs. Matthews comes in to check on us. I get a kick out of that. And sometimes I exercise my old skills, just to show off. The Cloverleaf is going to raffle off a station wagon, and the one who sells the most tickets gets a free Christmas turkey. I've already sold so many we're planning on a great feast.

But mainly I pick up bottles of this cheap and perfectly palatable wine. I lie here in the twilight and think. I blow smoke in a bottle and watch it sink. Hey. That rhymes. Patricia would be proud of me.

Getting Rid of the Ponoes

•

BY PETER MEINKE

W HEN I WAS 10 years old I couldn't sleep, because the minute I closed my eyes, the ponoes would get me. The ponoes were pale creatures about two feet tall, with pointed heads and malevolent expressions, though they never actually said anything. What they did was approach me, slowly, silently, in order to build up my fear (because I knew what they were going to do); then they would tickle me. I was extremely ticklish in those days; in fact I could hardly bear to be touched by anybody, and the ponoes would swarm over me like a band of drunken and sadistic uncles, tickling me till I went crazy, till I almost threw up, flinging my legs and arms around in breathless agony. I would wake up soaked, my heart banging in my chest like the bass drum in the school marching band. This lasted almost an entire year, until the Murphy brothers got rid of them for me.

Because the ponoes would come whenever I fell asleep, I hated to go to bed even more than most children. My parents were not sympathetic; ponoes didn't seem that frightening to them, nor were they sure, for a long time, that I wasn't making them up. Even my best friend, Frankie Hanratty, a curly-haired, black-eyed boy of unbounded innocence, was dubious. No one else (including myself) had ever heard of them. They seemed like some sort of cross between elves, dwarves, and trolls. But where did I get the name? I think my parents felt there was something vaguely sexual about them, and therefore distasteful.

32

That year — 1942 — I was always close to tears, and my bespectacled, watery eyes must have been a discouraging sight, especially for my father, who would take me to the Dodger games at Ebbetts Field and introduce me to manly players like Cookie Lavagetto and Dixie Walker. I had a collection of signed baseballs that my father always showed to our guests.

Because I was terrified, I fought sleep with all my might. I read through most of the night, by lamplight, flashlight, even moonlight, further straining my already-weak eyes. When I *did* fall asleep, from utter exhaustion, my sleep was so light that when the ponoes appeared on the horizon — approaching much like the gangs in *West Side Story,* though of course I didn't know that then — I would often wake myself up before they reached me. I can remember wrestling with my eyelids, lifting them, heavy as the iron covers of manholes we'd try to pry open in the streets, bit by bit until I could see the teepeelike designs of what I called my "Indian blanket."

Often I would get just a glimpse of my blanket, and then my eyelids would clang shut and the ponoes were upon me. It is possible, I suppose, that I only *dreamed* I was seeing my blanket, but I don't think so! Sometimes I would give up trying to open my eyes, give up saying to myself *This is only a dream,* and turn and run. My one athletic skill was, and remains still, running. But in my dreams the ponoes would always gain and my legs would get heavier and heavier and I'd near a cliff that I would try to throw myself over but it was like running through waist-deep water with chains on, and I would be dragged down at the edge. This, I suppose, with variations and without ponoes, is a common enough dream.

During this year, since I scarcely slept in bed, I fell asleep everywhere else: in the car, at the movies, even at dinner — a true zombie. In the winter I liked to curl up on the floor near the silver-painted radiators, whose clanking seemed to keep the ponoes away. I constantly dropped off at my desk at school, once actually clattering to the floor and breaking my glasses, like some pratfall from The Three Stooges, whom we would watch every Saturday afternoon at the Quentin Theatre. Eleven cents for a double feature — it was another world! But Miss McDermott was not amused and would rap my knuckles sharply with her chalkboard pointer. She was a stout and formidable old witch, and when she first came at me, aiming her stick like an assassin from *Captain Blood,* I thought she was going to poke my eyes out and leaped from my seat, to the delight of my classmates, who for weeks afterward liked to charge at me with fingers pointed at my nose.

We had moved from the Irish section of Boston to the Irish section of Brooklyn, and my father, Little Jack Shaughnessy, liked to hang around the tough bars of Red Hook, where (he told me) there was a cop on every corner looking for an Irish head to break. My father was Little Jack and I was Little Jim (or Littlejack and Littlejim) because we were both short; but he was husky, a warehouse worker at Floyd Bennett Airport. Though he was not a chronic brawler, he liked an occasional fight and was disappointed in my obvious fear of physical violence.

"Come on, Jimmy, keep the left up." He'd slap me lightly on the face, circling around me. "Straight from the shoulder now!" I'd flail away, blinking back the tears, the world a blur without my glasses, like a watercolor painting left in the rain. To this day, when I take off my glasses, I have the feeling that someone is going to hit me. Oddly enough, it was fighting that made me fall in love with the Murphy brothers, Tom and Kevin, though love may not be exactly the right word.

I was a natural-born hero-worshipper. Perhaps I still am, as I believe unequivocally that our country has gone to the dogs since President Kennedy was shot in 1963, despite all the revelations of character flaws and administrative blunders. When I was young, most of my heroes came from books — D'Artagnan, Robin Hood; or movies — characters like the Green Hornet and Zorro, or real actors like Nelson Eddy, whose romantic scenes with Jeannette MacDonald made my classmates whoop and holler. I would whoop and holler too, so as not to give myself away, but at night, fending off the ponoes, I would lie in bed in full Royal Canadian Mountie regalia singing, in my soaring tenor, "For I'm falling in love with someone, someone . . ." while Jeannette would stand at the foot of my bed shyly staring down at her incredibly tiny feet or petting my noble horse, which was often in the room with us. This fantasy was particularly ludicrous because I was unable to carry a tune and had been firmly dubbed a "listener" by Miss McDermott in front of the whole music class, after which I spent the term moving my mouth to the words without uttering a sound.

The Murphy brothers were tough, the scourge of P.S. 245. Extorters of lunch money, fistfighters, hitters of home runs during gym class, they towered over most of us because they were older, having been left back several times. Tom was the older and meaner; Kevin was stronger but slow-witted, perhaps even retarded. Tom pushed him around a lot but was careful not to get him too mad, because there was nothing that Kevin would not do when in a rage, which became increasingly evident as they grew older. Pale, lean, black-haired, they wore white shirts with the sleeves

34

rolled up and black pants and shiny black shoes. For brawlers they were very neat dressers, early examples of the Elvis Presley look, though they never looked so soft as Elvis. Most of the rest of us wore corduroy knickerbockers, whistling down the halls as we walked, with our garters dangling and our socks humped around our ankles. Small and weak, I wanted nothing more than to be like the two fighting brothers, who seemed to me to resemble the pictures of tough soldiers, sailors, and marines that were posted everywhere.

The Murphys had strong Brooklyn accents (they actually called themselves the Moifys), but the whole neighborhood was heading that way, and the schools fought valiantly against it: accents were bad in 1942. I still remember the poem we all had to recite:

> *There once was a turtle*
> *Whose first name was Myrtle*
> *Swam out to the Jersey shore . . .*

Tom Murphy would get up in front of the class (like many others), grinning insolently, scratching obscenely, ducking spitballs, and mutter:

> *Aah dere wunce wuz a toitle*
> *Whoze foist name wuz Moitle*
> *Swam out to da Joisey shaw . . .*

We would all applaud, and Tom would clasp his hands above his head like a winning prizefighter and swagger back to his seat. Miss McDermott never hit the Murphys — she had wise instincts — but tried to minimize their disturbance (distoibance!) by pretending they weren't there.

But there they were: they had the cigarettes, they had the playing cards with the photographs that made us queasy, they wrote on the bathroom walls and the schoolyard sidewalks. Of course they must have written obscenities, but in the fall of 1942 they mainly wrote things like KILL THE KRAUTS and JAPS ARE JERKS: they were fiercely patriotic. I thought of the change when I visited my daughter's high school last week: painted on the handball court was YANKEE GET OUT OF NORTH AMERICA.

And, suddenly, Tom Murphy adopted me. It was like the lion and the mouse, the prince and the pauper. Like a German submarine, he blew me out of the water, and I lost all sense of judgment, which was, in 1942, a very small loss. Perhaps it was because I was so sleepy.

On rainy days, when we couldn't go outside to play softball or touch football, we stayed in the gym and played a vicious game the Murphys loved, called dodgeball. We divided into two sides and fired a soccer-size ball at each other until one side was eliminated. The Murphys, always on the same side, firing fastballs the length of the tiny gymnasium, would knock boys down like tin soldiers. I was usually one of the last to go because I was so small and hard to hit; no one worried about me because I was incapable of hitting anyone else and eventually would get picked off. But one rainy September week, while our Marines were digging in on Guadalcanal and Rommel was sweeping across Egypt, they had to call off the game twice in a row because the brothers couldn't hit me before the next class started. They stood on the firing line and boomed the ball off the wall behind me while I jumped, ducked, slid in panic, like a rabbit in front of the dogs, sure that the next throw would splatter my head against the wall. Even when the coach rolled in a second ball, they missed me, throwing two at a time. The truth was, I suppose, that the Murphys were not very good athletes, just bigger and stronger than the rest of us.

The next day was a Saturday, and I was out in front of our house flipping war cards with Frankie, who lived next door, when the brothers loomed above us, watching. Kevin snatched Frankie's cap, and he and Tom tossed it back and forth while we crouched there, waiting, not even thinking, looking from one brother to the other.

Finally Tom said, "Littlejim, go get me a licorice stick," and stuck a penny in my hand. "Fast, now, get a leg on." Mostroni's Candy Store was three blocks away, and I raced off, gasping with relief. The thought had crossed my mind that they were going to break my glasses because I had frustrated them in dodgeball. I'm sure I set an East 32nd Street record for the three-block run, returning shortly with the two sticks: two for a penny, weep for what is lost. Tom took the sticks without thanks and gave one to his brother, who had pulled the button off Frankie's new cap. Frankie still squatted there, tears in his eyes, looking at the three of us now with hatred. He could see I was on the other side. I sold Frankie down the river and waited for new orders.

"Can you get us some potatoes?"

"No," I said. "I don't think so." Tom glared at me. "Maybe one."

"Make it a big one," he said. "I feel like a mickey." Mickeys were what we called potatoes baked in open fires: all over Flatbush you could smell the acrid aroma of charred potatoes.

"My cap," said Frankie. Kevin dropped it in a puddle from yesterday's rain and stepped on it. Ruined. Frankie picked it up, blindly, holding it with two fingers, and stumbled up the steps to his front door. We lived in a row of attached two-story brick houses, quite respectable though sliding, with a few steps in front (on which we played stoopball) and a handkerchief-patch of lawn, surrounded by a small hedge. In front of our house was the lamp post by which I could read at night, and next to it a slender young maple tree, which my father would tie to the lamp post during strong winds.

I went through the alley to our back entrance and found my mother working in our "victory garden" of Swiss chard, carrots, radishes, beets. My father went fishing in Sheepshead Bay every Saturday, a mixed blessing, as he would come back loaded with fish but in a generally unstable condition, so we never knew what to expect. Today I was glad, as it would make my theft easier.

My mother looked up as I passed. "Littlejim, are you all right?" My mother has always been able to look right into my heart as if it were dangling from my nose, a gift for which I frequently wished to strangle her.

"Of course," I said with scorn in my lying voice, "I'm just thirsty."

"Well, have a nice glass of milk, sweetheart," she said, wiping her forehead and peering at me. I trotted into the kitchen and looked in the potato pail beneath the sink. There were around 10 left, so I took a large one and a small one, stuck them in my shirt, and went out the front door. The Murphys were waiting down the street by the vacant lot, the fire already going.

Thus began my life of crime, which lasted almost eight months, well into 1943, for which I showed natural gifts, except temperamentally. I was always trembling but never caught. I graduated from potatoes to my mother's purse, from packs of gum at the candy store ("that Nazi wop," said Tom) to packs of cigarettes at the delicatessen: the owners watched the Murphys, while my quick hands stuffed my pockets full of contraband. Under the protection of the Murphy brothers, who beat up a German boy so badly that he was hospitalized, who dropped kittens into the sewers, who slashed the tires of cars owned by parents who tried to chastise them, I collected small sums of money from boys much larger than myself. Like Mercury, god of cheats and thieves, I was the swift messenger for Tom and Kevin Murphy.

I loved them. They needed me, I thought, not reading them well. What they needed was temporary diversion, and for a while I provided that. Kevin was virtually illiterate, so beginning with the Sunday comics one afternoon, I became his official reader. He read (looked at) nothing

.

but comic books — *Plastic Man, Superman, Captain Marvel, The Katzenjammer Kids; Sheena Queen of the Jungle* was his particular favorite because of her lush figure and scanty clothing.

"Get a load of that," he'd squeak (Kevin, and to a lesser extent Tom, had a high, nasal whine). "What the freak is she saying?"

" 'Stand back,' " I'd read. " 'There's something in there!' "

"Freaking A!" Kevin would shout. He got terrifically excited by these stories.

It was not long before I was talking like the Murphys, in a high, squeaky voice with a strong Brooklyn accent, punctuated (in school) by swear words and (at home) by half-swear words that I didn't understand. My mother was horrified.

"What the freak is this?" I'd shrill at some casserole she was placing on the table.

"Jimmy! Don't use language like that!"

"Freak? What's wrong with that?" I'd say in truly abysmal ignorance. "Freak, freaky, freaking. It doesn't mean *anything,* everyone says it." This is 1943, remember.

"I don't care what everyone says," my father would shout, turning red. "You watch your lip around here, and fast!"

On weekends we sat around a fire in the vacant lot, smoking cigarettes I had stolen (the Murphys favored the Lucky Strike red bull's-eye pack, which showed through the pockets of their white shirts) and eating mickeys that I had scooped up from in front of Tietjen's Grocery. About six of us were generally there — the Murphys, myself, and two or three of the tougher kids on the block whose faces have faded from my memory.

One spring day, when rains had turned the lot into trenches of red clay among the weeds and abandoned junk — people dumped old stoves, broken bicycles, useless trash there — Tom Murphy had the idea for The Lineup. This was based on a combination of dodgeball from school and firing squads from the daily news. The idea was to catch kids from the neighborhood, line them up like enemy soldiers against the garage that backed onto the lot, and fire clayballs at them. They would keep score and see who was the best shot.

"Go get Frankie and his little brother," Tom told me. To Tom, almost everyone was an enemy. "They're playing 'Three Steps to Germany' in front of his house. Tell him you want to show him something."

Since the cap incident, Frankie had become much more alert, darting into his house whenever the Murphys appeared on the block. He often looked at me with reproach during the past months, but never said anything, and I simply dropped him like a red-hot mickey, though he had been my only real friend.

"He won't come," I said. "He won't believe me."

"He'll believe you," Tom said. Kevin stepped on my foot and shoved me into the bushes. It was the first time he had turned on me, and I couldn't believe it. I looked at Tom for help.

"Go get Frankie and Billy," he repeated. "We'll hide in the bushes."

I walked miserably down the block, sick at heart. Shouldn't I just duck into my own house? Shouldn't I tell Frankie to run? Somehow these alternatives seemed impossible. I was committed to the Murphy brothers. While my childhood went up in flames, I spoke through the blaze in my head and talked Frankie into coming to the lot for some mickeys. I was bright-eyed with innocence, knowing full well what I was doing, cutting myself off from my parents, my church, selling my friend for the love of the Murphy brothers, whom I wanted to love me back.

"My ma gave me two potatoes; they'll be ready in a couple of minutes. You and Billy can split one."

Frankie wanted to believe me. "Have you seen Tom or Kevin today?"

"They went crabbing," I said, glib with evil. "Their Uncle Jake took them out on the bay. They promised they'd bring me some blueclaws."

The walk down the block to the lot, maybe 200 yards, was the longest I've ever taken. I babbled inanely to keep Frankie from asking questions. Billy was saved when he decided to go play inside instead — he didn't like mickeys, anyway, a heresy admitted only by the very young. I didn't dare protest for fear of making Frankie suspicious. The lot appeared empty, and we were well into it when Kevin stood up from behind a gutted refrigerator; Frankie whirled around right into Tom, who twisted his thin arm and bent him to the ground.

"Lineup time!" shouted Kevin, "Freaking A!" as they carried the kicking boy over to the wall. There they threw him down and tore off his shoes, making it difficult for him to run over the rusty cans, cinders, and thorny bushes. They had made a large pile of clayballs already, and the three other boys began firing them mercilessly at the cowering figure, their misses making red splotches on the garage wall. This was the first Lineup in our neighborhood, a practice that soon escalated so that within a few months, boys were scaling the lethal tin cans their parents had flattened to support the war effort. The Murphy boys held back momentarily, looking down at me.

"Where's Billy, you little fag?" Tom asked.

39

"He wouldn't come. He doesn't like mickeys." I was wincing at Frankie's cries as each clayball struck him.

"Maybe you ought to take his place," Tom said. "One target's not enough." Kevin reached from behind and snatched off my glasses, plunging me into the shadowy half-world in which I was always terrified. Without my glasses I could hardly speak and I said nothing as they pushed me back and forth like a rag doll.

"You see that hoop there?" one of them said. "Bring it over to the garage and stand in it, you four-eyed freak." Squinting, I could barely make out a whitish hoop lying near the fire. I bent down and grabbed it with my right hand and went down on my knees with a piercing scream that must have scared even the Murphy brothers. They had heated the metal hoop in the fire until it was white-hot and my hand stuck briefly to it, branding me for life. The older boys whooped and ran off, firing a few last shots at Frankie, Kevin not forgetting to drop my glasses in the fire, where my father found them the next day.

I knelt doubled-up, retching with pain and grief while Africa was falling to the Allies and our soldiers battled through the Solomon Islands: the tide had turned. I went home and had my hand attended to — first-degree burns! — and slept dreamless as a baby for the first time in years.

The Sugar Maples

•

BY ARTURO VIVANTE

N EAR THE HOUSE along the drive they stood, the sugar maples, untapped sources of sweetness, to make his life less bitter, if he willed.

He remembered, as a boy, in Canada — there from Italy, by way of England, during the war — one year in early May, deep in the woods some two hundred miles north of Montreal, where spring came late and where he had gone on a summer job in the forestry department, he struck with an ax a yellow birch, not with the idea of felling it, but just to set the ax in full view rather than on the ground where he might lose it, and the tree's sap gushed out abundantly, like blood from a deep wound, though color- less, and though the birch, of course, made no lament. As the sap contin- ued to pour out, he watched it in amazement, stilled by the sight, then pulled the ax out and wished that he could staunch the flow. The man he was with said that, like maple sap, it too was sweet and that syrup and sugar could be made from it, though it took even more boiling down.

Ever since then, from time to time he thought of the faraway tree that he had wounded, and the sap that he had spilled sometimes was lymph, sometimes the sweetest liquid. It suggested both pain — deep cuts, hospi- tals, and gauze — and pleasure — pancakes, breakfast tables, campfires. Sometimes he even thought of the birch with its gold limbs as of a woodland nymph he had violated. Then the thoughts went beyond pain, pleasure, and shame, and he saw yellow and white birches clothed in

41

liveliest green and heard their leaves flutter in the wind. The slightest breeze — a mere breath of a breeze — was enough to stir them.

Now his thoughts were with the maples, a more stable tree. It was March in Vermont. Spring was filtering, seeping in like a wave in its tentative, halting, sometimes backtracking fashion — slow up the mountains, fast along the valleys — on its long sweep from the Gulf toward the Arctic, penetrating into the core of living things, imparting its own motion to them. Least to man perhaps, most or soonest to crocus and snowdrops, and — in the animal kingdom — to peepers. It stirred them into a choir. Oh, what a din they made, those heralds of the spring.

Not outwardly yet, though their stems seemed heedful and their buds glistened, but deep within, the maples knew it too, and were affected. The sap was running. Buckets hung from the trees along the road even a quarter mile from town. One, two, three, even four buckets to a tree. What a good kind of farming, he thought. No animals to slaughter. Maples — you don't have to prune them, till them, or climb them. No tedious, poisonous insecticides or fertilizers needed. Nothing of that sort. Just a tap and a bucket.

At a hardware store he bought, for ninety-nine cents, a maple tap — a small metal, funnel-shaped device with a keel-like projection for striking with a hammer and a ring to which a bucket could be attached — and off he went home, quite happy.

Home was a four-windowed bedroom he rented in an isolated house that belonged to the college where he taught. Five other teachers had rooms there, but they stayed only two or three days. They arrived from New York on Mondays and departed Thursdays, leaving him alone for four nights. Then the house — with kitchen, living room, and garden — was his, and sometimes he cooked or lit a fire and sat in the living room by the fireplace or wandered in the garden. A long time before, when the house had been a private home, a woman lived there who was fond of wild flowers. She had transplanted many varieties of them into the garden, and they still grew — the previous April the lawn was carpeted with violets; there were trilliums and bloodroots in a copse. The garden extended nearly without demarcation into a field. It had been seeded for corn the year before, and in September it was so tall he had almost gotten lost in it. From his windows, north and south, he could see distant mountains, and west, a wooded rise. Since he missed a full view of the sunset and the ocean, he hung on the bare walls a painting he did of a fiery sunset on the sea and one of mauve clouds with streaks of gold and saffron over a line of mountains. Yet another he did of a daffodil sky just after sunset.

Dale, an elderly Vermonter, lanky and mild-mannered, came twice a week to clean the house (all except the bedrooms) in a sparkling red van, the only flashy thing about him. After a dry spell, of which he had complained, there was a storm and he asked Dale if he thought it had rained enough.

"Oh, yes, the ground got a good soak."

It pleased him to hear him say the word "soak." It was exactly the same word that the farmers in Tuscany liked to use — "*zuppata.*"

"Do you have some land here, Dale?"

"Yes, a field back of the house."

"Ah, good. Is that a sugar maple?" he asked him, pointing to a huge tree in the middle of the front yard.

"No, that's what we call a split-leaf maple. But those along the drive — that one there, and the other, and the other, all the way down to the gate — are sugar maples."

"Did they plant them along the road so it'd be easier to collect the sap with the horse carts?"

"Yes, that could be. It would make sense now, wouldn't it?"

"I was thinking of tapping one of them."

"Now's the time."

"I bought a tap downtown. How deep should I set it in?"

"Oh," he said, crossing one index finger with the other to show a little over two inches. He smiled; he seemed amused and pleased that an outsider should want to collect sap.

"And how long will the sap run?"

"A month maybe, till it warms up."

"It doesn't harm the tree, does it, to bore these holes for sap?"

"No, it don't seem to. They heal right up."

"I think maple syrup has the most wonderful flavor. There's nothing quite like it. It's unique."

"That's right. Unique."

"I hear you can make syrup out of yellow birches, too, but it must taste different."

"I've never tasted it. All plants have sap, but there's nothing like a maple. The first sap is the finest. That's called fancy, or grade A. Then, a little later in the season, there's B. But they are all good — not much difference there. Cold nights and sunny days — that's what does it. Last year was a great year. A good tree will yield a bucketful in two or three days, if the weather's right."

Again Dale reminded him of the way Tuscan farmers spoke of the olive tree. They had the same love and admiration for it that Vermonters had for maples.

With a screwdriver — he could find no gimlet in the hardware store, only drills that cost more than buying the syrup (he had in mind to make only about a pint) — he bored a hole into the nearest sugar maple, inserted the tap, hammered it in a bit, and hung to its ring with wire a large empty grapefruit-juice can stripped of its label and with its top incompletely opened so as to serve as a lid to keep the rain out. Almost immediately a drop flowed down the tap, and soon another. He left and went to his office. When he returned in the late afternoon, the can was already a quarter full. He drank some of the sap — faintly, very faintly sweet, certainly not tasteless, not like distilled water. That sap was spring, and he was drinking it — drinking spring from a source purer than the mountain springs or the brooks fed by melting snow from which, in his walks, he also drank.

Did spring really show least in man or move him least? No, the very love that in the spring, more than at any other time, he felt for nature — especially the flowers that were so beautifully made in their every tiniest detail; and the new sticky leaves, between rose and gold, issuing from the buds; and the wooded mountains, slowly turning from brown to green; and the nearer trees, gaining in their intricacy, in their hatching and crosshatching, so that the view of houses was concealed little by little — wasn't that, too, a manifestation of spring, spring in him? Surely it was. He felt one with them, a tenderness. And, not least, love for his own kind.

That month, at a college party, a woman who taught French, seeing him alone hanging around rather gloomily with a glass of wine in his hand — his sixth or seventh — had said to him, "Aren't you talking to any of these pretty girls? Look, there's one. Her name's Astrid. She's one of my students."

Her hair was the lightest brown, the color of a walnut shell, and it went down to her shoulders in ringlets. She had a bright look, enlightened eyes. Though alone when the French teacher had pointed her out, in a moment two boys approached her and the three entered into lively, merry conversation. He watched her laughing. Pretty — and unattainable, he thought. But a little later, while he was sitting on a long sofa with plenty of room to his right, unaccountably she came to sit beside him. "Who are you?" she said, cheerfully.

"Fortune's favorite child. You are sitting next to me."

She smiled. "That's a nice compliment."

"Sitting next to you I feel invisible."

"Invisible?"

"All eyes are on you."

"I don't think that's true."

"Well, if not invisible, inconspicuous, beside you. I thought I saw spring outside, but it's within."

"Say, I'm not used to this!"

"Oh, you must have scads of admirers."

"No! You are quite wrong. I have none."

"You have me. But you are 'a metaphor of Spring and Youth and Morning' while I am one of fall and age and evening."

"They have their beauty too."

"Evening and fall, but age?"

"Yes, age too. There's more time in it, and I love time."

"You are very kind."

"I'm being truthful. I know you teach here, but what do you do?"

"I sketch."

"Don't worry, then," she said. "Artists never age."

Later he walked her to her house — one of the college dorms.

"Do you want to see my room?" she said.

"Oh, it's so late."

"I have a nice room."

"I'm sure it's nice, but — "

"Come," she said.

The invitation was made with such innocence, trust, and sureness that he was baffled. He followed her up the stairs, feeling anything but invisible or inconspicuous. What was he doing? Was this accepted? A couple of girls saw him and paid no attention. She led him down a corridor that seemed twice its length to him and finally reached her door. There were plenty of conversation pieces in her bedroom, and he wasn't short of words anyway, but at last they fell silent. He touched her arm. She stood motionless, inscrutable, looking at him. "Well, I must go," he said.

"You know your way out?"

"Yes, I'll find it."

"Good night," he said, and kissed her on the cheek.

He bought a second tap, hung another can from it on the next tree on the road, and it too began dripping. Amazing — and yet so natural. In a couple of days the first can was full. In the kitchen he poured the sap into a pan, and boiled it down to a fraction of its volume — till he had only about half a cup. And this precious, straw-colored liquid — which tasted just like the one in stores, and better, he thought — he decanted into a quart bottle, which he stoppered and placed in the refrigerator.

The next day, Dale was over, and he showed it to him.

"I saw your two cans out there," Dale said, and, smiling, took the bottle, held it up level with his eyes and shook it. "Haven't boiled it down quite enough. Just a little more will do it; it's almost there."

"I'll boil the next lot down a good deal more, make it really concentrated, add it to this, and they'll average out just right."

"Yes, you can do that."

"Do you think the Indians knew about maple syrup?"

"I'm sure they did," Dale said without hesitation.

It was good to talk to Dale. He knew the lore of the land that most, if not all, had forgotten. He talked about the Indians and the first settlers as if he had witnessed their doings, with an assurance that touched him and amused him. Often, in his teaching jobs, more than with his colleagues he made friends with the maintenance people. He remembered a lab boy at N.Y.U. with whom he would go and drink beer in a Third Avenue bar, and a cleaning lady in Indiana for whom he would go to his office just in order to be there and talk to her when she appeared around midnight. And others, in almost every place he had taught — and he had taught in about a dozen. Such were his luminaries.

One batch of sap he inadvertently boiled down to the point at which it very nearly crystallized into sugar. He was left with a tacky, chewy substance, which he tasted. It seemed as good as anything he had ever set his teeth into.

This business with the maples was a welcome relief from the teaching routine. Going back home, he would invariably look into the cans, and his joy could almost be measured by the amount of sap that had accumulated. It's the only thing that gives me any pleasure, he thought.

He took a drive with a middle-aged friend and talked to her about tapping the trees.

"Poor trees," she said. "It sounds cruel."

"No, it don't hurt them. At least, it don't seem to. They heal right up during the summer. That's what Dale said, anyway."

"Who's Dale?"

"The caretaker at my house. An old Vermonter."

"He ought to know."

"Yes, and yours, my dear, if I may say so, is misplaced pity."

After three weeks he had more than a half a bottle of syrup. Then the weather turned warm, and no more sap flowed. "It's all over," Dale said.

The syrup in the bottle had some impurities — bits of bark and other matter. He went downtown for a little sieve, explained to the saleswoman

46

what he needed it for, and picked one out. "Oh, you want to strain it for the dregs," she said.

Glad she had supplied him with the right word, he filtered the syrup through the sieve, and now it looked clear — like the kind you buy. He took a spoonful of it. In Europe they had nothing like it. It couldn't be bought, except perhaps in some gourmet shops in Paris and in London, at exorbitant prices. As a child in Italy he had never seen it used in dishes. And yet its subtle taste evoked a memory. It eluded him, though he knew it was a memory of very long ago — one that had nothing to do with all the times he had had maple syrup in the United States and Canada. "Tastes and smells you don't forget." So where had he tasted it in his childhood? And the spoon gave him the clue — in medicines, as a vehicle to disguise bitter drugs. Yes, pharmacists used it there, importing it from far away at prices that were prohibitive for grocery stores and restaurants. A vehicle for bitterness.

He took another spoonful, and pondered on his life. Here he was alone during the long weekend in his solitary house. Every weekend and much of the rest of the week, too, except when he taught and was around the heart of the campus. And he thought: Astrid — there's another kind of sweetness. And a line of Boccaccio's recurred to him: "All pleasures are trifles as compared to love." Yes, if, under cover of darkness, he could cradle her body with his, and share the air that she breathed, and bask in the warmth that they engendered, then the magical world he'd inhabit, which the crocus's petals enclose. He thought of the crocus, the tulip, and other flowers outside in the garden, closing up at night, and he a tiny creature resting in that chamber, feeling whole, safe, sheltered, comforted, protected. With her here in bed it would be like that, only better. But to hope for such bliss was to falter, was to falter and waver besides. For how could such heaven descend on earth that was already half ashes, on earth that was withered and spent? Yet, he reasoned, winged seeds land on stark rocks, land where no softness receives them — and cinders on richest of sods. But to invoke such a fate on a loved one was a sign less of love than of hate.

The thought of her worried him. He had often talked to her since that first meeting, and she looked at him with such loving eyes. She brought him flowers to his office, left some brownies in his mailbox. She wrote him notes and seemed unable to dissemble a certain slight displeasure if he had lunch with other students or if he even walked with them. If he wanted to — he was almost sure — he would be able to cradle her body with his, yes, under cover of darkness. But she was so young, so very

47

young. Yet one of his colleagues was surprised or didn't believe him when he told her that he had never had an affair with a student here. "I've never even kissed one," he added. "Not passionately anyway. Just affectionately."

"You are so young," he said to Astrid in his office.

"I am a senior."

"You a senior. I am the senior. A senior citizen; well, though I don't exactly qualify, how many times — in stores, in restaurants — haven't I been asked? In one restaurant I went to — Denny's — there was in the menu a listing, at reduced prices, for senior citizens — 55 or over; *55 or over*, and according to that description, I did qualify." There, now he had just about told her his age, though he hadn't meant to, for to tell his age was against his principles. Passport dialogue. But he *had* to discourage her, had to ward her off. He hoped she had more sense than he. He didn't trust himself. Oh, God, she kept coming to his office, after classes, if she saw a light. And he would try to keep the conversation on her studies, on poetry and painting and the weather and cities and her family; but it was difficult. Only a week more and she'd graduate; she'd be gone far away and in September she would not be back. Luckily. How so, luckily? She was so warm, so good, generous, abundant, shapely, *beauteous.* He wanted to hold her in his arms. Sometimes he did, but gently — when she left and he gave her a parting kiss, like the one in her bedroom, to which, though she had invited him again, he had never returned.

She laughed at what he'd said about senior citizens in the menu. It seemed to mean nothing to her. It slid off her, left about as much of an impression as a drop of rain on a duck's feathers. She laughed, then turned serious and stared at him, her face flushed.

"Do you know how to cook pancakes?" he said.

"Yes, why?"

"Because I have half a bottle of maple syrup from that sap I told you I was collecting. We could have pancakes, over at my house, before you leave."

"That's a grand idea. When?"

"Weekends there's no one there, and the kitchen — the whole house — is ours. Saturday? Around six?"

"Fine."

"I'll buy the mix," he said.

Saturday, around six, he was looking out his bedroom windows for her, expecting her to come walking down the drive like Little Red Riding Hood, when he heard the telephone ring.

"Do you still want to have pancakes?" she said.

"Yes, aren't you coming?"

"I'm with Jennifer; can she come too?"

"Sure."

He watched the two girls cooking one pancake after another, pouring the thin and subtle syrup, eating.

"Your maple syrup's yummy," Astrid said.

"And so are your pancakes. Just right," he said. He paused a moment. "In fact," he added slowly and in another tone, "everything is . . . as it should be."

Jennifer hummed appreciatively, but Astrid gave him a swift, knowing look.

Soon they left; he opened the refrigerator, took out a bottle of champagne that he had bought for the occasion, brought it up to his room, and poured himself one glass after another to the end.

The Encounter

·

BY ARTURO VIVANTE

Y EARS AGO WHEN I was a college student in Montreal, there used
to be (and perhaps there still is) off a trail on one of the highest
ridges of the Green Mountains of northern Vermont, a log
cabin, built, I think, by the state, or possibly by lumberjacks, for people to
take shelter in during storms and blizzards. It was a simple, windowless
structure with an unlocked door, a wooden bunk, a shelf, and a rudimen-
tary fireplace made of rocks. I stopped there with some friends during a
cross-country skiing tour. We lit a fire, made some coffee, then went on to
a lodge we had rented in a village down in the valley.

In the months that followed, I often thought of the cabin, remote and
vacant up there in the mountains, and one weekend in late October I went
to the village again, alone this time, meaning to retrace the trail we had
taken through the woods. Beautiful as they had been in the winter, the
woods would be even more beautiful now in autumn.

I had a knapsack with a good blanket, some food, and a flashlight,
and rather than stay at the lodge, which I could hardly afford, I decided to
climb the mountain and look for the log cabin on the ridge.

It was evening, the air crisp, invigorating. A few clouds in the west
matched the crimson of the leaves. As I climbed higher and higher up an
open ski run, the clouds had golden hems. The trees, too, I thought, had
just such colors. I reached the top of the run and went on deep into the
woods along the trail we had taken. I couldn't see the bright clouds

anymore. The day seemed darker, as if half an hour had passed in a second. But the sky straight above me — what I could see of it through the leaves — was still light-blue. I walked on and on, ever looking to the right, for I remembered that the cabin was on that side. The trail seemed narrower now than in the winter and it wasn't as easy to follow as when there'd been tracks in the snow. Tall maples and birches stood on each side of it and rustled in the wind. It's like music, I thought, the music I like best.

Despite the knapsack, I felt light and free, felt almost like skipping along. The trail followed the ridge, up and down and curving. Downhill at times I broke into a run; uphill I took the short, slow steps of mountaineers. Sometimes I paused and listened. I heard only the wind and once or twice a branch scraping on another — a sound that also was the wind's. The birds had gone to sleep. Soon I'll be asleep too, I thought — if I can find the cabin. I'd had supper in the village, and having got up very early that day, I expected I wouldn't have any trouble sleeping. Maybe I'd light a fire, sip some of the apricot brandy I carried in my knapsack, and then go to bed.

After a few miles, before it was quite dark, I came to the cabin. It was just where I had thought it was — about 50 feet off the trail on the right — and I congratulated myself on my memory and sense of direction. Like the trail, it looked less prominent than in winter. It was almost hidden by the leaves, its wood weathered gray and brown and rather shaggy. The door was wide open and I went in. I shone my flashlight around. Though bare and primitive, the place was quite clean. There was the bunk, there the shelf, and there the fireplace with ashes and cinders, perhaps the same left by the fire that my friends and I had lit.

I set the knapsack on the floor, unrolled the blanket and laid it on the bunk, then went out to gather firewood. Soon I had a good bundle of twigs and deadwood and a strip of birch bark. They were dry and caught easily, the birch bark burning even better than paper. The chimney drew well, just as I remembered. I closed the door with some difficulty — the latch was loose. Then I sat gazing at the flames, reached for the apricot brandy, and took a few swigs of it. The flames leaped and danced. My shadow danced to them on the walls. The wood crackled. I stayed up till it had burned itself out. "And now I'll go to bed," I whispered. It was strange to hear my own voice. I took my shoes off. The bunk was hard. There was no mattress, but wrapped in my blanket — a soft blue English plaid — I felt snug. I closed my eyes, and, turning around, I settled on my right side as I usually do before going to sleep. I opened my eyes again to see if any of the embers still glowed in the fireplace. None did. The place was absolutely

51

dark, and I closed my eyes again. The wind had died down. It was so quiet and still in the cabin I could hear the sound of my heart and my breathing.

But something seemed odd. I heard a sound of breathing — not in time with my own, but slower, and deeper. I stopped breathing — I don't know whether from anxiety or to make sure I wasn't mistaken. The sound went on. I wanted to jump out of the bunk, but I lay perfectly still, barely breathing, as if the slightest motion might give me away. The breathing was coming from below the bunk, and it was peaceful, regular, and deep — the breathing of someone sleeping soundly. That, at least, was reassuring, and I took a big breath. But still I didn't move. I couldn't seem to.

Who was it? What was it? Was it an animal? It must be an animal. No human would sleep *under* the bunk. Was it a raccoon? A skunk? No, it must be something larger. I couldn't remember hearing a cat — a healthy cat — breathe. They made practically no sound. A bear? Could it possibly be a bear? Yes, very possibly, I told myself, and thought of the open door and the loose latch. And yet it might be something smaller, and I wasn't going to leave my warm bunk, my cozy cabin, for a raccoon. I wasn't going to be made a fool of by some small creature. I had to find out. Where was my flashlight? Where were my shoes? Slowly I uncovered myself. And very carefully my fingers inched along the floor searching for the flashlight. I couldn't find it. I made wider and wider arcs with my fingers and at last reached it. I brought it up onto the bunk and lit it. Perhaps I shouldn't shine it under the bunk. No, definitely I should not. Again I put my hand on the floor and moved it even more gently than before toward the hollow under the bunk. But I found it impossible to move my fingers inward more than a couple of inches, and not because there was anything in my way. It was the unknown.

I clutched the flashlight and, muffling it with my hand, I brought it over the edge of the bunk and hung my head down. The breathing went on unruffled, and I took courage. But still I was too high. Was the animal hibernating? But wasn't it too early in the season for animals to hibernate? Whatever it was doing, it must have had a very large meal for it to sleep so soundly. Leaning out and down farther and farther and shining the flashlight under the bunk, I saw fur — black, mountainous — obviously a bear's. Instantly I recoiled and in doing this struck the flashlight sharply against the edge of the bunk. There was a terrific knock under me. The whole bunk seemed to heave. It quaked, throwing me off balance against the wall. And the animal got out from under the bunk and stood on its paws in the middle of the floor between me and the door, a black bear so big I wondered how it could have fit under there. It shook sleep off like a

52

dog shakes off water. Recovering somewhat, I shone the light in his eyes and he blinked as if dazed. I tried to be brave. I got out of the bunk and stood my ground. Any sign of fear on my part, I thought, and he would bound forth and claw me apart like a plaything. Where were my shoes? I didn't know where my shoes were. But there was my knapsack. I grabbed it by its metal frame and held it in front of me like a shield. He nudged it with his muzzle, perhaps smelling the food inside it, and held it with his forepaws.

"Good, bear, be good," I said in a soft, warm, imploring voice.

He rubbed his nose against the side of the knapsack harder and harder and tugged at it with his paws.

I was born and had grown up in Italy till I was 14, and somehow it came more natural for me in a crisis to speak in Italian. *"Buono,"* I said, *"stai buono."* But the Italian didn't help, and in a mixture of Italian and English I went on, *"buono* now, good, good boy, *buono,* be quiet, gently now, good, good bear."

I had in my knapsack a large chocolate bar, a slice of cake, a loaf of bread, and a package of cheese. I pulled the loaf out, unwrapped it in a hurry, and gave it to him. He gorged it down as if I'd given him a crumb. I gave him the cheese. I gave him the chocolate bar. I gave him the cake. Soon everything was gone. Only the apricot brandy remained, and it was on the floor by the fireplace. I reached for it, and there, incidentally, were my shoes. I slipped into them, opened the bottle, and poured the syrupy fluid all out onto the hearth. He lapped it up with some relish. And now he looked at me. I had nothing else to give him.

He came closer. *"Buono, buono,"* I said, moving toward the door. I opened it. "Go home now, go." But he didn't move. And suddenly I thought: He *is* home; this isn't my house; this is his. And while he stood contentedly watching me, I picked up my blanket and holding onto my knapsack, empty now except for my toothbrush and a change of clothes, I returned to the doorway. He didn't follow me. He looked at me sadly, as at a departing guest, and turned toward the bunk. Slowly he crept under it. And I thought: He's going back to sleep, drugged by the brandy; I could get back to the bunk, too, but no — I would never sleep.

I made my way back to the trail, and along the trail to the ski run, and down the ski run to the village and the lodge. I got a room there. In the lounge people were drinking and dancing. I wandered among them. I sat at the bar hoping to find someone to tell my story to, but no one seemed right. When the bartender asked me what I would have, I ordered a glass of apricot brandy. I drank it and then went to bed between fresh sheets, with a telephone on the bedside table and a private bath opposite. I switched the light out. And still I couldn't sleep. I went to the window and looked at the mountain; for a long time I watched it. The moon, a gibbous moon, was lighting it now, and the moon mist hung over the village. I thought of the thousands of creatures in some kind of shelter or home for the night. "Home, home, everyone where he belongs," I said to myself, "lair, nest, cradle, bunk, bed."

"Bed," I repeated, getting back into it and closing my eyes.

Walking the Trapline

•

BY REBECCA RULE

MY BROTHER THOMAS'S snowshoes were bigger than mine, though he was not. Father made the snowshoes. It took a long time because the ash for the frames had to be aged and steamed into shape. The deer hide had to be soaked in the brook until the hair floated off and then tanned in our cellar. One year the neighbor's dog dragged the hide out of the brook and chewed it. Father saw the tracks. He found the ruined hide. Later, he shot the dog. I think the neighbors knew, but they never said so.

On winter evenings, Father sliced the stiff hides into strips to soak in coffee cans till they were supple and slimy. He knotted them to the frames. His big, scarred hands squeaked each strand tight and even into place.

The small finger on Father's right hand was a shiny stub. The beaver trap had "snipped the little feller right off," he said, when he told the story. But I remembered the bloody mitten.

Father cut my leather harnesses plenty big for me to grow into. When the insides were webbed, dried, and varnished over, he sliced the harnesses thick and measured them to my feet. As he knelt to adjust the buckles around my rubber boots, I saw his pale scalp through the thinning curls.

He was a young father just the same, with a hard jaw, all his front teeth, and blue eyes that made you feel dirty when he stared at you. Mother said I had eyes like my father and asked me what I was staring at all the time. She never asked him.

When I was eleven and Thomas was nine, Father began to teach him about the trapline. He allowed me to come when the weather was fine and the dishes done.

Father trapped beaver through the ice, mink in the brooks, and fisher in the trees. He got good money for the pelts. He said his job at the tannery, which made him smell so sour, wouldn't be enough to feed us but for the animals he caught.

When Mother complained that Father ought to be tending to the woodpile or the roof or the broken cellar steps, he'd say he trapped for the money and she should be glad. She'd stare him in the eye just a second till her face had to twitch away. She knew he trapped because he wanted to, and that was all.

Father tended the sets he had to drive to in the evenings after work. On Sundays, he made the rounds of the traps in the big woods out behind the house.

"Father, do you think we'll catch anything today?" I asked, snow-shoeing behind him and Thomas up the hill behind our house. The snow was new and light and clean. It barely held the imprint of my webbing.

"Your Ma would rap me a good one if I came back with nothing, Elizabeth."

I laughed. She would never rap him, though she might get cross and not make supper if she thought Father had wasted the whole day. When Mother did not make supper, Thomas and I went to our room early to get away from her silence.

I liked to step on the tails of Thomas's snowshoes and make him stumble when we walked downhill. Sometimes he'd stumble too far and jar Father. "Watch it, boy," Father would growl. And Thomas would look back at me real ugly. He was the only one in our family who frowned with his nose. I guess that was because it was so short and high on his face.

"You see those tracks down over that banking?" Father stopped so quick I almost walked over Thomas.

"Yup," I replied.

"You see them swish marks and how square they are?"

"Yup," I replied. I could have told Father what kind they were, but he always finished a lesson once he started it.

"A little female fisher," he said. "She's moving on a new snow. We might get up here a-ways and find her hanging in my little trap."

"I hope so," I said.

Father stared at Thomas until he looked up. "Wouldn't that be dandy, boy?"

56

Thomas nodded.

I curled my thumb in my mitten. Mid-morning by the sun, and the air was still cold enough to stiffen the skin in my nose.

We found the trap empty and sprung. The bait was gone. Father picked up a feather. "Sprung by a christly blue jay. Fisher came along, just climbed right up and ate that bait slick as a bean." He stomped the feathers into the snow. Thomas and I stood silent and close together, elbows rubbing. Better not make matters worse, we thought. Thomas and I thought about some things the same way. We'd catch one another's eye and understand that we were thinking and feeling the same.

"She'll be back," said Father.

"She'll be back," I repeated to Thomas, who knew as well as I did that fisher travel in great circles and always come back.

Father pulled the pack basket off his back as if it wasn't heavy a bit. He laid it up against the leaning birch tree beside the ice chisel he carried like a staff. My father was strong. When the beaver trap sprung on one hand, he opened it with the other to free himself.

"Can we build a fire?" Thomas asked.

"What, you cold?"

"No," said Thomas, shivering. I kicked him in the ankle, meaning "Tell him you're cold." Thomas knew what I meant, but clamped his mouth shut. Thomas could be stubborn about things that didn't count.

"I'm cold, Father," I said. It was all right for me to be cold.

Father didn't hear.

Thomas and I played tag to keep warm and threw snow at one another because we liked to. We were careful not to throw snow at Father. When he played snow fight he'd run us down one at a time and rub our faces with snow.

"You kids get away from this set if you're going to raise hell," Father said.

I sat by the pack, tired of the game anyhow. Thomas walked away.

"Reach in that bag and find my bottle of scent," Father ordered without looking at me. His scents were secret. He said they were made of deer glands, skunk juice, fish oil, and other secret things that no other trappers could know and we could never tell.

He had strung up the new piece of beaver carcass. He plucked a branch of hemlock and wired it over the meat — to make it look natural, he said. Fisher didn't know hemlock branches did not grow on birch trees.

Father didn't catch many fisher in a season; there weren't too many around. I had never seen one in a trap, only in the cellar when I watched the careful skinning and stretching. He had to peel the fur away from the flesh whole with his blunt skinning knife, even to the tiny toes. Thomas wasn't allowed to skin. One rip ruined a good pelt. Father let Thomas skin our cat that died. Afterwards, Thomas whispered to me that skinning Fluffy had made him throw up in the bathroom, quiet so Father wouldn't hear.

I glimpsed a fisher once. Father had said, "Look up, quick," and in the tree I'd seen the flash of darkness, the bouncing of the branch. "Fisher," he'd hissed, and the hiss made me tremble to think I'd seen one.

With a twig, Father dribbled the scent over the bait wired high as he could reach on the leaning tree. The scent was tangy as skunk and fresh as pine needles. One Halloween Father smeared it on the doorknob so when the neighbor's kids came begging, they'd get that smell on them to last a while. Father and I laughed and laughed to think of them eating their chocolate.

The steel-wire trap was nailed just below the bait. When set, it made a square for the animal to reach his head through grabbing for the bait. The trap would snap around the neck.

By the time we reached the farthest-out pond, the sun was gone, the day turned gray. Father left us the matches and told us to warm up while he made a set at the upper end of "the meadow." I called it a bog because of the ice; a beaver bog where dams had backed the water over part of the woods and the trees had died and silvered. Trunks stood straight and silent. Stumps tipped to the air and groped with twisted roots. All my nightmares occurred in beaver bogs. I told Thomas they were haunted.

Father saw the snow melted at the top of the beaver house. He knew the beaver were there, breathing. The single beaver he had left alive last year had formed a new colony. He never trapped all the beaver out of this pond because it was so handy to home: just five miles straight out the back door, a new colony almost every year.

Thomas and I watched Father stride away up the bog. His tracks were wide apart and straight in a row. "I wish I hadn't come," Thomas mumbled.

"We're going to catch something pretty soon," I told him. But I knew he meant we had walked too far and the air was too cold. His black buckle boot had a barbwire hole in it that let snow on his sock. His left foot had been frostbitten the winter before. He liked to complain about it.

"I don't care about this," said Thomas, who knew it might take Father hours to make the pole sets for the beaver. Then five miles to walk home; six with the side trips we had to make for the other fisher traps. We wouldn't be home until dark.

We broke pieces from dead trees. Thomas chopped some low pine limbs at the bog's edge. I peeled birch bark for a starter.

The ice melted around the log Thomas and I shared. We took off our boots and rested our sock feet on spruce branches almost in the blaze. Our thawing toes hurt. The smoke rose straight in the air. We ate the cans of sardines Mother had tucked in our coat pockets. We shared the roll of lifesavers and the strong cheese wrapped in brown paper. The snow did not quench our thirst.

Far down the pond we saw Father chopping with his pick: steady, straight-backed, forceful. We could hear the ringing of iron on ice.

The mink traps had been empty when we'd followed the brook in to the pond. One was frozen over so a mink could have walked right on it without harm. Father had smashed the ice without a word. He made Thomas reset the trap, plunging bare hands and arms into the black water. Water seeped out from the fire and turned the snow to gray slush at our feet. Cinders floated. I gathered sticks and watched them flame. I held a brand to the back of Thomas's bent neck to make him jump and knock it away. I threw bits of snow into the fire to hear the sizzle.

Thomas huddled over the warmth. "You didn't have to come, you know," I told him.

"Yes, I did," he said with red eyes. Father didn't always have to punish Thomas to bring the redness. Sometimes he just shook his head or set his jaw so the skin was tight, and Thomas would shut up and be red-eyed.

"Are you still cold?" I asked.

"Not so much," he murmured. I wished I hadn't asked. I wanted him to say, "Course not, damn you."

"He won't be much longer," I said.

"You don't know."

Before Father finished the beaver sets, the flakes had started. They were slow and scattered at first so we hardly noticed, picking up to sting our cheeks and melt on our faces.

I watched the swirling against the sky. I welcomed the snow. Thomas watched it accumulate on his sock through the hole in his boot.

"Should we put the fire out, Father?" We refastened our snowshoes. We pulled hats down and scarves up for the long walk home.

"What's it gonna burn in all this snow, little girl?" Father struggled to button his coat around his neck, still sweating from work.

Thomas kicked snow on the fire when Father's back was turned. "Where's it gonna go, Thomas?" I asked.

Father snapped around quick at Thomas, but did not speak. He hurried us. He knew the snow would not stop. The flakes were tiny, fast, wet-falling.

Father walked too fast. He walked fast enough to make my side pain and to make Thomas stagger. I watched the tails of Thomas's snowshoes, while the snow fell so heavy I could only see looking down. I thought we might go straight home and leave the two last fisher traps for another time, but Father left us sitting in the snow while he took the side path up to the first one.

He'd be right back if the trap was empty. If not, the resetting would take some time. The snow piled on Thomas's shoulders. When Father didn't come back and didn't come back, I stamped my feet, clapped my mittens, and danced in the snow. "Come on, Thomas, dance with me. We'll do a snow dance to be warm." Sometimes in our room Thomas and I danced until we were dizzy and red-faced. I could barely see him through the snow, but his words were clear and sharp in the silence of woods where even the birds were hiding until the storm passed. "He's taking his sweet time, ain't he."

"He must of caught something," I said.

"I don't care," said Thomas.

"You should be glad."

"You gonna be a trapper when you grow up, little girl?" he mimicked.

"Shut up," I said. "I don't know why you're so mad just because you're cold. There's worse things than being cold."

I followed Father's trail. I would walk to meet him. I would help. "He told us to stay here. You'd better stay here." Thomas grabbed my wrist at the bare part where the mitten didn't meet the cuff. The snow on his mitten stung me.

"I ain't tired," I said. "Are you, Thomas?"

I met Father. "I told you to wait below," he said. His eyes gleamed.

"What'd you catch?" I asked, knowing.

"A pretty little female, Elizabeth. Peek in the pack." He knelt. Female fisher had the finest fur and brought the best money.

She rested in his basket on top of his traps and ax and scent pouch. I pulled her out and rubbed her back against my face. The fur tickled.

"Can I carry her?"

"Don't drop her or drag her. I don't want no fur rubbed off."

I pulled off my mitten and touched her with my bare hand. The body moved with my pressing, the flesh still soft. Carrying her in my arms, I felt as if I had tamed a wild, living animal.

The snow piled on our snowshoes till we had to kick and push it off. Thomas and I strayed from the trail and tripped on invisible rocks and bushes. Father set too steady a pace. We followed, though, and did not fall far behind because he said not to.

Thomas breathed loud enough for me to hear even when we rested while Father went to tend the final trap. We sat close together under a spruce. The low branches kept the snow from striking us directly. I could smell the spruce needles. The snow bent the branches to the ground.

Father disappeared in darkness. Night had come early with the storm.

The fisher lay stretched across my lap, her tail in the snow, her head on Thomas's knee.

"He's not coming back," Thomas said through his scarf. "He's going to leave us here and tell Ma we got lost."

"He might leave you the way you act," I said. "But he wouldn't leave me."

Thomas cried, I think, though I really couldn't see.

"You talk foolish, Thomas. You don't talk like my brother."

"I'm cold," he said.

"Just because you're cold . . . "

"He don't care about us, you know," said Thomas.

"We'll be home pretty soon. You'll thaw."

"He don't!" he shouted.

"How do you know?"

"It's just the way he is," Thomas said. "He just does what he wants. He don't care about nobody."

I knew lots Father cared about. He cared about Mother because she was his wife. He cared about us because we were his kids. He cared about animals and outwitting them.

I held the fisher's face to mine and rubbed the length of her across my lips. She was warm and quiet. I imagined her my pet. If she'd been alive, though, she'd have been clawing and biting and fighting me. I loved her dead.

"Your mouth flaps too much," I said, the way Father would have said it.

"If we freeze up, he'll be in trouble."

"Why'd he be in trouble 'cause you were so stupid to freeze yourself?

61

Why'd you want to get your own father in trouble? You're crazy."

"I hate you," he said, and meant it.

I hugged the dead fisher. I stared out through the close spruce. My eyes strained to follow the tiny flakes that bent the thick branches. I would watch for Father, and he would come. Snow could not stop him.

Saturday Night at the Hi-View Drive-In

•

BY REBECCA RULE

I F YOU PUT TOO MUCH syrup in the bubbler, the cola will come out as thick and bitter as coffee that has set too long. If you put in too little, it'll be thin and customers will accuse you of watering it down. So I leave the mixing of cola to Paulie, the snack-bar manager. I don't want to hear about it if it turns out wrong. Same reason I pin my name under the collar of my blouse — the "Judy" hidden, the "Burley" only sticking out part way; I don't want to hear about it. I figure Paulie gets paid to manage, let him manage. Alphonse is Paulie's boss. Al works days for the state crew; nights he runs the drive-in, so he pulls in two salaries all summer long. Winters he puts in a lot of overtime during snowstorms. All in all, he makes good money. He's killing himself, of course. He doesn't sleep. I don't think he sleeps more than three or four hours a night all summer. Al's a young guy — not much older than me really, though he seems older because he's been working a long time. Also, he looks old. Three hours of sleep a night will do that — make your eyes red and tired all the time, cave your cheeks in, thin your hair. Well, maybe the thin hair he inherited from his father.

Al's saving his money to buy a camping area. He believes in 10 years there'll be as many tourists around in the summer for camping, hiking, and swimming as come winters to ski. He says they'll be swimming in the river! The river has been cleaned up. No more toilet paper in the mud; just bloodsuckers sticking to your feet when you accidentally touch bottom.

63

My winter job is behind the counter at "Bradley Mountain — the Pleasure Place." We call it the P.P. More skiers come every winter. Last year they began to complain about the lines, which is a real good sign. If I had to guess, I'd say there were more tourists around this summer than other summers. I think the camping area is a good idea. I think Al knows what he's doing.

Paulie asked Al once why he wasn't married. Paulie's married with three kids under six. They all have round faces just like Paulie, though theirs aren't as red. They'll get redder as they grow up — like Paulie. High blood pressure, I think. The boys have crew cuts like their father. The little girl looks like somebody (Paulie, maybe) put a bowl on her head and cut around it. She's cute. Paulie thinks the world of her, but he treats his wife like dirt. She probably doesn't think so, but I do. I don't think Paulie beats her, but he makes her stay home with the kids — gives her 25 a week for groceries, tells her if there's any left over she can spend it on herself. Generous, huh?

She had a chance to work at the drive-in. In fact, she could've had my job, but Paulie said he saw enough of her at home. He said that to her face. If I were married and wanted to work, I guess I'd work no matter what my husband said.

Anyway, one night when the three of us were cleaning up — Paulie washing dishes, Al wiping counters, and me sweeping — Paulie asked Al why he wasn't married. I just kept on sweeping as though I hadn't heard. I thought Al might be embarrassed to talk about not being married in front of me. I was curious, though. Al's a good guy with ambition. I was as curious as Paulie.

Al said he wasn't married because he worked too hard for his money. He said he'd seen too many guys get married and a year or two later end up divorced — with nothing. The wives got the house, the car, the upright freezer, whatever there was. "They don't care if a guy's been working two jobs since he was 16 so he could own his own house and put a few decent things in it. And it doesn't seem to matter if you've been married two months or 20 years. They want it; they get it," he said. "I'm not stupid enough to be taken to the cleaners by a woman."

I felt bad for him when he said that. He's a lonely man, I think.

Tonight I have to work the glass box. Taking tickets is my least favorite job, especially on X-rated nights, and that's when I usually get stuck with it because that's when the high-school kids — the part-timers — have to stay in the snack bar. It's the law: nobody under 18 allowed outside during an X. They're allowed to serve popcorn and listen if they want (there's a speaker behind the counter), but God forbid they should be outside where they might take a peek. Of course, they *do* watch. Business gets slow and the boys sidle out the side door to stand in the shadows near the men's room. They take it all in. Sometimes the cop will come up and stand right next to them. He doesn't care. He's watching, too. They're all watching.

And here I sit, just about the only female in the place, on a bar stool in a fluorescent glass box. The light's so strong inside the box that as soon as it gets dark, as soon as the movie starts, I can't see anything except my own reflection on three sides. My hair starts out smooth and pulled back in a barrette. Then the booth heats up, I begin to sweat, the hair strings around my face, sticks across my forehead. I look like hell but I can't comb it — not sitting there all lit up with the cars backed end-to-end all the way to the highway. They can see me, but I can't see them. That's the way of it, since most of them don't come out of the woodwork until after dark. They don't care about catching the beginning of the movie; they just want to be sure nobody driving by sees them waiting to get in. It's worse than standing in line at the rest room; you don't mind doing it if you have to, but you don't want an audience.

Some leave their headlights on while they wait. Beyond my reflection I can see five or ten sets of headlights, smaller and smaller down the line. When customers pull up, the booth lights hit them and they kind of draw back — like clams when you poke them with a fork tine to see if they're alive; they draw back just a little as if the light hurts their eyes. Then the hand comes out with the money. I reach through the half-moon window and replace the bills with tickets and change. They drive on.

We need the lights so I can count how many in each car. Usually on X nights, the counting is easy. A man alone — dollar seventy-five; a man and a woman huddling, the woman's face upturned on the man's shoulder as if to prove she isn't embarrassed, or turned away as if she sees something real fascinating out the side window (like a spruce tree or cat's eyes) — three-fifty.

As darkness comes on strong, my hands stiffen with money dirt and the windows turn to mirrors. I can see every blemish on my face, but mostly I notice my double chin, pale and soft, which I hate and can't seem to get rid of no matter how much I weigh. If I lost 20 pounds, the chin would still plague me. I *should* lose 15; I can tell by the way my mother looks at me when I take second helpings at Sunday dinner. She expects me home Sundays.

I have gained weight since I moved out. The trouble with cooking for yourself is that you cook just what you like, so you eat too much. One of these days I'll start cooking food I don't like — fish sticks, liver, turkey tetrazzini.

Without the double chin, I wouldn't look half-bad. Even now, when I smile the chin stretches out of sight; my nose is straight enough, my eyes big enough, blue enough. One ear is bigger than the other, but you can't tell under my hair. Sometimes I believe if I combed my hair just right and could hold a smile for six or eight hours straight, I could maybe attract a decent man — someone more decent than that creep Mark Ham with his curly red hair and sideburns, so full of himself he wouldn't notice another person half-dead across the room.

He thinks *he* broke up with *me* and I let him think so because, basically, I am a kind person who'd just as soon not hurt anyone's feelings, though I know Mark would have trouble imagining — even if I told him so — that a girl like me, double chin and all, could get sick of him, could become repulsed at the thought of his slimy hand holding hers, his slimy arm around her shoulders. Slimy freckled hand, slimy freckled arm. The man has freckles all over — as far as I know. I mean I never saw *all* of him, although once at Hampton Beach I saw him in a pair of those black, skimpy swim trunks like the Canadians wear. We sat in the sun for about six hours. He burned, of course, all over. He pulled his knees up to his chin and, with his mirror shades in place, watched the girls bounce by. To me he looked like some kind of red squash curled up there in the sand, the freckles like a brown blight all over. So there I sat in my pink one-piece with the ruffled skirt designed to hide unsightly bulges while he ogled other girls.

Why he asked me out in the first place is a mystery. In the city shopping, I met him on the street. Pleased to see someone from home, I smiled a big smile and talked to him like he was a long-lost pal: What are you up to? Do you have a job? Have you seen so-and-so? That kind of friendly talk. I forgot myself; I'm supposed to be shy. In second grade I heard someone describe me as shy and figured, why not? I started acting shy and kept it up. In high school, if there'd been a yearbook page for "Most Shy," they'd have put my picture in. Shy is a good safe way to be, though it does wear on a person after a while because of all the things you have to pretend you're too shy to do.

Anyway, the next night Mark called and asked me out. I couldn't believe it. Maybe I did so much smiling that day on the street, he hadn't noticed my chin. Maybe he thought I was pretty. Maybe he thought I was nice. Maybe he was just hard up. I don't know. In high school he went out with pretty girls like Sheri Pritchard, the short cheerleader. Maybe he was sick of her type. I don't know. I didn't know then and I don't know now.

One thing, I don't smile *at all* while selling tickets from the glass box because somebody might get the wrong idea.

The trouble with Mark is . . . well, his name for one. I couldn't seem to pronounce it the way he wanted me to.

"My name is not Mac," he'd say. "It's *Ma-er-k*." He pronounced the first sound "Ma" like what I called my mother. He growled the second and choked on the third.

"I know," I'd say. "Mark."

"Not *Mac*."

"I didn't say Mac; I said Marrrrk."

Where he learned to pronounce r's in the middle of words is beyond me, but I just can't seem to get the hang of it. Finally he told me to call him Baby. Isn't that a sickening name for a grown person? So I ended up calling him nothing at all. He called me Baby once; I told him to cut it out. "I'm not *your* baby. I'm not *a* baby," I said. "I like to be called by my name." He looked shocked. Maybe he thought I had no opinion about what anybody called me. Maybe he thought I ought to be happy to be called anything at all.

Same thing, when we rode in his truck he always wanted me right next to him so he could slide his arm around me. I didn't find that a comfortable way to ride, particularly with the floor shift between my legs, but he insisted. Maybe he thought I didn't, or shouldn't, mind being uncomfortable.

The other trouble with Mark — the main trouble with Mark — was that's as far as it went — the hand holding, snuggling in the truck, kissing on Main Street. One night he grabbed me in front of Laverdiere's and kissed me like we were in a movie (PG, not X). He kissed me for a long time while running his hands up and down my back. I thought I was in heaven. At the same time, I hoped nobody I knew was watching.

But that's as far as his affection went. When we were alone, he lost interest. Not that I wanted to be mauled or anything, but I wouldn't have minded some PG hugs and kisses, some flattering whispers, a wrestling hold or two.

After a few months I began to wonder what was wrong with me. I was sure he'd done more with Sheri Pritchard than sit on the couch and watch TV. At first I thought he was holding off because of some notion that I would be embarrassed to be loved. Eventually though, I began to feel there was something so ugly about me inside or out or both that he couldn't force himself to get close.

So I started not answering the phone when I knew it was him. I was sassy and sarcastic when we met. Besides telling him not to call me Baby, I complained about the vertical hold on the TV. I complained about the flat root beer and stale potato chips he liked to feed me. I complained about the radio stations he tuned in and the floor shift between my legs. Once I even told him his after-shave turned my stomach, which it did. After a few weeks of that treatment, he said, "Judy, you've changed. I don't think I want to go out with you anymore."

Subtle, huh?

I replied sweetly, "I don't know what you mean, Mark. But if that's how you feel, then I guess that's how it's got to be."

The trouble is I broke up with Mark nearly a year ago, and nobody decent has asked me out since. Sometimes I wonder if I should have been more patient. Sometimes I wonder if I'll ever get another chance.

Behind me, make-believe lovers slurp and groan. The music dies down making each lover-sound more distinct. Of course I'm curious. Of course I want to turn around for a peek. My neck aches from wanting to turn around for a peek. I mean, I *know* what's going on, but I'm curious to see for myself. Sounds like they ate something bad at supper — some overripe turkey tetrazzini, maybe. They slurp it up. Then, when it hits the stomach, the groaning starts. Of course I know that's *not* what's going on, but I have to entertain myself somehow sitting here all lit up and alone in the ticket booth. Even when they scream, I don't look back. I *never* look at the screen when I'm in the glass box.

Five minutes before intermission, Al will be down to take over so I can work the snack bar. Maybe he'll come down early so we can chat a while. I like visiting with Al, though our chats are never what you'd call chatty. He'll say something kind of sarcastic like: "Big turnout tonight. I guess the word's out." Which might not be sarcastic except for the way he twists his face when he says it and for the fact that I know he doesn't think much of the movies he shows. For one thing, he could be arrested at any time. Whenever a new movie comes in, the town sends a contingent — chief of police, a selectman or two, sometimes even the county sheriff — to decide whether or not it's pornography up there against the sky. Usually they all arrive together in an official vehicle with writing on the door, bubble lights, and a floppy radio antenna. How they decide about pornography, I don't know. Maybe they sit in there voting. "All those who think this is dirty, signal with a 'yea.' . . . All those who think it's just good fun? . . ."

68

They haven't closed us down yet; Al hasn't had to go to jail. Though I don't suppose jail would bother him much. He's the kind of guy who takes things in stride, though I know he'd be upset about missing work if they kept him locked up too long. He doesn't like to miss work; he likes to keep the money coming in.

"Yup," I'll say to Al, "looks like they're coming out of the hills for this one. I've sold . . ." and I tell him how many tickets I've sold to make him feel good. Instead of being paid by the hour like the rest of us, he gets a percentage.

"Yup," he'll say, "the word's out."

Maybe neither of us is a fast talker. Maybe that's why I feel comfortable talking to him. I don't feel like he's analyzing everything I say or counting my r's. When he shows up, I can leave the glass box and move up to the snack bar where I'll stuff lukewarm meatballs into submarine rolls for impatient customers. I'd much rather do that than take tickets, even though the sauce dribbles down my fingers and stains my cuffs, even though some people give me the cold stare like I should get my fingers off their meatballs. "My hands are clean," I feel like telling them, "probably cleaner than yours." Al's strict about clean hands in the snack bar. He keeps a can of Boraxo on the counter by the sink; the sign says "Use me." When customers give me the cold stare at the snack bar, I give them the same right back. If you act shy when you're waiting on people, they'll begin to make demands: "A little fuller," they'll say, wanting four meatballs when I'm supposed to put in just three. "More butter," they'll say, when I'm supposed to squirt just once on a small order of popcorn and twice on a large. Not that Al would say anything; Al's never spoken a harsh word to me, not even when I came out seven dollars short at the ticket booth. Paulie's the one who makes the rules about how many meatballs and squirts are allowed. And Paulie has a temper that I don't care to stir up. So when a customer demands more butter, I put it on quick and hope Paulie doesn't notice. I don't like scenes — not with customers, not with bosses.

In spite of all that, I'd rather work in the snack bar than the glass box. Two hours in the box and I begin to lose my breath. Tonight, as usual, I've forgotten my watch and the clock's broken, so I try to read the upside-down watches on the hands that slide in and out of my half-moon window. Frayed shirt cuffs, hairy arms, tattoos, bug bites, warts, Band Aids, open sores, oil stains, freckles — a hand covered with freckles. I recognize those freckles.

"Mark?" the name slides out before I can catch it. I forgot to pronounce the r.

I haven't seen him for a long time — months. Not face to face like this, nose to nose, since he's in the pickup, sitting up there pretty high. I've seen him in the distance a couple of times, on the street with time enough to cross to the other side and avoid him. Not that I *need* to avoid him, just that I have nothing to say. Here, with lovers behind me 50 feet high, wrestling across the night sky, and the man who might have been my lover in front of me with the booth lights in his face, I find myself with less to say than usual. Yet I feel like I should say something.

Under the lights every freckle shows. His eyes are pink, unblinking. I feel like I'm in a who-will-blink-first contest. I quit. I blink.

"One," he says.

"Dollar seventy-five," I say, taking the five and handing back a quarter and three bills. He's wearing his class ring — sapphire blue in a white-gold setting. It is a big, fat ring. Once he offered it to me — to wear, you know, how high-school girls do with yarn wound around a hundred times for fit, or on chains around their necks. I told him that was kid stuff, which it is.

"How long you been working here?" he asks. He still hasn't blinked. Maybe his eyes are glued open.

"Since spring," I say. Then, because there are no cars waiting and because he's staring as though he expects more, I add, "It's easy work. What about you? Are you still at the tech school?"

"Part-time," he says, pronouncing the r carefully, spitting out both t's. I guess they teach you how to pronounce t's at the tech. He stares beyond me, at the screen. He's pretending to be talking to me, but staring at nude people on the screen. (I assume they're nude from the look in his eye.) He shuts his engine off like I've got nothing better to do than watch him watch the movie, than wait for him to decide whether he has something else to say to me. He's sitting there like I've invited him.

I never liked his attitude. I only went out with him because . . . because I wanted to see what it was like to go out with someone. Sad but true. He has no right to sit there in his big black truck staring at me and through me and beyond me with his little pink eyes. Men alone who pull up to this booth keep their eyes down. They don't look at me, and I don't look at them.

Mark told me once that he's the type of guy other guys like to pick fights with. He claimed something about the way he walks or carries himself seems to antagonize the guys who socialize on street corners —

young guys who quit school and work the graveyard shift if they work at all, guys with bottles in the pockets of their leather jackets. He seemed proud of his ability to cause trouble. "I can talk my way out of a fight," he said, "if I want to. Most of the time I just keep walking by. I just ignore them. They don't really want to fight me; they just think they do."

He's acting like he wants to fight me. My father says never stare a mean dog in the eye. He says that makes the dog feel like he's got to defend his territory. I feel like defending something. I feel like he's mocking me — and I hate to be mocked. The glass is between us though, so I couldn't punch his face even if I wanted to — which I do, sort of. It's a strange feeling; I've never wanted to punch a face this badly before.

He seems proud to be alone at an X-rated movie where he can sit in his comfy cab in the dark and think whatever obscene thoughts he wants to think, do just as he likes. He seems pleased that Judy Burley, the girl he dangled for months, *knows* he'll be thinking obscene thoughts and doing just as he likes, alone. On the other hand, maybe he's not so proud, maybe he feels found out, maybe he's embarrassed to be 20 years old and all alone at the Hi-View on Saturday night. Maybe he's bluffing. Maybe he's been one big, freckled bluff all along.

Then Al's behind me in the booth. I jump a little because I didn't hear him open the door. The whoosh of fresh air feels good. Close quarters, though; we can't help but brush shoulders as I move off the bar stool and he moves on.

"Paulie needs you at the snack bar, Judy," he says. Al hardly ever calls me by my name. I like the way he says my name. No doubt he's wondering why this joker is parked in front of the ticket booth. No doubt he's going to say something about it if Mark doesn't move along soon. I can hardly wait.

Mark tries the stare treatment on Al, but Al won't put up with it. He laughs a kind of clearing-your-throat laugh and says, "What's the matter, buddy? She give you the wrong change, or is your truck broke?"

Mark doesn't answer. He turns the key fast, lets the clutch out too quick so the truck lurches forward. Al and I are silent for a minute or two as we watch the truck lights travel down one row, up another. Mark's being choosy about where to park it. Somebody toots; they don't like his lights and noise this far into the movie.

"What a jerk," Al says.

"He *is* a jerk," I say, meaning it. If Al says he's a jerk, then he must be one, he must have been one all along. I give Al a big smile. I feel my double

71

chin stretching right out of sight. I wonder if he knows what I'm smiling about.

"I can't believe I ever went out with him," I say, just to let Al know I'm the kind of girl men sometimes ask out; it seems important to let him know that if someone were to ask me out I probably wouldn't hurt his feelings by saying "no," even if the guy were a jerk, which, of course, Al isn't. "Thanks for getting rid of him," I say. "He can't take a hint."

"No problem," he says quietly.

I run between the parked cars from row to row toward the lighted snack bar. I'm careful not to look inside any cars; I don't want to see what's going on; I don't want to know. I concentrate on rear bumpers, license plates, and speaker posts.

Paulie's behind the counter looking harried, as usual. His white apron is buttered up and his forearms are orange with meatball juice. The coffee machine's broken, so he's been mixing instant in little styrofoam cups on the spot. The counter is brown with coffee, and sticky. Neatness is not his strong suit. Sweat has streaked his face and plastered his collar to his neck. The collar's in love with him, clinging when he pulls at it with a thick, orange finger. Even with the top button open, this shirt, like all his shirts, seems too snug at the neck, riding up, riding down with his Adam's apple. He won't unbutton a second button. I don't know why: maybe he's got a tattoo on his collarbone or something; maybe he's bald-chested. Paulie's all right to work with as long as you don't make him mad, but he treats his wife like dirt. Maybe buying shirts a size too small is her way of paying him back.

I think of Al down in the glass box, waiting for those last few customers to straggle in — dollar seventy-five, three-fifty, dollar seventy-five — his percentage night after night adding up to a campground on the side of the mountain: electric hookups, running water, one-holers nice and clean, firewood for sale by the bundle or cut-your-own deadwood. His own place, his own work, no more moonlighting. The man will be able to sleep eight hours a night in his own little cabin in the woods. He'll have time to rest, time to think about something besides work, time to think about the help he needs and how lonely he is — time to be lonely and do something about it.

I wonder how long it'll take him to realize that I'm the kind of woman who would *never* take him to the cleaners.

Timepiece

·

BY DIANE COPLIN HAMMOND

S INCE ERIC'S BEEN COMING here I've started hearing the clocks
again. There's at least one in every room in my house — cuckoo
clocks, digital clocks, clocks that glow in the dark and ones that
play tunes on the hour, a plastic Snoopy clock that's still in Bradlee's room
— and when you're very quiet you can hear the whole house murmur. It's
peaceful, in a way, this steady drone of time. Those clocks aren't in any
hurry, they're making their way towards eternity. Left alone they'll get
there, too. Bradlee did a good job. He fixed them to last forever.

Eric picked up on the clocks right away. He seemed to know they
were private. He didn't make any comment about them the way most
people do; he just looked them over, sort of counted them up (there are
five in the living room alone), and then looked out the window for a while
like he was trying to figure something out. Then he looked at me. Whatever he came up with still seems to be troubling him, but I'm not about to
ask about it.

Eric is a gentle man, a shy man, the type you expect to have narrow
shoulders, although he doesn't. He's a music teacher at the high school,
but what he really wants is to be a concert pianist. It's clear he won't make
it; he's already 35. He knows this, I'm sure, although he has never brought
it up. He is a man who accepts facts.

Even before he saw the clocks in my living room, Eric did things for
me. If it was cold outside, for instance, he would bring my scarf to me and

73

tuck it around my throat. Solicitous things. Yesterday he convinced me to take a nap, and while I was asleep he did my laundry.

Eric is a good man, a man to trust. I know that. Even so, I have no intention of telling him about Bradlee. You start giving things away to people, pretty soon there are just that many more things you'll never have back again.

Mrs. Muriel Truesdell, Bradlee's and my mother, was an alcoholic. Why mince words? I simply state it as fact. She was a good-natured alcoholic, after all, and she was usually pretty discreet, at least when I was growing up. It wasn't too difficult for her to pull herself together for a Parents Weekend once in a while.

She had a lot of class in a vulgar sort of way. She was a pure type. The Mrs. was strictly honorary, of course. It went with the flashy emerald wedding ring she bought herself on credit at Tiffany's. She was a big, tobaccoey blonde, a sales representative for all kinds of office equipment, copiers, business forms, you name it, whatever was hot. She lived all right for a while; she had money to burn. She worked hard, I'll say that for her, and then her men were generous. I was in nine different girls' boarding schools from the time I was eight until I was eighteen.

I don't know how it was for Bradlee, but I liked Muriel. She let you know that however much you might think about hating her, she'd beaten you to it. Pretty soon you were lying about how happy you were just to cheer her up. I don't remember her ever calling me by name. She called me Baby. Oh, Baby, look at this place I've put you in this time.

And how the hell she did it when she was never around I'll never know, but she always made you understand that she loved you like nothing else on earth. Love drove her crazy, though. She wasn't built to withstand anything stronger than a good time. She never once visited me when she didn't break down within the first hour over something stupid like a bruise I'd gotten playing field hockey or the fact that I was wearing a cardigan that was too small. She'd be awash all day. Muriel sure knew how to cry. She could really let go. She was pretty, but she looked tubercular when she'd been crying.

But mostly I didn't see her. Most of the time it was like being an orphan whose mother has died and gone to Trenton or Poughkeepsie. You couldn't get in touch with her, and she was never around when you needed her most or anything like that, but she was out there somewhere loving the hell out of you, and that was some help. It's even some help now. She's dead, of course, but in Muriel's case that's really only a detail, a technicality.

As I say, though, I don't know how it was for Bradlee. He was one late

74

arrival, and by then Muriel was on a slide. She was selling advertising novelty items for a greasy Italian in Newark. Ashtrays, party balloons with some company's logo on them, gimmick business cards. She'd run through more companies by that time than you could call off in one breath. She just couldn't keep her hands off the clientele. In the early days, of course, that was good for business. But when a woman hits 40 and looks like she's pushing 50, it can be an embarrassment for everybody.

I don't know what-all Muriel did with Bradlee the first few years, without money for boarding schools. Just because she believed that Bradlee had a right to life didn't mean she'd ever intended for him to have a life with her. All I really know is I got a call one day from one of Muriel's sleazy boyfriends telling me that Bradlee needed to come stay with me for a while. A few hours later Bradlee stepped off a bus at the Greyhound terminal talking to some stranger like he couldn't imagine anything better to be doing in the world.

He was five years old.

From the time he saw the clocks, it turns out, Eric thought I was terminal. Shopping around for a farm to buy. Dying. The way he explained it, he'd figured out something was wrong from the very start. I can see how he might have come up with that. For one thing, I'm pale as the devil. Of course I always have been; I got that from Muriel. Not a pearly, delicate pale or anything, more a sort of bluish pale, and I don't wear makeup. I also don't sleep much anymore; I average about three hours a night, so I'm usually tired.

So when Eric spotted the clocks — and he picked up on them so fast I think now that he was looking for something like them, some clue — it merely confirmed for him that I wasn't in it for the long haul. The way he pieced it together, I had surrounded myself with time because I must not have enough of it, must need to savor it, know it inside out.

He told me this very gently, sitting on my sofa holding my empty gloves in his hands. He wouldn't even look at me. The whole thing had come out because my furnace had nearly blown up the night before, and we were waiting for the repairman to come. The house was freezing and Eric kept asking me to go to his apartment, where it was warm, while he waited at my house alone. Even after he explained and I told him he was wrong, he kept trying to get me to put a hat on, wrap another blanket around myself.

Here was a man who had faced the fact that I might check out at any minute, and he was still sitting with me in my living room freezing to death waiting for the furnace man to come.

75

I've decided to tell him about Bradlee.

When Bradlee first came to stay with me, I had never seen him before. I recognized him at the bus terminal from photos Muriel had sent me, though. He was a real chipper kid; he had these stained-glass eyes. He even had freckles, like he'd come right out of some corny Norman Rockwell painting. He was carrying this little plaid suitcase and some man had hold of his hand until he was sure we were squared away. Bradlee had that effect on people.

On the ride to my apartment — I was in college by then, but I'd had enough of dormitories — I asked him what-all he'd brought in his suitcase. He said spacemen. I said how many spacemen can you stuff in a little bag like that, and he said only a couple. The rest were coming in the morning by parcel post. When I got him settled down and opened up his suitcase, there wasn't a thing in it. Not so much as a toothbrush. Muriel had forgotten to pack. We managed with what we could get Bradlee at Kresge's.

Bradlee sure could talk that first visit. Not about anything real most of the time; for instance, I could hardly ever get him to tell me anything about Muriel. He did say he spent a lot of his time with a Mrs. Consuelo Gonzales — that's how he referred to her, Mrs. Consuelo Gonzales — and that Mrs. Gonzales liked to dress him in three or four outfits a day from hundreds she kept in a closet. I didn't know how much to believe. Some people pray, others drink. Bradlee made up stories.

The spacemen he brought in his suitcase lived in my broom closet for a good two months. Their names were Petie and Gee. The others, the ones that came by parcel post, Bradlee sent back by return mail. He said there wasn't room for them in the closet and besides, Petie and Gee didn't like them all that much.

Petie and Gee weren't any problem to have around. I mean, Bradlee didn't try to give them half his dinner or anything like that. He said they lived off specks of dust in the air. The most he did was leave pieces of dental floss on the closet floor for them. Bradlee was meticulous about hygiene.

But after a while, I noticed Petie and Gee weren't around much anymore, and I asked Bradlee about it. He said they were down the road in a vacant lot putting together a spaceship. Gee's birthday was coming up, and he wanted to get home for that. On a hunch I managed to get a call through to Muriel. I was right: Bradlee was going to turn six in four days. We went out to a spaghetti house to celebrate the night after Petie and Gee blasted off.

Because his birthday was in November, Bradlee wasn't due in kindergarten until the next year. I couldn't afford day care, so I took him to all my classes at the university. He was real good about that, too; he figured out just how to act. He latched onto one of my empty notebooks, got a pencil, and pretended to take notes like everyone else. He couldn't write a word, but he did a first-rate job of faking it.

In early May I got a call from Muriel telling me to send Bradlee back. Baby, she said, I'll never be able to forgive myself for sticking you with that child. Oh, Baby, did you ever hear of such a mother? She was crying to beat the band; you could practically wring out the phone. Listen, Baby, I'm starting out fresh, she said, I'm changing my ways because my family doesn't live long, and I can't stand the thought of dying the kind of person I've been. Baby, no one, not even me, should have to die like that.

We argued about Bradlee a little, but there was really nothing I could do. Muriel was bullheaded when she got onto something, and my university let out in another three weeks. I had almost no money left, what with Bradlee and all, and I was going to have to work two jobs to make up, which meant I'd never be home. For the summer, at least, I figured he'd be better off with Mrs. Gonzales and Muriel.

I pinned my phone number and address inside Bradlee's suitcase lining when I took him to the bus terminal. He didn't seem to mind going back. I called him a few times at first, but then they must have moved again because the line was disconnected and Muriel wasn't listed anywhere in Newark. I kept hoping Bradlee would call, but he didn't. When I graduated from school, I moved to a better part of town, and I was careful to check directory assistance every so often to make sure I was still listed in case they tried to find me. They never did. I didn't hear anything again until Bradlee was 10.

It's taking me a long time to tell Eric about Bradlee. It's been three weeks, and I haven't even gotten to the clocks yet. I haven't been talking nonstop; it isn't the sort of thing you want to ride right through to the end in a hurry.

When Eric and I are together now we rarely go out. If we're not talking, we're making love. Once we went ice skating and Eric put on these wicked-looking black hockey skates he said he'd worn in high school. He looked different, surer, standing so quietly on those long, thin blades. That's the way he makes love, with a sureness and strength you wouldn't have expected. Afterwards he holds me until I fall asleep. Until Eric, being held was always rare and strictly compensatory.

I owe that man. I owe him.

It was late August when I got the call from a Mr. Anderson. At first I thought he was another one of Muriel's boyfriends, but he turned out to be a lawyer, calling to tell me that Muriel was dead. She had developed kidney and liver failure and died within five weeks.

Muriel left me $10,000 in life insurance, $12,000 worth of debts, and Bradlee. The lawyer seemed embarrassed about the whole thing. Did I have adequate housing? Yes, I did. Did I consider myself fit to raise the boy? Could I be less fit than Muriel? Did I have sufficient income to provide for Bradlee? Just.

So I drove up to Massena, this godforsaken town in upstate New York, and fetched Bradlee back. By then I had my house, a homely little stucco place in one of the working-class neighborhoods just outside the city. Everyone on my street except me is retired. I bought the house and all the furniture inside as part of an estate sale. The place was chock-full of lace doilies, antimacassars on the chair backs, hutches full of lead crystal nut dishes, cupboards full of glass, that sort of thing. Lace curtains, dark furniture. I didn't change a thing. I love it and so, I think, did Bradlee. I'd find Bradlee sometimes cleaning the things in the hutches, turning knick-knacks over and over in his hands, dusting the crystal figurines.

Our household, once I'd gotten Bradlee settled in, could have doubled for the set of "Leave It to Beaver" any day. I wore bib aprons and carried tea towels around. I even started wearing some old flowered shirtwaists I found in an upstairs closet. I fixed us nutritious, all-American meals like meat loaf and mashed potatoes, pork chops and green beans. I was learning to can vegetables from my garden. I had fixed my schedule so I would be home when Bradlee got back from school.

Bradlee was still a pretty kid — you kind of wanted to see him turn his baseball cap sideways, he was that kind of good-looking. But he'd gotten very quiet, very intense, and he still didn't talk about Muriel much. He did tell me she wouldn't let him near her at the end. While she was in the hospital dying, she made him stay with a neighbor named Margaret Jackson, a fellow dropout of Muriel's from Alcoholics Anonymous. The last time Bradlee saw Muriel was a week before she died. She sent him out for cigarettes.

I enrolled Bradlee in the neighborhood school right away so he could start off fresh with the other kids, but he didn't bring anyone home, and I don't think he was ever invited anywhere. He didn't seem lonely to me though. What he did was he began to collect clocks.

At first he'd bring home old busted ones he'd found in the trash or had gotten from the neighbors, and he'd tinker with them down in the basement by the hour. Then he discovered Mr. Henry down the street. It turned out that Mr. Henry had made his living repairing clocks, and pretty soon Bradlee was spending every weekend over at his house working on clocks. Bradlee would stop off there after school sometimes, too, if he'd found a real treasure he couldn't wait until the weekend to show off. For Bradlee's twelfth birthday Mr. Henry gave him a pretty miniature grandfather clock he'd built himself. For Mr. Henry's eighty-first birthday Bradlee gave him an electric space-commander clock where all the works were visible through this smoked lucite body that was in the shape of a spaceship. He'd been fixing it up for weeks and he was real proud of it, I could tell. They had plans to build a full-scale grandfather clock from a kit, and Bradlee was going to get a paper route so he could raise his part of the money. He never did that, though. Mr. Henry checked out before he had a chance.

Bradlee was the one who found him. According to the medical examiner, Mr. Henry had been dead for two days when Bradlee discovered him slumped over his worktable, still holding a pair of needle-nosed pliers in his hand. You'd expect a kid to get hysterical about something like that, but Bradlee was very calm; in fact, he was the one who called the county coroner's office. You'd think he'd been finding people dead all his life.

After that Bradlee spent more time with his clocks than before. He arranged them all over the house. He'd go around every day making sure they all read exactly the same time, and it upset him if I rearranged them in cleaning. I probably should have made him talk about it, but you don't make Bradlee talk about things. I figured he'd work it out for himself.

Which he did, in a way.

One afternoon when I came home I noticed Bradlee's book bag already in the front hall. That was unusual; I generally beat him home by 20 minutes. I went upstairs to look for him — I thought maybe he'd gotten sick during the day and was asleep. I found him in his room.

He was sitting in the middle of the floor, and he'd arranged 12 clocks around him in a circle. They were all different types and shapes, and they all faced him. When I asked him if he was feeling okay, he just looked at me. I wasn't sure he'd heard me so I asked him again, and he just kept looking at me with those stained-glass eyes of his, and it was then I noticed he was rocking. It was nothing obvious or anything, but he was rocking back and forth, back and forth.

He was keeping time with the clocks.

He had somehow gotten them all to tick at the same time, and he was just rocking back and forth, keeping time.

79

That was six months ago. He hasn't spoken a word since.

Eric has come to the state institution with me the last few times. He agrees that Bradlee's a beautiful kid. We both know he's never coming out of there, but we don't talk about it.

Eric rarely goes home to his apartment anymore. It's nothing we've decided on; it's just worked out like that. He has talked me into putting the clocks away. We've filled a trunk full of them and shut it in the attic. Eric was afraid of them for me — is afraid — and although I've tried to reassure him, it is difficult. Because privately I'm sure that sometimes, late at night when Eric is asleep, I can still hear them, even up there in that trunk. This is impossible, of course, because they're not even plugged in or wound up, but still I'm sure I hear them.

And it's not a frightening sound at all. I can understand how it must have comforted Bradlee that last year, may be comforting him now if he can still hear them. But they hold no answers for me the way they did for Bradlee. They are only clocks. And if I hear them sometimes, it is only mixed in with Eric's soft, even breathing, and when he sighs and shifts in his sleep to cup his hand over the top of my head, I know it is only his breathing I have been hearing all along, quiet and sure, keeping time in the night.

And this will do, for now. It will do.

Old Light

·

BY BARRY TARGAN

W E HAD COME UP to the farm for our four summer weeks, and Maine was all before us like a promise as various and new as the flow of the heavy tides. Blueberries, the sea, the pine-stained air, clamming on the mud flats, black bears at the dump. And there was the ritual of memory that she turned for us, like a massy key in the lock of the door to heedless days, a gift that each year increased its value as we grew ready for it.

Her house was her studio, a contrivance of light and space around her painting. Her work was everywhere, a dominant line. Sketchbooks, canvases, tubes, bottles, jars, frames, cans of brushes, until it all joined into its own controlling logic, but she moved about in it easily enough.

She painted anything that would hold light, but she was best known, well known, as a painter of people's faces. Not as a portraitist glorifying corporate presidents and dowager heiresses (though she had painted them all in her time), but a painter who tried to see, like her betters before her — Velasquez perhaps, Rembrandt — the soul figured forth in pigments. Her work hung in the world's great galleries and museums and private collections. And now young art historians wrote her letters and were beginning to construct treatises about her accomplishments and what they fancied was her glory.

But there was a greater glory. "Your father slept there from the time he was 12." She pointed through one of her large windows to a small barnlike shed. "Up top. Your grandfather and I, we slept here in the main house. And your Aunt Susan, well, we were never sure where she would turn up. With her you could never tell."

It was our delight to hear this, and our envy, I suppose. Against her indulgent but firm, creative chaos, we would compare the grumbling strictures we lived by, for our father, though an abundant man in all ways, was orderly and as accurate as one of his T-squares. "He gets that from your grandfather. He was orderly. But about the rest — meals and beds and clothing and where the children were — he never thought much about that and I suppose I didn't either. It must have put a mark upon your father."

And then, "Tell us about John Palmer," one of us would ask. Again. As always.

"Oh, you've heard all about John Palmer," she would say. "How about Winston Churchill? Or Eisenhower?"

"No, no. Tell us about John Palmer, how you met."

"I'll tell you about Rita Hayworth or William Faulkner. I met them too. Or Enrico Fermi."

"No, no. John Palmer. You and John." And the three of us, her grandchildren, would chorus her until she was borne back into that summer, into the salt-tanged days of war and love to come.

She had just graduated from art school in Philadelphia and now, in that summer, she went back to the Atlantic City boardwalk, where she had in summers past drawn quick portraits in charcoal or sepia pencil or full pastels. She worked in a boardwalk store that had been hollowed out to allow room for the 12 artists, their easels and chairs, and for the crowds who became their customers to stand behind them and watch them work. A man, Joseph Brody, owned the store — the Artists Village, he called it.

There wasn't much other work to get then, and what she had really wanted to do anyway, had wanted since childhood, was to visit Europe, to see the cathedrals, the paintings, Picasso, the Left Bank, the Paris night. But now, of course, Europe was aflame. Just weeks ago we had invaded it. Even as she drew the soldiers and their girls, many had received their orders. They would all get to Europe before her, but to a Europe she could not imagine now but could only fear for. Would the Cathedral at Ulm be standing? The Louvre? What would be left for her?

Atlantic City had been converted into possibly the world's largest military training base. All the hotels were made over into barracks, and all day soldiers would drill on the boardwalk. But at night and on weekends, even with the special precautions taken to keep the lights from shining out to sea, the city and the boardwalk turned back to play, as if the daytime business of preparing for war was just that, a business with regular hours and a set routine.

Everyone on the boardwalk then was from somewhere else, and that somewhere else was from anywhere in America — Idaho, New Mexico, Maine, the West Texas mountains, Louisiana, the cornfields of Kansas. And no one was staying. Everyone was passing through, to Europe or the Pacific. Nothing was standing still.

"Time and event was in charge of all our lives, sweeping us together and apart and yet toward a grand destiny that we all had a share in," she would tell us. "It was — the *war* was — terrible, but this, *this* was wonderful. A mad music. A heady wine."

About the end of July, maybe early August, in mid-afternoon when the temperature was very high and had driven everyone off the boardwalk and onto the beach, she and two other artists were taking their turns minding the store. It was a Monday, slow and tired after the hurtling weekend. Only Joseph Brody, from time to time, would whirl through and urge them to get up and pull someone in off the boardwalk, or maybe he even meant the beach. They paid no attention and Joseph Brody did not wait around to see if they did. This summer she was reading her way slowly through an anthology of American poetry. She had gotten to Whitman, and that day, remarkably, she had just read,

> *Give me the shores and wharves heavy-fringed with black ships!*
> *O such for me! O an intense life, full of repletion and varied!*
> *The life of the theatre, bar-room, huge hotel, for me!*
> *The saloon of the steamer! The crowded excursion for me! The*
>   *torchlight procession!*
> *The dense brigade bound for the war, with high-piled military*
>   *wagons following;*
> *People, endless, streaming, with strong voices, passions,*
>   *pageants.*

when she heard this man begin to talk to her. She didn't remember him *starting* to talk, just that he was talking when she finally heard him. He might have been talking to her for some time.

"You're the best one, you know," he said. "I've been watching you for two days and you are *by far* the best one. You should open your own place, or at least you should work on your own. Is the problem capital?

83

There are ways around that, you know. I've been looking around. There are three stores that would rent you space. Here, I've got the figures." He sat down in the customer's chair and pulled it over to her and produced a small notebook of figures — rents, percentages, equipment, paper, mats, bags, insurance, utilities. He had it all worked out. On paper she could have opened her own business in a week. She was astounded.

"Who are you?" she asked. And then, "And what's it your concern anyway?"

"I'm John Palmer," he said. "Corporal Palmer for the time being. And there's no point in getting angry. You don't have to open your own business just because you could. But if you ever think about it, this is the way to do it."

Just then Joseph Brody came by and saw John Palmer sitting close to her. "What is this, afternoon tea? You. Up," he said to John. John got up and Joseph Brody pushed the customer's chair back to its proper position and then he pushed John down into it.

"Now," he said. "You want to talk, so talk." To her he said, "Draw." And then he was gone.

"Go ahead, draw," John said.

"It's okay. You don't have to. Joseph is just a little crazy."

"No. It's okay. Go ahead, draw my portrait."

And so she did, and as she drew he talked on and on about her possibilities, about what she could do for herself if she wanted. And after a time she heard that it was good talk, that there was thought and fact and imagination to it and that what he had constructed for her was, indeed, as possible as he had claimed. Finally, when she got to his mouth, she told him he would have to stop talking so she could draw it. He stopped, but she could see that it was not easy for him, though it wasn't that he was *driven* to talk, it was only that he had so much to say.

By the time she had finished, a small crowd had gathered at her back, which was what usually happened, and when John got up another person sat down.

"Here," he said, and gave her the notebook with the figures and plans.

"Thanks, it's an interesting idea but I don't want to be that permanent. I've got more to do than this. But thanks. And good luck. Goodbye."

"I'll be back," he said. And he was.

Late in the afternoon three days later he returned with a wonderfully crafted artist's easel, unique and better than anything she had ever seen like it. It was made out of a lovely mahogany, elegantly jointed, with brass fittings and wooden buttons of a contrasting wood. It had drawers and compartments and arms that slid out of slots and turned in sockets. It even had places to hold extra canvases or boards. And most incredible of all, the whole thing could fold up as if into itself and could be carried about like a suitcase.

"For you," he said after demonstrating it.

"But wherever did you get it?" she asked.

"I made it. I designed it and I made it."

"You *made* it? But I don't understand."

"I'm a carpenter. A boat builder, actually, but they have me a carpenter now. I'm attached to a combat engineer unit bound for somewhere. I went to the shop and worked on this until I got it right, though I can think of ways I might change it if I ever do it again. That's the way I am."

He went to her regular easel and started to dismantle it, moving the lights, the chairs, her supplies, everything. Quickly he put the new easel — more a traveling studio — in place.

"But Corporal Palmer, how can I accept this? I don't even know you."

"It's not an engagement ring," he said over his shoulder. "It's just a piece of furniture." He turned. "And I sure can't take it with me, so you either have to take it or sell it or throw it out."

"What's going on here? What is this?" Joseph Brody descended and twirled like a tornado. "What is this?" He looked at the old easel before him and the new one in its place. He spun. He didn't know what to do. "You," he said to John, "what do you want?"

"My picture. I want her to draw my picture," he said, disarming Joseph Brody, neutralizing him.

"Oh . . . well . . . so," he turned to her, "so what are you waiting for? Draw him, draw him."

And she did. Then, and again and again and again four and five or even six times almost every day or evening right through August and past Labor Day.

And she would tell on, and as in any fairy tale, the three of us bore down upon the details, waiting to savor again the familiar, excited within our expectations the way you anticipate music that you have gotten by heart. John Palmer would come by at odd times, day but mostly night. He, like many others, was in a holding pattern, past training and now waiting for the exact orders to depart. Sometimes he had duties, but often not. He would come to the Artists Village and whenever she was not busy with a customer, he would talk to her, and when Joseph Brody would swoop down on them, he would sit and be drawn.

He would talk about *going on,* she would explain to us. It was as if he did not recognize the war, overlooked it, *refused it.* It would claim his time, but that was all. He was busy with other things that he could imagine. So busy that what he imagined became real enough to live by, as if he could actually see and touch what he was looking at through the mind's eye. And, oh, he looked at everything.

He was a boat builder born and reared in Warren, Rhode Island. But more than a boat builder. He was a master shipwright, the youngest ever in Rhode Island. He was a naval architect without the title or the schooling. He had taught himself their math and had read all their books, and then he added to that what he knew in his fingers and with it all built better boats. He told her about his triumphs, about the racing victories of Palmer boats through all of the Narragansett Bay and beyond. Clear over to Martha's Vineyard.

He designed and invented and built boats to any task — for racing or fishing or hauling or just to row in. He was 25 years old, but already had his own yard "stuffed with boats" waiting for his return, as he put it. But there was no arrogance to him, not a touch of it. It was confidence, rather, the self-assurance of a superb craftsman. To be so good at something that it could speak loudly enough for you, first you had to be absorbed by it, taken over and humbled by it. Finally, there had to be no room for *you* in your work. She knew what he meant. They talked about the discipline and intricacies of their respective crafts, though John did more talking than she.

And then, casually, he began to wait for her until she finished working, sometimes until one in the morning or even two on the weekends, when he would walk her home, to the room in the boardinghouse on a side street far from the boardwalk. But just as often they would stay on the boardwalk and walk its length talking about the things they had done with paint and wood and about the things they were going to do, the astonishing paintings, the magnificent boats. They did not talk about themselves. Or about each other, but who they were came clear, each to each, as they talked about their love of light and of straight-grained wood.

She had one day free each week, and they would go off. John was marvelous. He could produce anything. A car to take them away, a boat when they wanted, and just the right boat. He would rig a sail out of what he could find and they would poke about the sandbar islands and into the small inlets for crabs that they would eat late at night on a beach somewhere. Or he would sail them out to sea on a boat like a slab of wood with a sail not much more than a bed sheet, but he would tighten everything down and make the boat do just what he told it. She never worried then. She would have sailed around the world in those tiny boats with John Palmer at the tiller.

Those were filling days, the sea and the light bursting together, John Palmer sitting back with the mainsheet clenched in his toes like another hand, at ease in any swell, as she watched him, lean and effective, to remember and sketch later.

Sometimes a Coast Guard cutter would steam up close to them as if to board them for an inspection, but they were never stopped or questioned. The cutter would steam away, men along the rail looking at them, *glad* for them, for they were charmed.

They would fish and swim and walk through the starved sand grasses and the ground-up shells and sometimes they would walk across the sand stained with the oil from a torpedoed boat, oil that may have floated across from Portugal or hung about in the sea for years to come down finally on the beach.

And John Palmer could find anything. The moon snail alive creeping across the sand, the ripest beach plums, ghost crabs. Sometimes they would go down to Cape May, to the very point of New Jersey, and watch the birds of all sorts, and John Palmer would know them all. The birds and the stars and the trees and the curve and shape of everything and how it would weigh-out in water or air, how it would all balance.

"Gaiety," she would say to us. "It is the word I think of when I think of then."

Sometimes they would walk before the huge hotels, gray and ornate as sand castles, with the thousands of men in them sleeping, waiting to cross the dark sea just a hundred yards away, walk in the salty night carving the air excitedly into glowing images and animate shapes so sharp and firm that she always remembered them, even as the Coast Guardsmen with dogs patrolled the beaches at the water's edge against enemies, and airplanes from the mainland droned overhead looking out.

"Oh my, oh my," she would say, "but we were affirming flames."

Once they walked right into the dawn. They were not allowed to be on the boardwalk after certain hours, but by now the patrols knew them well enough and let them be. And that night they never turned back. They clambered their way out to the end of a rocky jetty and watched the sea slowly brighten into the day.

It was the first time that John Palmer was entirely silent. They just sat there closely in the darkness listening to the sea well up and hiss through the dried seaweed. They sat quietly thinking their own thoughts but each other's thoughts, too. When he finally did speak again he said, "Maybe after the war, I'll come back here."

It was the first time he had ever mentioned the war. "Maybe I'll come back here and build boats. There are special problems to water like this, different from the Bay." And he explained the problems. "And there are advantages." The easy cedar he could get, the oak, the wider-ranging markets of the Delaware and the Chesapeake. As ever, he had worked it all out first, not as a daydream but as a plan as exact as the boats that he would design even if he might never build them. John Palmer went about his life doing things one way.

"But what about your yard in Warren?"

"Oh, I could sell it off easy enough. A yard's not worth much more than the man who runs it."

"But you would be starting all over again."

"I don't see it as starting over, just as continuing in another place."

She thought he was going to say more, and she thought she knew what more he was going to say, but he had not thought her out fully enough for him to figure her into his calculations yet. Not yet, though she was sure he was working on it and the time would come. Then what would she do?

But the war came before them, swiftly. Orders. Packing up. No time for a gentle leaving. John Palmer came up to the boardwalk at a busy time. It was the Sunday of the Miss America Pageant week and she had customers waiting in line. He took his place. She did not see him until he sat down once again before her. He told her that he was leaving in a few hours. He talked on as if the audience at her back were not there. He had found a sawmill on the mainland that had stacks and stacks of perfectly dried planks waiting. He had made an informal contract with the operator. He went on as if the orders in his pocket and the ordering of his life were not in contention. He was, as always, *going on.*

But she could not put it all together as well as he, not nearly so well. The blue marine September day, Miss America in the air, the clog and density of people everywhere, the rivulets of perspiration that ran down through her charcoal-smudged face, Joseph Brody flying about like a trapped pigeon, John Palmer calmly figuring the length of his dry-dock runway against the average of the tides. And the battle lines in Normandy defined in the maps that the newspapers were now printing each day. She could not hold it together in a pattern.

Then John Palmer was gone. She had not even time for a proper good-bye. Before he left he gave her a portfolio of all the drawings she had done of him over the summer. And he would write. Make plans. Yes. But where? Where would she be? But he was gone. Someone else, another soldier, was sitting in his place. She drew him and how many others she could not tell. She saw nothing more. Not even John Palmer. Only a blankness.

Only much later that night at the bone-weary end of work did it all come together and she fell and kept falling into winter and into her life alone. The war had come suddenly true, and the fire that was John Palmer that had burned the mist of the war away was banked down now, and she grew cold.

She went back to Philadelphia and set up a studio and spent days doing nothing, hearing the radio, walking about, sitting in Rittenhouse Square for hours until it became too cold, sometimes doing freelance artwork that a friend would call about. Her money was running low, but she was listless, a cork bobbing about. There were parties to go to, and young men who were interested in her, and professors whose pet she had been who were anxious that she should begin her promising career. But she could not take hold, as if she had broken without being hurt and was mending now.

She grew cold with waiting for what she did not know. Only some-times the thought of John Palmer would warm her, his exuberance and confidence and energy would ray through her and for an hour or two or a morning she would start up, mix paint, spring at a canvas, paint at what she had talked to him about in the long summer nights and on the beaches and at sea. Then she would take courage. Make plans. But the winter wore on, bore her down in the snow and the shortness of things so that even John Palmer grew vague and thin and as fleeting as all of her life felt to her just then.

And the war bore down on her too as the terrible cost of moving the battle lines in the newspaper came clearer. By February she was as vacant as February can be, as toneless as a raw umber wash on an unprimed canvas.

And what was worse, she could not say what had happened to her. She was not suffering, exactly. She was not depressed or worried, only empty as if a plug had been pulled and she had drained out.

In late March a friend showed up at her dreary studio with a letter from Joseph Brody. She had worked for Brody too and he had sent the letter to her friend because he did not know how to reach her. She had given him no address, for she had no thought of returning to his Artists Village or to her indentured status. She had left the village. His letter thought otherwise. It was the same letter she had been receiving since her senior year in high school, a letter of instructions, work schedules, arrangement of pay. She dropped it on the table. But in his envelope there were other letters to her, six of them, from John Palmer. She opened them and arranged them in order, smoothing out the thin blue paper, and read them, long letters and thorough.

In the midst of war there was no war. Only the intimacy of personal effort and the sweep of his imagination doing this to some building or that to some machine. And the boatyard somewhere along the south Jersey coast grew more tangible in his letters even than in his talk. There were sketches, bills of particulars, lists. He even asked her to send for information from certain manufacturers whose names he included.

But he saw Europe, too, and reported to her that Chartres was intact, the Louvre undamaged though all the art was hidden away, that the Cathedral at Ulm was standing. He had remembered everything, every detail that she had told him about her European dreams and, as best he could, he had gone about seeing Europe for her. And he saw it clearly, not only the splintered streets, rubble-strewn and broken, but the spirit and the hope and the achievement of civilization. She knew enough about the destruction from the daily news. It took a John Palmer in the midst of it all to remember that there was more, and that time would come and maybe men like him to make life whole again.

She read all the letters and she read them three times again. And she stirred like life itself in March begins to stir. Who was John Palmer? She would see.

She found the portfolio of portraits she had drawn of him through the summer. She had stored them in the miraculous easel that he had built for her. Like his letters, she arranged the portraits in an order. There were 174 of them, and through that long March afternoon she watched herself as she came to know this man almost as if for the first time. And she discovered herself, too, how she had a great magic, and that she could find a person's humor in a charcoal line, his wit and compassion and strength and courage and fear. Through that summer she had been discovering John Palmer layer by layer. And discovering herself, too. Though she had found neither of them until now. And now she knew what she was supposed to do.

In the easel in which she had stored the portfolio there were other things — her hodgepodge of art supplies, broken shells and pieces of beach glass, sketchbooks. The easel was like opening the summer again. There was even sand. And there was the anthology of poetry she had been reading when John Palmer began to speak to her. The page was marked still, the poem at which she had stopped as he began to speak.

Give me the shores and wharves heavy-fringed with black ships!
O such for me! O an intense life, full of repletion and varied!
The life of the theatre, bar-room, huge hotel, for me!
The saloon of the steamer! The crowded excursion for me! The
  torchlight procession!
The dense brigade bound for the war, with high-piled military
  wagons following;
People, endless, streaming, with strong voices, passions,
  pageants.

She had fallen in love. And now what was she to do? Could she write to the APO address on his letters? The last letter was dated in January. She had answered none. What could he have thought? Did he imagine she worked at the Artists Village all year long? But of course she had told him that she would go back to Philadelphia, but she had no address to give him then. Would he understand that she was not receiving his letters even as he dutifully went on writing them? But she decided that John Palmer would figure out whatever was necessary if anyone could and that what he was doing was *going on.* The important figuring out to be done was for her. What was she to do? And where begin?

She would write, of course, but she would go back to where she had stepped off into nothing. She would go back to where she had gotten off of any path. And, of course, she was going back to wait. With the kind of faith that comes to us in life once only, when we are young enough to believe *completely* in anything we want, she went back to Joseph Brody's Artists Village because she *knew* that someday John Palmer would come back there to do what he had said, and that he would come back there for her too. And that they would walk off down the boardwalk again as if time had not happened, as if the bridges of the Rhine had not happened. He would come back and they would pick up their proper lives.

But he did not. The war claimed him after all. And her story would end.

In other years her story would end and we would ask clamoring children's questions like after a tale by the brothers Grimm, intense with the child's literal necessity of where and when and what and why, until the excitement of the story wore down and we were beckoned away by other pleasures.

But we were older now. *I* was.

"That's a sad story, Grandma," I said.

"Yes," she said. She had gone to the great window above the sea and watched the snake-necked cormorants resting on the exposed reefs. "Yes, it is. Sad. But it is a lovely story, too. I've remembered, you see. And proudly. Proudly."

I came to her by the window. My sisters had gone off. There was more to the story, this part of it now, as if she had waited until I had turned, was turning, into life myself. She had waited for me to allow her to come closer.

"He was a special man, John Palmer. A gorgeous human," she said. Then, "We all need — *must have* — someone like that happen to us, or else nothing will ever make enough sense. Do you understand?" She turned to me, hard and nearly vehement, but she was imploring, rather, and not angry, granting a trust now made good. "I love him still. I won't put that aside. I would not willingly lose him or give him up. Not in all these years. There's room in my life for him and your grandfather and for all of this." She waved her hand around her kingdom in and out of the house. "John Palmer made it large enough for that. I've had all the luck."

In the Surprise of Life

•

BY Sharon Sheehe Stark

T HIS IS A STORY OF Christmas past and of a grandmother; yet there is Lilly wilting in the wash of now; Lilly barefoot by the river. Deepest, thickest summer, the river's listless groping over stones, sky damp and colorless as a cough. Her husband's passion is the soft clay bank. Again and again his spade makes careful vertical incisions; the soil slices off like fudge.

These banks are lavishly nuggeted with Indian artifacts. Other weekends his toil was rewarded early, easily. Today the earth itself is a stony squaw, sullen with secrets, yielding nothing. Lilly's efforts are all *against* the mud, keeping her knees clean and her toddling daughter out of the soggy river bed. At 37, she is an old mother; this is hard work. The sagging air, the rhythmic scrape of his tool, swallows sweeping in to sip. She thinks of fern beds, of putting greens, of shade, of sleep . . . . Suddenly, what? A hardly remarkable stir: a deeper stillness. Whatever its shape, the moment is marked; it is hers. She goes to her husband, thrusts out the child. "One second," she says. He hands her the spade. With hardly a pause she chooses her spot. She sinks the shovel deep. One confident cut; moist clay curls stiffly away, crumbles. The psychic nudge does nothing to tame the thrill of what she sees. Not just an arrowhead but a splendid find, a polished jasper paint pot, partly uncovered; a timid eye blinking the scree of centuries.

And stooping to retrieve one muddy treasure, she discovers another,

93

as if the latter had simply dropped like a rock from her bent head. A relic of her own past. Something she had not thought about in years. Some events are like that: humble in the happening, meekly abiding a brown oblivion in the wrack and scrap of time; memories working in the lapse like the virtuous dead aching to be canonized. Digging carefully now with bare hands, her body begins to hum with remembrance and visions of the child she was.

Lilly McShea in seventh grade. Tall and toothy, knobby with popping bones. Everybody's case in point of the Three Poors — attitude, posture, Palmer Method. Her life reads like an inventory of things misplaced or lost: records, radios, homework, lunch money, even her best friend, Gretchen Loobie, because she borrowed her slambook and left it in the ladies' room in the uptown Rialto. A Tuesday's child despite Mrs. McShea's sputtering insistence that Lilly was born on a Friday night "easy as throwing up supper."

Her dumbness and disadvantage are issues she routinely raises in hope of kindly avuncular rebuttal, rarely forthcoming: and the proofs, in any case, leave little room for debate: (1) the rigid corps of D's on her last report card; (2) down at the Teen Canteen only one person has ever asked her to dance — a stubbly geezer reeking of camphor who was later led kicking back to the Lutheran Home; (3) the regular chalk eraser drubbings from Sister Emory, which keep her hair prematurely, if lopsidedly, gray; (4) she killed a dracaena once, as best she can figure, by breathing on it.

They say she "writes well," but what is that when every paper is at the mercy of the school-issue pen which routinely up and punctuates her best sentence with a monstrous blob of midnight-blue slobber: *this,* for pity's sake, is *not* her fault. Her chin describes an oscillating arc between bashful and belligerent. A blushing brat. One of those hell-bent, but-but-butting teacher baiters about whom lurks the mushroom cloud of an endless classroom groan.

Her "folks" are a decent, soft-spoken sort holding everything — mortgage, conviction, outrage — as tenants in common. ("We like our peace and quiet, our coffee black. We *loathe* shirkers!") Lilly has refashioned their faces into pliant molds of matched dismay, unstable stares she fears will distort in the hardening, twist to grimace or bunch in irreversible disgust.

In the kitchen, Mrs. McShea is filling miniature pie shells she'd cut out with Coke bottle bottoms. Lilly understands these are for Canasta Club and, as the filling happens to be creamed peas, it's just as well. "Can I have one?" she pipes anyhow. Just to see her mother's supple *come-now* face, hear her sigh. Hear her say, "Have a banana." The flatness of the woman's voice makes Lilly blurt, "How the heck can I help it if some jerk steals one freakin' sneaker? Just tell me, how's that *my* fault?"

A blast of bitter air rattles the cupboards. The door slams shut, appears to shove Muzza into the kitchen. She's wearing a karakul coat, her plaid babushka gabled high over a crown of iron gray braids. Two cold red bunions poke through holes in outsized brown corduroy Keds. On her lapel, a plastic Rudolph pin, the face painted mean as a mink's. Despite the temperature and Mr. McShea's willingness to "fetch" her, she has come stubbornly on foot from Bantell Street, down through the steep rooty woods, down the easy Grade, across Estey and up, up, up their own merciless Hill Street. She gathers Lilly close against her cold coat, the smell of cold clenched deep in her fur.

"Vell, Mutska," she says. Her Ajax smile, wire glasses low on a plunging nose. "You ready paint town red with *starababba*?"

The suspicion that she is too old to go tooting around town with a funny-tongued grandmother is mixed with the laggardly lure of the marked trail. Known hazards. Let Muzza do the talking, drag along like something dredged; hard to lose a gym shoe on Main Street. "I don't care," she says, shrugging.

Now Muzza points to the dough scraps left on the rolling board. "Anna," she admonishes, "don't trow 'way. Ve come back. I roll up with little cinnamon, sugar, bake. Last dough good as first."

"See that dirty skillet on the stove, Mother," says Mrs. McShea, being droll. "Shall I save it so you can make soup?"

"That depend what you fry. Lamb chop? Kielbasi? I put little water, garlic . . . "

"Out of my kitchen, you two greiners. Go, go." Laughing, she shoos them with her floury apron. "And don't bring home any chicken's feet or pig's knuckles."

Lilly grabs her pea jacket, her green toboggan cap, and they leave, two rangy ladies tilting stiffly downhill to the Estey Street trolley stop.

The face of downtown Christmas has already dulled to a shopworn sorriness. Holly collars around the light stanchions have a lusterless, brittle look. The beards of sidewalk Santas are ashy, their suits mustard-stained and dingy. In a mill town the skies rain grime regardless of season.

First the errands: the light bill, the coal company, the bank. They cut over to Market Street, dawdle in front of Jurcic's Funeral Home where Muzza studies the somber black and white sign board. If the deceased happens to be Slovenian or even close — Croatian, Polish, Slovak — she will press upon Lilly a clean handkerchief and the two of them go trundling in. *Amidio J. Vizzini,* Lilly reads with relief, even though the muted pleasures of past occasions — when these affairs limned the dominant social motif of her childhood — still linger. The pinkened gladiola air, priests and nuns nodding like limp black flowers; the foreign syllables — thickly sibilant — compressed to a rich, mysterious, gummy hum. In a way, she had grown up in this house, had in fact grown tall, if a little spindly, around the procession of gun-metal gray coffins, the biers of perfect — oh, better than perfect — strangers. And Muzza holding the baffled widow's hand; Muzza suddenly, coruscatingly beautiful, transfigured with tears. Nobody ever said, who are you? What do you want with our grief?

On then to Bender's Yard Goods where they settle on a celery wool for Lilly's Christmas dress. "Don't make it too long," she says. The whisper of conspiracy is the sound that hushes their history — too many schemes to count, this one against Mrs. McShea and the nuns who would hold 1958 hemlines to mid-calf. In compliance with Lilly's directives, Muzza has been sneaking up her skirts a half inch at a time. "You bet," Muzza says now. "American way. Short and sweet." She cocks her head, eyes beguiled. "Short and sweet, short and sweet," she intones, her tongue on the words tasting and zestful. She rocks back on her heels, sways, dips, flutters her meager chest. The pulling surf of girlish, self-conscious laughter. "Don't get started," Lilly chides, "or you'll pee your Pechglos."

At the Rexall Muzza picks up a bottle of Father John's tonic, a tin of talc. While they wait to pay, Lilly slips a roll of Tums off the rack and into her pocket, believing by some private logic that the store has invited this: something about the sourness of life, something about the way the wan little clerk answers Muzza's sportive friendliness with a waspish, superior reserve. Muzza draws two singles from her small, black, principled coin purse. The potato-digging hand, coarsened and stained, her middle finger broken in one of those willful treks down from Bantell Street is permanently crooked like a comma; next to it, the diamond Tata bought her at 70, when he understood finally that he was dying. Lilly's clear claim on the Tums fuzzes. In plain view of the priggish clerk, she pops them back on the counter; she meets his eyes coldly, smartly: a wordless challenge between equals.

Later, on Main Street, Muzza notices the green toboggan cap is missing. Lilly punishes her skull with both fists. "Oh spit!" Then, "Somebody must have hooked it. Some grubby Front Street kid, no doubt,"

Muzza pinches her cheek. "You big little palooka," she says with such effortless delight that Lilly is tempted to question the wrong in her wrongheadedness, to, indeed, credit herself with some rare elusive charm.

"Anyhow, I hate ugly ting," Muzza is saying. "Look like Ravnik peasant hat. Ve go over Edelman Brothers, get something nice color. Maybe red. Maybe sexy as heck."

It's no secret that Muzza is soft on American. She prefers the fluff of Sunbeam to her own hefty loaves. She loves and loves to say Snickers bars and Dairy Queen, soda jerks and Snooky Lanson. Shamelessly, she mines conversations for new clichés and snappy phrases; takes them home, drills till they're perfect, polished as her kettles. Eventually she tries them out in public, sometimes ruinously. At Tata's wake, when Father Navenshek finished his sour-cream *strukla,* yawned, and looked at his watch, Muzza leaned over — her tone profoundly solicitous — "Fadder," she said, "vot time you have to beat it?"

After buying the cap — a soft confection of raspberry angora that matches nothing Lilly has ever owned — they go over to Foodfare for the *potitsa* ingredients. What was once the main event of a gleeful spree is now just another errand. But early joys have a way of embering down, burning low, and the old woman's renewed ebullience catches in Lilly, fans small pockets of pale, watched fires. Their selection is careful. "Peticular," says Muzza. They choose the walnuts one at a time, examining the color of the honey. "Your eggs nice and fresh?" Muzza asks the stock boy. He nods minutely. "You better slap them," she cracks. She always says this, in just this genial, enjoying way, and yet now Lilly sways with the shock of sudden embarrassment. She bucks off with the cart, lurching far ahead of Muzza, past the dairy case and around the corner. Up the next aisle, briskly, as if she is no stranger to purposeful hustle. A competent young woman entrusted with the family food shopping. As if she is a *real* person. At the flour section she stops and guiltily waits for Muzza, but what overtakes her first are simple hunger pangs fed with irrepressible visions of *potitsas* puffing and crusting in Muzza's oven. To consider now the rich spirals of nut-crumbly filling would be unbearable. For each of her three daughters' families Muzza will make one great loaf, rolled and plumply coiled, bigger than a bread box. By Christmas Eve they will be snugly in hand, but not until after Mass the next day will anyone dare do more than snitch a pinch of loose crust or a fleshy gouge from the bottom. Her stomach grumblings, she understands, betoken a ritual rightness: in the excitement of these jaunts, they have always neglected to eat, and soon anyhow Muzza's purse will be flat as Lilly's pocket, empty as her heart.

That night Muzza stays over at Hill Street. For want of a spare room, Muzza always sleeps with Lilly in her pineapple poster bed. It used to be she would implore Muzza to spend the night, each time prompting an unvarying exchange. Muzza: "What crazy person like sleep with skinny old hunky lady?" Lilly: "Skinny hunky kid." Muzza: "How you can be hunky kid with such name like McShea?" Lately, though, the practice seems sadly tarnished, tacky as downtown Christmas. Like undershirts or drinking buttermilk (which she and Muzza did, by the gallon, in the stuporous summers, in the Bantell Street kitchen).

Nor is she much disposed anymore to badger the old woman for "stories." Over the years her rapt enchantment had goaded Muzza to outrageous perjuries, the same old-country sagas reworked, enlarged, enlivened with late-night liberties and silliness, so that, in the end, preposterousness became its own fulfillment. And within the framework of these mixed fictions emerged a separate secret, collaborated reality that dried epoxy-hard between them. Far into the night the bed rocked with laughter (Muzza has a high unruly giggle somehow connected directly to her bladder). And Mrs. McShea would have to come in and, as if they were a couple of slumber-party cut-ups, whimperingly plead her need for sleep. "*Starababba!*" Muzza would whisper when her daughter was gone. "Old woman."

More recently, when a tale is told, the teller is likely to be Lilly. And the practice is inexcusable, a dark and shameful breach of a firm family taboo: *Don't tell Muzza. She'll fret herself to death.* Inside, her grandmother is all melt, oceans of ready sympathy that can be tapped like a vat. For months now, under cover of night, Lilly has been slipping her worries, feeding her woes. Whispering sadness into her heart like a slow poison. Every lump and bump and blister, the mad dog, the lurking maniac, a sliver of glass Muzza will understand is wending a deadly course from Lilly's finger to heart. She's addicted to Muzza's tears, floats blankly in their lenient broth as something yet to be and loath to be born.

Now she draws a breath before launching a barrage of recent wretchedness. Indifferent young men, abandonments and betrayals, injustices and mortifications. Spiteful Gretchen Loobie. "I'm cursed," she snivels. "Jinxed forever." And seeing that Muzza's grief has not yet ripened in her eyes, she scrambles to the crest of the worst she can think of. "I have nothing to live for," she says. "How long do I have?"

"Vot how long? Vot you mean?"

"How long till the glass zaps my heart? It would truly be a blessing," she says, borrowing the words, the pious tone from the widows of Jurcic's.

In the beginning Muzza's weeping is soundless, perceptible only as luminosity of darkness, the night billowing silkily around them. Then, "How can you can say such thing?" Each word strangled, each word the bitter core of a separate sob. Bony hands dig into Lilly's arm. The shuddering mattress. Then long raking, ragged gasps. They lie side by side on their backs. Tears pour from Muzza's face onto Lilly's pillow. No bottom to this welling. What has she started? Panicked imaginings of tears like blood. How many pints can a person lose? Visions of Muzza lying dry and cheekless as an apple doll. In the end Muzza turns to the wall, hoards her grief, baffles it the way proud people hide pain from the puncher. Soft sobs of lament, private, estranged, and Lilly comes frightened across the distance, awkward with retraction, sodden with remorse, "Don't mind me, Muzza. Just one of my stupid moods." She drapes herself over Muzza's shoulders, tries to suspend an upside-down grin in front of her face. "Look, I'm smiling." And that having little effect, she draws back and says, "Maybe I'd get real happy if you'd tell me . . . tell me about the time you pulled the plug on your daddy's mean wine." "No!" Muzza says.

Long minutes pass; time running for dignity, smoothing itself like a rumpled apron. Muzza dabbing her eyes with a soft white sleeve. "I vill tell you instead sad story, terrible story." She pauses, sniffs. "First Christmas your Tata and I are marry, he come home from number two mine, eat and go to bed. Always this his habit for he must get up again at four. It is lovely silent night, holy night. Snow is falling deep on street. I go over visit my friend Mrs. Svoboda. Ve talk little, eat *sganzas*. I have small glass gooseberry wine. Ven I come home it is late, maybe half past hour of nine. I am careful not to wake him. Take off shoes, put on nice lawn nightgown. Suddenly he sit up in bed, eyes big like gold piece. I see hate, murder. I see my skinny neck snap like chicken's. Next ting he holler, 'Now I got you, *hoodich.* You svine. By holy Rochus, now you vill pay.' Tank God I am near door. I run so fast like never in life. Down dark back steps. Out on street. Two block I run with nekkid feet and pretty nightgown back to house of Mrs. Svoboda." She pauses significantly. Her next words spew whispery reprimand "How you like such crazy mix-up Christmas? How *you* like, Mutska?"

Her words, swirling, fragile as snowflakes, deliquesce into darkness. Gone, gone. Tata, too. Given to Lilly *after* the rage, in the season of his shy, venturing tenderness. A man with fruit trees and a thousand gimmicks for giving quarters. Gone, seamlessly as the words. She tries to envision Muzza at 19 or 20, a graceful wraith haunting the bleary street, but sees only this bony old woman in desperate, squawking flight, the big yellow bunioned feet slapping the blameless snow. The adult solemnity in which she and Muzza lie nodding, sage as pensioners, dissolves too, and the sounds that rip from her are not unlike the yips of a terrier.

"What he tought?" Muzza says now. "I was big Welsh crew boss?" Her chest starts to heave and within seconds they are choking, rocking, gasping like bad motors, laughing and crying, catching back in tandem only long enough to listen for suffering footsteps down the long hall.

Late on the afternoon of Christmas Eve Muzza comes stomping in out of the weather. She is empty-handed. "I bring bad news," she reports grimly. "It is *potitsa.*" They stare at her, incredulous; the woman is immune to culinary failure. "Of course," she says, "*potitsa* is fine, like always." She spreads the fingers of her left hand. In the middle of Tata's ring is a raw, shocking hole where the stone had been, and the sight makes them cry out as if pinched. "Only ting," she says, "*potitsa* have new ingredient this year. I only notice when loaves are on table to cool."

They are talking diamonds, talking Tata; yet nobody bothers to suggest the obvious; that any halfway reasonable person would have panicked and clawed those breads to shreds. But Muzza lives by the law of use; in her heart and on her table, an exalted place for leftovers. What curse, what hellish thing would rise from the rubble of three plundered *potitsas?* "So," she is saying. "I tink I have figger out vot to do. Everybody come up Bantell Street after church, eat *potitsa* under nose of cook, so I can keep eye on operation."

Muzza's table has but one extra leaf, and the relatives gathered around it form a rictus as of crowded, uneven teeth. They appear uneasy and, at the same time, tautly expectant, as if they'd been herded here to witness some startling revelation. Lilly finds it wonderfully new and comical. Her hefty aunts and their strapping steelworker husbands, the male cousins — hellions all three — held to a tea-party daintiness. The nibbling bites, the thoughtful, dubious chewing. Muzza slices the bread herself into thin volumes like poetry. Then she sits back, watching around the table, her eyes widening with each committed chomp, shuddering as each Adam's apple signals a fully executed swallow. The stillness swells, the air as densely sacrosanct as just before Communion. But solemnity sits uneasily on Muzza's face, the slack muscles struggling to uphold the look of an elder presiding gravely. When she catches Lilly's eye, she comes apart like a slow-ripping seam, laughs into her hands. Her shoulders shake; her glasses bump down her nose. Her eyes brim and when her mouth molds a surprised O, Lilly knows she's wet her pants.

The family laughs, but tightly, in the provisional manner of people trapped in someone else's hilarity. They take up a sparse chatter. "Don't the Chinese or somebody make traitors swallow diamonds?" "Not at today's prices, Alice," says Mrs. McShea. "You're thinking of glass," somebody else offers. "Ground glass — shreds your innards."

It is not, nor will it turn out to be a white Christmas, but Lilly senses the moment the same as late, late at night you know it's begun to snow; a yielding thing. A subtle shift, as if the weather is inside you. Her heart quickens, her cheeks warm. Hands trembling, she breaks her slice in two. The stone is cool, restrained, smugly coddled in a plump yellow raisin. It clings for an instant, then drops ringingly onto her plate, seems to come awake in a tantrum of polychromatic sparkle, punching back the bold hues of Muzza's dome lamp. Like a tiny, somewhat feisty, fallen star. Everybody cheers and applauds. In the glow of her own starshine Lilly grins brazenly. She reels with the sudden weightlessness of someone unexpectedly sprung or plucked in the nick of time from certain catastrophe. Someone favored by heaven. Is it possible she is, after all, rather splendid? A genuine benefactor? And reshaping her face along more modest lines, she lifts the stone from the crumbs and places it in Muzza's mud-yellowed palm.

The grandmother stands. Squared shoulders. The face of a matriarch, even if Lilly does catch a rakish spark in the slanted Yugoslav eyes. "I have many," she says, "how you say — people vot live after me. Only one ring. Today I decide finder keeper. Ven I kick bucket" — and a protesting pulse trembles the room — "ven time come," she says firmly, "Tata's diamond go to Lilly. Fair is fair."

•   •   •

Late afternoon. Drawn shades squeeze fiery wands of light across the bed where the child naps between her parents. Ceiling vents breathe jets of cooling air. A blissful dimness, the river afternoon lingering in the smell of sun and mud and sweat, swaddling them damply in fatigue and a dreamy kind of contentment. On the dresser sits the jasper paint pot: the polished fact of their good fortune. In Lilly's hand the ring, retrieved from its ancient cotton, for she has been telling the story, telling the husband as he drowsily nods; telling it mostly for her own amazement. "Know what I think?" she says now, excitedly. The rise in her voice flutters his eyelids. "Muzza was a practical sort," she says. "Every Christmas she got me what I needed most."

"You needed a diamond?" he says.

101

"That low-down dreadful year, what I needed most was luck."

Yawning, he says, "Love? Did you say love?"

"Well, that too. Maybe luck needs love to recognize itself. But what I'm trying to say. It never dawned on me till now — why, I'd lay odds that *potitsa* was rigged from start to finish. Like a prisoner's cake, you know. Like Tata's quarters turning up in socks."

His lips vibrate softly. *Hmmmmmmmmm, Hmmmmmmmmmm.* His breath evens out and it doesn't really matter that nobody hears her words go by easy as water over stones. She'd never told him she says, touching the girl's cheek, that after 11 years of childlessness, she had felt the fusion of their cells in her belly, a soft pop like a thread breaking as she made the bed that day. She'd touched the spot. "I knew. I knew," she whispers.

And then what she doesn't speak but merely thinks; that the time came when Muzza began to prefer her native expressions, hunger for black breads and mushrooms from the Ravnik woods; gift chocolates sat pat, unoffered on her lap, hoarded like that long-ago grief, and her eyes traveled imperturbably past worries. And the family met Muzza's daily dimunition with baffled panic, tried and found they lacked her gift for inventive tenderness; and that, worse, nobody knew how to make the foods she craved — the *potitsas,* the *struklas,* the *sganzas* — even when she was full. And one night, long after Lilly married, her sleep had opened like an awed eye upon the moment of Muzza's death; and the grief too was open and outward, translucent as the pink pulsant mystery of Jurcic's Funeral Home. When the phone rang, she picked it up and said, "I know," and began a lifetime of missing her.

And what is more tenuous, softer than thought. A view perhaps from the soul — of what is unknown to her and yet known, here and yet gone; of the way she lives once in the surprise of life, like a tiny miner masquerading in street clothes; of all the things that encapsule things and those still others and on to the smallest, most infinitesimal amazement; of the meanness and rage that also yield; but mostly of all that is good and bright and sometimes funny locked in the obdurate mud, the stern, pretending faces.

And in *her?* Deep, deep, deeper than she could ever reach or explain, a persisting expectant thing, warm like love, sharp like joy — often unreasoned and perfectly unprovoked — embedded there, as it were, in the heart. As if she had, indeed, not found but swallowed that diamond, and it burned, burned, burned but had hardly harmed her.

Her husband stirs, speaks thickly out of his torpor. She leans her ear to his mouth. "I believe you," he says, and sleeps.

The Appaloosa House

•

BY SHARON SHEEHE STARK

M Y FATHER'S GIRLFRIEND'S NAME was Dolores and my mother
went by Dusie because she was one. As in pip, as in pistol, as
in humdinger. In those days men waited until after the holidays, so he left us on the second of January while the ya-ba-da-ba-do
cartoons on TV tried, by their jangle of Saturday morning sameness, to
deny it and just as it was starting to snow.

For three days and three nights Dusie observed an oddly formal
mourning, in the manner of an Irish wake. She called in her friends; she
wept and laughed. There was cake and wine, coffee in the fine Belleek
cups that had come from Kilkenny. On the fourth morning she came
downstairs and said, "Maybe if I'd kept the trash baskets emptied and got
somebody out to paint the house last summer like your daddy asked . . . "

I stopped stirring my Sugar Crisp into whirlpools and rolled my eyes
up at her.

"But, oh, no, I have to be Madam Nobody-tells-me-what-to-do, Mrs.
Stand-on-my-rights, stubborn Irish smarty-pants. Maybe if I'd kept the
toilet paper roll on the holder?"

We exchanged rueful looks that answered all her silly questions. We
alternated weak, well-meaning chuckles and then she put the coffee on.
"Did you know he took *both* bottles of Lavoris?" she said, like it was
something she'd read in Ripley's. It was shortly after that she kicked off
the campaign.

Right after breakfast, in fact, she drove us down to Cherry Street; she parked in the loading zone in front of House of deLuca, which was the cruddy yellow brick building where my dad manufactured his line of budget neckties. I waited in the car while she tramped out her message in the strip of snow between the building and the sidewalk. She was wearing a big orange fur coat nearly the same color as her hair. I watched her face turn splotchy as a washerwoman's hands in the cold air. She was that other kind of Irish, not dusky-haired and delicate, but ruddy, raw-boned, and sturdy as a pack mule. In funny little schoolgirl shuffle steps, her stadium boots tamped along in the snow. The letters were 20 feet high — "S" then "O." She came around the bottom belly of the "B" with high marching steps and finished with a flurry of furious double-barreled stomps — SOB.

"Ma-ah!" I squeaked when she got back in the car.

"What?" she said. "What's wrong with sob? You know, sob, sob, sob. Boo hoo, the rooster flew the coop."

Next day she called Western Union and made arrangements to have a singing telegram delivered to Dad at work. "What can you give me in, well, a crumb-bum medley?" she asked in the crisp tones of a suburban matron. As carefully as if she were choosing music for a wedding, she made her selections: "Your Cheatin' Heart," "Why Do You Do Me Like You Do?" and "Toot-Toot Tootsie Good-bye."

She called the printer and had him make up announcements. When they came, I helped her stamp and address them. Very plain, very tasteful, which was a distinct departure in a family partial to purple velvet and plaster lawn statuary. But Dusie had the unerring Irish instinct for effect. The message, too, was simple and painfully to the point: MR. AND MRS. NUNZIO DELUCA RESPECTFULLY SUBMIT THAT NUNZIE IS FAT, FORTY, AND FOOLING AROUND. NO GIFTS. SEND MONEY. HE'LL NEED IT.

Once we had these projects cooking, it was just a matter of time till they boiled over. We lived to hear the affection lurking in the hells and damns of his false indignation. Dusie would take the call on one phone; I'd hang on the hall extension. Or sometimes he'd come by; it didn't take long after the announcements went out. I remember how he went right to the kitchen and, as we stood gaping, proceeded to make himself a peanut butter banana; it was hard not to draw a mental circle around that scene, hard not to start feeling cozy. A trick, I decided, and for the first time I saw him not as a father but as a man — *somebody's* man — a man with a middle like a flour bag and stumpy legs. His overlarge face and well-tended mustache, combined with two great symmetrical wings of thick salt-and-pepper hair, gave him the look of expecting to turn handsome at any moment. Wild eyebrows and wet brown eyes; he was growing more like a Nunzie every day. I couldn't picture him with this Dolores person, who probably ate corn off the cob row by row and carried Pretty Feet around in her handbag. I wished him a speedy old age so Dolores would see that the old rattletrap wasn't good enough for anyone but us.

"Listen, Kathleen" (he never called her Dusie when she was acting like one), "I'm just the poor son of an Italian immigrant. How about giving the old boy a break?" Talking with his mouth full meant he couldn't have been too mad. He was a sucker for her stunts and Dusie knew it. She'd always been able to butter him up with monkeyshines, romping through the neighborhood in sheets, baying at the moon like an escapee from the state hospital down the road. And dying. She "died" all the time. Strokes before breakfast, poisonings at lunch; I grew up thinking everybody's mother "did" heart attacks, but probably not as well as mine. And Dad boasted the way some men crowed about their wives' cooking. "You're not gonna believe it, Herb," he'd say, his voice rushing the start of another Dusie story.

Several weeks later, after the weather had made that indisputable turn into spring, we went down to Cherry Street and picketed my dad's plant. Dusie had handpainted a huge sign that read NUNZIE DELUCA UNFAIR TO WIFE AND KIDS. For most of that sweet spring afternoon, we paraded up and down the walk, Albert on one side of her, I on the other. She carried 10-month-old Teena Jo papoose-style on her back. The soles of Albert's shoes flapped and slapped as he walked. I was 11 and wearing one of her size 14 house dresses cinched at the waist with gold and green Christmas ribbon. Stretched-out bobby sox bunched miserably around my ankles. As an afterthought, she'd tucked the Doctor Dentoned baby in an onion bag. The worst of it was Albert and Teena Jo weren't even ours.

"Wait till Mrs. Stefka finds out," I taunted. Dusie was supposed to be "keeping an eye" on them while their mother went shopping. "You're gonna get it, you're gonna get it," I singsonged softly as we pounded the pavement. I was getting too old to be her loyal sidekick anyhow; I was learning to feel "dumb," especially when a fussing old woman came up and gave Albert and me each an orange and a nickel.

Inside the building, Dad's employees, most of whom knew us very well, kept rapping on the dusty panes. They waved and looked vivified; in due course my dad came out and flagged down the Mr. Softee truck. He bought us all frozen yo-yo sticks. Then he whacked my mother once on the behind and went back in.

She packed the next four months with sometimes inspired, sometimes second-rate shenanigans. Crazy calls to his office in assorted foreign accents. The "Beware of the Stud" sign on the factory lawn. She bought us both Orphan Annie wigs that made us look like a pair of dried chestnut burrs. In those and dark glasses we followed Dad and Dolores all the way down to Pimlico in Maryland. They never noticed we were behind them or if they did, didn't let on. Not knowing what to do with ourselves once we got to the track, we ended up going to see *Invasion of the Animal People* at some local movie house. "Lotta good that did us," I said to my mirror image in the theater washroom. Framed in that bonnet of curls, my face lost some of its stronger points. I wanted to think flowerlike, I wanted to think fragile. I had his dark popping eyes and sloped forehead. Dusie's sharp nose. I remember thinking my father left us for all the pretty little girls in Dolores's belly; he would buy them horses like the one he'd promised me. I dreamed I drowned their children by the dozens, as fast as they were born, but sometimes they were my own babies and, ashamed, I hid them in sandy coves and giant potted plants the likes of which have never been seen in our city.

I'm not sure when it was exactly, but there came a point when Dusie's intrigues broke away from the mainland and assumed a shape, a life of their own — became, in a way, an island of compulsiveness. She plotted on paper, drew diagrams, made greasy jottings while stuffing pork chops or frying the garlic peppers Grammy DeLuca had showed her how to make. She started jobs and never finished them. She called the house painters and then couldn't settle on a color. So the men went away disgusted. All night long the house creaked with her meanderings, the hall light flashing on and off, and in the morning her eyes would be bright as fever, her body pulling in six directions, her hands too shaky and eager to pour coffee. "Now listen," she'd say (and sometimes I'd only pretend to), "this oughta give the old guinea pause."

In late summer, around the time the three of us would normally be taking a place at the shore, we went down to House of deLuca with two men and a U-Haul. Lucky for us, my dad wasn't around. In the space of an hour we had a cutting table and three sewing machines and whatever else she needed to start a business in the basement, a mini necktie factory in competition with Dad's. One night I awoke to a gentle pressure on my shoulder and two incandescent eyes beaming into mine. "House of Spouse," the voice said, and the night sifted shut again. My dad claimed

106

such apparitions all the time; they told him where to put his money at the track. But in the morning Dusie was at the breakfast table ordering labels. "House of Spouse," she reiterated. Wasn't it scrumptious? We'd blow House of deLuca right out of the water.

Before Dad booted her out of the office, she used to keep the company books. Not well, I understood, but adventurously. He used to say she gave him bottom lines that would knock Jefferson off Mount Rushmore. I suspect she learned the business better than she let on because hers was off the ground in weeks. She knew just whom to call for supplies, hired machine operators, a cutter; she and I tacked on labels, pressed, and packed boxes. Profit being the least of her worries, she was able to call Dad's jobbers and offer House of Spouse 20 percent cheaper than "House of de Dummy," as was her wont to call it. Shameless, she even promoted the idea of a "label with a story behind it."

That brought him around, of course. He came up the driveway in his new canary-yellow T-Bird. He was wearing a turtleneck shirt, Levi cutoffs, and a wide belt with a chunky gold buckle in some kind of zigzag design.

I kept right on playing "Oliver Twist Can't Do This" against the side of the house and was dying for him to say the ball was leaving marks on the paint so I could crack how his opinion didn't mean beans around here anymore. But he just stood quietly by watching, so I finally said, "A longer line at the waist would make you look taller, you know." I said this in a monotone, without missing a single catch, as if there was no meanness at all behind it.

He noticeably sucked in his stomach. Then Dusie came out and as she strode toward us, he said, "One of these days, sister, you're gonna go too far." Last year he would have boomed this in what she called his hotshot-Italian-husband voice. It occurred to me at that moment that "Italian husband" could be a kind of unstable species, one that outside its element reverted quickly to an original state — soft, sweet, and perfectly defenseless.

"I had that equipment coming to me," she said. "The business is half mine."

"That's true, Duze," he said agreeably. "Mind if I get myself a Coke?"

"Be my guest." Her arm swept a grand gesture toward the house.

"Maybe we can discuss this over a Coke."

"Maybe the sky will rain rhubarb."

"Ah, Duze, always gotta be a wiseacre." He threw up his arms and as he turned to go, I saw that his belt buckle was really three big fat letters spelling YES.

Dad needn't have worried his head about the business. Though we were getting orders and holding our own financially, Dusie soon let things slide out of sheer lack of interest. There were no major goals in her life, only ways and means to short-term spectacles. She rarely even talked anymore of Dad coming back, but the scheming and stewing went on, a ceaseless scudding across her storm-green eyes. There were days I stood in oblique, reluctant awe of her reckless creativity and could see that all those external events — my dad and Dolores and heaven knows what else might strike her — were often only springboards to her intractable genius.

I owned an antique toy, a rusty tin man my grandmother had brought from Ireland when she was 10. He clutched an enormous curved pole in both hands and rocked back and forth on one toe from a high perch the size of a dime. I never learned to stop doubting the rickety principles that brought him back each time from his heart-stopping dip over the edge; neither did I trust whatever it was that kept my mother sane and both of us out of prison. Especially after the business with United flight number 101. Up until then whatever she did at least evinced a token respect for limits, a sense of comic proportion, as though she'd struck some sort of begrudging bargain with the conventional world. What happened was this: somebody let it slip that Dad was planning to take Dolores to Cincinnati on the eighth of November for the Eastern Haberdashers' Convention. So Dusie did what any self-respecting spurned American housewife would do: she called United and booked that Cincy flight solid. And I assisted. We spent days on the phone. In several different dialects and in the names of every prominent citizen we could think of — Dr. Ferguson, J.T. Bigatel from the bank — we made reservations. At some point, the girl said, "Goodness, such interest in this flight. Is there something big going on in Cincinnati?"

"Oh, my, yes," I explained. "It's the annual running of the pipkins. We never miss it." I heard my voice and it was unmistakably Dusie's: her puckish expression on my face, her face on my neck, her neck patching red on my body. Her body standing smart as a new broom in my shoes. My shoes. A pair of dirty white sneakers and a broken shoelace. They were mine, and they were still on the ground. "Hey, Ma," I said. "Isn't the airline going to be mad as hell?"

She looked at me, recognition spreading like a rash. She curdled her mouth and hunched her shoulders up around her head. "Oh, Mother Machree," she said between her teeth.

United *was* furious, and if Dad hadn't convinced them she "wasn't all there," Dusie would have been in a peck of trouble. What's more, as it turned out, Dad and Dolores had reservations weeks in advance and as the result of our finaglings, had the whole plane to themselves all the way to Ohio. Not quite what Dusie had in mind.

It was nearly winter again when my father came home. Maybe in those days men could be driven back by the first rush of cold through the alleys, the beseeching bells of street-corner Santas. He came in and set his two-suiter down on the rug, flopped into his old Naugahyde chair. You'd have thought he'd just come home from work. He seemed limp and shapeless. His skin could have been an ill-fitting suit and inside nothing but sawdust and old rags. And something else — in some imprecise way he looked strangely subtracted, denuded.

"Just like that, Bart?" Dusie said, and whatever else she wanted to say wouldn't come unstuck, so she said, "Just like that, Marvin?"

He gave her his cow-eyed look and laid his hands on his thighs, and then I noticed it was his mustache that was so oddly gone and how shamelessly he sat there stunning us with the sudden pale pink of his unprotected mouth, his naked face.

"Well!" she said, all the rancor and resolve bobbing wildly around in her throat. I watched her swallow and swallow again. With all her stubbornness and sass, she could be sliced like scrapple.

"What can I say, Duze? You're the best and the craziest. You're the screwy broad I married. I missed ya, kid."

And I would be tough and dry enough for the two of us. "Where's your YES belt?" I said with a dispassion that was not in my genes.

After dinner he went into his den and sat alone in the stiff December darkness. I came in pretending it was just to bedevil the daylights out of him. I spoke very quietly, my voice gritty with malice, the sugary kind I was good at. "What's wrong?" I said, "Did good old whatshername" — and I slit my finger across my throat — "skiiiiick!" His dark, sad eyes working against mine made me sick and sorry at the same time. He held out his arms and I went to him, sat on his lap, laid my head cautiously on his chest. His smell: it was like no other, and I remembered how the day he left I buried my face in his old Woolrich shirt and breathed and breathed and breathed. He began to stroke my hair with awkward hands, hands heavy with the contemptible syrup of his melancholy, and though it is also possible that I only dreamed it, I have always believed the next thing I did was bite him, my teeth digging down into his shoulder until I could taste the fat salt root of all the tears I never shed.

Then I went in to say good-night to Dusie. She sat on her bed stunned

109

and sunless as a widow. Over the past months she'd lost a lot of weight; her face was round-eyed, a crumple of planes and angles. "He's home!" I said, "He's home!" acting joyful, acting like a child. And after a while, in a voice full of the old music — my grandmother's voice, the voice Dusie used only for ominous or solemn high occasions — she said, "The harvest is past, the summer is ended and we are not saved." In the arc of lamplight her hair sparked gold and copper around her lost white face — Katy Keenan, whose mother had come from Kilkenny, and she hung her head and said no more.

And not that night or the next, but soon thereafter I sat up in my bed knowing exactly what she'd meant by those words: first the loss, then the time of "taking measures"; our mischief had outrun the demons; we were home free and now he was back and now we were at risk again. I was grateful and yet grief made me thin as paper.

Dusie observed a period of mourning much longer than the first. She spoke little and took long solitary walks in the cold evening air. Once I awoke and looked out to see the freshly blanketed lawn already littered with snow angels, each one just her size. She devoured mystery stories and the poetry of Yeats. Calmly, methodically, she performed any chore my father asked. His bereavement, too, went on, over and over again announcing itself in his dragging step, his slow, forgetful speech. It was a sorrow I prayed the Lord to forgive, for I could never.

But then on the morning of St. Patrick's Day my mother got up and made us all green waffles, and later that week she did something with freshly baked brownies rolled between her palms that made my dad think Miss Kitt, our cat, had used his pillow as a litter box. We were like a house settling, aching down to itself. The creaks of cautious laughter, the night whispers, the easing of protocols; all the old angers and tyrannies cracking back, snapping into place.

Under the penitential circumstances, it was inevitable that I would get my horse, a magnificent Appaloosa we named Dandy Orbit, after the space program, I suppose. Dusie and I both learned to ride and though I was at "that age," I soon became another age, the one that preferred to hang out after school smoking cigarettes by the ice machine at the superette or doing the circuit with high-school motorheads. So Dandy-O became my mother's horse by default and by destiny: was there any doubt that they belonged together? Dusie with her healthy limbs and flaming hair sat resolute and proud as a Celtic queen. And later she would groom him and croon softly, gently stroking his mane. The vegetable crisper always full of carrots and apples.

And when she wasn't on Dandy-O she was riding the crest of a new wave of eccentricity. She "died" more frequently than ever, staging dreadful falls and electrocutions. I learned never to take my excuse forms back to school without reading them first. On the blank designated "Reason for absence or tardiness," she'd write bubonic plague or hoof-and-mouth disease or St. Vitus Dance. I looked triskaidekaphobia up in the dictionary: fear of the number 13. I handed it back to her: "Just say I had a cold if you don't mind." She liked to enter buildings through windows and doors that said "Do not enter," but I would not say she was a classic madcap. She did not, for instance, dance naked in hotel fountains or go barefoot to the opera or hire skywriters except that once, to say her name.

By mid-August of that year the house had still not been painted so Dad said he was going to be in Dallas for two weeks and she'd better have it done by the time he got back. Or else! (The "Italian husband" was starting to shine through.) I remember that as she gave the painters their instructions they argued a little. In the end they shrugged and carried out her orders to the letter.

The evening Dad's plane came in, I sat waiting in the yard on the big white rock that said THE DELUCAS in capital letters, then Nunzie, Katy, Connie, and Miss Kitt in small. I wasn't going to miss this moment for anything. Way down the road already he must have seen because the car started to drift onto the Madsons' grass. Then he continued on up and made the turn into our driveway, and the car crept slowly along a short distance before coming to a faltering halt. He got out and stood alongside the car for a long time, just staring at the house. The first section, which included the garage and family room, had been done conservatively enough in a nice polite beige. The rest was painted paper-bag tan and mottled with great splotches of brown and black. His face looked dumbfounded, then perplexed. Then he bumped his forehead in the Calabrese way. "An Appaloosa house," his lips said without sound.

I think we both caught sight of her at the same time. On the lower, the garage roof, straddling the peak: Dusie in her western boots and flannel shirt, Dusie with her riding crop. Dusie astride her house in the deep summer evening, behind her the row of poplars like dark feathers against the green and gold sunset.

My father sat down on the rock beside me. He said nothing, nothing, and then he put his head in his hands and began to cry. "What the heck," I said, tipping my head for a second against his shoulder, meaning to give comfort, "Eloise Bumbaugh's mother still wets the bed." I patted h s arm. He wiped his eyes and went in and minutes later I saw him emerge head-first from the guest-room window. On his hands and knees he scraped across the sugary shingles. When he reached Dusie he grabbed her belt and untangled his limbs. He sidled in tight behind her, as if he were setting himself snug in the back of a double saddle. He held on, hugging her close, both of them digging in, clinging to beat the band.

It was the summer of my thirteenth year. My parents will not give each other up; they rage and they cling and six years later my father will die in a late-night accident in the company of a girl named Emma Jean Candy. It was a sad house they rode in the dense August twilight, but it was somehow exultant, inexcusably blessed with the grace of their special madness. These things I began to know as I sat forgotten on that flagrant family rock, and still I knew nothing and dared not move or speak for the mysterious forces suspending the thin moon over the black poplars and all the strange and delicate rhythms holding us all safe in this dusky dream, keeping holy the sacrament of balance.

The Sound from Inside

•

BY EDWARD GALE

R AY COBURN PRETTY MUCH ran his farm by himself. He had his
dog Bear to help him catch any of his cows or chickens when
they got loose or ran away, and Bear kept out any varmints that
might want to find their way onto Ray's land. Bear was as big and old as
any dog in East Calais, and he probably had a part in fathering any other
dog that was anywhere near half his size. He didn't have any particular
breed in him, but he was all black and left a footprint you could almost
step in. Bear was getting slow in his old age, though, and it was probably
the memory of him more than anything else that kept the varmints and
the cows in line. So Bear mostly made his presence known, and the rest of
the time he lay in the sun and kept Ray company when he was out working
by himself.

In June while school was still going on, I worked for Ray, and Ray saw
to it to pay me what he felt he was going to. I stopped at Ray's every
afternoon on my way home, and since I went home right after work, Ray
couldn't figure off anything for room and board. Ray never kept track of
any hours, and he paid me at his pleasure. It must have been his pleasure,
for what he paid me, but I guess it must have been enough, because I kept
stopping in to work for him, and with the help of me and Bear, Ray kept
his farm going.

All that was until Fleeroy came.

Fleeroy McConnel took Ray Coburn by surprise. The way I heard it,

113

he didn't give Ray much of a choice — he walked in Ray's door, saw Ray eating breakfast, told him he was cold and hungry and needed a place to stay and some food to eat, and he said he was willing to work in exchange for it. Ray had plenty of room — in his barn — and he wasn't so much opposed to trading food for an extra hand, and Fleeroy had a job.

Fleeroy's real name was Leroy, and then that wasn't right, because that was the name they gave him when they drafted him into the army. Fleeroy was born Michael Lerioux, but it got changed around somewhere in the last-name-first, first-name-last forms. Then when folks got to know him, they started calling him Fleeroy, and he didn't mind because Leroy wasn't his real name in the first place.

Fleeroy wasn't the most conventional-looking of characters, and if he had been standing on the street unemployed, I don't think Ray would have pulled him away and put him to work. Fleeroy wore glasses, and his hair was long, and he had a beard and squinted eyes that were big and round and bloodshot whenever he found it in himself to open them, and his head bobbed when he talked. He was in good shape, though, and he looked like he could work, even if he was a little skinny. If what he told Ray was right, he hadn't eaten in a while, and after a few good meals the weight would come back.

I worked with Fleeroy some that week, pulling weeds out from in between the furrows in the potato field and helping him put in new fencing where a weasel that probably hadn't met up with Bear yet had burrowed his way into Ray's chicken coop. Fleeroy would smile and nod whenever Ray told us what needed to be done, and he'd get the tools out and start to work. Then it would get hot, and Fleeroy would sit down and curse Ray and call him a capitalist and say we should get together, me and him, and form ourselves a union. It got to be 90 degrees out that day, and if it was going to get any hotter, Fleeroy was set to walk off. It never did get any hotter, and we never did walk off. It was just as well, though, because me and Fleeroy never did have much to bargain with, and Ray didn't much care if Fleeroy slept in his barn or not.

The fifth day Fleeroy worked for Ray it rained all morning. I watched the rain through the window in my classroom at school, and I couldn't decide if I wanted the rain to stop or not. If it did, I wouldn't have to walk home in it. If it didn't, I could get the afternoon off because Ray wouldn't need us going out in the rain. But the rain stopped, and the puddles were dry on the walk up to Ray's farm, and I got my mind set on going to work.

Ray's truck wasn't in the yard when I got there. I looked around and couldn't see any sign of him anywhere, and I figured he must have took advantage of the rain and run down to Calais to take care of all the things that needed taking care of every time it rained. Fleeroy wasn't around either, and I figured maybe he went into town with Ray. That didn't make much sense, because Fleeroy wasn't going to impress people if Ray brought him into the bank with him.

I walked around out to the back of the barn, just to make sure they weren't around, and there wasn't anything different, except for a barrel by the chicken coop with a piece of plywood on top of it. I was wondering what that was doing there, when I heard something rustling in the grass past the yard. I looked and I could see it rustling, but I couldn't tell what it was, other than it was big, and it made a good part of the grass move around! And then it stopped.

I'm not known to be one of the bravest in the world, and I wasn't terribly excited about seeing what it was that was making so much grass move around. But I suppose my curious streak is a little stronger than the yellow one down my back, and I went to find out what it was. I walked up real slow and quiet as I could. The ground was still wet, and my boots squeaked whenever they got soggy, and it wasn't the easiest thing in the world to plan a surprise on whatever it was lying in the field. But I kept myself down low and tried not to make too much noise, and I snuck up to where it was hiding in the grass.

And then I couldn't believe it. Fleeroy was lying there, stark naked, with his arms spread out and a smile on his face and not even a towel under him. I turned my head quick and sat down so I wouldn't see all of him, and I closed my eyes and opened them again to make sure they were working all right. "What is it you're doing?" I said.

Fleeroy lay there, and he didn't even open his eyes. "Lying in the sun," he said.

"But shouldn't you at least have some clothes on?" I said. "You're going to get yourself burned in an awful way."

"It ain't going to hurt me," Fleeroy said, and he smiled like the sun was pushing the corners of his mouth further and further apart. "Just feel it. Nothing that feels this good is going to hurt you."

I looked at him lying there, and I hated to think what there could be in the grass crawling underneath him. "The bugs aren't biting you in the back?" I said. "Don't you want something between you and the ground?"

I wasn't looking, but I could tell by the way Fleeroy's shoulders were moving that he was wiggling his bottom into the grass. "It's still wet," he said. "They're all washed down. Bugs aren't anything, anyway. They won't hurt you if you don't bother them." Fleeroy turned to me and opened his eyes, and they were big and round and bloodshot. He raised his eyebrows way up on his forehead, and his smile got bigger. "It's nice and soft. Take your clothes off and grab a spot."

I jumped away when Fleeroy said this. I looked at him, and I could see that it was harmless, but I still thought he was acting a little strange. I looked at his bloodshot eyes. "Have you been drinking?" I said.

Fleeroy's body shot back, and I think the question hit him by surprise. "I've only been drunk twice in my life," he said. "Once was in Paris."

"What were you doing in Paris?" I said.

"Drinking cognac," Fleeroy said. "There's something I wanted to tell you," he said, "but I can't remember what it was. It's on the tip of my tongue. Here, read it for me." Fleeroy stuck his tongue out at me.

Now I never had read the tip of anyone's tongue before, and he only stuck it out for a second, so I couldn't be sure if there was anything written on it or not. Knowing Fleeroy, he probably wrote it down there just so he could remember it.

Then Fleeroy remembered what it was he wanted to tell me. "Did you see it?" he said.

I didn't have any idea what Fleeroy was talking about. "See what?"

"In the barrel," he said. "You didn't see it? Last night me and Ray, we got the weasel."

"How'd you do that?" I said.

"I heard him," Fleeroy said. "Sometime in the middle of the night. Didn't hear *him*. I heard the chickens. He had them all wound up. Sounded like me when I used to play the accordion."

I couldn't help but ask him. "You play the accordion?"

"Used to," he said. "I hated it. My mom and dad made me. They were both musicians. Dad played the piano, Mom played the harp. We used to play all the Grange halls around Lewiston. I was good. Mom's still got the posters stuck away somewhere. Had my name on them. Didn't have my picture. I wasn't that good. Probably sounded a lot like the chickens."

"So how'd you get him?" I said.

"Get what?"

"The weasel."

"Oh, yeah," Fleeroy said. "I snuck in the chicken coop. Kept to the ground and kept the lights out so he couldn't see me. I could see his eyes. Maybe he could see mine. Maybe it was a chicken's eyes, now that I think about it. Anyway, I flipped the light on, and me and the weasel couldn't see a thing. I screamed. 'Ray!' I screamed. 'Get your fanny out here, Ray! I got the weasel!' Ray came running out in no time, still pulling his suspender straps up over his shoulders. My eyes were just getting good then. Ray got in the light, and his closed right up. Then he told me to get the barrel. When I got back, Ray had set his sight again, and he had the weasel trapped in the corner. It sat there and whined at us. Ray put the barrel in the corner and forced him into it." Fleeroy stopped and thought a minute. "Pretty humane on Ray's part. I guess he couldn't have shot him with all those chickens around. Would have scared them to death. I bet they wouldn't lay for weeks."

It occurred to me what it was Ray had the weasel in the barrel for, and I was afraid to tell Fleeroy. I hadn't ever seen it myself, but I knew it was something Fleeroy wouldn't enjoy watching, and I wasn't so sure I'd enjoy seeing it myself. I figured I'd tell him anyway, and at least we wouldn't have to be mending the fence on the chicken coop anymore. But then I heard Ray's truck pull up in the yard out front. I decided not to tell Fleeroy anything. "You better get your clothes on," I said, and I turned and walked away so I wouldn't have to watch him do it.

I walked pretty fast out front because I didn't want Ray walking out back and seeing me there with Fleeroy putting on his clothes. I came around the front, and I saw Ray just as he was getting out of the truck.

Ray had his dog Bear with him. Bear bounded out of the truck and sat next to Ray with his tongue hung out, and his body lurched up and down with each breath he took. Ray walked around the truck and Bear followed him, and then they both stopped when they saw me walking up. "Holden," Ray said, "we got the weasel."

I got up by Ray and Bear and the truck. "I know," I said. "Fleeroy just told me."

Ray looked around. "Where is he, anyway?"

I was afraid Ray might know about me and Fleeroy out in the back, but I could see he didn't. I didn't want to volunteer any information, and I didn't say much. "He'll be up in a minute," I said.

"Oh," Ray said, and nothing seemed to be funny with him.

Fleeroy came walking up from behind the barn, and I was glad to see he had all his clothes on. "What you got next?" he said to Ray, and he wrung his hands together like he was trying to massage them after they had been working hard.

"Gonna take care of the weasel," Ray said, and he started walking for the barrel.

Me and Fleeroy filed in behind Ray and Bear and walked quiet

117

behind them. I looked at Fleeroy, and I could see he didn't know what Ray was going to do. I wasn't sure what I was feeling. I was a little nervous, but I guess mostly I was excited. I hadn't ever seen Bear be weaseled before. It didn't happen that often, and when it did, it wasn't always on Ray's farm. People knew Bear, and they called Ray whenever they had a weasel to take care of. Ray brought Bear over and Bear made short work of it every time, and now I was going to get to see it.

Fleeroy seemed as interested in what was going to happen as I was, but I think his interest was more of concern. He walked up next to Ray. "You aren't going to shoot him, are you?" Fleeroy said.

"Nope," Ray said, and he didn't slow his stride.

Fleeroy looked relieved. "Then what are you going to do?"

Ray got up to the barrel. "You'll see," he said. He took the piece of plywood off the barrel and handed it to Fleeroy. "Hold this."

Fleeroy took the piece of plywood in his hands. "Is he going to jump out?" he said.

"Nope," Ray said. He looked down in the barrel to make sure the weasel was still there. "He's been pent up a while. It'll take him a minute." Ray looked at Bear and took a deep breath. "You ready?"

"What are you doing?" Fleeroy said.

"Watch," Ray said. Ray wasn't that old for his age, and he could still throw a bale as good as any man in East Calais. He bent down and wrapped his arms around Bear and lifted him like a newborn calf. Bear was quiet and lay limp in Ray's arms, and Ray held him over the barrel.

"Wait a minute!" Fleeroy said.

"What?" Ray said.

"You're not going to drop him in there, are you?"

"Sure am," Ray said.

"But you can't do that."

"Why?"

"He'll get killed," Fleeroy said.

"No, he won't."

"Of course he will. You've seen that weasel."

"He's done it before," Ray said.

"I don't care," Fleeroy said. "He's going to get killed!"

Ray looked Fleeroy in the eye. "You done this before?"

"No."

"Shut up, then."

Fleeroy's eyes got bigger and rounder than I had ever seen them before. "Look at the barrel," he said, "and look at the dog. He's too big.

118

The barrel's too small. He won't be able to move."

"He's done it before," Ray said, and he gave a grunt and lifted Bear up over the barrel and dropped him in.

There was a silence then. Fleeroy was looking at the barrel, stunned. I looked from Fleeroy to Ray, and I didn't know what to say to either of them. Everything was quiet in the barrel, but I waited for it to explode.

Ray looked at Fleeroy. "Put the cover on!" he said.

Fleeroy stared at the barrel and didn't move.

"Put the cover on!" Ray yelled.

Fleeroy still wouldn't move, and his knuckles grew white around the plywood.

"God damn it!" Ray yelled. "Give me that!" He reached over and ripped the plywood from Fleeroy and stuck it on top of the barrel.

I can't really explain what followed because I hadn't ever seen or heard anything like it before, and I wish I hadn't seen or heard it then. It was like for some reason everything was different, like things stopped moving. Fleeroy was froze where he was, and all the muscles in his neck were tight and bulged, and his head twisted slowly to one side. Ray stood still and stared at the barrel with his arms folded, and he didn't even flinch, but it wasn't normal the way not a hair on his body was moving. The barrel didn't move, but it made a sound from inside that blocked out every other sound that could have been made around Ray's farm. I don't know what sounds there were that I didn't hear because there was nothing else but what was coming out of the barrel, and I don't know how to describe what that was.

And then it was quiet.

Ray unfolded his arms real slow and put his hands on the piece of plywood. He lifted the corner, then lifted the entire board and held it to his chest. The weasel jumped up out of the barrel and ran off around Ray's barn. Ray stared at it where it ran around the corner, and he kept the board to his chest.

Fleeroy still didn't move. I looked at him, and I don't think he knew where he was. I stepped up and looked in the barrel, and Bear was lying on the bottom of it. He was covered with blood, but his eyes were open and his chest breathed up and down. I looked up at Ray, and I wanted him to do something. "Ray," I said, "he's still alive."

Ray kept staring at the corner of the barn where the weasel ran around, and his eyes got squinteder and squinteder. "He's still alive, Ray!" I said. Ray wouldn't even look at me. He kept staring at the corner.

Nobody was saying anything. Finally Ray took his eyes from where the weasel ran around the corner, and he looked in the barrel. He leaned down and lifted Bear out, and Bear was quiet and hung limp in Ray's arms. Ray held Bear close to him, and he turned and walked to his house, and he never once looked at either me or Fleeroy. And that was the last I ever saw of Bear.

After a while the muscles on Fleeroy's neck began to relax, and his body got back to normal. He stared at the ground and shook his head from side to side. He put his hands in his pockets and walked away.

And then I was left by myself. I looked in the barrel, and Bear's blood lined the sides and around the bottom. I closed my eyes, but I could still see him lying there with his chest lifting up and down and his eyes looking up at me, and it wouldn't go away. I walked home, and it wouldn't leave me, and in the middle of the night I heard the sound coming out of the barrel, and I thrashed around and woke up and saw I was in my room. It was quiet, and the window was open and the curtains wafted in the breeze. I laid back down and tried to get to sleep, but I couldn't because I was afraid it was going to come back.

Bear died that night. That next afternoon I stopped at Ray's on my way home from school, and Ray was gone, and I didn't see any sign of Fleeroy either. I walked around the back to make sure he wasn't lying in the sun again, and that's when I saw where Ray had buried Bear. It wasn't marked at all, and I only knew because the ground was turned up fresh and the plot was about the size of Bear. I stood silent for a minute to pay my respects, and I thought about what Ray had told me once about his being in the war. I sat in the back of his truck, and he was throwing hay bales to me, and he wouldn't answer any of my questions. "There's a lot you don't want to know!" he finally said, and I thought how maybe he was right. Then I looked around the farm, and no one was there, and I made my way home.

The next morning it rained. It didn't just rain. It poured. I walked down the road on the way to school, and the mud was deep and my boots sank in it. I walked past Ray's farm, and his truck sat in the yard, but nobody stirred outside.

I kept walking past Ray's farm, and the rain came down hard so I couldn't see far ahead of me. I thought I saw someone else walking in the road. I got closer, and it was someone in the road, and I sped my stride to catch up.

It was Fleeroy. He was standing in the road, and he sort of waited for me. At least he stopped walking until I caught up with him. Then he turned and started walking with me.

Fleeroy didn't have a raincoat on or anything on his head. The rain soaked his hair and ran down his beard and dropped on his glasses and looked like it blinded him. He had a pack on his back with what must have been the clothes he carried around with him, and they were getting wet, too. He had something tucked under his coat, and it was probably the only thing on him that was keeping dry.

Fleeroy and I hadn't had any words between us since Bear died, and I didn't know what to say. I don't think Fleeroy did either, but he broke the silence for me. "Going to school?" he said.

I looked over at him. "Yeah," I said. "Where are you going?"

"I don't know," he said. We were quiet, and we could hear the rain beating down on the puddles in the ground, and we were both feeling uneasy. "I'm supposed to meet up with a band in South Carolina."

"You still play the accordion?" I said.

He laughed at me. "No, I play bass now," he said. "I can play Hendrix to a T. Don't know if I want to, though. It's a country-western band."

"When were you supposed to meet them?" I said.

Fleeroy looked down on the ground. "Last week. I don't know. Maybe they'll still be around."

"Oh," I said. "Maybe." Then I saw whatever it was under Fleeroy's jacket start to move around, and a tiny black dog stuck its head out between the buttons on Fleeroy's chest. "What's that?" I said.

Fleeroy looked down at the dog sticking its head out from underneath his jacket. "What, that?" he said.

"Yeah," I said. "What is that?"

"A dog," Fleeroy said.

"I know that," I said. "But what are you doing with it?"

"I'm taking it with me," he said.

"Where'd you get it?"

"I got it from Ray."

"Where'd Ray get it?"

"I don't know." Fleeroy petted the dog on the head. "He came home with it yesterday."

I looked at Fleeroy surprised. "Does Ray know you have it?"

Fleeroy's eyes got serious, from what I could see through his glasses. "Ray doesn't even know I'm gone yet. I hope he doesn't know for a while, too."

I thought about what Fleeroy had done, and it seemed to me he was stealing. "You think that was right?" I said. "Ray's going to miss that dog. You never saw him go anywhere without Bear." Then I thought a minute

121

more. "It wasn't supposed to have happened like that. I thought Bear was going to tear the weasel apart. Ray must have, too, or else he wouldn't have put him in there with it."

"I don't care," Fleeroy said. "You know what he's going to do with this dog?" It hadn't ever occurred to me, but I knew what Fleeroy was getting at. "He's going to raise it and get it big and strong and put it in a barrel with another weasel. He doesn't care about this dog. He just wants to see that weasel dead. Or any weasel. He doesn't care."

"You sure?" I said.

"Of course I'm sure. We buried Bear yesterday. All Ray said the whole time was 'Never again.' Then he went off into town, and he came back with this dog."

"But you just said he wasn't ever going to do it again."

"I was there," Fleeroy said. "That wasn't what he meant. He meant a weasel was never going to get away with it again. That man wants revenge."

The dog squirreled itself around and pulled its head back in under Fleeroy's jacket. "You sure you're doing the right thing?" I said.

Fleeroy stopped walking and stood in the rain. "You remember I told you I've only been drunk twice in my life?"

"Yeah," I said, and I wasn't sure what he was getting at.

"The other time was at my sister's wedding. I got in a fight with my six uncles. I can't drink. I get too violent. Ray told me he was in the war."

I waited for Fleeroy to say more, but he didn't, and I couldn't draw the connection between what he said. "Yeah," I said. "I know. He doesn't like to talk about it. I know he saw something awful, but he never said what it was."

Fleeroy started walking again. "Some things you just can't talk about," he said. "You can still see it, you can still smell it, you can even feel it. Sometimes it will make you want to run crazy in the night. But you can't get yourself to talk about it." Fleeroy stopped walking, and he stared me straight in the eye. "And Holden," he said, "Ray didn't see anything."

I didn't understand what Fleeroy was talking about. "He must have," I said.

"He might have saw something, but he didn't see anything."

Fleeroy kept staring at me until he thought I knew what he was talking about, and then I could see he didn't want to talk about it anymore. I still didn't know if Fleeroy was doing the right thing, though. "What makes you think he won't get another dog?"

Fleeroy started walking again. "I don't know. Probably he will. I don't think Ray's ever going to change, but I don't know what I can do about it. Maybe someone else will." He looked at me, and he didn't say another word.

We kept walking through the rain to where the road joined another dirt road that went over the hill to Fletcher. It occurred to me that Ray might come driving down anytime with his truck, and he might see me and Fleeroy on the side of the road. I stopped, and I pointed down the other road. "You might want to go that way," I said. "You can get to Route 12 once you get over the hill. You should be able to get a ride there." I looked Fleeroy over. "Unless they mistake you for a drowned rat."

Fleeroy looked at himself, and then he looked at me and smiled. "I've been mistook for worse. I'll be seeing you," he said, and he turned and walked down the road.

I got myself through the rain to school. It kept coming down and pecked on the windowpane, and I spent the day watching it run down the glass. The drops met with other drops and got bigger and bigger until they were too big and broke apart again. Then before school got out the rain stopped, and I watched the drops dry on the window.

It was still wet when I walked home, and I didn't want to stop at Ray's. He probably had a lot that needed doing because we hadn't gotten much done the last two days, but I figured it was too wet. It was too wet, I told myself, and I went straight home.

The Sheep, Jimmy and I

.

BY KIM YONG IK

ONLY 20 MILES TO GO to Corea, Maine, and I can't get a ride all morning. As I buy doughnuts and Coke at the roadside store, the man says, "Don't count on those summer people to pick you up." Are there winter people, too? I ask myself. Away from the fast car road, I walk along the rock shore toward the headland, taking my lunch. The sea is open, its wind bringing the same smell as my faraway hometown seafront.

After finishing the large Coke, I stop to piss. My water arch sparkles in the sun reflecting blue and orange. "Muzige!" I shout the Korean word for rainbow as I often did in my childhood. Startled at my own loud voice, I look around to see if anyone is nearby. There at the bend, two or three boulders away, a man in blue jeans and a faded sweater is standing. He is mumbling something, not noticing me. In the shade behind him a sheep moves about, a bell on its neck tinkling like a wind bell on a pagoda.

I take a long strip of kelp from the barnacled rock and bite into its tender coils. The chewy fiber tastes deliciously salty. Why didn't he hear me shouting "Muzige"? His face is lonely and blank.

Curious, I try to listen to what the lone man is saying, but hear only the tinkling of the sheep bell and the sound of wind over the pines. I say, "Hello," then a louder "Hello!"

His head slowly turns to me, his mouth loosely open. I say, "My name is Kim."

124

He blinks his large eyes and looks at me like a deaf mute. I say, "An Yung." His eyes growing bigger, he watches my mouth intently. "It is our Korean greeting, 'Are you in peace?' " He says nothing but still watches me. Is he a shepherd? I turn to the sheep which moves forward until the rope tied to a pine trunk pulls him back. I have a strong urge to cut the rope to release the animal. I go to the animal to give it a bit of kelp. It jumps and snatches it from my hand with a sharp tinkle of its neck bell. It takes it like a starving refugee. I like the good wet feel of its tongue on my palm. I remember my mother would lick my skin for the telltale trace of salt to find out whether I had gone into the sea. As I feed the sheep with more kelp, the man joins me, laughing as though tickled each time the animal's mouth touches his palm to pick up kelp. From the pine grove a dog runs down, barking, followed by three children. "Let me feed the sheep, Uncle Jim. Let me, let me . . ." They stretch their hands toward him, fighting for the kelp in his hand. A bald-headed man with a camera comes after them.

I hold out a piece to a girl but she quickly puts her hands behind her. "You can eat this, too," I tell her.

"I wouldn't eat seaweed, would you?" says the bald-headed man, turning to spit. He takes away the children.

Several men and women, well dressed, carrying baskets, come down talking and laughing. The man in the old sweater runs toward them, shouting, "Mother, I found a Korean!" His high voice sounds young . . . not more than my age.

A woman in a large-brimmed hat moves forward. "I'm Jimmy's mother, Mrs. Thayer." Her way of talking is so friendly that I feel flushed. Beside her, Jimmy is laughing to himself, tilting his head. The men and women go by, ignoring me. "Jimmy found a Korean, eh?" one says.

"What are you doing in Maine?" Mrs. Thayer looks at my knapsack.

"I go to University of Kentucky. When I look up a map, there are Oriental name towns, China, Corea, so." I try to explain.

"Oh, I see," she laughs. "You thought you'd come home for the summer. Where are your family?" As I don't answer, she asks, "In your country?"

I nod slowly. I don't tell her my mother died last month.

An erect white-haired man in a gray sweater stands before me. "I'm Mr. Thayer." As he shakes my hand, I bow.

"Will you join us in our picnic lunch?" Mrs. Thayer invites me. The men and women are unloading their baskets.

I can eat more but say, "I am not hungry."

Mr. Thayer says, "You are near Corea, all right. Early missionaries used to spell the name of your country C-O-R-E-A, and that's the way the town got its name."

Mrs. Thayer turns to the tall man walking back and forth laughing alone. "Jimmy, do you want him to stay?"

Jimmy halts. "Yeah," he says, then moves his head to and fro, repeating to himself, "Anyong; are you in peace?"

Mrs. Thayer introduces me to the children's father who has a funny name, Dr. Little, and to his plump wife. "What took you to Kentucky?" asks Dr. Little.

"In Korea I learned 'The Sun Shines Bright in My Old Kentucky Home.' So I chose."

"You mean 'moonshine' there, not sunshine," he says, the corners of his eyes turning to others. Some laugh. I don't understand but sense he is joking. I remember the rain on the day I arrived in Kentucky and laugh with them.

Jimmy brings to me a huge steamed lobster on a paper plate and a clipper-shaped metal. I smash the lobster open with a stone, not with the metal, and start to eat. Jimmy looks amazed. Under his gaze, I feel uneasy and ask, "Why is the sheep alone away from the rest?"

"Every summer when we shear our sheep in our island corral, we bring one here for eating," he says. Must the animal whose tongue just touched me die so soon? I don't feel like eating.

Mrs. Thayer talks to Jimmy. "Show Kim around our house."

"Yeah," he says and walks away.

I follow him on the trail going through the grove. He walks lightly on his tiptoes, moving his head to and fro. The trail thick with soft pine needles stops abruptly at a concrete floor and a swimming pool surrounded by tall trees. "Why a pool? When you have sea?" I ask.

"The sea water is too cold," Jimmy says.

Maybe the winter people swim in the sea and the summer people in such a pool. Beyond the low door of a shed by the pool I see a shower. I have not taken a bath for many days. I ask Jimmy, "Does it work?"

He goes through the swinging door and turns on a knob and hurries out wiping his wet hair. I take off my knapsack, undress myself and go under the shower. With no one around, I sing "My Old Kentucky Home," thinking of how wonderful Kentucky seemed before I left for America.

Jimmy waits for me in orange swim trunks, his legs so long. He is handing me swim trunks. Although I didn't take the shower for swimming, I slip them on. They are too big, but I jump into the pool. As I frog-kick, the swim trunks slide down to my thighs. I pull them off and go underwater only to come up toward the blue sky, making a large fish mouth for air.

"Mom, look at Uncle Jim!" cries a high child's voice. "He is swimming with no swim trunks on." I see the two boys on the other side bending over near Jimmy in the pool. I didn't know Jimmy had taken off his swim trunks. I didn't even know he had come into the pool. Then a shadow hits my head as I hear a little girl giggling. "This Chinaman is naked, too." The father holds her. Trying to free herself from his grip, she shouts, "It's true, he has nothing on. Look!"

Late in the afternoon I walk with Jimmy up the sloping lawn to say thank you and good-bye to his parents. Facing the bay, Mr. and Mrs. Thayer and their guests sit at a stone table in front of the house. Dr. Little holds his camera to take a picture of us, but Jimmy leaves me and goes into the house.

Mrs. Thayer asks me, "Could you stay with us for a while? Until you came, Jimmy hardly talked or laughed. He didn't swim even once." As I hesitate, she glances at the upstairs window and goes on. "Except at mealtime, he always stays in his room doing some mathematical problems."

"That mathematical side of his brain was least damaged at his birth," Mr. Thayer explains, but adds, "When it comes to sociability, he is zero."

A maid in a white uniform collecting glasses says, "Jimmy is lighting the fire in the living room."

"He is waiting for you, Kim," Mrs. Thayer says in a hushed, excited voice. "Let's go into the house."

I follow her. The room is so big, its ceiling so high that the dining table at the farthest side looks small. Jimmy sits at a small table, staring at the flames in a huge fireplace. "Who made such a good fire?" Mrs. Thayer says admiringly. "Jimmy, Kim might want to stay with us. Show him how to play chess."

Jimmy takes out a board from a box laid on the table and chessmen. I sit before him. Moving a man on the board, he demonstrates to me, "Rook goes straight," then another with "Bishop goes diagonal." As he goes on explaining to me, Mr. Thayer says, "Jimmy likes to show off."

Learning that the American game is little different from the Oriental chess, I start to play with him. Before every move, Jimmy takes much time. He moves his man on a certain position and without taking his fingers off it, he looks left, right, front, back, just like a cautious driver before crossing a crowded street. He seems to have some strategy and knows what he is doing. I hear Dr. Little saying, "Kim has an Oriental patience." Why Oriental, I think.

At one point I move my Queen and call "check." He moves his King back and forth in every direction. At long last he gets up slowly. Dr. Little, interrupting his conversation asks, "Who won?"

Jimmy says, "Kim," and leaves with his head down.

Mrs. Thayer comes over and says, "I'll show you where you will sleep."

In the bedroom upstairs, she whispers to me, "Jimmy gets upset when he loses a game. Let him win sometimes." She talks on. "He goes to a special school in Boston, but during the vacation in Maine, he doesn't want to see anybody or do anything."

When I come downstairs, Jimmy is alone in the living room, mumbling while walking back and forth. The maid brings in a tray and puts plates of food on the table. "You guys hurry up and eat your supper," she says rather rudely. "Mr. and Mrs. Thayer are gone out for dinner."

I tell her I am too full to eat, and sit on the sofa looking at magazines in a rack. I leaf through a woman's fashion magazine, then pick up *Reader's Digest,* still bound with a strip of paper addressed to James F. Thayer. He hasn't opened it yet. If Jimmy would read the magazine aloud, I could listen to improve my English. When Jimmy finishes his supper, I ask, "Will you read this for me? I still miss many words when people speak."

Sitting beside me, he starts to read . . . right from the front cover. He pronounces every word so slowly and loudly that I can understand. The kitchen door is ajar; the maid peers into the room, then the other kitchen people . . . all whispering and smiling. He doesn't notice them but keeps on reading. He never stops.

When Jimmy is halfway through the magazine, Mr. and Mrs. Thayer return. Standing at the door Mrs. Thayer, one arm still in the sleeve of her coat, watches Jimmy reading. Mr. Thayer waves his hand toward me and quietly moves about the room. Jimmy finally raises his head from the magazine and sees his parents. "What is it, Mom?" he asks, looking around him. "What is it?"

"Nothing, Jimmy," she says, and turns away, taking off her coat.

I know some wonderful thing is happening, but I don't know quite what.

I stay on with the Thayers. Jimmy never says what he wants to do. When he stays in his room, I take the chessboard with me, or appear carrying a towel to show what I want to do with him. After a little

128

hesitation, he always comes down to join me. I only wish no one would ask us, "Who is winning?" or "Who won?" for Jimmy is always a loser, yet I don't want to lose any game just to please my hostess.

One time, after supper, I want to go to bed right away, but do not want to leave Jimmy alone. Half-asleep, I play chess with him. I don't know how long I stay with him when I hear Jimmy calling, "Check." I try to move my King but cannot. At last I say, "You won." His nostrils enlarged, quivering, he gets up and walks back and forth, every once in a while closing his fists, making a strange sound.

Coming to my bedroom, I open the window for cool air. The stars are out. I hear a car coming. Jimmy rushes outside, shouting, "Mom, I won!" His laughter is followed by, "I moved my Bishop, then my Queen. I checkmated him!"

I hear the sheep bell but cannot sleep. I am tired. The tinkling of the bell makes me think of Mother's funeral service which I did not attend.

I often go to the sheep to feed him some kelp. When the gardener Joe comes to give him dry cereal in a bowl, I take the bowl and feed the sheep with the cereal in my hand, talking to him in Korean. I like the sensation of his tongue on my palms, which are always wet with sweat even in cool Maine. Seeing me laugh while feeding the sheep, Joe says, "I have to take the sheep to the town butcher this Saturday."

When Jimmy comes down from his room, I ask, "Do you know he is to go to the butcher tomorrow?"

"Yes," he says. "Don't you like to eat mutton?"

"No." I ask him what I have been wanting to ask. "Shall we take the sheep to the island?"

"What for?"

"Maybe he wants to be with his own kind."

With his eyes whitening he grins, and slowly unties the rope from the pine, and pulls the sheep to the landing dock.

Reaching the side of the boat, Jimmy lifts the sheep, the veins in his neck standing out. The animal, raking its paws in the air, struggling, is hauled into the cockpit, dropping dung. By the time I clean the sheep droppings from the floor, the boat is passing the lobster traps. A yellow butterfly fluttering low over its reflection in the clean water lands on the railing by the sheep.

Coming close to a shadowy marshland before the spruce-covered island, the boat stops at a long pier. Jimmy carries the sheep out of the boat. The animal pulls at its rope, tinkling its neck bell. It trots down the meadow toward a corral fence at the island's edge. We run after it

129

toward the shore where glistening pebbles make a passage to an islet.

I take off the bell and untie the rope from his neckband. We take him to the edge of the woods and run from him.

That night I decide it is time for me to go. Early in the morning I call the bus station to find what time to leave, and make a last big fire to enjoy. The gardener Joe comes in with an armful of logs. After putting them into the storage bin, he asks, "Kim, did you see the sheep?"

I don't answer but put more logs into the fire. He doesn't ask me again, but says, "The fire is too big, not that big . . ." and leaves the room.

Soon Mr. and Mrs. Thayer come downstairs. Jimmy is not up yet. At the breakfast table Mrs. Thayer says, "Kim, do you want to stay with us as a companion for Jimmy? You will be paid a salary, if you want to call it that."

She glances up at the ceiling where Jimmy's room is. "Jimmy has had a number of companions, but you get along with him best. The last companion he had was a graduate psychology student at Harvard. Jimmy didn't like him. All that one did was sit on that sofa, reading *The New York Times*."

"He was a paid dinner guest for a month and a half," Mr. Thayer says, laughing bitterly.

If I take the job, do I have to lose at chess to please her? I find myself saying, "I should return to school."

"I told you Kim has to go back to school," Mr. Thayer says to his wife and asks me, "When do you leave?"

I want to leave before they find out that I turned the sheep loose on the island. I say, "Soon after Jimmy gets up."

"He would be upset to see you off." Mrs. Thayer lets out a long sigh.

"I don't want him driving to town." Mr. Thayer gets up. "Maybe I should drop you off on my way to the post office."

I feel bad about not saying good-bye to Jimmy but pick up my knapsack quietly to leave in Mr. Thayer's car.

In Kentucky every time I think about my summer experience, my folks in Korea come to my mind, and I wonder how they are managing without Mother. While washing dishes at the Bamboo Inn restaurant to help pay the university, I often regret that I came to America. One day when the Chinese cook doesn't show up, the owner lets me cook some Chinese dishes. He is so pleased that he fires the Chinese and has me cook for less money. Whenever I pick up the order a waitress lays down on the counter, I always look through the slot to find for whom I am cooking. For a poorly dressed or worried-looking customer, I put more food on the plate. One day in May the owner counts loudly and angrily how many shrimp I put in the ninety-five-cent shrimp-fried rice. I match his loud voice by shouting, "The customer ordered shrimp-fried rice, not fried rice," and walk out of the restaurant.

At the end of the month, I return to the Bamboo Inn to receive my final pay. While waiting for the owner, I see a group of students I know. I ask them what a companion job really is, talking about Jimmy and the summer people I met in Maine. They all urge me to write to the Thayers to find out if the job is still available, and one practically jumps out of his chair to get a piece of paper from the cashier and draft a letter.

A week later a special delivery letter comes. When I open the envelope, a check falls out . . . for $200. She wants me to come. The letter goes on, saying that before I came last summer, they had thought about sending Jimmy to a private mental institution. She even mentions the sheep humorously. "Jimmy said he took the sheep to our island because Kim doesn't like mutton."

I travel by train. At Ellsworth, Maine, Joe meets me in the car. Jimmy is not with him. I ask how Jimmy is doing. Joe says, "Not too good."

I wonder if the sheep we took to the island found the way back to his own flock. "Does he often go with you to the island?" I ask.

"Nope," he says. "When we all go next week to chase sheep into the corral for shearing, he might come along."

Dandelion seeds fly all along the road. Summer is just starting in Maine. At the door Mr. and Mrs. Thayer greet me. "Jimmy, Kim is here," Mrs. Thayer calls, looking toward the stairs.

No answer comes. I run upstairs and knock at his room. I say, "It's me, Kim. An Yung. Are you in peace, Jimmy?"

I hear his feet close to the door, but without opening the door, he says, "I'm doing something."

Puzzled, I come downstairs slowly and enter the living room. Mr. Thayer says, "Don't feel bad, Kim. Jimmy is always like that." He leaves the room.

Then I hear Mr. Thayer talking loudly upstairs. "Jimmy, don't be so stubborn."

"I don't trust him." It is Jimmy's voice.

Mrs. Thayer hurriedly gets up, saying, "I'll take you to the room where you will stay."

We go out of the house across the lawn to a shed near the road. The room has no window. She turns on the light and says apologetically, "We call this the photoroom. We haven't had a bathroom installed yet."

131

Against one side of the gray wall is a blanket-covered cot. After she leaves, I sit on the cot blankly. Maybe Jimmy is angry with me because I left him last summer without saying good-bye.

At dinner Jimmy faces me across the table, but his eyes are gazing outside the window; sometimes he mumbles silently. Mrs. Thayer does most of the talking about her grandchildren to Mr. Thayer and tells me happily, "Kim, Jimmy's sister will have her baby soon."

Jimmy stamps his foot, saying, "I hope the baby will be born dead."

No one speaks. Jimmy alone moves his spoon slowly. Mr. Thayer asks Jimmy to leave the table.

Jimmy stays in his room and comes downstairs only at mealtimes. I finish eating before he does and bring out the chessboard and sit at the small table before the board, but he hurries back to his room. With nothing to do, I pick up a book to read, but seem to stare at the same page until my eyes hurt.

I say to Mrs. Thayer that I think I should leave, but she says, "Stay here until our Fourth of July picnic. A crowd will go to the island to pick berries and chase the sheep into the corral."

I stay on, hoping to see the one I fed last summer among those in the corral.

On the day of the picnic, the boat is packed with people — everyone at the Thayers' and their neighbors along the Bay. Jimmy comes and sits beside me at the side of the boat. Many of the youngsters carry sticks and clubs. One picks up the sheep bell and rings it. The sound reminds me that the bell will soon be used for another unlucky sheep.

Out in the sea, the lines of white water, sea gulls, and waving seaweed remind me of home. Amid the chugging sound of the boat, a loud radio, and the noises of the children, my own lips mutter Korean words. Is Jimmy a bit like me in his aloneness, I wonder.

The boat passes the shadows of the marshes and reaches the pier. I go down the meadow to the corral. With the tide in, the islet is separated from the island shore. Not caring to join the picnic crowd, I start to walk through the woods. Later I come down to the shore where Joe sits yawning and smoking. Taking out a sack of food from his pocket, he tosses it to me. "I kept a sandwich and cookies for you." Feeling hungry, I finish a ham sandwich and, munching one of the cookies, go to Jimmy, who is walking back and forth near the corral. Suddenly women picking berries run away from the corral and disappear behind rocks. "Jimmy, don't stand there," calls a hushed voice.

Jimmy moves forward. At the edge of the woods stand a group of sheep, the head sheep looking to and fro. Someone shouts, "Quick, move back!" The youngsters in the woods move in, and hoofs sound on the brittle twigs close to us. Jimmy still stands at the mouth of the corral and the head sheep halts abruptly. From the woods a high voice calls, "Get out of the way, you idiot."

Defiantly I stand up in front of the entrance. The head sheep turns away. Then out of the flock a sheep moves, alone, toward me. The sheep with the neckband. I stretch my arm to offer a cookie. The sheep comes and nibbles the cookie from my palm. The head sheep halts and comes after him, followed by the flock. I quickly take off the neckband. Without going away, my sheep licks my empty palm. I slap the sheep and kick his shoulder with the sole of my foot. The animal jumps back, colliding with the oncoming group of sheep. They trample one another. All the sheep run away wildly, splitting the youngsters at the woods' edge.

"What is that for?" "Chink!" Angry voices come. Some throw sticks at me.

I walk away. Jimmy is with me. The older people are calling back the youngsters in the woods. I am thinking of the one sheep; he is alive and he knows me. The pleasant feel of his tongue on my palm stays with me all the way to the pier, and even in the boat among the angry glares. Jimmy sits still, neither laughing nor talking.

In the evening I don't go to dinner but go to bed early. Early in the morning I walk to the local store and buy chicken to cook Chinese style. I want to make a "good-bye" gift. In America I have learned little but cooking Chinese food.

When I come back carrying the groceries, Jimmy is looking for me. "Mother wants you to come for breakfast." He won't leave until I go with him. The Thayers' grandchildren have come for blueberry pancakes. As I sit next to the older boy, he says, "I don't like Kim." "I don't like him either," the youngest says. The girl looks around the table. "Everybody hates Kim."

To break the awkward silence, I say, "I like Kim."

Mrs. Thayer smiles. "Kim has at least one vote."

Mr. Thayer says, "Jimmy might vote for him."

"No, Uncle Jim can't vote," the older boy says. "He'll be locked up soon in a mental hospital."

Mrs. Thayer sits still, a honey jar in her hand. Mr. Thayer lets out a dry cough. "What a terrible thing to say about your uncle."

"That's what Dad said," the older one says. The others laugh, kicking each other under the table.

133

Looking at no one, I tell them that I am leaving by the evening bus.

Coming back from breakfast, I wash the chicken clean and season it and come to the seashore to broil it over a driftwood fire. Each piece of driftwood I collect makes a different flame. The aroma of chicken rises. I fill a pan with the chicken pieces, but I'm not sure I feel like giving it to the Thayers. Then I think of Joe's birthday sometime this summer and decide to give it to Joe.

On the way to his house I pick wild mint and decorate the pan. When I knock at the old shed, Joe is not home. I put the chicken in my knapsack and go to the main house to call a taxi. Mrs. Thayer says, "Jimmy is in his car to take you to the bus station."

"Do you think Jimmy should drive at night?" Mr. Thayer asks.

"Why not?" Mrs. Thayer says. "With the headlights on he can see like anyone else. Why not? He can drive. He's not an . . ." she cries.

"If you talk that way, I don't care," Mr. Thayer shouts angrily and walks upstairs.

After I get into the car, Jimmy drives away. Before the empty road, he stops the car long and turns his head to left and right just as in a checker game, then quickly moves out on the road. At every turn he stops, stretching his neck to look farther on the road. He goes so slow, cars behind us begin to honk. In the town he drives around and around. A bank clock shows it is already close to my departure time. I ask Jimmy, "Can you stop?"

"Oh, no. Not on the road." The car moves on as he says, "There isn't a parking place."

A half block ahead I see a car moving out of a parking lot. I point to the spot, "There, Jimmy."

"I don't want to pay for parking," he says.

I insist he stop his car and let me jump out, but he refuses until he reaches the dark part of the street way out on the headland. Getting out of the car, I hurry along the bay to the bus station.

At the ticket office a man says that the bus has just left and there won't be another until midnight. As I walk out, Jimmy is right behind me. It starts to drizzle, and Jimmy and I go to his car. Feeling heavy and tired, I close my eyes to rest. When I open my eyes, I find the road moving. Not a car ahead. I see rain in the bright headlights. Jimmy is holding the wheel. "Where is this?" I ask. Jimmy doesn't answer but watches the white-lined wet highway. Wide awake, I raise myself and grasp his arm. "Jimmy, stop." The car doesn't slow down. "Listen, Jimmy. If you don't stop, I'll call the police."

134

At the junction the car swirls around to a side road. As though chased, the car is running fast, the speed meter hand reaching 80. I clutch his arm to stop his car. "Let me out. You go home."

"No. I'm not going home."

I look around for a police car but soon stop looking . . . I don't want to get out into the cold rain. I ask Jimmy, "Where are we going?"

"Anywhere you want to go," he says.

It occurs to me that to be with me, he used a strategy just as in a chess game: driving deliberately slowly on the way to the bus station, then around and around the town, pretending to look for a free parking place, following me around until I dozed off in his car. He checkmated me by taking off.

When Jimmy finally stops at a gas station for fuel and goes to the rest room, I call his parents. Mrs. Thayer asks, "Where are you?"

"We are getting close to Canada."

"Could he drive that far?" she sounds relieved, even proud. "Well, as long as he is with you, Mr. Thayer and I will call off the police. But call us again to let us know where you are." As Jimmy comes out of the rest room, I hang up.

In the morning light I see a few farmhouses along the mountain road. The rain has stopped. Jimmy yawns loudly. The car jostles on a dirt road and stops abruptly. Jimmy goes out of the car and walks behind it. The car is stuck in the mud. I help him push from behind, but it refuses to come out of the mud trough. Hungry, I take out the broiled chicken from my knapsack and share it with Jimmy. The hours pass.

Finally a truck stops. Long-haired men and women, some barefoot, jump out of the rear and cab. Without waiting for us to explain what happened, they go behind the car, their boots, shoes, bare feet collecting mud, and push it out of the mud hole. As they climb into the truck, one with a headband asks, "Where are you heading?" As we don't answer, he says, "Need a pad? Come along."

Jimmy drives after the truck, moving along the ever-turning mountain road. Going through a tunnel of moonlit leaves, we come to what seems to be a farm. In front of a large building, the truck stops and everyone goes inside.

No light inside except from the moon. Not invited, we stand near the entrance, watching. The men and women make a fire in the dug-out ground at the center and put in pots and jars. In the flickering fire, I can see the high wooden ceiling and the large dirt floor. Each moves around, getting dishes, mugs. One picks up a large jar from the fire and calls us,

135

"Care for black beans? If you stay more than overnight in this commune, you can earn your food by doing some work — fetching spring water and collecting deadwood."

Jimmy and I join them, picking up bowls from a wooden board nearby. As we find only one spoon, I break a twig into two with which I pick up the beans.

"Chopsticks from a hazel twig, very clever." The man with the headband smiles at me. "This farm is owned by my uncle. He arches a forked hazel twig and wherever it bends down, he finds water."

"Oh, a water dowser!" Jimmy says. They smile and nod. No one seems to think Jimmy is odd.

They scatter around the room to sleep. We go to a corner of the wooden floor and, finding blankets, we help ourselves.

In the morning when I get up, Jimmy is walking back and forth at the entrance, mumbling and laughing to himself. Everyone else is asleep.

Carrying water buckets, we follow a narrow trail and find a stream by tall grasses and sedges. Scooping the water in our hands, we drink, then wash ourselves. It is good to watch the cold clean water moving and thin sedges springing from a crack in a large stone.

The sound of water comes to me clearly. "Jimmy, how would you like to stay here all summer?"

He turns to me, his large, clear eyes unblinking. He gets up slowly and steps in the stream, letting the water run around and above his feet as he clenches his fists, shouting loudly, "Anyong! Are you in peace?"

On the way back, each of us with a bucketful of spring water, Jimmy picks up dead tree branches in his free hand with great concentration. At the barn, we find a "Gone to the fields" sign in front of the dug-out fireplace and a thin man alone reading newspapers, looking cold and miserable. Jimmy helps him pile wood to make a fire and goes out to get more.

As I fold the blankets at the barn corner where we slept, I see the thin man place some of the papers on the pile and light them. Only the paper burns. Jimmy, bringing in an armful of logs, says to him, "*The New York Times* goes under the logs, not on top."

The man makes room below the woodpile and puts the remaining papers underneath and lights them. The logs soon catch fire. The man, surprised at how the fire grows, mutters, "I never made a fire before."

As the flames rise, he turns his back, then again turns, his face toward the fire, in a motion of dancing. Jimmy and I join him circling round and round, all of us.

Doors Made to Order

•

BY MARCIA YUDKIN

T HE SOUND OF the hard rubber tips of her walker against the floor
was blunt, but not as curt and indignant as Vivian wished. Murray was late. Any second the grandfather clock would strike
eight, and Murray knew that in order for her to be seated for the musicians' first note he had to pick her up by 7:45. This year at least they had
aisle seats, but people still would glare at her for making the suspension of
the first break more difficult. Murray would flash concern at her, as if to
say, "Mother, if you're embarrassed I can take you home." Vivian would
ignore him and follow the walker step by step at the limits of her strength.
Never was he apologetic himself; he was the loving son devoting his
evening to his mother.

Vivian knocked the walker against the door, which yielded easily.
Each scrape ahead opened it further, until she had passed through and the
door swung closed without rebounding at her. That Jack Mycklowski had
done a wonderful job. "I see," he'd responded. "You need them
lightweight and fixed so they won't clobber you." Then he'd plunged into
the task and turned her apartment into a new neighborhood of sawdust
and tobacco. He'd left it a neighborhood too, still sectioned but without
barriers. Murray's suggestion would have cost one-tenth as much, just
removing the doors and disguising the vestigial hinges, but so what? It
would have meant surrender to her disability. Murray seemed to want her
stuck in helplessness — or almost stuck, so he could rescue her.

137

Vivian halted in the position she'd aimed at, beside the front door with her back to the coat closet. That way they'd waste the least amount of time when Murray buzzed. She'd be set for him to negotiate the two remaining doorknobs. When he'd visited halfway through the carpenter's week, he'd furrowed his high brow: "Mother, why not leave the closet and the front door as they are? You won't be going out alone anyhow." Stupidly, reasonably, she'd conceded that much.

A familiar rumble prepared her for the footfalls and the rasp of a key in the lock. "Goodness, Mother, they haven't fixed that elevator yet. I'll call Marvin about it tomorrow." Murray pecked Vivian on the forehead and tossed his long hank of hair back over his bald spot. "Have you been standing here long? You know Dr. Katz said standing in one place isn't good for you."

Vivian jiggled her purse against the walker. "I'll have the stole, please," she said, her voice verging on sharp. It would be chamber music tonight, and she especially hated to miss the first piece on the program. Less familiar works by composers she loved were her great passion. She caught the message more clearly when there weren't passages and themes she could already hum. The sheltering weight fell on her, distributed as cockeyed as usual. Murray hadn't learned to drape the fur like his father, but the nubby dress she'd chosen should keep the silky lining wrapped around her shoulder. "Onward," Vivian ordered.

"I talked to Rubenthal," Murray remarked in the elevator.

"Oh?" Vivian scoured his pleasantness with her ready sarcasm. "Did you convince him?"

"He said you insisted." Murray rattled off his monthly warning about her "risky investments." He was a very old 40, she suddenly noticed, with a deceptive earnestness around his hazel eyes and droopy nose. He counseled conservatism for her and meanwhile scattered the business in directions her husband would have disapproved. But he was her only son.

"Thanks for taking me to the concert," she interrupted, reaching for and squeezing his hand softly. He brightened and shut up, helping her in and out of the car and up the three steps in solicitous silence.

"Heavens, we're not too late," she exclaimed when they turned the last corner. The hall clock read 8:30, and the ushers were still seating people. Maybe the cellist's bow had come unstrung — that had happened once, during his warm-up, fortunately. He'd sped to his hotel and back for his spare while the audience coughed.

"Mother, it's a contemporary program." Murray crackled their pro-

138

grams beside her in the aisle. "It looks weird. We can turn around and go home."

Vivian faltered. An evening of clicks and strident screeches wasn't what she wanted. But the musicians had begun filing onstage to subdued applause. She pressed on and gestured for him to slip ahead of her. Her heart beat hard; a bead of moisture trickled by her ear. But there was no reason to feel self-conscious. The musicians sat utterly still, as if meditation were their performance. A program landed in her lap, and she read in astonishment.

YALE CHAMBER MUSIC SOCIETY
Opus 27 (1951)   Wolf Lehrmann
Neal Mellenger, oboe
Jackson Willard, cello
Pierre Gaspard, piano

NOTE: Since this work begins and ends with an undetermined length of silence, the audience is requested to refrain from applauding until the musicians rise from their seats.

INTERMISSION

Opus 48 (1953)   Wolf Lehrmann
Julius Bologna, violin
John Miller, violin
Kathleen Miller, viola
Jackson Willard, cello
Pierre Gaspard, piano

And no program notes! It was a scandal. The tenseness in the hall was palpable, all eyes on the motionless three men on the stage, all ears confronting nothing. Vivian thought she saw the neck of the fat cellist twitch, like a subtle signal, but the oboist stayed solid in his pose, the pianist kept his long-lashed concentration. Just when the silence seemed about to explode with frustrated expectations, the dark-locked man at the piano raised his hands to the keyboard.

What she heard was even more startling. The music was rippling chords, dissonances melting and reappearing in a pattern she couldn't catch although she thought it was the same thing repeated with slight modulation. It wasn't pretty; it was faintly diabolical, complex and ambiguous, unsettling and sinuous. Vivian shifted uneasily in her seat and

139

the cellist came in. He began to weave a mesh with his bow — delicate, strong, intricate, going around and around like an expanding afghan square. The two lines seemed obsessive and independent, yet peculiarly in harmony. Then the third entered, the oboe with a singing part that dipped and soared and hooted in staccato, lay low and rose again in triumph. Her mouth fell open and sensation overcame her, like the time she was five and experienced something known by reputation. She had spilled from a wheelbarrow. "Pain": a concept became real. Now this was — what?

She had no words for what she heard and couldn't hold on to her impressions, which followed the shifting colors and dynamics as they supported and contradicted one another. But it was a revelation, showing that a wall of the world she lived in was pliable and could be peeled aside like a curtain, disclosing a realm that was rigorous and lush. The oboe had parted the curtain, and she tried by squinting at the oboist to fix her vision of the vista. But her eyes were moist; she was losing it; the oboe was dipping to a low note and fading away. The cello became quieter too, weaving slower and more finely until a thread, dangling, diminished to nothing. The piano continued its weird clashing harmonies as Vivian despaired; the wall was opaque and hard again. She glared at the handsome pianist as he lifted his hands and folded them in his lap, let his eyes drop closed, and left a depressing stillness, the silence heavy and turbulent. Behind her a pocketbook hit the floor; lipsticks and pencils clattered; the scene on the stage remained dead and cold.

Without any apparent signal, the three rose in unison, faced the audience and strode offstage. Here and there hands clapped, but the applause didn't reverberate. Vivian rocked with the stark, troubling mood. The lights went up.

Murray's smile, as he bent over her, broke her entrancement. "Mother, shall we go? No need to sit through any more of that."

Vivian looked at him with withering surprise. "Are you in a hurry to get somewhere?"

"Actually, yes." A contrite acquiescence settled over his face. "The men's room. I'll be back."

When he left, her impressions were more jumbled. It seemed she had been shown another world, but not initiated. What had the music revealed? Perhaps the chatter around her held clues.

"It had a nonretrograde rhythm. Did you notice?" That must be one of the bohemians behind her.

"You mean retrograde." Brisk certainty. "It was positively Romantic."

140

"Negatively Romantic. The guy's a nihilist. That went out with Dostoevski."

Vivan turned to another cluster of voices more lighthearted in tone.

"When I come to concerts I like to lean back and forget my troubles. They put this junk on the series one more time and I cancel my subscription."

"It reminds me of your charge account, dear. It goes round and round and there's never a final payoff."

"Did you hear that Kramer's is having a sale?"

Vivian retracted her attention. Restlessly she wondered when the intermission would end, whether Murray would spend the second half out in the corridor. He had once, claiming an important contact had kept him talking. Vivian worried her gold charms and finally noticed the lights dimming without her son.

This time four men and a woman came out and instead of sitting in silence, tuned up. The string players rotated pegs to match the pianist's note; when the violinist at the front nodded, everyone began. Vivian sat erect in her seat, watched the violinists scrape and ping, but couldn't get it. The terrain was guarded by the piano, with brutally refused access, ponderously pacing on a high concrete wall. Five devotees of a foreign system; what could get her admitted?

She sat back, surrendered as she might to a party of distinguished guests parleying in Turkish. Her mien was still polite; she had influence; she'd bribe someone who could translate when the time was right. Vivian folded the program into her purse and began to summon strength for the slow journey back. Murray's aid was pinched, but she had other resources.

In the next month Vivian tried everything. There was so little time, it seemed, and each simple inquiry was turned back after a while. No, Lehrmann wasn't in the *Harvard Dictionary of Music*. No, there were no Lehrmann records at Cutler's. No, he wasn't listed at the Yale Music Library. No, Linda Saven's friend Lawrence had never heard of him. Perhaps Louise, who did her errands for her, didn't know how to use a card catalog, maybe friends and reference librarians lied upon hearing the fierce urgency in her voice, but Vivian began to suspect that there was a brotherhood so exclusive that the announcer of her classical music show was left out. In frustration she ordered a set of porcelain that elicited gasps from her friends and remonstrations from her son.

She was troubled by dreams about the failures in her life that she thought she'd forgotten. Accompanied by a repetitive score of discordant fragments, she would awaken angry with herself, cursing the necessary trudge to the bathroom. She would recoil from the mirror when the fluorescent shimmy made her skin look transparent. If she was as old as she looked in that harsh glare, she should know everything. Then she'd count up the years and take heart, until compelled to inch the walker through the custom-designed swinging door. Nighttime used to rejuvenate her, but no longer, not when every experience or image stressed her limits.

With her friends, she would careen from bored to attentive. When Lily, Diane, and Elaine animated the bridge table with grandchildren's names and the exploits of decorators, she faded into her cards. Then she perked up suddenly with a daring bid and the news that she might, next winter, move to Miami Beach. "Really?" Vivian wondered herself where the idea had come from. Lily drove her home and asked if she would mind a stop at the drugstore. Vivian consented, trailed in when Lily was ready to leave, and turned gay and acquisitive at the cosmetics counter. Once she interrupted Elaine to plead, "What do you know about the other world?" When Elaine prattled on about God and religion, Vivian padded toward the phonograph.

Music had been her consolation. But now melodies that soothed made her uncomfortable. Luxurious textures and resolutions she had liked raised her hackles, as if the orchestras were straining to hide something. Sometimes she listened so hard she would start at the baritone announcements on her radio program. Couldn't they take a cue from that "Opus 27" and provide a silence for the effect to reach full force? Vivian pored through her record library one afternoon for the liner notes and found only one offhand hint, on a Beethoven quartet set, that music could be profound. Beethoven's tormented lyricism, though, was equally beyond her.

Murray's Sunday telephone calls continued. Vivian didn't speak to him of her turmoil. Instead she asked about the books he was reading, the plays that he went to. Her prompting led him into such detail about a World War II general once that she dozed off and the receiver tumbled into her lap. He always inquired after her health and counseled caution with her assets. On Mother's Day Vivian checked the acidy retort she had prepared and startled both of them with an unaccustomed "Why?" "The bottom line, Mother, is that you might lose the principal," her son replied. Suddenly she knew what she would do; she had formulated a plan.

• • •

142

The gold charms clanged as Vivian reached down for another dab of foundation. Maybe she should remove the bracelet. She expected to sit perfectly still, but if she didn't, the small noise might be distracting. Vivian decided to keep it on and focused on her makeup. Her blue eyes sparkled today and were not ringed so much with wrinkles. She might even be considered attractive for her age, at least discounting her poor legs. Vivian hurried through her daydream; she wanted to post herself by the front door before the trio buzzed.

Vivian turned and surveyed the bathroom. A woman's space, but with nothing to make men snicker. She pressed through the swinging door to her yellow bedroom. The pills were stashed in the closet with the baubles she knew shouldn't be for guests' eyes; only the framed picture on the bureau made the room personal. Should there be another hard chair in there? The musicians might wish to warm up privately before the performance. She could have asked Anna Sondheim's advice and hired Louise to set up, but this was her show. Vivian pushed the walker at a brisk but not quite headlong pace, checking all the sights on the way.

When she reached the foyer, the elevator's rumble tautened her nerves. She followed the chorus of steps in the hall and called out firmly at the knock: "Please come in. It's open." She stretched out her hand to the middle man of the three, who had to shift his black oblong case to grasp right hands.

"Mrs. Slater?" His voice was gruff, like a hibernating bear's. "I'm Neal Mellenger. Glad to meet you." He indicated the youngest man, with lashes so long and dark they hardly looked real. "This is Pierre Gaspard."

"Enchanté." He nodded, keeping his hands in his pockets.

"And this is Jackson Willard." The man was very large, with a bulky inanimate companion.

"Hello. Have we beat the crowd? I'm crazy about parties."

"I'm afraid there won't be a crowd tonight. I did say a private party, didn't I, Mr. Mellenger?" Vivian flashed a hard smile and beckoned them into the living room. "This is where you'll be playing, gentlemen. The piano was tuned this morning, Mr. Gaspard. You can warm up here or in the bedroom. Just let me know when you're ready to get started." Vivian headed her walker for the kitchen to leave them to their puzzled glances. She hadn't hired them under false pretense. Even if she had, she'd paid more than the fee they'd asked, in advance. They ought to have suspected, in any case; who would request "Opus 27" for a *party?*

The door whisked shut behind her. Through it leaked whispers and lulls she interpreted as shrugs. If she were they, she'd be glad to play

143

without the pressure of reviews and without having to gauge applause. She crept close to the thin barrier to spy — another advantage of that nice carpenter's work. But there were no remarks to hear, only arpeggios leaping from the piano, a thunderous chord and a lullaby reply. The cello growled at its lowest reaches while the notes of the oboe poured upward in a defiant stream. The instruments circled, flirted, and ignored one another like the patterns that had disturbed her. Had they started already? The instructions were to let her know.

Vivian banged her metal helper through the door and apologized to the startled cellist with a quick mustering of composure. "Everyone's here who will be here," she announced. "But please wait until I get seated." She flushed when she realized that here, in her own house, the musicians waited on her slow movements. The pianist flexed his fingers, the cellist rearranged the loose pages on his stand, but the oboist, gray-haired with a subdued complexion, watched her. His gaze didn't waver until she had settled in her chair, nudged the walker aside, and nodded just as gravely. He nodded at the two others, who, although they weren't looking at him, at once became transfixed like statues. Vivian thought she knew what to expect but was again caught off guard.

The silence started out cushioned, as sound would be by her rugs, soft chairs, and drapes, but it changed. It felt like the automatic car wash she'd dared once, a track jerking the car forward through onslaughts of suds and brushes. Provoked by nothing, the sequences now were all in her head. First appraisal of the stone-still men, gratitude that the roles weren't reversed; worries about the refreshments and whether she'd really turned the clock's striker off; estimation of the lapsed time, wondering when they would begin; the mounting strain of expectation with hostile ideas breaking in; suspense so taut it brought on revulsion and the thought that this was their revenge; and a tumultuous cauldron of feelings that rebounded louder and louder. Vivian thought she would faint, with no relief to be counted on.

When the pianist came alive, his passagework wouldn't let her relax. The shifting chords seemed to go nowhere and so sustained her discomfort. The cellist's entrance didn't spare her either. But when the oboe touched down and took off, she catapulted with it through the cracks in the disorder. Exhilarated, she hung on for the ride, accepting the vertigo of the unfamiliar. Yet the thrill stole all of her energy and let her down too soon. Where had she been? The cello was retracting its support; the oboe was mum. Now there was only the piano, plodding steadfastly in indefinite directions. If she'd been in the other world, now she was lost, navigatorless. The chords ended too, without a resolution, infuriating her as the three played dead again. She'd paid them well, and they'd better tell her what it was all about.

An impatient flick of her wrist sliced the silence, and the cellist took the cue to open his eyes. He blinked, and Vivian noticed that he had the look of a big eater starved and unhappy. The young man at the piano exposed dark eyes fringed all around with boredom. Obviously he preferred glory and large halls. A gourmet spread during intermission wouldn't win him over. The oboist emerged last, his wide face weary and spent. No, it would have to be the stout man. Vivian struggled in her chair while staring at him.

"Oh, thank you, Mr. Willard," she said, accepting his arm crooked in front of her. "Thank you all, gentlemen. I'll see to the refreshments now."

The cellist was harder to walk with than her metal contraption, but he held the door for her without her having to press through it. "Ah, cake!" he exclaimed when he saw the counter, and let his support drop. "Chocolate cake. Neal and Pierre never eat during concerts."

"Oh? Please, help yourself." Vivian grabbed the refrigerator handle for balance. "Why is that?"

"Neal says eating wrecks his embouchure and Pierre claims crumbs always stick to his fingers. Mm. Did you enjoy the concert?"

"Yes, as a matter of fact. But I have a question." Vivian steadied herself and plunged. "What is that piece about?"

"About?" The cellist scooted crumbs from the corner of his mouth to the interior. "It's about nothing."

"Oh, come, now." Vivian edged into the tone she used with Murray. "Do you take me for some rich fool?"

"Oh, no!" He stopped gobbling cake, his no longer greedy eyes innocent and sincere. "I'm serious. That's what Neal says when he lectures. Lehrmann was a discovery of his, a cranky genius teaching deaf children in London. Neal says the pieces with silence especially are about nothing. But don't ask me." He looked pointedly at her hand on the refrigerator handle. "I just play what's put in front of me."

Vivian pulled and extracted a colorful plate of fruit, then let out a quavery distress signal that sent the man away to fetch her walker. Pineapples and melons made her mouth water as she tried to think. She exchanged the fruit for her walker when the cellist returned and indicated that she would bring out the cake herself. The door closed after the musician with its stroke that was never a slam, and Vivian contemplated its perfect fit in her life. Wouldn't getting the lecture be like removing the door? She liked the knock of light metal against thin wood and watching herself progress against the obstacle. Take the door away and there'd be no surprises, no scenes hidden beyond her sight.

When she pushed through, the tableau was different from what she'd imagined. The bored pianist was absorbed in cantaloupe, the cellist was browsing in her porcelain collection, and the oboist slouched, whittling at a reed. The leader looked up, raising one bushy gray eyebrow.

"Some cake, Mr. Mellenger?" Vivian advanced and dropped the plate on the coffee table. "It's all right because I don't need the second half of the program. Haydn is nice but what I really wanted was to experience "Opus 27." In fact, can I engage you for a repeat performance, at your convenience?"

"I'm afraid our fees are going up," he replied. "It will cost one-third again as much for an evening like this."

Vivian didn't blink, although Murray's unctuous warnings slid through her mind. She'd just tell Rubenthal to sell some stock. She smiled. This was her best investment.

Upland Game

•

BY HOWARD FRANK MOSHER

W HEN MY BROTHER CHARLIE and I were growing up in Kingdom County, a number of itinerant specialists could be
counted on to visit northeastern Vermont each year. I had no
idea where these exotic wayfarers hailed from. My earliest impression of
United States geography had been formed by the American League baseball standings, and until I was nine or ten I thought New York lay somewhere to the north of Boston because of the Yankees' perennial position at
the top of the column. "Away," we called anywhere more than five miles
beyond the county line. Or "the other side of the hills." All I knew for
certain was that since we could not go to them, the mind readers and
barnstorming baseball teams and one-elephant family circuses came to
us. Then they departed, leaving Charlie and me with a day of desolation
on our hands, and maybe a fifteen-cent souvenir: a tattered poster, an
autographed snapshot, a handful of spent shells from the Manchester
Arms Company sharpshooter, which still gave off a faint and exciting
aroma of gunpowder after six months in a dresser drawer.

Of all the itinerants, the sharpshooter was my favorite. Actually, he
was an ammunition salesman, a drummer of rifle and shotgun shells,
who, as a sideline, put on marksmanship exhibitions at county fairs and
rod and gun club suppers and sometimes, on an impromptu basis, out
behind the general stores and four-corner filling stations where he sold the
company's line. He was a small man of 45 or 50, with pale eyes narrowed

at the corners from driving into ten thousand suns and squinting over a shotgun barrel at a million clay pigeons. He was slightly hard of hearing, and when he spoke, which wasn't often, it was usually to complain about the weather in what I believe was a mild southern accent. His suit looked as though he'd driven two weeks straight in it, and unlike our other showmen, there was no hoopla about him at all. In fact, he didn't seem to care whether he shot or not, and it was this odd quality, his apparent indifference toward his talent, that appealed to me and annoyed my brother, who by the time he was 18, was considered to be one of the two or three best shots in our neck of the woods himself.

"He's here," Charlie said, pulling in behind a dusty gray Pontiac in front of our Uncle Clarence Kittredge's general store in Kingdom Common.

It was a warm and hazy Saturday morning in early October, and Charlie and I had already been out doing a little road hunting in the new Hudson Hornet he'd bought the previous summer with money he'd earned working in the paper mill at Groveton and playing baseball up in Canada. I had just turned 12 and was enormously proud to be out riding the roads and hunting with my grown-up brother. And here, out of the blue, was the Manchester sharpshooter. It was almost too good to be true.

The shooter and Uncle Clarence were standing across from one another at the store counter. Uncle Clarence was thumbing through the company's latest catalogue. The shooter was reading a Socony road map and frowning.

"New line of sixteens, I see," Uncle Clarence said.

The shooter nodded without looking up from his map.

"Good shell?"

"Fairly accurate upland game shell," the shooter said.

"Wouldn't care to pop a few out back for the boys here?"

The sharpshooter gave Charlie and me a quick, aggrieved look. He reached in the inside pocket of his suit jacket and got out a half-full pint bottle of Southern Comfort and unscrewed the cap and took a sip. The whiskey was the color of standing water in a cedar bog. As it went down, the shooter winced. "I got to be up in Memphremagog by 11 o'clock," he said. "I might snap off a round or two first if it ain't too cold."

He went out to his Pontiac and unlocked the trunk. It was neat as a pin and contained several cartons of ammunition, a battered leather suitcase with straps and buckles, and three long canvas cases wrapped up in a wool overcoat. He handed me two of the cases and took the third himself. It was as warm as a morning in June, but I noticed that he was shivering in his suit jacket. When he shut the trunk lid the Pontiac shuddered all over, and so did he.

"Big old gas hog," Charlie said.

The shooter gave a dyspeptic grin, as though pleased to hear his car disparaged. "She's a guzzler," he agreed. "Burns gas and oil like they was both going out of style. Throw a rod clean through her block one of these days. Brakes ain't the best. Heater's shot. Trade her in five seconds flat if the right deal come along. Lug them around back for me, will you, bub?"

We went around behind the store to my uncle's garden in the vacant lot at the foot of Anderson Hill. Half a dozen men and boys from the street followed us. We laid the cases down on the short bench where Uncle Clarence sat to shell peas and husk corn.

"Unzip that shorter one," the shooter told me.

Inside was a light, single-shot .22.

"All right for a kid starting out," the shooter said.

He stooped over and picked up a Coca Cola bottle cap. He walked out around the brown corn stalks and frosted Kentucky Wonder pole beans and jammed the bottle cap into a rotten fence post at the base of the hill. He came back to the bench, put a shell in the .22, and fired at the cap without seeming to take aim.

I ran to get the bottle cap. One side was ripped flat, like a penny flattened by a locomotive on the Boston and Montreal tracks. I ran back to the shooter, who looked at the cap and scowled as though he'd missed it entirely.

"You ought to go on Broadway," my brother said.

"Kid gun," the shooter said, shoving the .22 back in its case. "All right for gray squirrels and such."

"There aren't any gray squirrels up here," Charlie said. "Too cold."

"I believe it," said the shooter, and turned up his jacket collar against a warm south breeze. "Man dear, it's chilly!"

He unzipped the second case I'd brought around and got out a .30.30 rifle. It was a bolt-action rifle, the kind most local deer hunters used. A couple of men moved up closer.

"You got a fifty-cent piece on you?" the shooter asked my uncle.

Clarence reached under his apron for his black change purse. He unsnapped it and stared inside for some time. Finally he removed a half dollar.

"I believe," he said slowly, "that it is unlawful to destroy a coin of the realm."

"Trade you Mr. G. Washington's picture for her," the shooter said,
going for his back pocket.

"That isn't necessary," Uncle Clarence said in a dignified voice.
"Heave it up?"

"Not too high. Wouldn't want to miss and pick off some old lady
raking leaves up top the hill."

Two or three of the men chuckled at the thought of picking off an old
lady.

"I thought you never missed," Charlie said.

"You say?"

"I said, I thought you don't miss."

"Miss quite frequently," the shooter said.

He slid a shell into the chamber and rammed home the bolt. "Heave
her."

My uncle threw the fifty-cent piece out and up. It spun over and over,
flashing against the red sumac and yellow popples on the hillside. The
shooter fired, and the coin vanished in thin air.

"Yes, sir," Clarence said with a note of finality.

"Anybody," said my brother, "can learn to do that. There's a trick to
it, just like shooting a woodcock. You wait until it's at the top of its arc,
then you've got a stationary target. All it takes is practice."

"There you have her," said the shooter and shoved the rifle back into
its case like a man hanging an old saw up on a nail. "Practice is the thing,
all right."

He took another sip of Southern Comfort. Then he unzipped the
third case and slid out the loveliest gun I'd ever seen. It was a 16-gauge
pump-action shotgun with a rich dark stock and a barrel the color of Lake
Memphremagog on a gray day in duck season, engraved with two pheas-
ants flushing out of a wheat field.

The shooter looked at my uncle. "You got any spoiled hens' eggs on
hand?"

"I do not. I don't pass spoiled eggs off on my customers. You want
eggs from my store, you'll have to settle for grade-A fresh."

The shooter considered. "All righty. I'll purchase half a dozen grade-
A fresh hens' eggs."

My uncle went inside. A minute later he came back with a half carton
of brown eggs. The shooter gave him a dollar and Clarence handed him
back eighty cents.

"It's on the company," the shooter explained to the men and boys. By
now there was a gallery of 15 or so, lounging against the back wall of the

store, hunkered down on the edge of the harvested garden. Among the men I recognized some who were crack shots themselves.

The shooter put six shells into the shotgun.

"How many eggs?" my uncle said.

"Try three. Three grade-A eggs. Fling them out away. They spatter."

Three brown eggs sailed over the garden at intervals of less than a second. The shooter fired three times. Before the third egg left my uncle's hand, the first two had burst in midair into small, yellow omelettes. The third egg burst, raining yolk and white and fragments of brown shell onto a heap of dead pea vines. I scrambled for the ejected shells, smoking on the ground at the shooter's feet.

My brother was already haranguing the onlookers, patiently, yet with an argumentative edge to his voice, the way years later he would talk to certain undecided juries in the courthouse across the common. "What he is, boys, is fast. I don't say he isn't accurate; he's accurate enough for trap and trick shooting. But mainly he's fast. Out in the woods, fast isn't all that important. Accuracy is what counts in the woods."

"I never was much of a hand to hunt in the woods," the shooter said to no one in particular. "Sun never seems to get down between them trees and warm things up good."

He shivered at the thought of the sun not warming things up in the woods. He extended the gun, barrel first, toward my brother. "Care to try her?"

Charlie jumped out of the way like an infielder avoiding a sliding runner. "Watch where you point that thing, mister. It's still loaded."

"Safe's on," the shooter said. "Go ahead."

Charlie took the gun, turned it around, and hefted it. "How many shells left in this cannon? Three?"

The shooter nodded. Some of the men squatting on their heels stood up.

"Three eggs," Charlie told my uncle, and snapped off the safety.

Uncle Clarence sighed. One, two, three eggs sailed into the air. My brother shot three times. A lone egg burst in the air. The others fell back into the garden. One landed intact on the pea vines, and the shooter went over and picked it up.

"Fetch me a glass, will you, bub?"

I went inside and got a clean coffee mug from the counter and took it out to him, and he broke the raw egg into it and swallowed yolk and white and all in two gulps. "Breakfast," he explained to the crowd. "Only way I could ever get one down."

He handed the two rifle cases and his car keys to me. "Round one goes to the boot," he said.

He stuck the shotgun back in its case, and we started for his car. Singly and in pairs, the spectators came along behind.

"Sharpshooter!" my brother called after him. "I'll bet you my brand-new Hudson Hornet with 10 gallons of Flying A in the tank against that fancy shotgun that I can shoot two birds in the woods for every one of yours."

The shooter kept walking.

Charlie ran up and met him by his car. "You hear me, mister? My vehicle against your gun I can outshoot you in the woods."

The shooter unlocked the trunk of the gray Pontiac. One by one, he laid the three canvas gun cases on the overcoat. He shut the trunk lid with a puff of dust and turned to look at Charlie's Hudson.

"That your rig there?"

"That's my rig. Under 4,000 miles on her, radio, doesn't burn a spoonful of oil — ."

"Heater work good?"

"Mister, that automobile kicks heat like a Round Oak stove in a one-room school."

The shooter walked around to the driver's side and looked in through the open window. The keys dangled in the ignition. He rested his hand on the door. "You mind?"

"No, sir. Go ahead and try her out. Take her for a spin around the common. Go out on the county road and open her up wide. Whatever."

The shooter got in and rolled up the driver's window. He leaned across the front seat and cranked the passenger window up tight. He switched on the key and stepped on the starter, and the engine popped right off. He gunned the motor a little. The Hudson idled smoothly.

I expected the shooter to pull away from the curb; instead he reached down and turned on the heater. Outside on the street in front of Uncle Clarence's store it was a warm fall day. Inside the Hudson, it was getting hotter. Beads of sweat stood out on the shooter's forehead and slid off the tip of his sharp nose. He bent over and turned the heater on full blast and the sweat rolled off his face like water and he gave a small grin like Sam McGee from sunny Tennessee, and shut off the engine and got out of the car.

He took a round two-dollar watch out of his pants pocket and frowned at it like a hunter looking at his compass and wondering if he might be lost.

"Be here at two o'clock," he said to Charlie.

Evidently the shooter decided to postpone his run to Memphremagog. At 1:30 we found him sitting in the barroom of the Common Hotel, drinking from a new pint of Southern Comfort, and looking as though he'd just been informed on good authority that he had six months to live.

"Are we still on?" Charlie said.

"If you say so," the shooter said unenthusiastically.

My brother pointed at me. "He wants to come too."

"No doubt," the shooter said without looking in my direction. "You boys lead the way. I'll follow along in my old icebox."

Charlie drove once around the common for luck, past the commission sales barn, out the macadam county road, over the red iron bridge onto our dirt road, and up the lane onto the ridge. When we hit the lane, I looked back and saw the chrome Indian Chief on the Pontiac's hood bucking up and down like the figurehead of a ship in a stormy sea.

We left the cars in the puckerbrush at the upper end of the lane, where it petered out into an old logging trace. The shooter opened his trunk and got out his shotgun. He got a pair of rubbers out of his valise and sat down on the rear bumper and pulled them on over his scuffed dress shoes.

"The springs in your rig are all shot to hell and gone," I said.

"No call for barbershop talk," he said, yanking at the heel of a rubber. "You was my kid, you'd be cutting a switch about now."

"You ever have any kids?"

"No, praise be."

He stood up and struggled into his overcoat and buttoned it up to the throat. In the overcoat and rubbers he did not look like a salesman, much less a sharpshooter; he looked like a tramp just in off the B & M tracks.

My brother stared at him. "Aren't you going to be hot?"

"I hope so," the shooter said. "But I doubt it."

He loaded the shotgun and turned it upside down and shut one eye and squinted down the barrel with the other. I noticed that the safety was off.

"How is it," he said into the gun barrel, "that you ain't off in college? A smart young fella like you."

"I might go next year," Charlie said. "I have to get my car paid for first."

"He knows more than most of the professors do already," I said.

The shooter straightened up and gave a sardonic cough.

"Go ahead," I said. "Ask him a question. Any question at all."

"I just did."

"Ask him another one. Baseball. American presidents. Whatever."

The shooter looked off through the fall haze at the hills. "All right," he said. "Where are these so-called birds?"

On the way up to the woods through the dying steeplebush and orchard grass, Charlie and the shooter agreed on ground rules. As the shooter put it, they would shoot turn and turn about. He would take the first flush, Charlie the second, and so on until one of them had the daily bag limit of four birds. No one mentioned anything more about 2 to 1 odds.

The remnants of an apple orchard straggled thinly along the fence line between the grown-up field and the woods. The few apples they still produced were wormy and shriveled; nobody bothered to pick them. It was a good spot to see game.

A dark, good-size partridge flushed out of an ancient Red Astrachan a few yards ahead of the shooter. He fired twice after it had already disappeared into some thick softwoods to the left of the trace.

"Man dear," he said. "What in Ned was that?"

"Grouse." Charlie grinned at me, and winked.

"Why didn't you warn me ahead of time they made such a commotion? Sudden racket like that could give a man a stroke."

We continued up the trace into the woods. It was mixed hardwoods and softwoods, with most of the softwoods sloping off to the left, toward a deep ravine and a brook. To our right, maples and birches and beeches spread out over the hillside. Here and there among the tall hardwoods were coverts of barberry, shadblow, hazels, and wild roses with bright orange hips. It was ideal terrain for birds, plenty of feed with heavy cover nearby.

Charlie didn't have to wait long for his first shot. Twenty feet in front of us, a partridge was dusting itself in the trace. It flew straight out ahead, the easiest wing shot there is; probably he could have gotten it with the shooter's .22.

"One of this year's brood," Charlie said when I brought it in. "Poor little dummy. Easy shot compared to yours."

"Don't be second-guessing yourself," the shooter said. "You got him, didn't you?"

He took a drink, stumbled into a swaley depression, stepped over the tops of his rubbers, said Ned and man dear, fired three times at a bird rocketing out from under a yellow birch into the softwoods, and missed all three shots. He looked down at his shoes and said with a certain degree of grim satisfaction, "Sopped through."

"I probably wouldn't even have gotten off a shot," Charlie said, grinning at me again.

The shooter was picking stick-me-tights out of his overcoat sleeves. Without looking up he said, "Let's get on with this."

We climbed higher up the ridge. The woods grew denser, the trace fainter.

"Good place to get lost in," the shooter remarked.

"A man can't get lost in this country," Charlie said. "You just walk downhill, find a brook, and follow it out to a road."

"Some of us," said the shooter, "might freeze to death before we hit the road. Are we getting up toward the tree line?"

Charlie grinned at me. It was so warm we'd both taken off our jackets and tied them around our waists.

We came into a scattered stand of beech trees. The beechnuts had started to fall, and their prickly brown husks lay open on the leaves around the bases of the big, smooth gray trunks. Charlie stopped on the edge of the grove. I knew he suspected that a bird was nearby, feeding on the nuts. Maybe he'd heard one walking on the dry leaves.

"He calls this being his own pointer," I whispered to the shooter. "If you're perfectly still, they can't stand to wait very long."

"Neither can I," he said. "Winter's drawing closer by the minute."

A bird went up at the far side of the beech trees, a hundred or more yards away. It flew laterally to the trace, appearing in dun-colored flashes between the beech trunks. Charlie's gun barrel followed its line of flight. He waited longer than you would suppose even a patient man could wait, and finally the partridge veered and came into the opening where the trace ran, and he knocked it cleanly out of the air and into a small copse of fir trees on the edge of the gully.

My brother was ebullient. When I got back with the dead bird, he was saying he'd like to be a sharpshooter too, travel around putting on marksmanship demonstrations and selling ammo. He wondered if the shooter could use an assistant.

The Manchester Arms Company representative looked off in the distance at the red and yellow hills. Somewhere he had lost one rubber. His shoes and socks were wringing wet. His pants were splashed with mud up to the fringe of the overcoat, which was bristling with several varieties of burrs. A livid purple welt zigzagged across his right cheek, where he'd been raked by a blackberry cane.

"Enough's enough, boys," he said, and started back the way we'd come.

Before he'd taken 20 steps, a partridge flushed out from under a lone wild apple tree we'd walked past not five minutes earlier and came zooming straight back up the trace at our heads. The shooter took one wild shot, then dropped to the ground. I jumped aside. Charlie ducked his head, whirled around, waited until the bird was far enough away for his pattern to spread, and dropped it into the leaves as leisurely as plugging a Campbell's soup can on a stump — turning a nearly impossible shot into a routine one.

"They do that this time of year," he explained to the shooter, who was gulping Southern Comfort like Coca Cola. "They get drunk on fermented apples and fly straight at you. Smash into car windshields, picture windows, trees even. What do you think about that assistant?"

Without a word the shooter headed down the path toward his car.

When we were halfway to the field he stopped suddenly. "What's over yonder?"

"Over where?" Charlie said.

"Yonder." The shooter jerked his head toward the ravine.

"Oh, there. A brook runs down through there in the spring. It's mostly dried up this time of year. It's all full of brush."

The shooter veered off the trace toward the gully. He walked purposefully and quickly for a winded and defeated man who had gone through a pint and a half of whiskey since mid-morning, and there was an alarming desperation about the set of his back and the back of his head.

"Watch your step," Charlie yelled. "There's a big drop-off over there."

The shooter stopped short at an old barbwire fence strung up to keep cows from falling into the ravine years ago when the woods were open pasture. I ran up beside him. We peered over a rusty, single strand of wire embedded inches deep in the trunk of a half-dead maple tree. Far below I could hear the trickle of the diminished brook, but I couldn't see it. It was concealed from bank to bank by softwood slash and brush, and brush trailed down the steep side of the ravine over boulders and stumps and dense berry thickets.

The shooter clicked off the safety of his gun. He put one leg over the fence, caught his overcoat on a barb, and tore a long, jagged rent in the lining. He lifted his other leg and momentarily lost his balance. He did a rapid little dance astraddle the fence, waving his gun over his head like a baton. I was afraid he was going to pitch headlong into the ravine or accidentally shoot himself or my brother or me. Then he was standing on the brink of the gully, looking as unhappy as an aging, wet, and exhausted salesman whose luck had played out at last could possibly look.

He got out his bottle of Southern Comfort and stared at it. There was less than a swallow left in the bottom.

"Story of my life," he said, and flipped the bottle high into the air. It fell into a great pile of brush in the bottom of the ravine.

"Don't take it so —" Charlie started to say.

He was cut off by a thunderous roar. The entire gorge seemed to be filled with birds. It was as if someone had tossed a springer spaniel into a covey of eight or ten partridges. In fact, there were only four; but four partridges flushing in four different directions can seem like 40.

I never saw the shooter's gun go up. That's how quick he was. His narrow shoulders swung right and he fired. They swung left and he fired again. He raised the barrel slightly and shot a third time and swung right again and killed the fourth and last bird of his bag limit just as it cleared the opposite bank. The air around us was full of smoke and the scent of gunpowder, and my ears were ringing. The shooter's voice sounded small and far away when he said, "Go out around and fetch them birds up, will you bub? That hollow down there looks colder than Ned's frigidaire."

When we came back into the meadow where we'd left the cars, it was beginning to get dusky. In the hazy twilight, the fall leaves on the hills had faded to a tawny orange. Crickets were singing. It was as warm as an evening in late May.

"All right," Charlie said. "How did you know they were there?"

The shooter leaned his gun against the rear bumper of the Pontiac and began to unbutton his overcoat. "Them birds? I watched which way the ones I missed flown. They all flown off in that quarter."

Charlie reached into his pants pocket and got out his keys.

"What's they?"

"You know what they are. You know damn well."

"Oh, them."

The shooter took the keys and unlocked the Hudson's trunk and peered inside. "Needs a good hoeing out, don't she?"

He handed Charlie his catcher's glove and gear and spikes and two 38-inch Louisville Sluggers. He gave Charlie his two-piece fly rod and fishing basket and toolbox, and his rolled-up sleeping bag. He unlocked the trunk of his Pontiac and transferred the cartons of ammunition and his valise to the Hudson. He took off his overcoat, picked out what burrs

157

he could get, spread it lining-up on the floor of the trunk, and put the gun cases containing the .22 and .30.30 on top of it. He picked up the shotgun and frowned at it.

"Coming back," he said, frowning at the gun, "it crossed my mind to give this to you. Tell you to practice up, you could maybe be a shooter, too."

He put the gun back in its case and put the case on the overcoat and said, "Well, you couldn't."

Charlie and I stared at him.

"That's correct," the shooter said in a voice that was almost cheerful. "Like you said earlier, it's 90 percent speed. And you ain't quite quick enough.

"Not quite quick enough," he repeated, and for the first time that day he seemed happy.

He shut the trunk and went around and got into the Hudson. Leaving the driver's door ajar and one foot on the running board, he got a fountain pen and a pad of ammo orders out of his jacket pocket and wrote something on an order blank and handed it and the pen out to Charlie.

"Legal bill of transfer," he said. "Sign it."

Charlie signed it and gave it and the pen back to the shooter. He did not say a word, but he looked lower than I'd ever seen him look, after losing a ball game in the last inning, or losing a girlfriend, or losing a record trout.

"So," the shooter said, "you ain't getting no nearly new demonstration model pump shotgun to fool yourself with for the next two, three years until you find out the hard way you ain't quite quick enough for gun club work, county fair work, and have to spend the next 30 years selling shells or clerking in some sporting goods store."

"I could learn," Charlie said.

The shooter shook his head. "Quick part can't be learned. Fella has to find what he does best and stay with her. But not this thing. Not for you."

He shut the door and rolled the window part way up and started the engine. Charlie turned away.

"You hold on a minute," the shooter said out the top half of the window.

He wrote something on the order pad, tore off the sheet, and handed it and the Pontiac keys out to my brother.

"Round one goes to the boot," he said. "Heater's shot. Keep up the Valvoline, she'll get you where you need to go."

He rolled the window all the way up and pulled off the hand brake. Then he unrolled the window six inches. "You might land on your feet yet," he said. "I doubt it. But you might."

He cranked the window back up as far as it would go, leaned over to turn on the heater, and drove unhurriedly down the lane and out of sight in the dusk.

The shooter's Pontiac ran all right, on what seemed to me like nearly equal amounts of gas and oil, for the next four years. When Charlie left Vermont for law school, I inherited the car and got another year or so out of it. Neither of us ever managed to fix the heater so it would work.

The shooter never returned to Kingdom County. His replacement, a young salesman in a white shirt and necktie like any other salesman, knew little about guns. He told Uncle Clarence that our man had requested a transfer to a warmer territory, but it was denied, and a few months later he'd landed in a sanitarium over in the Adirondacks. The next time the salesman passed through, he said the company had received a burial bill from there for $235. According to office scuttlebutt, it had been returned unpaid because the company was having financial troubles. The following fall Manchester Arms stopped sending a representative this far north and Uncle Clarence defected to Remington. He was still mad that the company hadn't paid the $235, financial difficulties or no; and besides, he told us, Remington shells were eight cents a box cheaper, and probably just as accurate.

Something Might
Be Gaining

•

BY HOWARD FRANK MOSHER

BARNSTORM FIRST MENTIONED the buzzing one night in early
September on a truck route in upstate New York. He and I were
riding up front in the pickup cab, and Royce and Paul were
sleeping in back with the Indian.

"There they are again," Barn said.

"There what are?" I said. "Headaches again?"

Back in June he'd cracked the Indian into the center-field fence out in
Missoula and been hospitalized for three days with a concussion. Since
then he'd been bothered off and on with headaches.

"Not headaches exactly," he said, fiddling with the radio dial. "More
like buzzing, Eddie. It's a buzzing and humming sound, like wild bees
swarming to hive for the winter. Hear it?"

He twisted the dial, trying to bring in Wheeling, but we were sand-
wiched in between two semis and all he could get was static.

"Sure I hear it," I said. "I hear it every night we get on one of these
tractor trailer speedways. We need a tape deck, Barn. If we had a tape deck
you could listen to Hank Williams all night long."

"That's what we need, Eddie. A tape deck. A tape deck and a charter
airplane and hotel allowances. Any night now I expect you'll be telling me
we need a pension plan."

I laughed. "You left out royalty checks for shaving on television," I

160

said. "Why don't you try to get some sleep now? I'll wake you up if I want you to spell me."

"Or if you pull in Wheeling," Barn said, snapping off the radio. "Wake me up if you get Wheeling."

He settled back with his head resting on his leather jacket rolled up between the top of the seat and the back of the cab. "Good-night, Eddie."

Driving on into the night while Barn slept, I thought back over my summer with the team. They were the last of a breed, all right, and after three months with them, I was beginning to realize why. We traveled all over the country playing town teams for a percentage of the gate receipts, our four against their nine, their umpires, and their grandstands. Here today, gone tomorrow, we slept in the truck or under it, and lived on coffee and beer and the cheapest truck-stop food we could find. If we sprained an elbow or pulled a tendon, we played anyway. It was a hard way to make a living no matter how you looked at it, and over the course of the summer all the romance had been scuffed off it like the gloss on a brand-new baseball after nine innings of hard use.

Royce handled the infield. He was about my age, 21, and fast and rangy in the field and a powerful hitter. When Royce had his batting eye, you couldn't throw a ball hard enough to get it by him. He liked Budweiser beer in red, white, and blue cans, girls, and baseball, in that order, and if he'd ever learned to hit a curve, he could have played professional ball, maybe Triple-A level. But he hadn't, and it didn't seem to bother him. Royce wasn't what you would call ambitious and actually seemed to like barnstorming.

Paul was the fastest and smartest pitcher I'd ever caught. He could have gone all the way to the top, probably stepped right into the starting rotation at New York or L.A. or wherever, if he hadn't been quite so crazy. Even if he'd been only slightly less crazy, I think the Red Sox or some other team that desperately needed pitching would have taken a chance on him. But every fourth or fifth game he would start to shake off my signs, claiming that he was receiving his instructions from certain mysterious voices that only he ever heard. These voices usually directed him to pitch left-handed or under his leg or behind his back in order to humiliate our opponents. The trouble was, we were usually the team to be humiliated when this happened, though Paul didn't seem to care about that. Obeying the voices was more important to him than winning. When he wasn't pitching, he divided most of his time between trying to save Royce's soul and writing up his wins in a journal he called "Letters to the Ephesians." He'd been with Barnstorm for nine or ten years and Barn was used to him, but I didn't think I'd get used to him if I caught him for twice that long.

Barnstorm was the star of our team. He played the outfield, all three fields, on an Indian motorcycle 20 years old, a bright red, unmuffled machine that had sustained a dozen bad wrecks and could still pick up from 0 to 60 between home plate and mid-center. The Indian could wheel on a dime five feet short of a fence and run two entire games on a tank of gas. Most of its parts, including the engine, had been replaced several times. When we were out in the field, Barn rode the Indian in great, sweeping ellipses, ready to go anywhere as soon as the ball was hit, and he easily covered as much ground as any two outfielders could cover on foot. He was up in his fifties, a big, rawboned man from Kingdom County, up in the northern mountains of Vermont. He'd been in the barnstorming business for 40 years and had a broken bone for every one of them.

I'd joined the team the previous June. Barn's team was playing an exhibition game against my college team, when their catcher got into a fistfight with Paul and quit in the middle of the fifth inning. I filled in for him, and after the game Barn asked me to stay on for the summer. I was a senior, ready to graduate. I'd just taken my last exam. It was a chance to see the country and play some more baseball. I signed up.

"I heard it again during the game this evening," Barn said.

"What did it sound like? Bees still?"

"It could pass for bees. Or electrical interference over the radio when you draw near a truck or go under a power line. It commenced about halfway through. About the time Paul beaned that short fella."

"That doesn't surprise me," I said. Going into the bottom of the fifth, we'd been leading Boonville by three runs. Their leadoff man that inning crowded the plate, so Paul winged the bill of his helmet with a fastball and spun it clear around on the man's head where a catcher wears his cap, with the bill projecting out behind. The grandstand was humming as I went out to the mound.

"The voices told me to brush him back," Paul said when I was still 15 feet away.

"Brushing a man back is one thing. You were trying to knock him down."

"If I'd been trying to knock him down, he wouldn't be standing over there on first base," Paul said in the direction of the runner.

The short man scowled at us from first base. He seemed to be scowling at me more than Paul.

"Don't do that again," I said, hoping the man on first would hear me. In a lower voice I said, "Do you want another Macon on our hands? Up

162

here in the north country, they don't furnish people they don't like with a sheriff's escort to the county line. They just take them out in the woods and shoot them."

"Don't try to scare me," Paul said. "I know better. And I know better than to disobey the voices. Get back there behind the plate now. I'm going to humble these rubes the way they've never been humbled before. That's what the voices want me to do."

He cleared his throat and spit in the direction of the grandstand, which by then was up and roaring. I glanced over at Royce, who was sneaking a drink from his hip flask. The umpire was shouting at us to play ball.

I returned to the plate and signaled for Paul's fork ball, a spinning, sharply curving pitch almost impossible to hit solidly. He didn't throw it. He didn't actually throw any pitch. He lobbed the ball, and it came floating up to the plate like a generous scoop of vanilla ice cream bobbing to the top of a drugstore soda. The batter was so jittery from seeing the leadoff man's helmet spun around on his head that he jerked out at the ball and missed it by a clean six inches.

Paul tossed the next one underhanded. This time the batter was ready. He didn't try to kill it. He swung crisply and sent it on a line toward left-center. Barnstorm was off and racing at the crack of the bat. As he neared the fence, he stood up, and somehow he managed to pull the ball back into the playing field and the Indian away from the board wall at the last instant. Two home runs and a long double later, he made a backhanded circus catch in the left-field corner. That got us out of the inning, but the score was tied, and I knew that the game was gone, and the 75 percent winner's share of the gate receipts along with it.

"Why don't you fire that man?" I asked Barn that night as we drove north through the dark, bulking Adirondacks. "He's the craziest pitcher I've ever seen or heard of, and that's saying something. Someday he's going to kill somebody or get one of us killed. He ought to be pitching for that state hospital team we played in Louisiana."

"Paul's a fine baseball player, Eddie. Maybe a man has to be a tad bit touched in the head to be that fine a ball player."

"Maybe. I'm glad you can be so tolerant. Or maybe charitable is more like it when he costs us a couple of hundred dollars a tantrum. Have you gotten out of the red yet from those hospital bills in Missoula?"

Barn turned on the radio. Through the crackling I could just make out Hank Williams, Jr., singing something or other from his new album, *Songs My Daddy Taught Me*.

163

"There's the boy," Barnstorm said. "I guess old Hank would be pretty proud of him if he were still alive, Eddie."

"I guess so," I said. From what little I knew of old Hank, I thought he would have been just as apt to be jealous of the competition in his own family. I didn't say so to Barn, who had once showed me a blurred snapshot of himself shaking hands with a very young Hank Williams in front of a grandstand in Texas. Hank was still his hero.

"Missoula weren't Paul's fault, Eddie," Barn said when the song ended. "He was throwing in good earnest that night. I just misjudged where the fence was."

"Go ahead and stand up for him. You've been around him so much you've probably started hearing voices yourself. No doubt that's what that buzzing in your ears is. The voices, telling you to give Paul a raise."

"No, it ain't no voices. It ain't nothing like that. Just a sort of humming noise that begins low and louds up as the game goes along. Just a pesky noise, is all."

I thought for a minute. "It's nerves, Barn. It's got to be nerves. I don't see how you do it at all anymore, after all those crack-ups."

"It ain't nerves," Barn said patiently. "I ain't fence-shy. Not now, not ever. I've tangled with fences enough over the years so if they was going to get to me they'd have gotten to me before this. It ain't fences."

"Driving that renegade Indian every night, night after night, would make a deaf man's ears ring," I said.

"Slow down, Eddie. See them bright eyes beside the road? Deer season's coming boy."

"Maybe a doctor," I said.

After losing to Boonville, we'd won three straight games. Barn had played well in all of them, but the better he played, the worse he looked. His appetite had fallen off, and he hadn't slept more than two or three hours a night for a week.

"I've seen doctors enough to last a lifetime, Eddie. I'll tell you something. A man starts in doctoring for every little ache and pain, and the next thing you know he's in the hospital. People die in hospitals."

For a while neither of us spoke. We were headed for Barn's hometown over in Vermont, where the team traditionally played its last game of the summer before starting its swing south. As we crossed the toll bridge up in the narrows of Lake Champlain near Canada, Barn told me a story.

"Eddie, more and more lately I've been remembering back. You do that when you start to get on in years. You can't recall what you had for breakfast, but all of a sudden you're recollecting things you thought you'd

164

forgotten years ago. When I was a boy growing up, I lived in a log house with my Grammy Moon away off at the head of Lord Hollow. Ma had passed away, and the big boys had gone off to war, and Pa he'd just gone off.

"Well, one afternoon in the fall of the year, I was out in the dooryard splitting wood. Grammy was denned up having a poor spell in the outhouse. I'd split a chunk and wait for the echo to come cracking back up the hollow. Then I'd split another chunk and wait, and so on.

"I don't know how long I'd been at it. Maybe an hour, maybe more, when all at once I heard a faint little sound from far off down the hollow toward the county road. I stopped chopping and listened, and it got louder. It sounded like high water in the brook after a big rain, but it hadn't rained for weeks and the brook was fall-low. I knew it weren't high water. It turned off over the plank bridge up to our place, and the planks clattered like gunfire. I hollered for Grammy and she came fast from the outhouse, hitching at her overall straps.

"By that time it was on us. There was one man driving and a second man sitting in a little hooked-on car beside him. Both men wore goggles and leather caps with flaps pulled down over their ears. And they was whooping and hollering like the old horned devil himself was after them. They drove by me and by Grammy, and they drove in through the open outhouse door, and clean through the boards on the other side and on around the house. Only then it was just one man driving and the other man setting in the car amongst the boards where the outhouse used to be, reading the mail-order catalog.

" 'Don't be scared, boy,' Grammy shouted at me. 'It's only Armand and Wilfred, home from the Great Global War. They've whipped Kaiser Bill and stolen his own machine.'

"Well, Eddie, I weren't scared anymore, but I hadn't any idea in the world what it was my brothers were riding except that I wanted one more than I ever wanted anything before — to shoot a buck deer or play in a World Series or anything."

Barn paused, reflecting in that absorbed way of older persons thinking about the past, so far away and yet so fresh. Then he shook his head slightly and said, "Well, it run along a few years. Grammy passed away. I stayed on at the house with Armand and Wilfred. They was wild boys, Eddie, wild as yellow bumblebees, and stove in their machine and several others and let the place go downhill fast and gave me pretty much of a free rein to stay out of school and do whatever I pleased. For a year or so I hunted and fished day and night, the way any boy would. But I was always more ambitious than my brothers, and after a while I began to hire out to neighbors. I put away what money I could earn haying and working in the woods and sugaring. Later on I made a little money playing town ball. That was when every town with a general store and a church had its own team, and a farm boy with a strong arm could make a few dollars pitching on a Sunday afternoon.

"When I was 16, I bought my first machine. I rode it, too. Up log traces. Through brooks. Out cross-lots. Pretty soon I commenced to jump it. One Independence Day I made fifty dollars jumping the high falls behind the commission sales barn in Kingdom Common. And wherever I rode it, I made believe there was a great grandstand packed full of people watching me the way I had watched Brother Armand and Brother Wilfred arriving home from the war. The summer I turned 18, I left Kingdom County with the fair and went to riding up the inside of a big barrel with a show. I was one of the first ones to ride up a barrel. A year or so later, after barrel-riding became popular, I went into barnstorming."

Barn laughed softly. "Eddie, I've rode before thousands of grand-stands and millions of people. I've had my picture in the papers, been written up all over the country. Now I want to ask you something. You're a young man. What is it you want most?"

I thought for a minute. Then I said, "I don't know."

"Good," Barn said as he switched on the radio. "Because if you did, you just might get it."

Up in Kingdom County it was a good night for baseball, cool and dry and breezy. Barnstorm spent the day hunting and got back just in time to put on a pregame show for the grandstand. I stood at the plate and poled out 25 or so long, high fly balls, which he speared bare-handed and over his shoulder and behind his back while riding the Indian. Twice a ball got caught in a sudden stiff gust of wind and sailed over the fence. Each time the grandstand gave me a mock ovation.

"You'll have to keep your pitches low tonight," I told Paul when I warmed him up. "That's a home-run wind."

"I always keep my pitches low," he said. "Unless, of course, the voices instruct me otherwise."

"I was hoping we'd left the voices back in Boonville."

Paul frowned up at the filling grandstand. "You never know," he said.

By dusk the grandstand was packed. Town ball was still very popular in Kingdom County, and I had been looking forward to playing in front of a big friendly crowd before heading south. It looked like a good place to pay ball. The diamond was very well kept up. It was laid out inside the dirt

166

racetrack in front of the fairgrounds grandstand. The infield was some-what higher than most but smooth and level. A new, unpainted snow fence was strung around the perimeter of the outfield. There were several sets of lights mounted on the grandstand roof and several sets on the long, low, concrete animal barns across the backstretch of the racetrack, be-yond the snow fence.

The game began, and I knew after the first inning that it was going to be a contest. Paul was in top form. His fork ball was lively, and his control was perfect. A few batters managed to topple weak grounders that Royce scooped up and tossed over to Paul, moving from the mound to first like a big, graceful cat. Nothing at all went out to Barn, circling slowly under the lights. From time to time, he was blurred by the dust blowing across the field from the racetrack behind third base, but I could always tell where he was by the sound of the Indian.

We couldn't seem to do any better at the plate ourselves. Kingdom County had one of the best pitchers we'd faced all season, a ringer from the Canadian league, Barn said. He threw so hard the ball kept dribbling out of their catcher's glove into the dirt in the batter's box.

By the fifth inning neither team was on the scoreboard. The grand-stand grew quieter and quieter. By the seventh they were so absorbed in the game that only a scattering of people stood up to stretch, a ritual small-town crowds pride themselves on observing. It was so still when we were up and Barn's Indian wasn't running that we could hear the long-distance trucks going by on the highway behind the grandstand, and every now and then a racehorse whinnying from the barns beyond the outfield fence.

There was still no score after nine innings. The Canadian was throw-ing as hard as ever, and Paul was holding his own, though he was going to the resin bag every three or four pitches to rest his arm. By the twelfth my legs ached every time I came out of my crouch. My arm was tired from throwing the ball back to the mound. I thought about Barnstorm, out under the glaring outfield lights riding that gut-wringing machine back and forth through the fumes and dust for hour after hour, with a steel plate in his back and steel pins holding his legs together and a pounding head-ache and that terrible buzzing in his ears.

With two outs in the bottom of the thirteenth, one of their batters caught a fork ball that didn't break in time and hit a low line drive into shallow center. Barn made the catch off his shoelaces, and the grandstand came alive. They applauded him all the way in and continued applauding after he shut off his machine. He flipped the ball to me in front of our

167

bench, but he didn't dismount immediately. He leaned against the handle-bars, breathing hard, and for the first time since I'd met him, Barnstorm looked old to me. For the first time I saw him as what he was — an old man in a cracked leather jacket, playing a young man's game in the hardest possible way.

"Up there," Barn said.

"Where?"

"There." He pointed toward the grandstand. Then he put his hand to his head. The crowd assumed he was tipping his hat and began to clap and stamp their feet all over again.

"Good Christ," Barn said. He got off the Indian and started for the bench. He stumbled, regained his footing, and sat down with his hand on his head.

I grabbed Royce's arm as he started toward the plate. "Get on base," I told him. "I don't care how, but do it. On the first pitch to Paul, steal second."

Royce took a quick look at Barn and nodded. Half a minute later he stepped into an inside pitch while appearing to fall away from it and got his base. Paul was up.

"Barn's sick," I said to him. "We've got to get out of this fast. Swing wild on the first pitch."

For once Paul followed instructions. The ball bounced out of their catcher's glove, and by the time he had it in his hand, Royce was standing on second. Paul struck out on the next two pitches, and I was up.

All night I'd been watching the Canadian to see whether I could detect a sequence in his pitches. His first pitch was unpredictable, but during the inning before, on two occasions when the first one was a ball, I'd noticed that the second one had been fast and straight. I stepped into the batter's box, hugging the plate. Royce took a big lead. The pitcher looked at him, then looked back at the catcher and threw. It was a ball, off the outside corner.

The next pitch was letter-high and smoking, just as I'd hoped. For the first time that night I connected hard, driving the ball over second. Royce was home and I was on first before the ball was back in the infield. One run was all we got, but I was fairly sure that would be enough.

"Oil up your shotgun," I said to Barn as he got on the Indian. "We're going hunting tomorrow."

As I strapped on my gear the grandstand began to buzz again. By the time Paul finished his warm-up pitches they were roaring. An inning ago they had been cheering for Barnstorm. Now they wanted their home team

168

to score. When Paul struck out their leadoff man on three consecutive fork balls they quieted down, but nobody started to leave.

The next hitter menaced with his bat. I signaled for a fastball. "You'd better start swinging right now if you expect to hit this one, Casey," I said.

Paul's arm swung back and up and came whipping down past his head like a big striking snake; and before I realized what he was going to do, the batter stepped into the pitch just as Royce had done and was on his way to first, hopping and limping and rubbing his upper leg and grinning. The grandstand was up and roaring like a World Series crowd. Paul motioned me out to the mound.

"That man shouldn't have done that," he said severely.

"No, but he did. We did the same thing a half inning back if you remember. Don't let it unsettle you. Just strike out these next two, and you can spend all day tomorrow writing the Ephesians about it."

Paul scowled up at the grandstand. "Don't mock the Ephesians," he said, looking at the grandstand.

"I'm deadly serious about them. Strike out these next two, and I'll write to them myself."

"Play ball!" the crowd shouted.

Royce trotted over to the edge of the racetrack behind third base and called something to a blonde-headed girl leaning out of the grandstand. He ran across the track and got out his flask and offered her a drink. In the outfield Barn circled slowly. The grandstand was thundering. I began to have the helpless sense that I'd had in Macon, that something I was part of was getting out of control.

"They crave instructions," Paul said, staring at the grandstand.

"Instruct them in the art of striking out," I shouted.

The man's face was rigid. He cocked his head intently, as though listening to something far away. He nodded gravely and said, "The voices have counseled me to load the bases before chastising them."

The umpire was on the mound telling us to play ball, and I knew there would be no more reasoning with Paul that night. I could only hope he would strike out two more men after loading the bases.

He threw four straight pitchouts to the next batter, and the grandstand went wild, supposing that they had finally gotten to him. The Canadian pitcher was up next. He stepped into the batter's box and watched two slow pitches go by a foot outside the plate. After the second one he looked at me. He grinned and said something in French. As the next pitch drifted down, he took two short steps and swung smooth and hard.

169

"He's out!" I screamed. "He stepped across the plate."

"Fair ball," the umpire said.

It didn't seem to travel fast. It rose out of the infield almost leisurely. It continued to rise on a line, the sort of home-run ball an experienced outfielder just shrugs at as it goes over. So when Barn whirled his machine around and started back, I thought the lighting had confused him. As the ball climbed, though, he kept going.

Barnstorm never looked back. He gunned the Indian through the snow fence, splitting it apart like a row of ice cream sticks. He picked up speed as he crossed the racetrack through the swirling dust 50 feet under the ball, which sailed out of the lights just before the orange flash of the Indian exploded against the barn wall below. From the grandstand came a low wailing sigh of ultimate despair and ultimate satisfaction. Then there was only the sound of the wind, blowing a steady, rolling wall of dust along the track.

Half the county must have turned out for the funeral. The minister said what you'd expect — how a hometown boy had gone on to bring pleasure to so many people across the country, and so forth. I stood back on the edge of the crowd and looked off across the hills. The sky was blue, with a few fair-weather clouds high overhead, and the bright fall colors were just starting to come over the trees. A good day to hunt in the woods, I thought.

What made me uneasy as the minister spoke on was the crowd itself. Decent, hardworking people they would call themselves, and taken one by one, I knew they were. Yet standing together on the fall grass of the hillside cemetery above the village, they somehow kept reminding me of one more grandstand, waiting for Barn to perform.

"Dust to dust," the minister said quietly, shutting his book.

But I had already turned away and started for the truck, thinking that Barn had eaten all of that for all the grandstands he would ever have to.

Catering

·

BY ELINOR LIPMAN

LIONEL BECAME INTERESTED in cooking the summer he took the
Massachusetts Bar. Quiche was just catching on that year; people
were eating their spinach and mushrooms raw, buying their coffee beans whole, saying "tofu." I gave him a gift subscription to *Bon
Appetit* when he was hired by Hill, Metcalfe in Boston. Soon he was
roaming the North End on his lunch hour in search of cracked veal bones.
After two years with the firm, he left law and me.

This is his job now: he shops and cooks dinner one night each week,
Sunday through Thursday, for five different women. His meals are delicious, healthful, feminine: poached fish fillets and boned chicken, vegetables in vinaigrette sauce, soufflés, lots of fruit and cheese and chocolate;
delicate, thoughtful meals that women love with their dry white wines. He
wanted only five clients, women with good taste. He says he found them.

There were no advertisements, no mass mailings. He simply left his
chocolate-brown announcements in a Newbury Street women's shop
which sells man-tailored suits and expensive pocketbooks. The cream-
colored calligraphy was the perfect touch:

CATERING TO YOU
Light Suppers and Conversation
for the Gourmet Professional
Lionel Berens, Esq.
References

They were so much like our wedding invitations, in color and size and succinctness, that I cried when I opened the familiar brown envelope, and ignored several days' messages from Lionel on my answering machine.

He tells me more than I can bear to hear about his clients — their preferences in food, their allergies, what they look like and, whether they have large breasts. They are all attracted to Lionel, who is tall and thin and looks very much like an off-duty attorney in his corduroy trousers and plaid wool shirts. His curly brown hair with its gray streaks, his rimless glasses and the way he hums "I've Grown Accustomed to Her Face" when he chops things on a cutting board only add to his appeal.

He arrives at their condominiums cheerful and confident at 5:45. The doormen and neighbors recognize him by his wicker basket and the wonderful smells. Some days he carries a thermos of hollandaise.

Cynthia, Sunday night, is British, and the only one who still likes red meat. She is very tall, fortyish, owns her own travel agency. Lionel tells me she is blue-eyed and freckled and rarely buttons the top two, sometimes three, buttons of her silk shirts. She calls him "Pet."

Monday is Marguerite, who never tires of omelettes. I know she is blond, and I picture her barefoot in Capri pants and boat-necked jerseys. Monday is so easy for Lionel, with Marguerite supplying the jumbo eggs and he responsible for the filling alone. She wants to videotape him making an omelette, and I know what she means. Even before his cooking began in earnest, when we were together, eating steaks and chops and relying heavily on the broiler, Lionel made omelettes beautifully.

Kathy, Tuesday, asked chummy, almost conspiratorial questions when she called me to check Lionel's references. "Would you say he is good company? Is he discreet? Does he buy prime meat?" Her questions caused me pain. I told Lionel that Kathy did not sound bright or independent, did not demonstrate a sense of self, did not seem creative or spontaneous, probably did not have a life of her own to draw upon to enrich the partnership, or, frankly, possess any of those qualities he values so dearly in women.

"She has a doctorate," Lionel said.

He accepted Kathy as a client, and we don't discuss her much. I do know that she doesn't own measuring cups or spoons, and that Lionel has to bring his own pepper mill each Tuesday. She is the kind of person who has only ketchup and margarine in her refrigerator and cans of Veg-all on her shelves, yet Lionel describes her as ebullient. She is a teacher, a high-school English teacher with a doctorate.

172

Wednesday is Robin, a graduate of the Business School. She is short and dark and talkative, but not in the way Lionel likes. Rather than going on and on about his cooking and demanding to know which herb it is that sneaks up on you in the grated zucchini, Robin asks Lionel about his marriage and divorce. She blames her curiosity on her MBA and Harvard's case-study method.

My favorite is Dee-Dee, Thursday, a free-lance actuary. Lionel says she is overweight and unattractive. Signing up with Dee-Dee says a lot about Lionel's changing values. We rarely socialized with overweight people, and he never accepted theories about sluggish metabolisms, or childhood fat cells determining adult weight. He always admired concave bellies and the kind of taut upper thighs that seem to be carved from fine-grain wood. To him, such things are effortless.

Dee-Dee talks to Lionel about her problems, and he cheers her up. "I told her my ex-wife has a weight problem, too," he reported pleasantly. "I told her you stir-fry in water now and are down to a size 8."

"Do you discuss my weight with the others?" I ask.

"It doesn't come up," he says.

I know this means that Lionel has not exhausted his list of prepackaged topics: The Summer I Drove a Taxi and Paid Teamster Dues; How Natalie Wood Surprised the *Lampoon* Staff by Showing Up to Accept Her "Worst Actress" Award; Why I left Law; My Amicable Divorce.

I do not have a weight problem in that version of our life together. I am nearly perfect, a saint. Our divorce was a paragon of civility, no, amiability. We are friends. Better than friends — best friends. We speak to each other frequently. Constantly. We like each other. We love each other in a special way. We never fight. We never fought! Our friends did not take sides. We renewed our symphony seats, our adjacent symphony seats! No children to complicate things. No alimony!

What a wonderful person Lionel appears to be, talking this way about me. He smiles and leans over the table to confide in his audience. He seduces women by radiating such warmth for his ex-wife. He has it all, they think: a fair, generous man. A lean, handsome, educated, single man who speaks of marriage with gusto. A man who remembers to tuck a vanilla bean into his wicker basket to grind with the decaffeinated French roast. No wonder he has a waiting list.

Lionel called me at work and suggested we meet for lunch. He wants me back.

I thought it a little graceless of him to choose the same occasion to describe his latest venture — marketing frozen entrées. He seems to be

173

carried away by the adoration of his harem, and particularly by Robin's B-School thesis on cottage industry. I am tough with him. I predict he will lose his enthusiasm as soon as he gets beyond the glamor of making envelopes of chicken breasts for his Kiev, and has to worry about ordering grosses of aluminum entrée plates.

Wanting me back is not out of character for Lionel. His impetuousness is legend in both our families. My mother thinks it may be chemical. No normal person, she says, leaves a job in a distinguished firm to cook for strangers when he can practically taste an offer of partnership, or throws away a loving wife because of what some magazine multiple-choice test says about The New Fulfillment.

I half-expected a reconciliation, the same way I knew Lionel might try out divorce, but his business proposal complicates things. I have to be suspicious: Does he need more cubic feet for freezer lockers and industrial ovens? Does he know something I don't about my building's zoning? Does he want my job skills?

I try not to read too much into his display of affection for me. When I run into him downtown, and I am with a date, he kisses my cheek, pumps my companion's hand, asks about my father's diabetes, says he will call, kisses me again. My dates are astonished to hear that this prince is my former husband. They spend the rest of the evening counseling me about reconciliation then never call back. Lionel says he cannot contain his genuine affection for me, that he has become more spontaneous since leaving law and will not be bound by antediluvian rules of etiquette that forbid kissing and fraternizing between former spouses. He is too caught up in the spirit of no-fault.

Over lunch he tells me that "Catering to You" has not been all fun. He is finding the comparison shopping and menu-planning less challenging, and is beginning to cook in large, reheatable quantities. He misses the national news five nights a week. He is on mailing lists for things he never knew existed: equipment that stamps Pennsylvania Dutch designs on pats of butter; fish-of-the-month clubs; edible muffin forms.

Lionel always thinks I want to hear everything — how, because her former husband had a germ phobia, Cynthia rebels by not washing fruit; Marguerite has taken herself off dairy products for no apparent reason; Kathy mashes all fish because she is afraid of bones; Robin has no counter space; Dee-Dee is not losing weight.

He reaches for my hand and doesn't let go when the waiter takes our order for one marble cheesecake and one black coffee. I know that in another setting, and without me due at work, Lionel would go over the less pragmatic reasons for getting back together.

Lionel insists it is his treat. He walks me back to my office and kisses me in front of my administrative assistant. "I've been thinking it might be fun to have a baby," he calls from the elevator, as its doors glide shut and I wave good-bye.

Lionel gave his clients two weeks' notice and promised to keep in touch through a monthly newsletter. He is going to try restaurant law.

They call sometimes to say hello and ask for recipes. They are dying to hear in my voice a clue about our relationship, which they put to the test by tempting Lionel. Would he do a cocktail party for 12? A single moussaka for a potluck brunch?

They call so often, but rarely leave a name. I know them by their questions and the longing I hear in their voices.

The Fling

·

BY ELINOR LIPMAN

WHEN I MEET CLAIRE in the market and ask her a question about herself, she thanks me for being such a good friend and is likely to send a small gift. A cup of coffee in my kitchen produces a thank-you note from her in the next day's mail. She apologizes for coming empty-handed when she stops by to retrieve a book I borrowed and didn't return. She tries so hard to please and to be liked that she appears frantic most of the time. I have left her apartment with a public television program guide or an unopened roll of paper towels as a parting gift because I refused to take the leftovers from dinner or the flowers she arranged for the table.

Claire's apartment is very nice, and, of course, immaculate, but she apologizes for its size and for the landlord's taste in carpet and wallpaper. When you admire the antique Persian rugs that cover the green wall-to-wall, she apologizes for their worn spots and faded colors.

Claire works, and has always worked, for nonprofit agencies that pay her low to moderate wages. Her nervous energy translates well into job performance, where her impeccable manners and graciousness come across as confident charm. She has worked for charities, hospitals, museums, foundations, and universities in the 14 years since we graduated from the same women's college, changing positions for a genteel salary increase or the illusion of nicer colleagues. My theory about her job history is that she has an unconscious wish to be a volunteer for the same

176

organizations that employ her. She was brought up to be the mistress of a home, the wife of a successful man who commutes by train into the city and whose tax bracket prohibits his wife from doing anything for a salary.

Claire grew up in a Massachusetts mill town — a wealthy Protestant in a city of ethnic working-class Catholics. Her mother called Claire's father "Doctor" when speaking about him to patients or friends: "Doctor likes his dinner at six," she would say. Or "Doctor has hospital rounds this morning."

Claire was their fourth daughter and next-to-last try before producing a son, who is now his father's partner. Claire apologizes for the size of her family. She feels, apparently, that her failure to be born male caused her parents to have an undignified, practically Catholic number of children. And she was named for her mother, as if all the favored girls' names were exhausted after three, and one already circulating in the large white house would do as a thrifty choice.

Claire insists that Deidre, the oldest, is the family beauty, and that Martha, Gwendolyn, and Charles Junior were exceptional scholars and athletes. Her parents never bestowed any titles on Young Claire, as they call her — not easiest baby, or kindest or healthiest or most artistic child — just last daughter, the unmarried one, who lives away from home.

I run into Claire every few weeks. We do our Saturday errands in the same village center, and she always insists on treating me to coffee. She has generally met a new man between these meetings of ours. She meets a lot of men. They are attracted to her from the other sides of airport terminals and at the national conferences she attends for her nonprofit agency employers. She is a little taller than average, about five-foot-six, with dark hair perfectly cut into thick bangs above gray-blue eyes and sleek straight sides that curve under slightly at her collar. She always looks wonderful, perfectly groomed and neat, and dresses in sundresses of expensive dark cotton in the summer and outfits of pastel wool crepe in the winter.

Except for Phil, none of the men Claire has gotten involved with since we've been having coffee has lasted more than a few months. In every case the man backed away first. Only one said why — that she made him nervous. The others just stopped calling. Claire would let a week pass, then write the man a note enclosing a newspaper clipping. They were always cut from *The New York Times* and were always a feature about a topic the man had mentioned in conversation: passive solar heat, making wine at home, Shaker reproductions, restocking the Connecticut River with salmon. She clips articles for all her friends and leaves them in our mailboxes. I am inexplicably irritated by these clippings, the way unnecessary thank-you notes and house gifts irritate me, and I can only assume that she irritates the men she clips for. When someone doesn't respond to her notes, she asks me if she should call him to save this most recent lover the embarrassment of calling after not calling for so long. Sometimes she asks my permission to stage a confrontation, and I dissuade her, knowing how apologetic she will be. If she is determined to see the unresponsive suitor one last time, I suggest she surprise him.

"I can't just drop over," Claire says. "But I was thinking of calling and saying I was going to be in his neighborhood and thought I'd pick up my pie plate if it was convenient."

"Does that sound like a confrontation?" I demand. "Do you sound like a person who's been hurt?"

"No," she says meekly. "You're right. You're so good at knowing what to do. You're a wonderful friend."

"And don't bring a gift," I warn.

Claire looks troubled. "I was going to bring him some flowers and a clipping on the restoration of a Victorian beach house on Block Island."

"No flowers," I say. And more emphatically, "No clipping! Go home and rip it up."

Claire sighs. She doesn't agree. I may as well be advising her to eat dinner at a friend's house and not rise after dessert to clear the table.

"What will it say to him, your clipping? That you've been thinking about him? That despite his rotten behavior — ignoring you and not calling for weeks then being abrupt and sarcastic when you call him — he still deserves your thoughtfulness? What kind of a message is that?"

"You're right," she says, crying a little from the cumulative pain of so many six-week romances that she didn't want to end and the inefficacy of so much niceness.

"Thank you for listening," she says. "Thank you for being such a good friend." The next day a note on pretty paper falls through my mail slot, thanking me for listening and for being such a friend.

It is a little hard on Claire that I am married and that my husband is a sweet man. If she telephones weekends or evenings, she begins and ends the conversation by saying how sorry she is to be taking me away from Neil. She is nervous in his presence and is her most frantically nice self. Her compliments pour out in run-on sentences that can't be interrupted or answered: "Nora tells me that you're both taking a week off to do *nothing,* just work around the house, which is just so perfect for you two because you're both so creative and energetic that you'll accomplish so much and enjoy each other's company and probably just cook those wonderful meals you collaborate on. I cut out a recipe Sunday from the magazine section for grilling fish steaks on the hibachi with dill. I'll send it to you."

Neil never knows how to respond to Claire's high-speed one-way conversation. He usually smiles, excuses himself, tells me later that she drives him crazy and asks what I see in her.

It was he who pointed out that Claire has only two speeds — nice and more nice. I suspect this is absolutely true in her relationships. When things go wrong, and the men begin to pull away, Claire tries even harder — more notes, more clippings, more pies. If someone says he can't go out Friday night because he's working until six and has to go sailing early Saturday, Claire offers to cook his dinner. If he says he's too tired and is picking up some take-out, she offers to buy the food and deliver it.

"I shouldn't have done that, should I?" she asks when she describes such invitations and sees me wince.

Claire is now having what she calls an affair. I have learned that affairs are what Claire has with unsuitable men — Catholic, Jewish, or non-Caucasian men; those who are younger than she, and those who are not attorneys, doctors, academics, MBAs, or executive officers of non-profit agencies.

I am keen on Claire's current affair, which is with Phil Casciotti, our produce man. He is bright and kind and makes the fruit and vegetable section the most interesting part of the market. When Claire first told me she was having dinner with him, she used the phrase "just for fun" about six times in her run-on explanation.

Phil told Claire that he does not generally socialize with customers, but was too drawn to her and too impressed by her unfailing courtesy not to pursue the matter. She always asked him thoughtful, earnest questions: where things were grown, which potatoes held up best in chowder, can you tell if a melon is ripe without squeezing it? She was one of the few customers who didn't sample the Bing cherries and seedless grapes, and she complimented him when something she bought tasted especially good. It began when Phil weighed Claire's fruits and vegetables and marked the bag with some price well below its actual cost. After several weeks of such conspicuous favoritism, Claire told Phil she felt guilty about the markdowns. "Would it assuage your guilt to discuss it over a drink some evening?" he had asked. Admiring his charm and vocabulary, she said yes.

Claire is apologetic about Phil and tells me that she hadn't had sex in 11 months when they met and, at 35, is supposed to be at the height of her

179

sexual energy. She is strongly attracted to him and repeats to me in a voice filled with discovery that Phil's family came from the north of Italy, where people look more Bavarian then Mediterranean, accounting for his straight fair hair and almond-shaped green eyes. She also says frequently what a good person he is, a genuinely good person, with a little bafflement in her voice as if to say that men of her acquaintance don't generally come that way, and isn't it ironic that Phil, a fling, is so much nicer than the future-husband types she has met.

She is further puzzled by Phil's love of children, the way he plucks babies out of shopping carts and holds them over his head and makes them laugh and memorizes the regulars' names. None of the men she knows through work or meets through her family carries on the way Phil does when a baby passes by in a backpack or a stroller.

Phil must have sensed, after seeing Claire's heirloom Persian rugs, her collection of sugar tongs, and her pale blue monogrammed sheets, that his credentials mattered. He feeds her details about himself that she feeds to me. He has a degree in fine arts and wants to learn the fruit and vegetable business from the ground up. He hopes to own his own market within five years and to run a wholesale business that will supply fruits and vegetables to fine restaurants. His store will have fresh herbs year-round and possibly a cheese section.

Claire doesn't want her family to know about her affair. Her sisters are all married to what seems like the same person — a big, athletic stockbroker with tortoise-shell glasses and a squash racket in his briefcase. She says her parents would not be pleased even with Phil's dream and would be repelled by his current position.

I prompt Claire to see her relationship with him as something other than an affair. She calls him "my friend Phil." When I ask how things are going, she uses phrases like, "We have a lot of fun together," and "It's nice to just enjoy the moment." He is younger than she, Claire reminds me, just 30, a Catholic, and he doesn't own a suit.

Phil would like them to live together. Claire says it isn't practical because he has to be at the wholesaler's at 4 A.M., six days a week, and she wouldn't be able to let him leave the house without making his breakfast. She says they have worked out a nice schedule of early dinners, early-evening lovemaking, and Saturday night sleep-overs. Meanwhile, when a divorced stockbroker gets her telephone number from a brother-in-law, or a single doctor who has attended a medical convention with her father calls for a date, she feels obliged to accept. She has to look down the road, she says, and she mustn't be rude to a friend of the family.

It is obvious that Phil is crazy about Claire, even though it has only been a matter of months since their first drink. He grins uncontrollably when we shop together on Saturday morning and reduces the price of my fruit, too, simply by association. The other produce people, who report to Phil, know about the romance and run to cold storage for the freshest still-unpacked produce when Claire appears.

Claire kept Phil a secret from her family for almost six months, until a sister dropped by unannounced one Sunday noon between church and a museum visit. Phil and Claire, who were reading the paper in bed, managed to scramble into their clothes and arrange the covers, but they couldn't dispel the air of intimacy and the look they both wore of having been recently asleep. Phil was introduced to Gwendolyn and her husband as Phil Casciotti, with no further designation. That night Claire's mother called and wanted to know who this fellow Cacciatore was. She corrected her mother without chiding her for the corruption of his name and said he was someone she was seeing. "What is he in?" her mother asked. "Fruits and vegetables," Claire whispered. Her mother was silent. "Commodities?" "Yes," Claire said, lying for the first time in her adult life.

She told me this over coffee several weekends later. She looked tearful and said her parents were being quite cool with her because they have figured out she is sleeping wth Phil. Getting engaged or married would not pacify them because they do not find him suitable. Gwendolyn had told them he looked quite young, quite physical, and not like a professional. Choosing Phil would mean estranging herself from her family, even though they would be polite and correct and invite them to the family celebrations of holidays and promotions. They had several nice men in mind, her age or older, whose parents they knew.

Claire didn't know how to break up with Phil because she had never had to end a relationship herself. She thought it would be best to cook dinner and tell him in person, and after that shop at another market for a while. They would both be miserable, but Phil was young and handsome and would find a woman to marry whose family would brag to their friends about his entrepreneurial skills. She would try to keep busy — have lunch with her sisters more often, learn to quilt, perhaps look for a new job. She would write a note to Phil's mother, whom she had never met but might have hurt, to explain things and apologize. She thought she would send a gift to the produce people to thank them for their help and courtesy, and now their understanding. And she would keep in touch with Phil — cards at his birthday and at Christmas, and a split-leaf philodendron for the opening of his store.

Willow's Mysterious Sense of Humor

•

BY ERNEST HEBERT

OLLIE JORDAN STEPPED from the family truck onto the soil where once his home had been, turned to his son Willow and said, "Wiped clean." A bulldozer had scooped out a cavern in the hardpan and buried his shacks. All that was left were the caterpillar tracks of the dozer. Already some wild grasses had taken hold in the soil. Willow tugged at the chain that bound him to his father. Willow was looking at the back of the great sign — BASKETVILLE EXIT 8 — in whose shadow the Jordan shacks had sprouted. He wanted to climb the sign, swing among the steel struts, holler, exercise what his father called his mysterious sense of humor. Someday, thought Ollie, I'm not going to be strong enough to hold him, and he'll drag me where he wants as now I drag him.

Ollie began at the north corner of the sign and walked 32 paces southeast. Here had been the sleeping shack, which he had built for Helen and himself and which he called the "boodwar." He had overheard the word "boudoir" and deciphered that it meant a place for lovers. He had analyzed the word and found it a good one. The meaning of the "war" part was clear enough, for what were lovers but ceaseless battlers? As for "bood" — he figured that was one of the less ugly terms referring to copulation. He walked 20 more paces. Here his cousin Tooker had settled with his family in a converted school bus. To the right was the shack he had built for Adele and her baby, and behind that the room that his children, Turtle and the twins, had fixed up so that they could call it their

182

own. Now, as the wind quieted and the early summer sun fell upon the earth, his earth, Ollie Jordan caught a remnant of his home that the bulldozer could not remove — the smell of his clan.

Ollie's place sat on half an acre on top of a hill. It was bounded by steep ledges and hemlock trees whose roots gripped the granite with all the determination of dying millionaires clutching their money. Here, where the porch had been, a man could sit in a rocking chair, drink a beer, smoke a pipe, hold forth. Here he had said to his friend Howard Elman, "A man fishes to catch his natural-born self. You'll see a banker casting a fly to a rainbow trout, a mailman throwing plug at a smallmouth bass, and a man like me offering a worm to a hornpout. You can keep your trout. I don't want no fish that walks on water when it feels the hook." If the sign blocked his view of the Connecticut River valley below and the Vermont hills beyond, at least he could listen to the music of the interstate highway, which ran beside the river, and to the bitching and moaning of the wind like a woman too long without comfort. He said to his idiot son, "Willow, there ain't no place left here for a man to sit civilized."

Willow tugged at his chain. He wanted to climb the sign.

"What to do next?" Ollie said, bringing his mind to bear on the immediate problem, which was the only kind of problem that he considered. To Ollie the only truth of a clock was the ticking, and that was how he took life, tick by tick.

Ollie Jordan had returned to his former home in the vague hope that he might sneak back onto his land wth Willow. He never imagined that there would be nothing here but the sign.

After he and his family had been evicted, they had been offered succor by Ollie's half-brother, Ike. A professional man, in the Jordan sense, Ike was a successful burglar. Ike's wife, Elvira, introduced Ollie's common-law wife, Helen, to a social worker, and thus was born a great tension. Ollie was a traditionalist, in the Jordan sense. He feared welfare because he was afraid it would change him and his family's ways. Not that he was proud of himself or the family, but he did believe in the rough integrity of distinction among creatures, and the Jordans, whatever else they were, were as distinct from the run of society as mongrels were from poodles.

Matters reached a crisis when Ollie learned that the "Welfare Department," which was Ollie's phrase for any social service agency, had found a place for them to live in Keene. Helen urged him to move with her. Ollie was about ready to go along with the idea, partly because, as he would say about certain women, Helen could always "cast a spell over this frog," and partly because he was willing to sacrifice a philosophical point to get away from Ike's succor. But then Helen said that the Welfare Department wanted to examine Willow. They said, she said, that Willow might not be as dumb as he looked, might even be "educable," a word that Ollie translated as a marriage of the words "edible" and "vegetable." No one was going to examine Willow as long as his father was alive. He couldn't explain it so it made sense, but he held a deep conviction that in his son's apparent stupidity and odd behavior there was a seed of genius that someday would sprout, provided it was kept away from meddlers such as the Welfare Department. Willow's place was with him, and that was that. As was his wont, Ike entered the argument. "It ain't good for a man's spirit to have an idiot chained to him," Ike said.

"Everybody's got an idiot chained to him," said Ollie. "Only difference is mine is here to see."

Ike smiled. He had the narrow-mindedness of a successful man. Furthermore, while he was generous with his advice, he was cheap with his beer, which to Ollie demonstrated bad manners and a poverty of style. That night Ike drove Helen and the twins and Turtle to Keene. The next morning Ollie loaded his ancient four-wheel-drive International pickup with his tools, some personal items, and Ike's beer supply, and drove off with Willow. The truck and the few things he had in the back were all he had now. Broke and angry and knowing that as soon as the anger wore off he would be sick with loss for his family, Ollie drove at random on the back roads of Cheshire County, like a bandit with no hideout to go to. By accident, it seemed, they had arrived at the narrow dirt road that wound up the mountain from Route 63 to the BASKETVILLE sign. For a second, he had thrilled to the thought of returning to the shacks he had built. Now the truth was upon him. All that was here of home was an old scent that the rain soon would wash away.

Willow tugged at his chain, making a sound like a puppy.

"Oh, all right," Ollie said, and he slipped the key in the padlock that kept the chain around the boy's waist and released him. No doubt trouble would follow. It always did when Willow was loose, but at this point trouble seemed better than nothing.

Willow headed for the sign. At six feet, he was taller than his father by a couple of inches, but he seemed shorter because he walked hunched over like an ape. Willow paused before the sign to sniff the treats wafting on the air currents of the morning. Satisfied that at the moment the world was good, he grabbed one of the steel supports on the rear of the sign, and with monkeylike grace, monkeylike foolishness, swung from strut to strut until he was nearly at the top. Here he rested, draping himself in the crook made by two pieces of steel. Ollie watched Willow's performance, proud as any father would be before the athletic exploits of his son.

Ollie now prepared to make himself comfortable. He fetched a quart of Ike's Narragansett beer from the truck, searched about for a patch of ground just the right temperature, sat cross-legged, and lit his pipe to await developments. He figured that Willow, who like himself had not eaten breakfast, would realize he was hungry in about an hour and then would come down from the sign. How they would eat with no food and no money Ollie didn't know. He'd solve that problem when the hunger came. He had nothing but contempt for men who held full-time jobs, ate regular meals, made love at 10:30 P.M. every other night, mowed the lawn on Saturday morning, and showed any other evidence that they sought to order their lives in space and time. "There ain't no other time but now," he would say. Thus his despair at seeing his works destroyed lost hold for the moment as the comfort of the day, the comfort of the beer, the comfort of his thoughts settled in.

He watched white clouds gamboling in the sky, and they reminded him of his dogs. God, he missed them — their wet tongues and bad breath, their ridiculous insistence on protecting him from nonexistent threats. Dogs were loyal to undeserving men, as men were loyal to their own undeserving ideas about how to live. He supposed that after he had abandoned them, the dogs had stayed around until the bulldozer came. Some would raid garbage pails and thus would get shot. Others would attach themselves to humans, and thus stood a 50-50 chance of survival and a 50-50 chance of being gassed by the county. Ollie imagined that such a death would be without pain and also without the sweetness that follows pain. Perhaps one dog, say the shepherd, would learn to hunt alone again and return to the wild life to live in unacknowledged glory until his teeth went bad and he slowly starved to death or until he succumbed to his own parasites, eaten inside out as a man is by his beliefs. The dogs stood no chance with men, he thought. And men stood no chance at all. Men, like the dogs that they made over as their own dark inferiors, were neither wild enough to go it alone nor civilized enough to get along together.

To survive, the world needed some improved versions of its creatures. He had worked on this idea long ago, when he had sensed the strangeness in himself, and had sought to give it dignity and importance by contriving a theory around it. Soon, however, he realized he was not better than most men, nor fitter, but merely different. But in his son

Willow, Ollie saw possibilities. Indeed, he had concluded that Willow's idiocy was a departure point. He had gotten the idea by observing cater-pillars immobilize themselves in silky webs, to emerge later as butterflies. He had seen hints in Willow of the butterfly, in the boy's inscrutable and dangerous adventures, what Ollie called "his sense of humor." Lately, as more and more people, even Helen, had called upon him to shuck off the burden of his son, Ollie Jordan recognized the love he had for him as an instinctive, brainless duty, the human equivalent of a salmon swimming up river to fertilize some eggs and die. But also he saw in Willow his own shadowy love of self.

For almost an hour, Ollie's thoughts passed in review like the clouds above, to thicken into meaning and then dissolve into nothing. He had finished his beer, his pipe had gone out, and he was starting to doze when he was startled by a thump at his feet: Willow's shoes and pants. Moments later the shirt, then the underwear came fluttering down. The clothes, all in a bunch at his feet, reminded Ollie of a parachutist whose chute had not opened. He looked up to see Willow hoist himself to the four-inch-wide header at the top of the sign, stand, and — baldacky bare — face the Interstate Highway below.

"When you come down here, I'm going to beat you blue," Ollie said, but even as he spoke, even as he proceeded to give Willow holy hell, even as he shook his fist and jumped up and down at his own frustration, even so, Ollie Jordan thrilled at the sight of his mad son. "You stupid bastard!" he shouted, but added under his breath, "My, what a sense of humor that boy has got."

After a few more minutes of perfunctory ranting, Ollie fetched an-other beer, reloaded his pipe, and considered the situation. The worst, and unfortunately most likely, event that could happen next was that someone on the highway would report seeing a naked man on the BASKETVILLE sign, and in no time flat the Welfare Department would arrive and take Willow away in a white van with a red light and a siren that said wup-wup-wup. The second worst thing that could happen was that he would fall off and break his head on the ledges.

What to do? If he could go around the front of the sign, perhaps with a long pole — say a young maple sapling — he might be able to knock Willow off so he would land on the softer earth at the rear of the sign. "It won't work," he said to himself. "He's too quick." He calculated it would take a motorist 20 minutes to get off at the exit in Putney and find a phone. It would take the Mutual Aid dispatcher another 10 minutes to get somebody to the scene of the crime. Let's see, he thought, 20 and 10 is 30 minutes — half an hour, that ain't bad. Unless, of course, a state trooper saw Willow and radioed ahead. But Ollie, operationally optimistic if philosophically pessimistic, wouldn't consider that possibility. Half an hour, not bad, not bad at all. He had, oh, 15 minutes to enjoy this show before he had to do some serious thinking. He took a swig of beer and watched Willow.

Willow, arms outstretched, tiptoed along the top of the sign like some creature half-ape, half-dancer. He'd walk to one end of the sign, pivot, and walk the 75 feet to the other end. Through it all, he seemed to be keeping time to a music heard only by himself.

Suddenly Ollie Jordan heard a car churning up the dirt on the road that led to the sign. Moments later, Godfrey Perkins, the part-time constable of Darby, New Hampshire, stepped out of his cruiser, paused to adjust his stomach, and with studied nonchalance said, "I see Willow's got himself in a pickle again."

"It's his pickle," said Ollie.

"Not quite. It's a public pickle. He's disturbing the peace of the good people down there on the highway."

"Do 'em good to have their peace disturbed."

"If you won't get him down here, the law will," said Godfrey.

"Be my guest," said Ollie.

"He won't come down for you?"

"Nope. Got any ideas?"

"Not at the moment," said Godfrey.

The two men settled in, hands meditatively on their chins, like a couple of stand-up comics mocking intellectuals. Willow continued to perform. Occasionally he would do a handstand on the top of the sign while giggling loudly at the upside-down world, and then almost faster than the eye could follow, he would spring back to the world of right-side-up and continue his walking, or he would imitate Constable Perkins hoisting up his stomach by the gun belt. "If you could get a pair of pants on him, you could put him on the Ed Sullivan Show," said Perkins, who would have been surprised to hear that Ed Sullivan was deceased.

Godfrey Perkins was a passably tolerable man, for a cop, thought Ollie, who envied the constable for his stomach. It was a magnificent thing, a soft basketball-sized man's answer to pregnancy, especially remarkable in that it resided in the frame of an otherwise thin man.

A government car leading a cloud of dust came to a halt just behind Godfrey's cruiser. Ollie feared the worst — the Welfare Department had come to get his boy. A woman driver and a male passenger stepped out of the car. Ollie watched them walk the 100 feet from where the cars were parked to the sign. To Ollie, they looked like vacationers: tanned, pretty, dressed in colors instead of garments, it seemed, more ideas of people than actual people, the woman walking like a man, the man walking like a boy.

"Good morning," said the woman. "We're Kay Bradford, social worker, and George Petulio, intern, from the I-I? Independence for Independents in Keene?" Her voice traveled up slope so that it appeared she was asking a question instead of introducing herself. She glanced at Ollie, taking in his circumstance, he figured, like a loan company manager watching a stranger approaching his desk, but it was Perkins that she had addressed. "Ma'am, you're talking to Constable Perkins, and this is Mr. Jordan," said Godfrey, "and I must warn you that we've got a naked subject on top of that sign."

The woman smiled, "Have you tried talking him down?" she said.

"Not really. I just got here," said Godfrey.

Ollie could see that the woman was going to run the show. So it goes, he thought. Men talked big and fought big, and ran governments like fancy sportsmen's clubs, but when women chose to step in, they had their way. Women told you where to put the back door, what pan to spit in, and what pot to piss in, took, really, complete command of the important things. He believed that women were tough as oak knots on the inside and that displays of tears and hysteria were more techniques of control than emotions. As for Polio, which was how Ollie heard the name "Petulio," there was something peculiar about him, and it took Ollie a moment or two to realize what it was. He was big, not bear-big or bull-big like some men, but merely unnaturally outsized, as though in the universe in which he lived, things came bigger.

"Mr. Jordan," said the woman. "We want to help your son, and we want to help you help yourself." She knew him somehow, and Ollie was alarmed. They had papers on him, he guessed. These government people knew everything and they knew nothing. They were more dangerous than Christian ministers. "We're going to try to talk him down, and you can stand by and help," said the woman.

She walked over to the sign, placing herself just below Willow, cupped her hands and said to Willow in a strong voice, "Your mother and your brothers and sisters miss you. They want you to come home."

The woman must mean Helen, Ollie figured; she must have talked to Helen, who had given her some of the facts of their life.

"Have you had anything to eat today?" said the woman to Willow.

188

"If you come down, we'll buy you a biiiiig hamburger."

Willow continued his business on the sign, ignoring the woman.

"Willow . . . Willow . . . Willow," she called, but Willow seemed not to hear.

Constable Perkins was disturbed. He had a daughter just a couple of years younger than the social worker, and it bothered him that there was not a trace of shame on her face at the sight of a naked man. The crazy idea was forming in his mind that his witnessing the social worker watching Willow would somehow influence his own daughter toward depraved ways.

"Damn your soul, Jordan, get that subject down here," said Perkins to Ollie.

The woman turned a stern look on the constable. Clearly, she didn't like his approach, but then again hers wasn't succeeding. She seemed to consider the situation, and then she said to Ollie, "Why did he climb up there in the first place?"

"His reasons," said Ollie.

"Crazy reasons," said Perkins, as Petulio scribbled on a note pad.

"He looks frightened to me," said the woman.

"He ain't but he ought to be," said Ollie.

Kay Bradford thought she understood now. "Mr. Jordan, is that boy up there because you abused him?"

"I'm going to abuse him when he comes down," said Ollie. His voice was rough as granite. He was shocked by what he considered to be the woman's familiarity. It was clear to him before that they wanted to take his son away from him. Now it was clear that they also were looking for an excuse to put him in jail. They want everything, he thought. It wasn't the armies you had to fear. It was the truant officers and welfare people.

The woman caught hold of her emotions and said with a smile, "Mr. Jordan, you haven't been able to get the boy down. Why not give us a chance — alone? You just melt away. Maybe when he sees you're gone, he'll come down on his own."

"He always did like that sign. Course he never went up it bare before." Ollie stood his ground. The smile on the woman's face demonstrated to him a lack of cleverness that heretofore he'd thought she possessed. She was dangerous, he said to himself, but ignorant as a stump.

It was Godfrey who worried Ollie now. The constable had lost his sense of humor; he was beginning to become professionally annoyed by the situation. Minutes later, Perkins summoned the woman and the note-taker to the vehicles for a conference. Ollie could see that they were having a spat, and he could also see that Willow was not about to come down from the sign. When the woman returned, Ollie could tell by the urgency in her voice that something important had transpired at the vehicles.

"Willow, we don't have much time," she shouted. "Willow, it's hot today. You must be getting thirsty. If you come down, we'll buy you a . . . (she turned to Ollie) what does he drink?"

"Moxie," Ollie lied.

"Willow, we will bring you a Moxie," said the woman, then turned to Petulio and said, "Go to the store and buy Willow a Moxie."

Petulio seemed uncertain whether she really meant what she said — as well he should be, thought Ollie — and his uncertainty seemed to shift from mind to body, so that he swayed like a tree sawn through but undecided which way to fall.

Ollie sidled up to Constable Perkins and launched an exploratory mission for information. "She ain't doing too good," he said.

"It don't matter," said Perkins. His hands were cupped under his stomach; his manner was distinctly self-satisfied.

Ollie moved off. He had no doubt now that Perkins had called for help. He eased down to the vehicles, and there he heard the dispatcher speaking on the two-way radio in Perkins's cruiser. They were sending a fire truck with a hook and ladder from Keene, presumably to go get Willow. Ollie figured he had only minutes to act.

Back at the sign, Kay Bradford stood with her arms folded. She had given up.

"A sad case," she said to Perkins. "Child abuse, parenting without goals or objectives." She spoke as if to implicate Perkins in the sadness of the case.

"He ain't no child, Ma'am. He's as grown up as you and me," Perkins said, defending, it seemed, himself.

"Mentally still a child. Look at him," she said.

Why, Perkins asked himself, did he get the feeling he was being implicated in Willow's problems? "Whatever — still an idiot," he said.

The social worker breathed a sigh that obviously was an accusation, and Perkins for the life of him couldn't understand what she thought he had done wrong.

At this point Petulio put his note pad in his pocket and spoke for the first time. "Is that gas I smell?" he said.

Constable Perkins was alarmed. It struck him that he had made a mistake in not keeping an eye on Ollie Jordan. Then he heard, or perhaps felt, a *wump!* — a thing of substance that seemed to engage him with a

190

cloud of black smoke full of orange light, lift him off his feet, and carry him into the sky. So this is death — not bad, he thought. Seconds later he came to his senses. The social worker and her assistant each had a hold of one of his ankles, and they were dragging him along the ground. He could feel heat in the air. The indignity of being saved by a woman and a college student hastened a return of his manly bearing, and soon he was on his feet. The faces of his saviors — and his own, he guessed — were blackened. He thought about his brother, Andy, and how he would imitate Al Jolson singing, "Mammy, Mammy . . ."

"He's taking him." That was the voice of the social worker, and Perkins turned to see Willow scrambling down the unburning end of the sign, saw his father corral him in some kind of rope getup with one hand, beat him with a stick with the other, until off they went like a couple of guys in old movies being chased by cops. Perkins, too, found himself running — dead last. Ahead of him were the social worker and the assistant. He saw the Jordans get in their vehicle and peel out. Seconds later the social worker reached her car, but Perkins knew somehow that this chase would not amount to anything. Sure enough, Ollie Jordan had taken the time to slash the tires of his cruiser and the government car.

Perkins turned to look at the burning sign. It was a pretty fire. The people on the highway would thrill to it. He deduced that Ollie Jordan had siphoned gas into a can, crept along the ledge, and doused the front of the sign with the gas while he and the social worker were busy yakking at the rear. Perkins now could hear the fire truck that he had summoned pulling off the hardtop onto the dirt road. There was a good chance it would be too big to negotiate the steep turns. Oh, well, that was of little importance. What was important was that the world, as he saw it, was becoming faintly orange around the edges. He began to taste the hot dog he'd had this morning from Joe's wagon. Nausea — sign of shock, he thought. He touched his face. It was numb and left a dark, greasy smudge on his fingers. Under the black on his face would be red like a bad sunburn. The social worker and the assistant had gotten out of the car, and they were moving toward him, floating, it seemed, on a carpet of orange light.

"Oh, my God, what's happened to our faces," said the social worker.

"Mammy, Mammy," said Perkins.

Avoiding the Shoals
of Passion

·

BY DANIEL ASA ROSE

HE PLAN WAS THIS: After the graduation ceremonies, Beverly
would take her parents back to her room for 20 last minutes of
packing, Otis would take his parents on a brief tour of the MIT
campus, then both families would meet at 11:30 in front of the nuclear
engineering laboratory and walk together to the sit-down delicatessen for
lunch. (The delicatessen idea had been Otis's one contribution to the plan,
and Beverly had agreed at once: it would help make Otis's parents feel at
home. Also it was inexpensive, for whichever set of parents insisted on
picking up the tab.) Then after lunch, say 12:15, or as late as 12:30 if the
dark delicatessen beer put Otis's father in one of his toast-making moods,
they would carefully arrange the luggage in the two cars and take off for
Beverly's family homestead in Franklin, two hours north on 93. There the
parents could spend a couple of country hours getting to know each other
before Otis and his parents headed back to Jersey. It was an eminently
sensible plan conceived by eminently sensible people. Otis the astrophys-
ics major and Beverly the computer-math major had shaken hands on it
the night before. Only as an afterthought had it occurred to them to
pucker their lips and blinkingly kiss — which was fine. In their four years
of undergraduate life they had both seen enough relationships flounder on
the bizarre and treacherous shoals of passion that it was fine to base theirs
on friendship and good sense.

The wedding itself was going to be harder to plan, or at least they thought one part of it was going to be harder: the urban part, figuring out how much it meant to Mr. and Mrs. Spizer that their son be married back home among their thousand good neighbors in Newark. From what she could gather, Beverly sensed that it would mean a great deal indeed, and for their sake she was willing to do the block party, the dancing in the streets, whatever it was they did in Newark — but Otis was more concerned for *her* parents, who were quiet country people, white-picket-fence country. Thus it was planned, and thus the plan worked out, that after a delicatessen lunch of corned beef and tongue (but no beer — the liquor license had been revoked), Beverly rode out toward Franklin with Mr. and Mrs. Spizer in the meat-smelling seats of their beat-up silver Cadillac, Otis rode with Mr. and Mrs. O'Day in the straw-filled windiness of their shiny pickup truck, and on the way what needed feeling out was felt.

By the time both vehicles rolled into the smooth ruts of the O'Days' driveway a marvelous thing had been established: Beverly's parents and Otis's parents were all of one heart that the only important thing was for Beverly and Otis to be happy together and that all the rest of it — the "baloney on a bun" Mr. Spizer irreverently called it (he owned two butcher shops) — would fall into place wherever in the world it wanted to fall. It was remarkable. Beverly and Otis squeezed hands and then — right there in public between the pair of hot clacking autos — hugged. The two sets of parents beamed shyly at them, then came together themselves for the kind of embrace given only between people who are happily related or are planning to be happily related, the fathers clapping each other's back, the mothers kissing each other's cheek, and at their feet the O'Day chickens pecking at the tires of the unfamiliar silver Cadillac. Then it was time to be shy once again, people pulling apart and falling into the roles of guest and host, when suddenly Mr. Spizer shouted, "And now do I get to see your horse?" and turning to Beverly, planted a fleshy kiss upon her mouth, making her cringe the tiniest bit. Everyone else thought that it was an exuberant but sweet thing for this tiny, dimpled man to do. Beverly decided to smile.

Turning on his heel, throwing his arms open wide at the cloudless sky, the barn buildings, the tractor in the distant sunlight under a trio of white butterflies, Mr. Spizer cried: "I love this backwoods setting!" He flipped a jumbo-sized handkerchief out of his breast pocket and dangled it over his head while he kicked the air a number of times in a fancy little dance step that made everyone laugh, including Beverly. Then with no warning he stopped in his tracks and used the handkerchief to blow his nose, making everyone look away. Beverly looked at Otis but he was taking his mother by the arm and in a second all of them were walking toward the farm-house.

On the porch they ate cherry pie, homemade, of course, served on wooden plates with the thickest white napkins Beverly had ever seen her mother use. Mr. O'Day looked proud of the pie and the plates in his bashful, red-eared way. He was using the best manners Beverly had ever seen him use. Mr. Spizer preferred not to sit in the high-backed Shaker chairs occupied by everyone else, but rocked in the very old and fragile rocking chair in rhythm with his enthusiastic chewing. Four times Mr. Spizer told Mrs. O'Day how very delicious was her cherry pie, how much better than anything you could get in Newark, and then he grilled her as to what was in it, smiling and nodding very attentively as she listed her ingredients, though Beverly could tell he knew not a thing about baking. Finally, when Mrs. O'Day's cheeks were pink with the unaccustomed flattery, Beverly watched as Mr. Spizer turned his strange but rather charming curiosity onto the subject of the farm itself, in the form of quick, diverse questions to Mr. O'Day: how many acres did it have, was there a problem with insects, how could such a pretty little insect as a Japanese beetle cause the damage it did, was an acre bigger or smaller than an average city block, approximately? This last question was put to Mr. O'Day by Otis. Beverly was surprised.

They meant to merely pass through the bare, polished house on the way to the barnyard door, but the 16 hanging photographs of Beverly as a child before she had gotten spectacles kept Otis and his father busy in the living room, their four brown shoes moving slowly side by side along the perimeter of the braided rug. "I didn't know she wore pigtails," Otis remarked at one point, and Mr. Spizer replied, "Oh, what a nice-looking girl she's always been," and then the shoes went sidling along some more while everyone else passed beyond to the kitchen and the door they wanted. "Coming, gentlemen?" called Mrs. Spizer from the yard — it was clear that she was the strict one in the family — but it was nearly 90 seconds in the dusty sunlight before the group was once again complete.

Joining them with his jovial energy in this field that was called a backyard, Mr. Spizer clapped and rubbed his hands together as if a long-delayed treat was finally coming due. "Now to see the horse!" he said. "Yes?"

"Well, Beverly's mare can be jittery with newcomers," Mrs. O'Day said. "There are goats to see, or cows — "

There was a pause of black depression.

"We can see her if you'd like," Mrs. O'Day said.

194

Joy! Commotion!

"Is she truly dangerous?" Mr. Spizer asked Beverly as he danced along to the horse barn under the tidy blue sky. "How long have you had her?" Otis came up along Beverly's other side and looked at her with a similar eagerness. "Can you believe we've graduated today?" he said. "What did you do with your cap and gown?"

"I packed them in my book bag," Beverly told Otis. "Yes," she told Mr. Spizer, "yes, she is, if you don't handle her right." Beverly watched the way Mr. Spizer was lifting his brown shoes high out of the grass with each step, as if he didn't want to trample on any of the multitudinous wildlife that might live therein.

"Our whole lives ahead of us!" Otis suddenly shouted.

They were at the horse barn. It was a square building set under a large locust tree that filtered the light down through the leaves in a soft way. Beverly noticed that Mr. Spizer ducked under the leaves as if they were part of a plastic awning, something to keep the rain off one's head. When they got inside she kept an eye on Mr. Spizer because he seemed to be having trouble adjusting to the darkness. Beverly's mother cautioned Mr. Spizer to stay on the mare's left side, always on the left. The mare was fidgety with everyone crowded into the stall. Beverly went around front and kissed her nose hello, kissed her big humorless eyelids. Mr. Spizer asked Mrs. O'Day if he could touch, and when he got the go-ahead he placed his fingertips on her neck with great respect, as if it constituted an especially sharp-bladed cleaver. "Ah," he said, "so smooth," and he smiled, and everyone smiled. He wanted to touch the tail, and Mrs. O'Day let him do that, too. Mrs. O'Day showed him the hair in swirls on the torso, and the knobs on the knees, and the pressure points on the ankles. She went on to explain about the care and upkeep of the hooves, lifting one of the hooves and demonstrating, with two fingers, how the mealy underside should be ground out daily to prevent rot. Mr. Spizer giggled slightly with surprise to find a horse and a hoof and a hand so suddenly nearby him in the heat of the countryside. "What must it all smell like?" he asked, and without waiting for a reply he grabbed Mrs. O'Day's fingers and put them to his nostrils.

"Oh, like after you cut your toenails," he said.

Such an innocent thing to say! Yet Beverly's mother looked at Beverly's father; both looked at Otis's mother, who looked at Otis, who looked, with a sheepish smile, at Beverly, and it was at this moment that Beverly understood she would never marry Otis.

195

One Less Groundhog

·

BY DANIEL ASA ROSE

ELAX, I WOULD SAY, don't fight me. Open wider, wider, and think relatively happy thoughts. Don't tense up! Sit there with a tense jaw, you'll only get hurt, and I don't want anyone hurt in my chair. I won't have it. I don't care how old you are, if you can't show a little trust, off with the light and out you go with a nice smack on your fanny. Make another appointment.

That's what I told Roscoe, but he never made another appointment. I never saw him again from the day he left my office until we happened to buy adjacent farmhouses outside the fair city of Burlington. Here, dear world, was a fighting man.

We met again not as dentist-patient but as neighbors. This was years later when I was freshly retired. I won't say his teeth were falling out but it was obvious at a glance that I had done his last checkup. And I won't say his brain was falling out but it couldn't have been in very good shape, either. As a neighbor I had to take notice. He made things hard on himself, which is not a recommended way to get on in the country. He defied his new territory. Just as he had resisted me, so now he was set to fight nature. A big shot: what did he think, nature would lose? He wouldn't trust the land, and the whole thing was odd because he was way ahead of us in terms of being countrified. Here was this strapping young sculpture teacher from the wilds of northern Maine, a big, red-bearded genius at the crafts college with the earth in his blood . . . and you knew right off he'd flub his garden. It had to be deliberate. His kids could read the weather and pick up snapping turtles by their tails; our kids had been bred in cities, were now married to cities, and had outgrown the pleasure of our company. Yet this man was less at home out here than we were.

Roscoe's wife Mary was also discontented, but for a good reason. She didn't like the country and she didn't pretend she did. She, too, had been brought up in the wilds of northern Maine but she had thanked her stars the day she escaped to Burlington. So when Roscoe moved her out of their all-electric apartment in Burlington and popped her into the farmhouse she went into a tizzy that could have injured her health. She felt betrayed because Roscoe had taken her away from all that, and then had brought her right back. Moreover, she was allergic.

Big deal, she didn't enjoy country life — Roscoe wasn't about to let her stand in his way. Everyone else thought he was lovable, so let her think otherwise. Whom was she going to convince?

Roscoe was a "character" in the crafts college, always doing funny, lovable things like tying ribbons on his beard and spiking punch bowls with applejack. He liked people to see him pouring applejack into the punch with both hands held high and a big backwoods grin on his face. In the two months before we'd moved next door, Roscoe had broadened his country image: he'd drained the swimming pool and dropped in a mule, hoisted a scarecrow atop the roof to function as a TV antenna, and planted a garden next to the woods fully half a mile from the house. The hose for the garden was also half a mile and cost twice as much as all the seed. He planted only peas in the garden, so that when people asked him what he was growing he'd have an opportunity to make that big backwoods grin of his and say . . . "PEAS." He arranged to be working in the garden whenever guests from the crafts college would arrive. He'd lope back toward them on his bumpy mule; they'd stand in the driveway feeling uncountrified, yelling "halloo," shaking their heads with little academic grins on their faces and thinking what a character he was.

Dumb!

However, Roscoe didn't need our opinion so we decided to enjoy him. To speak honestly, though, from the day we moved in we both liked his wife better, despite her sinuses. I was in a walking cast because one of the movers had stepped on my foot, but I wasn't letting it get me down and we went over to make their acquaintance. Speaking as a sculptor, Roscoe said my cast was sloppy-looking. Speaking as a dentist, I could have told him I didn't like what came out of his mouth, but why look for trouble? He was rough, ambitious. I put my arms around them both and asked them over for a drink.

In the weeks to follow, Roscoe became more violent about what he called getting back to nature. We didn't know if it was because we presented competition as to who would get back there first, or whether the process had started before we arrived. Anyhow he now said "anyhoo," took to wearing overalls at parties, and cursed the weather. He went so far as to set loose a litter of piglets to give his land a barnyard flavor.

We weren't trying to rusticate faster than anyone else, but maybe it looked that way when we announced our intention to put in a garden ourselves. We figured the concept of a garden was general enough, but we figured wrong, because that's when Roscoe stopped talking to us. Just cut us off cold.

It was Mary who explained why he turned against us so suddenly. I was laid up for a few days — I had sprayed myself in the face with a pesticide — and she came over with a bunch of yellow cupcakes to cheer me up. She affirmed that we were competition. She helped us understand that the garden was a "symbol" to Roscoe and that he had placed it smack up against the woods for the greater challenge of keeping the varmints out. She reminded us of how heroically he'd worked to meet that challenge, digging a three-foot trench and hooking up an electric fence. She stressed the fact that it was a losing battle, and then she started crying. Then she sneezed, covering me with bits of yellow cupcake. Poor dear. Even though we could never get the hang of symbols, we acknowledged that it was a sad story: the groundhogs were bound to thieve all the peas.

Roscoe purchased a brown jalopy that looked just like the Depression and heroically made it into a movable sculpture. He filled the rumble seat with compost and tree stumps and he parked it at various sites on his land. It did nothing to enhance our view of the sun going down into the hills but we didn't say anything because what did we know about sculpture? His friends at the crafts college giggled. They were so tickled by the idea of sculpture on a farm that they threw a party to erect other sculptures: A-framed gizmos with bells hanging from the crossbars, facing our homestead like a musical hex. When we saw all those inebriated professors jumping up and down in their Asian clothes we looked at each other and said, "Life goes on," and we resolved to go ahead with our garden. Next morning we got it measured off parallel to the house, which we managed by taking turns up on top of the roof, hollering down instructions, and using probably more body English than was good for our old bones. Our garden became a perfect square, four railroad ties on either side, and before too long nature was obliging us with lots of colorful produce. (Lucky for us it wasn't one of those symbolic gardens because it really cut down on the grocery bills.) On one of her sneak visits over to see us, Mary told us Roscoe was fuming: he'd had a couple of months' head start, and the groundhogs were getting his goodies as soon as they appeared. We began giving Mary vegetables secretly; the man didn't have to know where his salad was coming from.

He still wasn't talking to us by mid-summer when he adopted the vile habit of chewing match sticks; nevertheless, I wanted to warn him about the danger to his overbite. I had some time on my hands since slipping on one of the piglets and putting out my back, so I watched him through my window, waiting for an opportunity to resume relations. At last I caught him in a pensive mood. He'd been rolling a boulder over to the jalopy when he unearthed something that intrigued him. He was gawking at it with his huge head, arching close, springing back. By the time I came up behind him he was whacking at it with the back of his shovel. I took a gander. It looked like a cocoon about to come undone, squirming around, snapping free of its elastic skin. He kept his back to me and he whacked faster, not curious as to what it might give birth to, not patient enough to wait; he judged it was safer to kill it at once and ask questions later. When I conjectured that it was someone's long-lost golf ball he threw the shovel over my head and called me an old goat.

Things were altogether bad now. I don't mind admitting my feelings were hurt and I made no more overtures. Let him feud. Let his overbite go hang. And if our garden intimidated him, so be it. He should have put his garden near his house where he could keep an eye on it. Instead, he pitted himself against the wild groundhogs with a vengeance that was frightening to behold. He stalked the woods, stuffing rags down every groundhog hole he came across, soaking them with gasoline and igniting them. First thing each morning and last thing each night he was down at the garden with a .22 rifle, straining to see or hear signs of a groundhog raid. One weekend he rented an automatic posthole digger to dig the start of another fence, outside the first one. The tool was dangerous — it was three feet long and worked like a corkscrew. He had to place it on the ground between his feet and ride it down. I was housebound the entire weekend because I had ruptured myself on a sawhorse, and it sincerely pained me to think of what he was doing.

Time brought its customary changes. I healed as usual, the air cooled, our garden pumped up new foods. At the end of the summer we had lots of corn to eat, more than enough. Mary was getting a couple of baskets of corn and cabbage and beets from us every day, and she cooked them right into Roscoe's supper without his knowing — until one night he figured it out. He asked her point-blank if they came from our garden and of course she didn't lie to him. He swept his plate to the floor and left the house. He walked back to his garden and saw a lone groundhog sitting in the ruins, nibbling. He tackled it and beat it to death with his bare hands, and he walked back to the house and cut open its stomach, right in front of Mary. He showed her the evidence, the peas piled up there inside, and then he fried that groundhog and had himself a meal. Mary spent the night at our house; we heard her crying into her Kleenex most of the night.

Roscoe left a couple of days after that. They didn't fight about it: they both knew that's what has to happen when half of a couple goes berserk. He dismantled his sculptures and went back to Burlington in a car brought by his friends. Mary and the kids stayed on in the country and ate pretty well, if I do say so myself.

Beginner's luck, that's all my garden proved, but Roscoe couldn't buy that. It was an accident my garden did so well, the sort of accident that happens when you look the other way, when you leave off fighting and forcing things all the time. I'm sorry he took it personally, because in retrospect I liked the man. I even found him lovable in a dumb kind of way. That's what I told my wife one night in bed while I was waiting for my liniment to dry. She wasn't surprised to hear me say it, though maybe she was too tired to show surprise. It was much later than we ordinarily stayed up — we'd had a little celebration, just the two of us, in honor of our son's birthday, instead of calling him up and making a bother.

I told her what I'd have said to Roscoe if he'd ever stuck it out in my chair, with a brace in his mouth so he'd have to listen. I would have told him to relax, settle back, don't try so hard. Don't play dumb! You know a farmer shouldn't make trouble for himself — he has enough trouble just getting by. Now maybe it's different for a sculptor but I suspect it's the same way for him: a fellow does better when he's at ease.

Roscoe, it's like lovemaking, son. Because there, too, you don't have to knock yourself out to get your point across. There's no emergency. You don't have to go around the North Pole and back. Mostly with the girls it's best to take your time, remembering the simple and elementary things like taking off your hat indoors. It has to do with manners.

I knew she was asleep then, but that was all right. She believed me.

Elmo's Fire

•

BY CARRIE SHERMAN

A WIDE, FLAT STREAM ran through Goshen. Its water was as clear
as the gas that Elmo pumped at Alfred's Country Store. Pebbles
shone up through it like wavery, illusory gems. In the deeper
pools the water looked green, and way down in it brown trout could be
seen dreaming and waving on the bottom as if the surface were light years
away. The bridge that crossed the stream marked the center of town. A
cluster of venerable, white clapboard establishments — Alfred's, the Goshen Inn, the Fairview Theater, the post office, and the First Congregational Church — made up Goshen. The place was that simple. That's
what summer people found so charming.

In the winter Goshen wasn't charming. Goshen was dead. Any native
would tell you that. They rode the last autumn show of bright red and
yellow leaves into the cold white drift of winter when the rocks froze and
the stream iced over through to those first muddy, green-speckled spring
days. But they weren't inclined to reflect much on it beyond comparing
the precipitation records cited by Harold Beane, the weatherman on the
local radio station.

Natives, that's what the summer people called them. Elmo Harp was
a native, if being born at Mercy Hospital and living and breathing in
Goshen ever since meant that, but some people in Goshen had their
doubts. People said Elmo was eccentric, a real character. Anything familiar would've been fine, but Elmo was solitary. Even in his own family,

surrounded by other Harps who had the same crooked teeth, oily brown hair, and shy fox-brown eyes, he looked like a second cousin twice removed. Maybe the Harps weren't regular churchgoers, but Harps had always lived in the hills around Goshen, and everyone knew that old man Harp made good maple syrup and could be counted on for dry cordwood come September. Everyone figured that if Elmo were really a bad apple, it would become apparent when it was time for a young man to show his fancy. Actually, no one paid all that much attention because come June, Goshen came alive.

Summer people in bright clothes swept off their grand porches, drank gin and tonics on their lawns, and walked barefoot right into Alfred's store. The candy-striped awning at the Goshen Inn rolled out, and the banners unfurled at the Fairview Theater. After performances of Chekhov, Agatha Christie, or some edifying modern thing, summer people wandered over to the Inn while younger ones might escape to kiss by the bridge. In that lambent light, Elmo Harp, the kid at the gas station, was an insignificant figure, but of course to Elmo that wasn't the case.

Elmo was 18 and pumped gas at Alfred's. All day long he drank one sweet bubbly tonic after the other and watched the heat ripple around the pumps and the shadows shift from one side of Main Street to the other. At first the job at Alfred's was like a vacation, but as one warm summer day stretched into another and Elmo watched the summer people laugh from one end of town to the other, he saw things differently.

The first time Susan Chalmers came by to fill up the family station wagon, she insisted on washing all the windows herself. "Oh, I can do it," she trilled. "I'm not helpless like some people. Where's the Windex and all that jazz?" She had a little bosom and thick legs. Like all the other Chalmers, Susan had big teeth, rough hair, and very smooth, lightly freckled skin. As far as magazine standards went, Elmo would've said that Ruby Turcot was prettier, but Ruby didn't have the slightest idea how to be pretty, and Susan Chalmers did. When she splattered window water on her dress, she just opened her eyes wide and said, "Oh, God, here we go," and giggled in a short nervous burst. From the sound of it she laughed that way a lot, and Elmo figured if you didn't like her, that giggle would drive you nuts.

And when Alfred waddled out onto the porch and asked Elmo what was going on, Susan was all smiles. She told Alfred that she was just learning how to pump gas, that it was something she'd always wanted to learn. Alfred stood there for a moment like a little pickle barrel, put his cigar back in his mouth, turned, and waddled back to his counter where he lorded over Muskol insect repellent, fireballs, Mennen skin bracer, Dr. Scholl's bunion pads, and an enormous jar of green eggs suspended in brine. Later Alfred said, "Well, she's a nice little nit." And Elmo thought so, too.

Each day Elmo waited for her to drive by. She drove with the utmost concentration, windows down, and the radio blaring. Since she was quite small, she just barely peeked over the steering wheel of the big station wagon. Actually it seemed that she really only guided the immense car by polite suggestion. But sometimes, when she thought of it, she'd look up and wave very quickly to Elmo. That signal amazed him. Looking at his own grimy, oil-stained hands, he'd think about how soft and little her hands were. Slowly Elmo discovered his own body thinking about hers until he just couldn't go any further.

So he watched her. She became a nightly goal. She didn't know it. Most people didn't know it when he watched them, he just looked. And if you want to look, you have to be prepared to see anything. He'd seen eels on autumn nights glide like big silver snakes across fields into the stream. He'd seen dogs eating deer in the woods. He'd seen Chester Weber shoot a sick cow in his barnyard last winter and cry afterward. Most people wouldn't have wanted to see those things. Elmo hadn't been exactly thrilled either, but it all seemed worth knowing.

Susan played tennis quite often with a tall, sandy-haired boy who drove a VW, wore a bandana like a pirate, and acted at the Fairview Theater. Elmo saw him everywhere — reading on the porch of the Goshen Inn, lying on the beach at the lake. He always looked as if he were waiting, ever so patiently, for a very important person who usually turned out to be Susan.

The Chalmers' house was a mile or so outside of Goshen on a dirt road. It was a standard old white box of a house. A hill rose up sharply behind it, and like most summer people, the Chalmers didn't hang curtains in the back of the house. Sitting up on the hill, Elmo could watch Susan plain as a drive-in movie while she took off her blue jeans, cut her toenails, and put on her gauzy summer nightgown.

But it got so that Elmo preferred to watch her in social situations, when she was genuinely animated. Elmo would wait until the Fairview Theater let out because she'd wait until the sandy-haired boy was done, and then Elmo would watch them stroll over to the Goshen Inn or down to the bridge. Sometimes, not too often, Elmo went over to the Inn to wait for her. The Inn was a place for summer people and Elmo felt uncomfortable there. The bartender was always quick to ask, "Will that be all for tonight?" Elmo always had another just to irk him and paid up when the bartender least expected him to.

One evening for variety, Elmo waited under the bridge. He had already had a couple of beers by the time he heard the clompity-clomp of her wooden sandals.

"Oh, Peter, don't be so discouraged . . ." she said. "It's just Goshen summer stock. It's good experience. If you go to Williams next year they have a terrific theater . . ."

The sweet little murmur of her voice ran on and on. Elmo even crooked his head out once to look at them. Peter, the sandy-haired boy, stood there looking sad, but still very important. What Elmo couldn't understand was why it took him so long to kiss her. As soon as Elmo was sure they were kissing, he crooked his head out again. Peter was better at smoking. Elmo knew he could've kissed her better than that by a long shot.

The next evening Elmo practiced smoking by the trout pool. Anyone looking would've been surprised even though it was just Elmo Harp in his dirty gas-station clothes. He was sitting on a rock with deep green water swirling all around. He held his head extra high as if he was English royalty and stretched out his arm so that the cigarette stuck up like a little flag. Then he'd cup the cigarette in his hand, bend down, and take a very serious drag on it. He was saying all sorts of important things to someone — maybe a movie star or an ambassador because sometimes he'd take the other part and nod his head in response. Finally he'd pretend that she was surprising him. It was all silent. The only thing that came out of his mouth was smoke.

That's the way Elmo Harp was by mid-August. If anyone had cared to notice him at the gas station while they were filling up, or buying a dozen of Alfred's home-grown nightcrawlers, they'd have seen his red-rimmed eyes, the sallow look under his grease-grimed face. If he'd made it through to November, the frost would've settled his bones, and he'd have been home free. But it was haying season, and hot — hotter than even Harold Beane could recall — and Herb Bishop asked Elmo to help out.

Herb and Martha Bishop were summer people, outsiders really, who had settled in Goshen year-round. Martha Bishop was always asking Alfred to order weird cheese, fancy chocolate cookies, and canned anchovies. Alfred did it, of course. He'd order five of whatever, and when the Bishops finally bought those up, he'd wait until Martha asked for more, then he'd order five more.

Herb Bishop was a forester by default. What else could a man do who'd inherited a couple of thousand acres? That's what everybody said anyway. Herb was a big, shambling, giant of a man. He seemed to be embarrassed all the time as if he were apologetic for owning all that land.

Elmo got to the upper pasture Saturday morning around eight. Martha was there in her old denim work clothes, her gray hair pulled back in a kerchief. She handed Elmo a thermos of hot coffee and smiled, which made her face all wrinkled and nice looking. "How are you, Elmo?"

That's what got Elmo about the Bishops. They always asked him how he was, and he felt he could say anything back. Why, once Herb told him he couldn't balance his checkbook. It still amazed Elmo that a man like Herb Bishop would tell him something like that.

All morning they pitched hay onto a baler. Other people that Elmo didn't know came by and worked also. By 10 o'clock the sky was like the bottom of a milk glass, and the dead heat had silenced everything but the rasping whir of a few insects.

At noon they walked down to the house where Martha had made lunch. Cold sandwiches, potato salad, and beer were laid out on the long porch table. But first, Herb, grinning, took off his shirt and hosed down his massive hairy frame. He did this unabashedly, with the simple, sensual joy of a man who's worked hard. The others followed suit. And lastly, Elmo, who instinctively turned his back on everyone and gingerly bent over so that the cold water ran off his narrow shoulders. Nonetheless, standing up, cold water trickled down to his groin making his insides cinch up tight. For a moment he stood there dizzy, blinking the water out of his eyes.

Over lunch Elmo listened while everyone talked about the President of the United States and articles they'd read in the newspaper. Their flushed faces were open, kind, and eager. They talked as if they knew the President personally and could really give him some helpful advice.

Looking down into Goshen from the Bishops' porch, it was hard for Elmo to believe that he'd sat on the little wooden chair outside of Alfred's for almost three months. Hard to believe he was sitting on the Bishops' porch like any other summer person. He couldn't follow what they were all talking about. The heat had enveloped him like a bad fever. He felt weak with it, and then he began to hear everything all at once — their talk, the car going by, a mourning dove. The sounds grew louder and louder until his head roared. As he looked from face to face, he wondered if they sensed his widening confusion.

Herb Bishop put his hand on Elmo's shoulder and said, "Ask your father about doing some cutting for me, will you?" To the table at large he said, "You know, Elmo's father probably knows more about trees than most university dendrologists." Elmo didn't know what a dendrologist was, but his heart slowed; the car continued down the road; the dove cooed softly in the tree; once more everything was in its place.

In the shuffle after lunch Martha looked appraisingly at Elmo and said, "If the heat gets to you, quit, okay? It got to me." And that determined Elmo then and there to work better than the best of them.

The Bishops' barn was zinc-white, spare, with a frontal span worthy of a Greek temple. It was topped with a running-horse weathervane which gave a rasping call every time the wind changed. Inside, bales of hay towered up to cathedral heights. Elmo stood balanced precariously on a topmost beam like a sailor on the high spar of a ship. Hay clung to his hair and the dry loft dust made rich, golden motes of light in which minute glinting particles were continually falling. Sharp, protruding stalks had pricked his hands till they were raw and tender. His eyes had trouble adjusting to the bright pool of light where Bishop, just a dark silhouette, was calling to him. Something about more hay.

Elmo was in charge of stacking the bales in an orderly, loosely piled pyramid. Bishop had sent him up there saying, "Well, Elmo, if anyone here knows how to do it, you do." Sometimes, as they both well knew, a hay barn improperly stacked with wet hay would in two or three days' time blossom into flame. Not that Bishop had to worry. His hay was perfect — dry, loose, shiny. Elmo didn't doubt that Herb would get the going price, if not more, for it.

The truck backed in and the fork grasped yet another bale and the antlike process began. Elmo saw then that the high part of the stack was slipping. He reached up to steady it, lost his balance, and grabbed at the lower bales. The whole top half gave way and an avalanche of hay slid by him. He braced his feet against the bottom of the stack while clinging to a support beam. Just the same, four hours of work was now strewn on the barn floor.

"Idiot . . . " muttered Herb, kicking the fallen bales. He was still just a black silhouette to Elmo. "Why didn't you keep things balanced up there? Christ, I thought you'd at least know how to do that."

No doubt hard work and the heat brought it out of Herb Bishop — the heat brought it out of Elmo, too, and it was much more than the heat. Whatever it was, it rose up in Elmo and it was ugly. "Stack your own damn hay, Bishop, you bastard." To emphasize his point, he shoved down two more bales of hay. He continued to blather as he slipped and stumbled down from the loft. On his way out the two men faced each other. Already

Herb's face — red and beaded with sweat — showed regret. "Look," he said, "I'm sorry. It's the heat. Let's just take it easy. . ." and reached out to touch him, but Elmo, stiff with anger, backed off. The others stood off to the side by the big hay truck, watching.

If Elmo had ever had much cause to bestow forgiveness, then perhaps that language would have come as easily to him as it did to Herb Bishop. Instead Elmo had been schooled in a stoicism that came from small, continuous deprivations. It came from helping his father handsaw all their winter wood because the chain saw was broken. It came from wearing his father's old, torn hunting jacket to school all last winter. Elmo had said what he said to Herb Bishop. There was no taking it back. He'd live with it forever. Later, if he thought it was wrong, he'd never let on. He left and he didn't turn around once.

Hands straight by his side, shirt untucked, hair all tufty, Elmo strode up Turner's hill. He was heading home. There were four switchbacks, three of them dirt, before the Harps' driveway. Elmo stopped dead in his tracks. He saw everything from the old, green, bug-eye pickup to the pile of wood in the front yard, to the peeling brown shingles and the little stovepipe sticking out the kitchen window. He could smell the pig and the chickens. The beagle stretched to the end of his rope and whined a welcome. A big mosquito landed lightly and confidently on Elmo's nose. Another on his arm. This deep in the piny woods it was always buggy and steamy unless it was winter. Angela, his youngest sister, straggled out from behind the house holding a gray kitten. She was barefoot, wearing bright red shorts and a dirty T-shirt. From inside Elmo heard the television and then his mother calling Angela back. Angela trotted absentmindedly in the direction of the woodshed.

Down the darkening path to the trout stream the very woods seemed to lean in and block his path, as if each leaf were a tiny, insect-bitten hand. The air was close and hot. He stood, dizzy from the exertion, holding onto a branch, panting, staring wide-eyed at the barely visible rock where he had once sat.

A barred owl hooted in the darkness. Elmo remembered Herb Bishop's face — the false gesture, his angry silhouette. And he remembered waiting and waiting simply for her to appear. It was a great anguished dawning. He turned from the rock in the stream, and stumbling down a path he knew by heart, headed toward town.

Elmo took the long way around past Bishops'. The barn was set back from the road — spare, blue-white, luminescent, and cold looking. Everything at the Bishops', including the day lilies, was shut up tight. The green clipped lawn was uncluttered. Elmo spit on it.

In town, applause resounding from the open windows of the Fairview Theater greeted Elmo. The banners fluttered and the wide yellow doors were open. People were laughing, and then all at once they came spilling out.

Jessie Warren, the sheriff's wife, was one of the first to see Elmo. She chose not to recognize him. So did her fat friend Ida. On the hottest night of the year these two older women carried sweaters over their arms. No one acknowledged seeing Elmo as he stood by the steps. But Susan saw him, and Elmo saw that. Her bright blue eyes turned on him quickly and away and back again, sympathetically.

The theater crowd and Susan with her brother and cousins drifted over to the Inn. Elmo watched them. His old clothes were soiled and littered with hay. His face was streaked with dirt and sweat, and his hair was uncombed. When he followed in their trail, even his walk had come apart.

Elmo sat at the far end of the curved wooden bar. "I'll have a beer." He hadn't meant to shout. It just came out that way. He was so exhausted he just stared straight at Teddy the bartender. Teddy had a wispy, damp-ended mustache and black eyes with long, mink-brown eyelashes. He wore one of those T-shirts with a white collar, and he was in the middle of preparing three Cape Codders, two gin and tonics, a manhattan, and for old Bucky Harriman, a regular and rather important figure in Goshen, a very, very dry martini. Harriman was head of the volunteer fire department. Just as Teddy looked down and saw that the cut limes were all gone, Elmo called down the length of the bar to him, "Well, you going to get me that beer or not?"

There was a slight hesitation in the noise of the lounge. A pause only a bartender would really hear. "Hey, buddy, I'll be right with you," Teddy answered. He looked quickly around the room with a tight, cheerful smile. Elmo stared at Teddy. He knew he had him pinned like a live bug behind that bar.

Another burst of laughter came from the pool followed by a splash. Someone had jumped in. Elmo saw Susan's bare shoulders and her bending over and turning to see if anyone was going to come out. She saw Elmo, and it seemed to Elmo that she smiled at him.

Almost joyfully, Elmo turned back to Teddy and shouted, "You going to get me that beer?"

This silenced the lounge. The little plastic swizzle sticks stopped stirring. When the conversation stopped, Teddy was talking to Bucky Harriman about the pros and cons of no vermouth while moving in the direction of pouring a draft for Elmo.

Old Bucky Harriman leaned on the bar and smiled down at Elmo. "Ahoy there, Elmo!" he said, and then he winked. It was the wink of a practiced politician, just as remembering Elmo's name was another pol's trick. He was well loved for those skills and got tremendous cooperation from everyone on anything that struck his fancy from sign ordinances to letting the belly dancers participate in the Fourth of July parade because, as Bucky pointed out, they were just local women who'd taken an adult education course.

"Alls I want is a goddamned beer," Elmo said flatly. He stood up like a boy in school and repeated his request.

Bucky smiled again. "Now take it easy, boy . . . Teddy here . . ." And Teddy sucked in the ends of his mustache. In an undertone to Bucky, Teddy said, "He's been trouble before."

Bucky nodded sagely, and Teddy, feeling that support, moved to the end of the bar and said, "Elmo, I think it's time for you to leave. Forget the beer. Just go home."

One of the men who had helped at Bishops' stood at the end of the bar and talked quietly with Bucky, who nodded some more.

That was it for Elmo. He was so frightened he didn't know what to do or how to break out of it. He was hearing everything all at once again. So he kicked over the bar stool and it got worse. "I'm gonna get you," he blurted. "I'm gonna get all of you. I'm gonna burn this place down . . . That's what . . . "

Big men got up from their little sociable tables. Elmo, wide-eyed with terror, bolted. He didn't see Susan, but he was sure she was laughing.

With each step he stepped out of himself into the woods, into the darkness behind the Inn, beyond Goshen. But whatever was left of him could still see, still move, still feel the night and the heat. He spied from the woods as men from the Inn came out and encircled the building. They stood 10 feet apart and called out to each other. Elmo had to laugh. He was the Indian and they were the pioneers on the plain. Elmo moved through the woods with windlike surety to the back of the store where he picked up the spare can of gasoline that Alfred kept for his motorboat. From there he proceeded to the back of Bishops' barn. Inside he constructed a teepee stack of hay and poured on the gas. He picked up the gas can, backed away to the door, and threw a lighted book of matches at the stack. Flames burst full from the pile and Elmo ran.

209

As the heat in the barn increased, hot air rose and the weathervane began to turn. Soon the horse was screeching round and round on its axis. Perhaps that sound was what called Herb Bishop to his bedroom window where he saw his hay barn lit up like a jack-o'-lantern on a hot August night.

Alarms rang. Volunteers raced into town. Many still had on their pajama tops. With toylike ferocity the fire truck rumbled out of the firehouse. Magically, Bucky Harriman sat shotgun, wearing his chief fireman's hat, waving and shouting. "Get over to Bishops'! Jump on it! Somebody call Chester!" As they roared through town, all the white buildings reflecting that revolving red light seemed to blush and blush again.

In the dark woods alive with the rustlings of night creatures, Elmo laughed. He laughed until the tears burst from his eyes. He stamped his feet like a wooden limberjack dancer and he didn't make a sound.

On tiptoe he ran with the almost empty gas can to the deserted west end of town. Looking up at the steeple of the First Congregational Church, he noted that it was 12 o'clock. Such dispassionate information defied burning; he ran on. Behind the Fairview Theater, Elmo watched an old man become young by ripping off a white pigtailed wig. When the actor ran out the back door, Elmo was so close he saw the actor's sweat rolling down his face.

Now Elmo proceeded slowly. Finally he settled on the bridge where he had watched her kissing. Using the last of the gas, he doused one corner, lit it, and sprinted up the back hill by Bishops'.

He lay down under a big pine. The barn was blazing now. He could see Herb and the other men manning the hoses. Martha Bishop and Susan Chalmers were there, side by side. Jessie Warren and her fat friend Ida had set up a card table for a coffee urn. It was almost a jolly scene. Alfred was passing out free doughnuts to the firefighters, and everyone was visiting and speculating about the fire.

The bridge fire was discovered soon and easily put out. But afterward many people went home to warn their families or just to stand on their lawns. Elmo seemed like a fire spirit, something the fates had blown down on them. Anyone's house might light up at any time.

Just when the roof of Bishops' barn really started smoking, Elmo saw his father drive in in the old green pickup truck with bug-eye headlights. Elmo saw his father get out and make his way slowly over to the front of the burning barn. He just stood there looking at it. Elmo could hear Herb Bishop call out, "Let her go . . . just keep it from spreading."

The roof caved in and the fire leapt out dancing. Great sheets of yellow and orange flame pulsed up into smoky, black tendrils. The crackling of the fire was loud, punctuated by small explosions and the heavy crashing of beams. The two men stood there and watched the barn go up in smoke. After a bit, Elmo saw his father look at Bishop.

As Elmo well knew, his father had a face that never told you what it knew. He was quick, too, even if he was as stiff as a new pair of blue jeans. Probably he told Bishop it was a damn shame. His father used that phrase a lot. Damn shame, he'd say, and then he'd spit. That's what he said when he heard how Ron Smith electrocuted himself using a power tool on his boat while standing in the lake. He'd said it when President Carter tried to rescue the hostages using helicopters and some of the helicopters crashed. A damn shame covered a lot of territory.

Even on the hill he could feel a lot of heat from the fire. He rolled over and looked up at the stars. They were so far away and tiny and cold, hard to believe they were great balls of fire. As a kid he'd sometimes feared falling into the sky. Looking up, he knew he'd never kiss Susan Chalmers; he'd never be a summer person; and he'd never find another home besides Goshen. He'd burned down Bishops' barn. It was a damn shame. In a while he knew he'd get up and go down to wait in Sheriff Warren's driveway. But for now he lay spread-eagled on the ground by the big pine and listened to the earth as if it were a big drum with the stream brushing across it, and he knew everything was held down by gravity.

Superpowerless

•

BY ALAN STERNBERG

T HOR, THE THUNDER GOD, and I generally flopped at cocktail hour. Vacations had their rituals; I was too young for this one and was considered a public nuisance.

"Thou art . . . um . . . pretty," I said, sidling up to my cousin Claire.

"Oh God," she moaned. "Will someone get him out of here?"

Harmon, her boyfriend, protecting his territory, threw an ice cube from across the porch. It whistled past my ear and knocked a plastic martini cup off the railing.

"And why does he keep talking that way?" Claire complained.

I talked that way because Thor did. Thor, as portrayed in the comic books, was much on my mind that summer. He used words such as "thou" and "art" and "hast." He also beat people up. There seemed to be no end to his talents.

Things were getting hot at the cocktail party — a lot of yelling, directed at me — and I left to go look at the cows. It was evening. The sun came horizontally over the lake and made the edges of things glow — bottles, glasses, adults, the posts of the cottage porch. All were largely above me as I sped past; I didn't cast much of a shadow in these surroundings. It was rough to be 11.

When it was dark I scaled the tree. The tree was a spruce that stood by the railroad tracks. At night I tended to lurk like a bat in the branches, holding a wooden replica of Thor's hammer and spouting Norse wisdom.

Occasionally I swatted mosquitoes. We filled three cottages, and the road to them wound between two cow pastures. Then it curved down a slight hill and crossed the railroad tracks. When cars came, they spewed rooster tails of dust and then stopped, purring softly, on the grass in front of the tennis court. When our car came, it lurched like a drunken Guernsey because it was old and — as my brother put it — frumpy. Gray smoke came out the back. My mother didn't like the car much, either. She and my brother weren't along this time to complain about it. My father looked relieved. I was in Vermont with him and a bunch of my mother's relatives. Mostly, the vacation had boiled down to getting on my grandfather's nerves and to hanging around with the cows. The cows were frumpy, too, I thought, but I liked them anyway, recalling that the last time my mother had gotten mad she had said that my father was frumpy but that Grandpa liked him anyway. She claimed it was because they went to the same college. After she said that she got even madder.

Through the branches I saw Harmon and Claire. They walked across the tennis court and into the bushes beside the rail bed. Claire wore a light summer dress and after a moment, as if there were ghosts, there seemed to be three people instead of two. This third apparition seemed to rise above Claire's head and after an instant it shriveled to the ground. That was a curious transformation — born, I surmised, of the mysterious world of cocktails — and later I told my father about it. He winced.

"Haven't you got better things to do than spy on your cousins?"

"I wasn't spying. I was just up in the tree."

"I'm not sure you should be hanging around in trees," he said. He paused to blow his nose. "Particularly that one."

"Why not?"

He ignored the question. "Your grandfather was looking for you, you know. He wasn't very impressed when I told him where he could find you."

Now *I* winced.

In the dark hours of the morning the freight train groaned from across the lake like a massive beast and I listened to it grinding slowly toward me and dreamt, as usual, of power. I was in search of magic moments, moments in which power was bestowed, such as when Peter Parker was bitten by a radioactive spider and became Spiderman, or when Dr. Donald Blake found an ancient walking stick in a cave and struck it against a rock, transforming himself into Thor. I often thought I could use a break like that.

213

Before breakfast it was chilly. I stood on the porch in a bathing suit and shivered and squeezed the edge of a newspaper between my toes. The sun struck brightly against the dock, the breeze riffled the water, and the sun turned the riffles to turquoise. On the hilly emerald pastures beyond the lake the cows floated like globs of cheddar cheese. I wondered suddenly: could this be a picture out of *Vermont Life?* I fervently wished it were. More to the point, I wished my grandfather hadn't found me. He had barged into my room at 7 A.M., in fact. "Hello!" he roared. "Out of the trees, are you?"

Now he dove into the water without a moment's rumination. He had a morning ritual: he swam 20 or so yards in a stiff crawl and then returned, emerging suddenly from the waist up, bellowing. The gray hair was plastered to his head and shoulders. The water in front of him was blue; beyond, it radiated into gold. My grandfather — the Scandinavian bear. He beckoned.

"No," I said.

"No?"

Grandpa looked at me with mock astonishment. It was a look exaggerated by the ravaged appearance his eyes had when he wasn't wearing his spectacles. "But the Norse gods," he intoned, pointing an enormous, wrinkled finger, "love to swim in cold water."

It was to avoid situations like this that I had purposely kept Grandpa ignorant of the comic books. Clearly someone had betrayed me. Grandpa was an engineer and thought logically. To him, comic books weren't worth much. They couldn't compare to a cold swim before breakfast. Grandpa, unfortunately, was a trying companion. I loved him to distraction, but hanging around with him tended to be painful. He required routine acts of courage that I would rather daydream about than perform. On one occasion he had tried to teach me boxing. I sniffed, remembering that disaster. It was true that Thor would have hopped into the lake without a second thought, but I couldn't say that without also exposing the real truth. The real truth was that I wanted to emulate my heroes, but only when it didn't hurt. How could I explain that?

Thor was tall and muscular and, it seemed at the time, the archetype of a man. I was short and thin and, it seemed at the time, a failure. Claire had long brown hair and long tanned legs and when she wore her swimsuit I was filled, it seemed, with strange thoughts.

My father on the other hand, was short and slight and, on the surface, a poor tennis player. But he wasn't what he seemed. In fact he was the best

214

tennis player there that summer. He ran raggedly about the court with a handkerchief fluttering from the pocket of his Bermuda shorts (he had allergies), but he also commanded an armada of chips and spins that were both devious and accurate. They tended to break up the normal pattern of percussive thumps that echoed over the field. He consistently beat Harmon, who was prone to fits of temper after losing. Now I was across the net. I was sulking.

"Grandpa threw me in," I sniffed.

"Your grandfather doesn't like his grandsons to be chickens. Why do you keep swinging your racket so hard?"

A ball soared against the back fence. I said nothing.

"I suppose you cried?"

I didn't answer that, either. I said, "You told him about Thor."

"That might have slipped out."

Father hit the ball into the net. I could see that I was disappointing him. I wasn't growing up according to plan. There was the hammer, for instance: he had made it, reluctantly, at my request, and now he seemed irritated that I carried it around so much. And there was the way he reacted to tears — they made him nervous. I was sniffling again and when I cried he looked about awkwardly, rolling his eyes, as if he were about to bolt from the scene.

There was a time when I was seven when I had nightmares. He used to come home at 3 A.M. from his job at the newspaper (via the Bulldog Lounge, I later found out) to find me sitting in the kitchen with my back against the dryer. I liked the dryer; when you turned it on it got warm and it vibrated. I also liked my father at these times; his tie was crooked and his breath was fragrant and he told good stories — his imagination seemed to have been unleashed. He also seemed to be more on my side than he usually was. Later, after I began to read comic books and after late-night arguments began to explode frequently in the house, I embellished some of his characters with capes and circular logos. They seemed to represent a magical era and I wanted to protect them.

My father squinted and shook his head. "You're 11 years old, you know," he said.

"Damn," I replied. A ball sailed over the fence.

I decided to apologize to my grandfather by waxing his car. Thor would have gone up to him and said something like, "Thou must forgive me for being a coward and for crying and for calling thee mean," but I couldn't. Grandpa was the real hero, and he inhibited such direct behavior from me. I couldn't bear his disfavor for long, but I preferred oblique approaches to penance. I took the hammer and the Kleenex box and walked down the railroad tracks. I had the Kleenex because I was coming down with a cold. I thought that was fortunate: I could blame it on him for throwing me in the lake. It was valuable ammunition, since our relationship functioned largely on guilt.

The rails were worn smooth and black on top and the pitch lay in sticky patches on the ties and the gravel was warm, for the afternoon had turned hot. The tracks curved slowly ahead of me as I walked, disappearing behind the trees. Grasshoppers erupted from the weeds and here and there I found uprooted spikes near the ditches and pondered them, holding the hammer, before walking on.

"You're a Skoglund, aren't you?" I was fidgeting among the flat discs of car polish in the dim back aisles of the general store.

"No."

"No?"

"My grandfather is."

"Same thing. What's your name?"

"Finch."

"What's the mallet for?"

I shrugged. I wasn't going to answer a personal question like that for a stranger. "Killing mosquitoes," I said. "Pounding railroad spikes."

"Do you read comic books?" I asked Claire.

"No."

Claire was 17 and it was obvious she didn't like to talk to me. I had given up using Thor's comic-book jargon on her; it only made things worse. Just now, she and Harmon were lying on the dock getting suntans. Like most of their activities, this seemed to be serious business that didn't accommodate interruption. The rituals of their romance were mystifying to me and they showed no willingness to explain them.

"My mother's at law school," I said.

"I know where she is."

I paused, having exhausted my shallow reservoir of conversational topics.

"At law school," I reasserted.

Claire scoffed. "In the summer?"

Harmon lifted his head from his arms. He had a sleepy look apparently cultivated by lifeguards from the South. He was a deep brown.

"Shut up," he said lazily to Claire. "You look like a jerk running around with that Kleenex box," he said to me. He was 18 and had large muscles. He stretched them now, as if he were just getting up in the morning. "Why don't you go up the hill and blow your nose?"

"People go to law school because they don't know what else to do with themselves," Grandpa said later, just before dinner. He and my father were drinking beer. I had asked my father about it, but Grandpa was doing the talking. He looked as if the subject pained him. "All over the country, people are deciding they're at loose ends, and they're running away to law school. Ten years from now, they're going to form their own political party. They'll outnumber all the Republicans and Democrats."

"When's she coming back?"

"I don't think she is," my father said.

He said it casually, but Grandpa stopped short. The beer bottle was several inches from his lips. "What did you say that for?" he said.

"It seems to be the idle gossip at this point," Father said. He looked at me with a sympathetic shrug. Then he pulled out his handkerchief and dabbed at his nose. "The kid had probably better get his facts straight."

"What?" I said. "She's never going to get out of law school?"

Grandpa picked me up and put me on his shoulders.

"Put the hammer down," my father said.

"No."

"The thing about gossip," Grandpa said, "is that the people directly involved are usually the last to hear it. You and me, for example."

I was thrilled. Grandpa rarely put us in the same category. Then he pulled the hammer from my grasp; as I clawed in resistance, he threw me in the lake.

"You'd really better be tough now, kid," he said.

While I changed my clothes, sniffling, he and my father were talking. When I came down, Father and I took a long ride in the canoe. We stopped at a little island in the middle of the lake. I was afraid he expected me to go swimming again, but instead we sat on a log and he said that my mother had met a man she liked at law school. She was going to go and stay in his condominium in Phoenix, out west. In fact, she was already there.

"Why does she want to live in a place like that?" I asked. My nose was running again, but there was nothing I could do about it: the canoe had a slow leak and the Kleenex box was floating, half-submerged, beside the paddles.

When we returned, Grandpa was still leaning against the porch railing. He had a steady look in his eyes I hadn't seen before. He was angry at my mother. He was her father and she had apparently done something very bad or, as he put it, "irresponsible."

My father shrugged.

Grandpa rapped the hammer absentmindedly against the railing. In the distance, thunder crackled. I watched warily.

"Have another beer?" my father suggested.

Grandpa looked slowly over the water, which was erupting into ripples from a sudden breeze.

"Why not?" he said.

Later on, with the thunderstorm past and violet clouds flying over the lake, I got to work on the car. It was the kind of blue that glows purple and hot in the sun, and it had a faded Yale University decal on the back window. Grandpa sometimes took us to football games, and we sat high up in the stadium while he watched the patterns unfold on the field below and growled that they weren't "precise" enough. My brother and I worshipped the car; Grandpa casually took it out each afternoon for vegetables. Now the hood was beaded with rain and the wax made dim swirls on the paint. I had to climb onto the fender, rubbing the sticky residue on my pants, to reach the vast dark area beyond the hood ornament. I made several curious swipes on the canvas top before abandoning the effort, half-done, to boredom and a strange sense of satisfaction. In the distance, Thor swung his hammer and rattled the heavens.

Later, in the dripping branches of a fir tree outside Claire's window in the other cottage, I waited, and after a brief period the light came on. She and Harmon had just had an argument on the porch; I had heard them yelling and I wondered if she was crying. I imagined that she would spend a lengthy period in front of the mirror, brushing her hair, but instead she began to remove her clothes, and after a stunned instant I descended the tree and sat on the dock. Strange things were happening to me, I realized after a moment — dark rushes of feeling followed by a physical turbulence I didn't recognize. Evenings as a rule filled me with emptiness. I lacked company, since my brother was at scout camp; and occupation, since my father had maliciously contrived to leave my comic books back home in Connecticut. But now it seemed as if a large chunk of my life had been cut off and was drifting away into the lake. My thoughts wandered in particularly strange directions. I went down to the tracks and climbed the fir tree and wondered if Thor was like the men who had walked down the rail line the week before, clad in orange vests, hammering in the errant spikes, cutting away the bushes near the track. Where did they come from? I imagined him walking the rails at night, alone, flailing with his hammer, his long hair and cape flaring in the wind as he tried to keep the railroad open while the bridges fell and the ties rolled away and new things began to replace them.

The train howled; it was terrifically slow. I shivered in the tree: if there were a magical moment, I felt, it was now; out of such a frightening enterprise I expected to get something, an infusion of superpower that would give me an unfair advantage in life's relentless competitions — or, barring that, a vision of Thor or some form of confrontation with my mother. "What the hell's going on here?" I intended to ask her. Grandpa would put it that way.

The ground vibrated at the base of the tree and the bushes were so starkly illuminated by the engine lights that they lost color. I descended; the train came on, roaring and squeaking, the wheels as high as my thighs, moving at a pedestrian pace and complaining at the irregular rails. The engine spelled itself out, L-A-M-O-I-L-L-E-V-A-L-L-E-Y, and then howled as it approached the road. Now the low, dark, horizontal shapes of the gondola cars jerked past, rocking and screaming, and the train seemed to pause for breath. It emitted a long hiss and then convulsed, sending a shudder that ran from car to car and out of view into the night. I threw the hammer on and climbed up.

In the gondola car there were blocks of granite trussed with cable. I sat on them and saw, looking up, that the stars were visible between the moving borders made by the trees. I rapped the hammer against the stone and mumbled "God of Thunder," "Enraged Asgardian," and other phrases gleaned from the comic books. Nothing happened. The car jerked and swayed and I saw nothing except, in the mist at the far end of the swamp, familiar shapes that were standing, dull and motionless, in the manner of cows. When the train slowed for the crossing by the general store I had had enough.

I rapped the hammer against the rails as the caboose receded. It was a half-hearted effort: my hands stung, but I remained without superpower, devoid of Norse wisdom, and, incidentally, chilly. The walk back was a somber one. The hammer I tossed disconsolately into the swamp. It made a concussive splash in the weeds.

There was motion at the end of the dock; I saw it as I approached the cottage — the swinging beam of a flashlight. My father and grandfather were looking over the water. After a moment I realized they were singing.

219

"We are poor little lambs that have lost their way," they said, "bah, bah, bah." There was a splash as Grandpa dove into the water.

"Backstroke," my father said. "You always crawl. You're some kinda efficiency nut. Want to see an inefficient, uncalibrated backstroke?"

There was another splash. Something glinted and floated in the water.

"Hello?" I called.

"Use to swim relays," Grandpa said. "Four by a hundred."

I sat on the porch. After a while they walked up the bank, sodden and gleaming in their undershorts.

"Grandpa," I said.

Grandpa sang, "Bulldog, bulldog, bow, wow, wow. E — li Yale."

He picked me up, soaking my shirt.

The flashlight swung. Father stopped short. "Holy smoke!" he said. "What happened to your car?"

The car stood in the field, spotted, covered with opaque swirls, inadvertently Jaguarish.

"Sorry," I said after a moment.

Grandpa shrugged. "I hope you're not going to turn into one of those weird artist types," he said.

"I rode on the train," I said softly.

The two of them stopped again.

"What?" my father said. "Are you crazy?"

They looked at each other for a moment, and then Grandpa laughed. "Hell," he said. "I didn't think you had the guts for that."

Living with Lura

·

BY ANNETTE SANFORD

A MOS WONDERED WHAT day, what year the shed fell down. It was true the last time he looked the roof had pitched forward a little, and there might have been a buckling in the west wall, but the framework was definitely standing. Now there was nothing but a pile of kindling topped by a preening catbird.

From the porch of the shack his milky gaze moved toward the fence and fixed on spindly wands of toad's flax waving in Lura's flower bed. Nasturtiums grew there once, and Dutchman's pipe had twined the pickets. In season, zinnias flamed beside red phlox. Mottled masses of calendulas, sweet peas, pansies, and verbena tossed their scents into the wind.

Lura planted by the moon, and everything grew.

The bin in the kitchen was never empty of potatoes. Spring and fall, dandelion greens simmered in a kettle on the stove beside carrots bursting orange and cabbage laced with green onion tips and a spoonful of sugar, to be certain — she told him — that afterward they didn't bloat.

Green beans, sauerkraut, beets, and corn gleamed in jars along the storeroom shelves. On the back porch dangled strings of peppers, garlic, and onions drying; and boxes on the floor were liable to hold on any summer day tomatoes, cucumbers, bell peppers, okra, and yellow squash all jumbled together, waiting to get the grit rinsed off.

She was a gardener that woman. And a fisherman, too.

How long had it been since he'd set his teeth in the flank of a big river hornpout? By doggies, hadn't she dragged those bullies up out of that muddy water though? And all before breakfast, too.

Amos had a quick picture of her, coming up through the weeds from the river, the sun behind her, and three or four slick-bellied fish flopping on a stringer, her face red and sweaty, her boots caked with mud. He supposed she was fat by then, but he never thought of her that way.

In his mind she stayed the cow-eyed splinter of a girl her pa said nobody'd ever in his right senses marry. Not unless they were hankering for a whittled-off witch instead of a wife. Goddam old fool.

Silas Brame — the biggest rogue in Webster county. He'd cut more throats than a meat market butcher. A good number of them at the domino table, a-chewing and a-drinking.

One time he'd took a spell and fallen right out of his chair at Stella's Beer and Game Palace, smack on the floor, his eyes walled back and tobacco juice spilling over his cheek like worm's blood.

"Heart attack!" somebody hollered, and the ambulance backed up to the door and hauled him off to the hospital.

"Drunk," the doctor said, but they kept him a week anyhow, just for spite.

Old nickel-milker. Wouldn't even give Lura a wedding. Only a dollar bill, all dirty, and a piece of sour advice. *Don't do it.*

She did anyway.

Amos was paying on a flatbed truck he used for hauling wood when the spirit moved him, and they ran off in that. Not very fast. It wouldn't go but 30. But it got them to the preacher and then the 10 miles across the river to the shack by nightfall.

Lura wouldn't put a foot inside until Amos chased out half a dozen alley cats from under the kitchen table. They left behind a rabbit they'd dragged from the field, and he chucked that out too, right past her nose just as she was coming through the front door in her peach-colored wedding suit.

He'd known in his soul she'd go home then. She ran back out on the porch and threw her head over the banister. But after a time she got all right — maybe she thought of Silas — and came back in, white-faced and furious.

Did she tear into *him!*

Who did he think he was anyway, bringing her to such filth? Animals! In her kitchen! And one of 'em dead!

"Git a mop! Git a broom!"

"It's our wedding night!"

"And you'll spend it in a clean house or yonder in the shed!"

They finished sweeping out somewhere around four in the morning. She even made him light a fire under the washpot in the backyard, and in the moonlight they boiled every piece of cloth in the house, from the sheets to his underbritches, and hung them to dry on low-bending oak limbs.

And still they ended up sleeping in the shed.

There'd been mice in the mattress.

"There's mice a-plenty out here!" he'd yelled because he was fighting mad himself by that time and wondering what in hell he'd got into.

"In a *shed* it's all right!" she screamed back, and they went to sleep in their clothes and didn't wake up till 10 in the morning.

Right away she commenced again, sending him around the house with a galvanized pail and newspapers soaked in kerosene to put a sparkle on the windows. After that he had to scrub the wood floor and haul out the mattress and burn it, and then if she didn't make him paint the kitchen shelves with the blue he'd bought for the truck fenders.

About mid-afternoon, they had breakfast in the yard under the crab-apple tree, blooming so pinky sweet it sickened him. He'd been ready to faint by then, but she was going strong, poking over the coals left from last night's washing and frying up bacon and eggs like it was six in the morning. Singing even.

"When we gonna rest?" he said when his watch hand got to five.

At that she stopped, lifted her head from the pot she was scrubbing, and smiled all at once like the sun coming up. "After we bathe."

She took him off by the hand then, down through the burdock and the Queen Anne's lace and the blackberry bushes crowding the river path. There were white butterflies, it seemed now, dancing on the milkweed blooms, and up in the sky maybe a hawk wheeling around like a slow spinning top.

They swam naked.

There was no mud in the river then, no log jams, or — further down — the government dam. Just clear, moving water, cold around their shoulders. Afterward, on a bed of sand and wild violet leaves, she gave to him with joyous laughter her cool body and her kisses.

She took a shiftless rascal and made a man of him, Silas Brame told his cronies.

Amos guessed it was true. God knows he didn't have a dime or a white shirt or a pocket handkerchief even. He'd been living in that cabin so long by himself, eating out of tin cans and laying his ear on the radio at night when he couldn't stand the silence, he'd forgot how it was to have another human being around.

She got on his nerves for a while. He wanted to get off by himself, and he did, saying he was going to shred weeds or out to chop bull nettle. Anything, so she wouldn't come along.

She sat on the porch and watched him go. He wondered now if she cried. If she had, she never showed it. When he came home, supper was ready, or there was bread rising, or she was lying on the bed in her petticoat, smelling like lavender water.

After a time he got to liking steady work. Clean sheets, good food. He got to caring if the hinges on the doors squeaked or the window ropes broke. He fixed the sag in the gate and plowed up the garden and learned to scrape his shoes before he came inside.

They had a baby.

The river was so high the bridge was covered. They couldn't get to town. Lura gave birth on the kitchen table. The same one the cats had huddled under when they gnawed the leg off the rabbit.

Tears ran down her face like sweat and soaked into the newspaper under her head. To Amos it seemed she was breathing tears instead of air, but nothing looked the way it was. The walls swayed, and the windows opened their mouths and screamed. The light bulb dangling in the space above their heads stared down like an angry eye, unblinking.

Amos had birthed a calf once. The heifer was blind. She'd fallen in a hole and broken her leg. He couldn't get her out before the calf came, so he stayed and brought the bawling, slimy thing forth into his lap. And now it was his son.

Dead, of course. Amos knew that as soon as he saw the cord circled tight under the child's chin and the little purple face, but he couldn't tell Lura, she was bleeding so.

Finally she knew anyway. There was no crying, and she raised up on her elbow and saw the baby where Amos had wrapped him in a dish towel and laid him on the drainboard.

She was different after that, but Amos didn't notice for a good long time. He looked up one day and saw she rarely combed her hair anymore or put on a dress. She slopped about the house in rubber boots and worn-out jeans, and most of the time she was dirty.

He hated her then for teaching him to be different from the way he used to be and to care about it. He wished she'd stayed with Silas in his unpainted house and left him to himself.

They screamed at each other, and he cursed her, but he never hit her.

A lot of men would have, he told her, but she only looked at him with those big, wide cow eyes, and he kept remembering the river bank with green violet leaves under her shoulders, and he wanted to cry.

She got better.

When spring came around again, he came home one afternoon, and she was down on her knees planting flower seeds. She'd walked out to the road and hitched a ride into town with a neighbor to buy them. Sweet William, they were. Little seeds, like pepper.

He'd gone into the house with a sigh, thinking nothing would come of that except another disappointment, but he was wrong. The plants sprang up thick as winter grass and bloomed and bloomed. Pink. Red, so deep it was black. Rose and white stripes, solid cerise, velvety maroon.

They got dressed up. He put a blossom in his buttonhole, and they went to church where they hadn't been since the baby was buried. Lura got religion that day. After that, they wore ruts in the road running into church every time the bell rang, but he didn't give a damn. She was back to like she was, and life became a sweet melon, full of juice running down his chin.

That June they had the baptizing in the river below the house. Lura went under, and seven more too, one an old lady with whiskers and long white hair that swam along behind her like snake ghosts.

"It ain't never too late!" she told Amos when she raised up out of the water, her dress plastered against her bones and her old woman's breasts showing through like dried apples.

Amos thought it would take a heap more than a promise of heaven to make him crawl out of that river wringing wet with everybody bellowing on the bank, and he went off with his hands in his pockets and had a little whiskey from a cough syrup bottle round back of the house.

There was dinner on the ground. Piles of fried chicken, potato salad, cucumbers and onions in vinegar, tapioca pudding colored pink and yellow and Paris green.

Lura went around shining like a candle was lit inside her, and Amos got scared thinking maybe she was changing into something he couldn't ever catch again. As quick as everybody was gone, he snatched her up and packed her into the house, just to make sure.

A long time went by.

They passed through happiness and came blinking out on the other side, contented. Lura spread. Through her hips, in her breasts. Amos grew a little belly that lapped over his belt and got in the way when he tied his shoes.

225

Lura made him tithe, and he found out what the Bible said was true. The money kept a-coming. Lura laid a wool rug on the living room floor and bought a butane cooking stove. Amos owned a pinstriped suit for both the seasons, and they got a truck that nearly always ran.

Then a bad thing happened.

Silas Brame came to live wth them.

The damned old fool was three-fourths blind and meaner than a sack of bobcats. He got the bedroom, and they took the sleeping porch. He got the chair by the radio and the footstool.

He talked all the time, balls of saliva shooting from his mouth like popcorn and lodging in the whisker scraggle on his chin.

Everywhere Amos went in the house, Silas was there first. Or his voice was. The sound reminded Amos of a shovel blade scraping flint rock. Worse was the whisper of his felt slippers following each other through the rooms like two old moles trapped in sunlight.

The best thing, Amos decided, was to keep him drunk. Except Lura didn't like it. Finally one day Amos took him to the doctor, and when they came back they had a new medicine, clear like drinking water, that Amos said might make her father kind of drowsy and thick-tongued and maybe a little crazy.

Sure enough, it did.

Amos doled it out privately from a bigger bottle in the shed, and after that, Silas didn't give a hang about the radio or which chair he sat in or where he fell asleep. He and Amos got cordial and even took to playing dominos with a set Amos hammered full of filed-off tacks so Silas could count the spots with his dry, yellow fingertips.

Just when it began to seem the old coot might last forever, like those two-headed pigs pickled in glass jars for carnival sideshows, he died, sitting straight up in his chair in the middle of the Grand Old Opry.

Lura took his going plenty hard. He hadn't confessed his Savior, so there wasn't a hair of hope they'd ever see him again, a hardship Amos raised a glass to, out in the shed, all by himself.

They began stepping out some then. Lura liked county fairs. She won blue ribbons on her potted plants and enjoyed sitting in the shade of the livestock barns gossiping with the country ladies while lambs bleated in the background.

Sometimes they rode as far as 30 miles to Putney just to look at the store windows and have a dish of ice cream. One March Saturday Lura bought a straw hat with a veil that came down over her face and made her look like an owl peeping out of a navy blue cage, but Amos didn't tell her

226

so and paid for it with a couple of five dollar bills the same as if he used them all the time for lighting up cigars.

In winter when the work was slow, they sat by the window piecing jigsaw puzzles on a sheet of plywood, or else, in the middle of the day, lay in bed wrapped together in a crazy quilt, kissing like kids.

Sometimes they crawled in the truck and rode slowly along the lanes, staring out at the lonesome houses of the country people, refrigerators on the front porches and swing chairs knotted high against the north wind.

Winter grasses of gray, beige, brown and russet spiked the roadside ditches. Hawks wheeled above; crows perched in skeletons of trees, black against the pearl sky. From time to time Amos pointed out stubbled cornfields frothed with flocks of geese.

Then it was summer. Winter. Summer again. Amos caught hot-weather flu and coughed for a month. Lura buried a fishhook in the palm of her hand, and the doctor had to cut it out.

They raised a flock of chickens that dressed out 40 hens. Taxes on the land went up. Lura put a black rinse on her hair. Amos called her a crow, but as soon as the roots grew out gray again, he bought her another bottle of Princess Mary Renewer and set it on the shelf above the bathroom sink.

A man in a white Cadillac offered them $200 an acre for their land along the river. They laughed. Afterward, they took the path through the Queen Anne's lace and the blackberries and saw that there were violets growing still, a deep sweet green, on the bank above the water.

All of a sudden Lura was sick.

A knot like a hen egg came up in her breast. Under her arm an abscess opened and didn't heal. It gave her a fever. Every day they stood by the window, and Lura raised her arm while Amos held a mirror, and they looked at it in the sunlight.

"Go to the doctor."

"No."

"Why not?" But he knew. If no one said it wouldn't, there was still a chance it might get well.

They made poultices out of comfrey roots, and Lura tied them to her with a worn-out stocking. She lost her appetite and grew thin as a girl.

She died.

At her funeral, three women Amos didn't know and a boy in a black-checked suit named Lawrence sang a song about the sunset. Forget-me-nots were blooming by the baby's headstone, and a red-headed lady in a polka dot dress cried.

227

For a while, Amos went on talking to Lura. He set two places at the table and served up her plate. He slept on his side of the bed.

The church people came out. When they saw what he was doing, they made arrangements to get him into the Autumn Leaves Care Center. The government would pay for it, they said.

Amos let them talk because they had bought a silver bowl and put Lura's name on it and set it in the church to hold Sunday flowers, but when they rode up to get him, he held tight to the door facing, and they went away without him.

Once he thought he saw a woman down by the river.

"Lura?"

He followed after her, and while she fished, he sat down to wait under a sassafras tree. When he woke up it was sundown and ants were crawling over his feet and mosquitos big as horses were biting his chin.

"Goddam old fool," he said.

He let the cats come back. One at first, then three and four. They curled up on the windowsills and licked their fur on the kitchen table. Mice got back in the mattress.

In the afternoon he sat in the shadows on the porch and looked over his property. He guessed there wasn't much he hadn't had. A son. But he got over that.

Right after Lura died he worried that maybe they'd missed a lot, but when he tried to think what, he only saw the two of them laughing in the ice cream parlor in Putney, or he smelled the lavender between Lura's breasts or heard the cry of geese.

Still, there was one thing.

If he could have caught a-hold of time. If every now and then he could have held it still with his thumb on its throat, just to feel it quiver, to watch that blue-black vein fill up along its temple and see its heart jump scared and foolish beneath skin thin as any tree frog's. There'd be a sweetness in that. One melons couldn't give. And he'd know for once and all just when it was the shed fell down.

Out from
Narragansett Bay

•

BY M. GARRETT BAUMAN

T HE BLACK MAN WAS the luckiest person in the boat. After an hour he had two bass and two weakfish. My younger brother Bobby and I had caught a medium-large flounder. Although Bobby hooked it, our lines tangled and we pulled it in together, our father saying that by the traditions of fishing it belonged to both of us. Later Bobby wobbled to the main hatch to lie down. Seasick. Yellow, flopping like the fish in the bucket beside him. I was sick my first times out, too. There's something about the emptiness. But you get over it if you keep going out.

The black man rented his gear, didn't even carry a burlap bag for his catch when he jumped aboard as we cast off the dock. His fish swung from the deck cover of the 30-foot boat, strung under the jaws with a few feet of line he cut with my knife.

Everyone else was jealous, especially my father, who uses three types of shiner spoons and unwinds his reel the night before a trip to check for snags. Two hundred feet of line spun into the living room like a spider gone beserk. Mother says he rechecks it because he's an accountant.

When the black man returned my knife, he thanked me and asked if he could borrow it again. I nodded. One of his strung-up fish was still alive; it swatted the mate's hat as he backed from the wheelhouse. The mate turned, man and fish eye to eye. I laughed.

"You want to keep them wet," the mate told the black man.

"Nah. I like to look at them."

229

I caught a stingray. Twenty inches of brown tail churned the surface, then the broad, flat fins rose like vampire wings. The black man reached over the side and lifted the line until the ray cleared the water.

"Watch out," my father said, "the tail's full of poison."

The black man laughed. "This here baby? Shoot! Give me a manta ray before *I* look out." There was a picture in my *Guidebook to Fishes.* A 30-foot manta ray, its wings pointed like the devil's, flapped half out of the water toward two fishermen cowering in a rowboat. Several times as a child I heard it rattle my bedroom window, and I knew it wanted to cover me with its dark mantle.

My father said to forget hooks and leader, just cut the line and drop the ray back. I protested. I wanted to carry it home in triumph, stuff it. Eat it, if need be. "Stingrays aren't edible," my father said.

The ray spun on the line, belly white, back brown with green speckles. Two fish in one. Its tail lashed the hull. "Aw, you can eat the wing tips," the black man said grinning. "Some folk call them nigger fillets." He whacked the fish against the side of the boat to free it. The ray turned green under water and spiraled down. The hook returned with white flesh on it.

After a few more stops other people began catching fish too, although the black man's string grew fastest. We still counted on our flounder to win the prize over his big bass. My father whispered to make sure we kept our fish wet so it wouldn't dehydrate and lose weight. He winked shrewdly, nodding toward our neighbor's fish, hung out like laundry in the breeze.

At dawn that morning when we came around the last bit of jetty at the end of Narragansett Bay, the ocean throttled into us. The boat smacked the waves, sending achingly cold puffs of mist over the bow. Next to me the black man's bare head glistened with beads of sea spray. "We're paying for this!" he shouted. I laughed.

My father leaned close. "Don't be scared."

"I'm not!"

Porpoises accompanied the boat a few miles beyond the riptides. Soft and brown, they suddenly appeared, puffing spray 10 feet away, diving over and under waves. My father said they were racing us. I asked if they'd eat people.

"No, porpoises are warm-blooded, like us."

"So what?" said the black man.

"They chase sharks from men in the water. Push you to shore. If the boat sinks, pray for porpoises."

"Trust those Charlies?" the black man said. "Sure, they'll stomp on sand sharks. But not big daddy white sharks! No sir! Porpoises save their own selves. Ain't one for miles. Saw a bunch of those white sharks tear up a tuna once off North Carolina. Bit each other's tails getting to the meat. Chewed up a gaff I stuck in them — just splinters come back. Bam! Bam! They go for the tuna, each other. Don't make *no* difference. Turn on their backs, choke down hunks big as bait buckets. Stomachs must be full of little sharks, they get so hungry."

"Well," my father said, "I heard porpoises — "

"Heard? Man, white sharks smell blood *through* skin. Everybody's meat to them. Porpoises ain't stupid."

The lady on the other side of the black man caught a blowfish — puffy, mumpy-mouthed with yellow sides and a white belly pimpled like a brand-new basketball. "Chicken-of-the-Sea," my father said.

"They're poison," the black man grunted, pulling it in for the lady. She wore knee boots and a slicker. Her husband was drinking beer in the stern with friends.

"It's a fish!" she said, wrinkling her nose. The black man asked if she wanted it. She glanced up at his string of starched-stiff fish and said, "What do you think?" The black man shrugged.

"Ought to blow him up like a volleyball," my father said. The black man grinned, then pulled loose the hook with a crunch. He held the fish behind the gills so its eyes bulged. Then he turned it belly-up and scratched the white underside with the hook. "That's it," my father said. "Tickle him."

The blowfish swelled, but not like a volleyball. The woman asked her husband what she should do with the fish. He waved it over the side, and the black man tossed it in. It floated over one wave but didn't come up the next. "Will it die?" I asked the black man.

"Nah."

The boat stocked chocolate Yoo-Hoo with Yogi Berra's picture on it, and ham and Swiss sandwiches. I used to look forward to the Yoo-Hoo as much as the fishing. My father bought Bobby a bottle, too, "to be fair." He boasted about treating us exactly equal, so we'd have the same chances in life. After my bottle was drained, I sidled up to Bobby, asking if I could have his. His cheeks puffed as he pushed it to me.

"Don't look over the rail," my father had preached. "Keep your eyes on the horizon, and you won't get sick." Each year he faithfully dispensed seasick pills at the wharf from the tiny blue box with lacy foil. They were thick and pasty, and we usually coaxed a soda from him to wash them down. They never did me any good. You stop being sick when you're ready. Pills can't help.

As we reached open sea, I learned to fix my eyes on the gray mist where ocean joined sky. After a few miles sea and sky blurred, and my vision wandered to nearer swells. But even when deliberately staring into the boiling foam next to the boat, I felt fine. Bobby, meanwhile, fastened his eyes on an undulating swell that had accompanied the boat since it left the bay. She rolled 20 feet to the side and rear, and his eyes rocked to her spindrift lullaby. Body and eyes weaved to different rhythms. Once I told him not to look, but then remembered that if he got sick I'd watch his pole as well as mine. The year before I'd caught two porgies on his line. Watch the wave, Bobby. Pretty wave. Green and blue, white foam like an embroidered pillow. Rest, Bobby. Then I searched the horizon for whale spouts among the scudding mists.

"Is it almost over?" Bobby groaned.

My father comforted him, leaving three lines to me. Three chances. So far the black man had six fish to our three, not counting my ray. It didn't seem fair. My father had built up our gear for years, while the black man just rented his.

"Up lines!" the mate yelled, clanging the bell. I reeled the baits furiously so none would snag in the propeller when the engine started. The black man assisted me. I stacked the poles against the railing, but the hooks and sinkers swung in and out precariously with the rocking. He showed me how to hang them so they no longer flicked in our faces, then told a story about a man who had a flying hook catch in his nostril. When the man jerked away, the barb sank in. "I told the mate to throw him overboard for a lure and see what we'd catch!"

As the captain searched for a new spot, we overheard the mate explain how they used radar to locate shipwrecks where fish gather. "Shoot!" snorted the black man.

A few times he peered over the side, shaking his head in disgust as the boat passed. When I asked what he saw, he told me, "A subway full of fish — at rush hour."

"How do you know?"

"The man knows," he whispered, tapping his temple. Then he grinned so I didn't know if he was teasing me. "But I ain't telling my secrets, boy." My father was bringing Bobby back from the toilet. Bobby shuffled heavily like an old woman. The black man stared at me with cold scrutiny. I tried to stare back but couldn't. Instead I watched a broken white pimple on his cheek. He must have picked it.

232

"You fish a lot?" I asked finally.

He grinned and turned to admire his catch. Most were already brittle. Flies scurried over one like pirates with more booty than they could bury. "Not a lot in the ocean anymore," he said.

My father overheard us as he climbed over the bench. "Fresh-water man, eh? Casting? Where do you go — Maine? Hudson?"

"Suburbs," the black man said.

By the next stop the woman who caught the blowfish had joined Bobby on the hatch. "Looks like we caught more people than fish!" my father chortled. All lines slanted under the boat, as though connected to one fish. A dozen people reeled in as soon as sinkers bounced on the bottom. Sea robins — mulatto brown with broad, bony heads and slender bodies. Just behind the head, wide, winglike fins. The black man held his robin on the railing. The fish spread its fins and seemed to glance around to see where it was. Fish eyes are usually cold and empty, but sea robins' eyes are blue.

The black man asked for my knife, grumbling to the fish, "You think you're a pretty boy, don't you? Blue eyes and wings! Who you trying to be, a flying fish?"

"They fly hundreds of feet," my father said.

"Where'd you hear that?"

"The boy's grandpa — "

"Shoot! This thing don't fly — jump a little maybe. These wings can't fly him down a slide." He yanked one fin up and down as if to make the fish fly. "I saw real flying fish once. On the way to Korea in '52. It was night. They come skimming over the water, two, three feet up mostly. Shining silver with the moon. Just glowing! Little silver spray trailed after them where their tails cut waves. Then thump! thump! they bang the ship — sounded like bullets there were so many. Must have lasted five minutes. Hundreds of them."

He paused, eyes far away. "Spooked me for days. Going to Korea. But this robin ain't like those. You just a bottom fish, ain't you? No silver." He bounced the point of my knife lightly on the sea robin's head until finding the crease between bones. Then he pressed down. The robin opened its mouth, and the black man plucked out the hook. Then he pressed harder. The fish made a gasping cry, like a frog croaking. Its eyes strained. The black man hammered the handle with the butt of his hand, and the fish cried again. "That's why they're robins," the black man said, "'cause they sing. You got to squeeze the music out of them; they hold it in, in the water." Although the robin's wings flashed out and back, it could

233

not take off. One wing nicked the black man's hand. "Stupid garbage fish." He pounded the blade all the way through. The robin still fluttered and cried. When he flipped it overboard off my knife, I could breathe again.

My father explained that the sea robins' great schools drive out bass and flounder. "Moochers of the sea," he said, eyeing the black man. He said they were voracious and no good to eat, that no fishermen like them. But the captain stayed at that place until everyone had caught at least one. My father said we mustn't count sea robins when announcing our catch. "Just say, 'I got two bass and some robins.'"

"What about my stingray?"

"Oh, sure, you can count that."

The black man caught two more robins and did the same thing to them. Someone else tried it but cut himself. The fish all cried. When the black man was done, he handed back my knife politely. I looked for traces of gore, but there were none. I wiped it anyway. The black man smiled and glanced at my father.

When the black man moved away, I told my father I did not want him to knife fish. He told me it was none of our business, that we'd show him when we won the pot. I said the pot didn't matter. "He shouldn't torture them." My father looked at me strangely.

When the black man returned, I told him I didn't want him to torture the sea robins. My father grabbed my shoulder and ordered me to apologize. The black man grinned and squeezed my other shoulder so I was trapped between them.

"That's all right," he said to my father. "The boy's got a right to say it, seeing I borrowed his knife. And he's right, too." Then he bent to me and said in a growly voice, "Once in a while, boy, there's a knife jammed up my back. My-oh-my! I hustle for the docks to find me some fish belly." His teeth flashed nearer. "The man says to waste garbage fish, right? Didn't I waste slants for him in Korea? 'Go for the belly and neck,' the sergeant says. 'Rip up those slants! Rip 'em up, nigger!'" He laughed sharply then snapped it off, leaning so close I felt the heat of his breath. "See, boy, next to that, what's a few blue-eyed robins matter?" His hand dug hard into me, although I don't think I knew until afterward that he'd hurt me.

My father touched my side. The two men stared at each other over my head. I couldn't see my father, but the black man grinned like Davy Crockett when he killed the bear. There was immense quiet, only the slapping of the hull on the water as the waves dropped away. The silence lay around us like a huge pillow, the rachet noises of the other fishermen's reels, their voices, little lost sounds the silence rolled into itself without a ripple.

Suddenly I was dizzy. Seasick? I glanced at Bobby, sighing on the hatch like a fish that has given up. If the men hadn't held me, I might have fallen. I imagined serpentining brown porpoises — will they chase sharks? The stingray spinning brown and white. Sea robins croaking, wings beseeching me. The broken pimples on the blowfish's belly, the one on the black man's cheek. Squid. Chocolate Yoo-Hoo. The manta ray. Silver fish flying. Did he stab anyone in Korea? Bait and fishermen, lines and hooks, sharks, fins. My stomach rolled like a cresting comber about to surge when the black man said to my father, "It's all right sticking a few robins, ain't it?"

The wave in my stomach receded. My father's hands quivered; it was his moment. He clenched my side and shoulder, then went limp and said quietly, "That's your business."

Then he let go of me.

Returning to Narragansett Bay, we threw the leftover bait to the gulls. My father refilled his dish just as the mate began stowing bait buckets. Bobby staggered to the bench to participate. Last time he hadn't gotten sea legs until reaching breakwater. Each time you go farther.

Gulls rarely miss. We threw bait as far as we could, but they always seemed to snap it up before it hit water. The black man told us to throw low, into the trough of a wave so the crest would dunk the birds.

After we emptied the bait dishes, the black man asked for my knife. I stared into his neutral brown eyes, waiting. He asked again. My father breathed loudly behind me. I wanted to ask what he was thinking, but the black man repeated his request. I extended the knife. The black man smiled and said thank you, then unhooked his fish and gutted the smaller ones. The big bass looked fatter than I realized — seven or eight pounds at least. He hefted it by the gills, inspecting, then looked at me just until our eyes met. He laid the big fish on the bench and slit his belly.

"What about the pot?" I said to him.

"You ain't supposed to remind me," the black man whispered.

"Don't you want to win?"

"Sometimes not so much." He scooped the insides and flicked them over the rail. The gulls pounced on the floating mass and dropped astern.

The mate weighed our flounder against the biggest fish from the other side of the boat. "They tie," he said. My father squinted at the scale, then reluctantly agreed. The mate asked the black man if he wanted to try his.

"No."

When the captain divided the pot, we got $9.50. "That's two out of three years we won, fellows," my father announced too loudly. The black man was severing heads and tails. My father said it again.

"We were lucky," I said.

"What!" my father protested. "We prepared. We outfished the whole boat, even your friend here." He cannot stand someone not acknowledging his accomplishments. I didn't understand the black man. He could have sliced my father up with a few words, but he only bent over his maimed fish. Did my father really think he won? Didn't he see? The black man seemed so indifferent. I would have screamed at my father if I were him, I thought. I never would have cut up my big fish in the first place. But he did nothing except pare the bass. Just once he glanced up at me as though to say something. But he didn't speak. Was it up to me?

Finally I whispered to my father, "He *let* us win. His bass was at least two pounds heavier than — "

"Nuts!" my father shouted. Although I tried to hush him, he would not whisper back, "He knew he was beat — that's why he didn't try. Maybe he wasn't in the pot. Somebody wasn't, or we'd have won $10 even. I counted 20 people aboard." The black man didn't even lose his slicing rhythm. The green ticket from the pot stuck in his shirt pocket.

A few minutes later the black man dropped several handfuls of chopped fish into my bait dish, telling me to throw it to the gulls, whose gray-white bottoms still hovered hopefully 15 feet overhead. I hesitated. How stupid killing fish to play a game with birds! I have always felt guilty on the ride in. "Go ahead," the black man coaxed. "They're dead now anyway. I'll teach you to work the gulls my way." I avoided looking closely at the pieces, not wanting to face an accusing eye. I tossed them up, the gulls snapping voraciously: fins, tails, muscle alike. Sharks of the sky. I passed a few pieces to Bobby. My father sat sullenly turned away, refusing the gift.

He put on his tan cap with crossed anchors on the brim. Mother bought it so he wouldn't get sunburned, his skin is so fair. He pulled it deep over his face so he was shadowed and grim, then recounted our prize money and folded it away, intent on preserving the victory. I didn't worry about him; I knew he'd want to try again next year.

"Behind those two," the black man said. "Hard! Now under that one. Make them twist. Make them hustle. There! See him? You're learning." His voice was soft, soothing, and I wondered if that was how porpoises spoke.

236

Rue

•

BY SUSAN M. DODD

MISS RAINEY ROTH, of Wyoming, Rhode Island, did not believe in luck. Sixty-one years old, a self-sufficient woman
with a business of her own, she had no time for hazy notions.
People who believed in sudden strokes of good fortune, she thought, were
simply seeking an excuse for idleness.

This sensible attitude was not the least bit undermined or shaken
when, on the 15th of September, Rainey discovered she had won $10,000
in the state lottery. She became a winner (the word seemed remarkably
foolish, applied to herself) not through luck, but through carelessness:
someone had dropped the ticket on the path to her small herb and spice
shop. Rainey had never bought a lottery ticket in her life, and she wasn't
sure whether her practical nature or her whimsical streak prompted her to
save the numbered stub, to check it against the winning numbers announced in the paper a few days later. Either way, she was sure of one
thing: she wasn't about to let the benefits of a rather silly accident alter her
realistic outlook. Luck, indeed. Luck was largely a matter of paying
attention.

Rainey was accustomed to making decisions. She rarely sought advice, but made up her mind with an almost savage authority. On the day
her winnings were confirmed, she remained in the potting shed behind her
house, where she put up flavored vinegars and scented toilet water, pot-
pourris and pomander balls. The scents from the drying sheaves of laven-

der and comfrey and sweet basil cleared her head. By late afternoon she knew precisely what she was going to do with the $10,000 that had fallen so peculiarly into her lap.

The private investigator's office was in a nondescript six-story building in downtown Providence, within sight of the state capitol. After checking the directory in the dim, narrow lobby, Rainey took the stairs to the third floor. At the top of the stairs, she followed a sign shaped like a pointing hand: "Franklin R. Alfino, Room 302." It relieved her that the nature of Mr. Alfino's services was not specified on the sign or his door. She thought this boded well for his discretion.

Its door ajar, Room 302 was just that — a room. Perhaps 15 feet square, windowless, uncarpeted. It contained one desk (gray metal), three file cabinets (one oak, two green metal), a small black safe, and a man in shirtsleeves who looked nearly as old as she was.

"I beg your pardon, I should have knocked," she said.

The man looked up slowly from the newspaper spread across his desk. "No problem. Mrs. Roth?"

"Miss."

The man smiled. "Miss Roth. Come on in." He waved casually toward a rickety folding chair beside his desk. "Have a seat." He did not rise or fold his newspaper. "What can I do for you?"

Rainey occupied the chair gingerly and with the utmost reluctance. She could already see she had made a mistake. The man was nothing like what she had imagined. A private investigator should, to her way of thinking, look alert, energetic . . . perhaps a bit sly. Franklin Alfino looked innocent and slothful. His narrow shoulders seemed pulled down by a center of gravity located in his soft, round belly. He had very little chin, no hair to speak of, and his brown eyes, too close together, looked sleepy. He reminded her of a Rhode Island Red laying hen. She was hardly surprised when he cackled.

"Don't like my looks, huh?" He leaned back in his swivel chair and stretched, exposing a rumpled shirttail. "That's the chance you take with the Yellow Pages."

"I beg your pardon?"

"Isn't that how you found me — the Yellow Pages?"

"In fact it is," Rainey said.

"Figures." Alfino nodded. "Started with the A's, right?"

Rainey felt herself flushing, as if she were caught in some ill-considered fib.

"Don't tell me Paulie Abrams is all booked up?"

"I think perhaps . . . "

"Looks aren't everything," Alfino said. "Let me tell you something — free advice." He was grinning, which made him look a good deal less sleepy. "There's 16 of us — private eyes — in Providence. Another five in Warwick. I know all these guys, and you can take my word for it — none of 'em looks much better than I do. Fact is, you could do worse."

Rainey said nothing, a doubtful and worried crease in her forehead. Finally, while Franklin Alfino continued to stare at her, she smiled. "Pretty is as pretty does," she said.

The detective cackled. "So what can I do for you, good lady?"

"I wish to locate my husband," Rainey said.

"I thought you said it was 'Miss.' "

"I prefer it. My husband and I have been . . . estranged for some time."

"Okay. . . Miss. What happens then — when I find him, I mean?"

"I would like you to make whatever arrangements are necessary for him to divorce me."

"You want to get divorced?"

"I want," Rainey said, calmly and distinctly, "for *him* to divorce *me*."

"But — "

"I am willing to pay."

Alfino shrugged. "Whatever you say. Name?"

"Lorraine Elizabeth Roth."

"His, I mean."

"John Amos Dudley."

Franklin Alfino scribbled in the margin of his newspaper with a ball-point pen. Without looking up, he asked in a monotone, "When and where, to the best of your knowledge, was Mr. Amos last seen?"

"*Dudley,*" Rainey sighed. "Commander Dudley. Point Judith Pier. He sailed for Block Island. The bluefish were running. He never came back."

"So he may have drowned?"

"He did nothing of the kind."

"How do you know?"

"Because he wrote and told me so. A postcard. Of the Watch Hill carousel."

"Have you got this card?"

"Certainly not."

"Don't suppose it'd help much, anyway. He tell you where he was going?"

" 'Where the spirit moved him,' he said." Rainey saw Alfino suppress a smile. "Even *I* had to be somewhat amused, Mr. Alfino."

Looking sheepish, the detective asked, "Why don't you call me Frank?"

"I'd rather not."

"I'm sorry?"

"Nothing to be sorry about," Rainey said firmly. "I am simply not one for informality in business dealings."

Alfino studied her, and she saw she had been mistaken: his eyes were as alert as a chicken hawk's.

"Back to business, then . . . Miss Roth. When did you receive this card?"

"I believe it was the first of July," Rainey said.

"Postmarked — "

"The first of July 1943."

Franklin Alfino rubbed his eyes with his knuckles, as if he'd had cold water thrown in his face. "Ho, boy. . . " he said.

"*You* can divorce *him,*" Franklin Alfino told her after a full minute. "Much simpler."

"So I understand. That is not, however, what I want."

Alfino sighed. "Have it your way."

"I intend to," Rainey replied. She did not leave until she had answered all the detective's questions and written him a check as a retainer.

Ten days later, Rainey was arranging bittersweet and marsh grasses in lacquered Chinese baskets when she heard a car coming up the drive. Footsteps scattered gravel on the path outside. She glanced through the small window and saw Franklin Alfino approaching the shop. She went out.

"You've found him?"

"Nothing yet. Sorry."

Rainey tried to keep impatience from her tone. "What is it, then?"

"Had to come out this way, your neck of the woods. How about some lunch?"

"You want me to give you lunch?" she asked faintly.

Alfino tossed back his head and laughed, scaring off a squirrel from some nearby shrubbery. "I want to *take* you to lunch. There's a little tavern not far . . . near Exeter. How about it?"

Rainey's usual lunch was a cup of sassafras or chamomile tea with saltines or a slice of buttered bread, and she frequently forgot to have that until three o'clock.

"Best cheeseburgers in Rhode Island. Chowder's homemade."

"I look a fright."

"Take off that smock thing and I wouldn't mind being seen with you. Besides, I want to talk to you. Business," he said.

He drove more like a tourist than a detective — slow, aimless, his concentration adequate but sporadic. Rainey leaned back and looked out the window, waiting for him to speak. He did not. When he pulled up in front of the roadhouse — a place she had never visited, but assumed disreputable — she regretted the ride was over. The leaves were beginning to turn, and she realized that she always worked so hard at this time of the year that she scarcely had time to notice the colors of the season.

The Hilltop Tavern was as dilapidated inside as its exterior promised. The air was stale, smelling of beer, tobacco, cooking fat. Several men in work clothes sat at the bar, drinking and staring at a television screen high in a corner. Alfino led her to a booth in the opposite corner of the room, and she chose the side of the table that placed her back to the television.

"Place doesn't look like much, does it?" Alfino said. The remark was offhand, but she got the feeling he was trying to gauge her reaction. She paused, pursing her lips.

"Pretty is as pretty does," she said at last.

The detective grinned. "Wait till the chowder — that's *beautiful*."

A stout middle-aged woman in a white nylon dress and an orange calico apron approached the booth. "What can I get you?" No menu was on the table and none was offered.

"Chowder and a cheeseburger?" Alfino asked Rainey.

"I believe just the chowder will do nicely, thank you."

Rainey waited until she felt sure the woman was out of hearing before she spoke. "Mr. Alfino — "

"I wish you wouldn't call me that." He sounded aggrieved.

"Please — "

"I know, I know . . . you don't believe in mixing business with pleasure." He hunched his shoulders and seemed to duck his rather large bald head. "But you did come out for lunch with me. How come?"

"I had nothing to offer you at home," Rainey said.

Alfino raised his mournful eyes and smiled. "You're honest, I'll say that for you."

"I'm afraid I never learned not to be. I'm a solitary person, Mr. Alfino. I've not had much need for tact and pleasantries."

"You went to college."

Rainey felt accused by the flat statement. "That has nothing to do with it."

"Don't get your back up. I just meant you talk like a person with education."

"A young ladies' seminary. In Boston."

"A seminary... you mean like a priest? What, were you going to be a missionary or something?"

"A seminary was like a finishing school, Mr. Alfino."

"Yeah? Are you finished?"

She smiled.

"What'd they teach you there, on the level?"

"To speak like an educated person. Tact and pleasantries, too, I suppose... but I lacked the aptitude. Or have forgotten, perhaps."

"You're all right," the detective said. "Pleasant enough for me."

"Thank you." She felt flustered, like a schoolgirl.

"I'm going to college myself. Community college. Nights. Getting an associate's degree in accounting."

Rainey blinked. "Why, that's very... commendable."

"Incredible, you mean." He laughed. "I'm 64."

"You look a good deal younger."

"Lady, you say you got no tact?"

Rainey squirmed uncomfortably, and the vinyl seat padding under her squeaked. "You said we had business to discuss?"

Alfino's face resumed its somnolent expression. "I haven't been able to turn up a thing."

"I didn't expect it to be simple."

"Did you expect it to be expensive? Because I gotta tell you, the hours are mounting up."

She raised her chin. "I'll decide when I can no longer afford your services."

"Hey, don't get me wrong — I can use the work. But this could take months, and even then, it might be a blind alley. I'm just trying to be honest with you."

"Of course . . ."

"I hate wasting your money, when it'd be so easy to get you a divorce without finding your . . ."

"Husband," Rainey said firmly. "I am still married to him."

"Sure. And you don't want to be — that I can understand. What I don't understand is — "

242

"You don't need to understand," she snapped.

The detective's nostrils and lips pinched, drawing together as if a swift and shocking blow had been dealt to him. The waitress returned, and Rainey looked away. Plates, bowls, and glasses were set on the black Formica table with unnecessary clatter.

Rainey felt sorely distressed by her unintentional sharpness. "I'm sorry," she murmured.

"You're right, though, it's none of my business — that part of it."

The waitress sauntered off again.

"I suppose that I *do* want you to understand." The admission was clearly difficult for her.

"Never mind."

"He left me, so he should divorce me . . . people must take responsibility for what they do."

"You loved him?"

Rainey looked severely at Franklin Alfino. He waited, watching her face with eyes that were alert under half-lowered lids.

"I did," she said finally. "But what's important is that I promised myself to him. And John Amos Dudley promised himself to me. Whether I loved him is beside the point, Mr. Alfino. I have kept my promise for 39 years."

Alfino shrugged. "No disrespect . . . but what's divorce gonna get you now?"

"Very little, I suppose you might say. But I've reached an age where I don't care to leave loose ends."

Franklin Alfino picked up a dented soup spoon and stirred thick white chowder in a gray plastic bowl. Behind wisps of steam, his face was troubled. Rainey reached for the pepper. Neither of them started eating.

"May I ask you a question . . . a personal question, Mr. Alfino?"

"Shoot."

"What makes you go to college? Do you intend to become an accountant?"

His cheeks seemed to sag when he smiled, and the dark pockets under his eyes deepened. "I'm a little old to start over." He picked up a greasy saltshaker and held it, right-side-up, over his soup. "But I'm not . . . 'finished.' Certain things still interest me, things I'd like to understand. . . . I never really had a chance to learn them until now."

"Precisely." Rainey nodded. "I want John Amos Dudley to look me in the eye."

"You think if he does you'll understand something?"

"I rather doubt it."

"But you'd have a chance to try?"

"I believe we understand each other, Mr. Alfino."

The detective leaned across the table and gently tucked a paper napkin inside the high collar of Rainey's blouse. The bristly back of his hand brushed her cheek. "Your chowder's getting cold," he said. "Eat."

Several weeks passed with no word from Alfino. Rainey was not surprised, but she was restless. She kept busy. She kept her feet on the ground. And she kept thinking of John Amos Dudley, who had courted her in a late Indian summer like this one, wed her the first week of Advent. Rainey had worn a silk shantung suit the color of champagne — it was wartime, and Chantilly and satin were considered frivolous. Her bouquet of white tea roses was bordered with lavender and rosemary. Lavender for luck, rosemary for remembrance.

John Amos Dudley was a local boy made good by war. A lieutenant commander in the Navy stationed at Quonset Point, he fought the enemy on paper. He was tight-lipped and clear-eyed when Rainey's father inquired about the specific nature of his duties.

Rainey met him at a tea dance at the Watch Hill Yacht Club on the last summer weekend of 1942. His dress whites were impeccably tailored and pressed, and his eyes were the color of the hazy horizon over Montauk. They waltzed — something by Victor Herbert, she recalled — and the plum-colored sleeves of Rainey's afternoon gown had fluttered in three-quarter time against the uncompromising white of Commander Dudley's shoulders.

Now the extraordinary warmth and fragrance of Indian summer revived her whirlwind romance, her scant months as a wife — continuing to live with her widowed father in the large shingled house on the pond at Haversham, while John angled for weekend leave. She had still felt like a bride when the bridegroom vanished, abandoning her, the war effort, and the United States Navy for bluefish, Block Island, and the spirit that moved him.

"The spirit that moved him" — even now, nearly four decades later, Rainey realized that she lacked the frailest notion what such a spirit might have been. On their wedding night, in a large cherry spool bed in the guest room at Haversham, John had wept in her arms, confessing his longing to be a warrior of the sea. He had petitioned to be sent to the South Pacific, attached to a cruiser or battleship. The Navy's continued refusal to make him a hero perplexed and unmanned him. Rainey had stroked his wet cheeks, reassuring him of his manliness, secretly hoping to conceive a son as the proof her husband needed.

By late spring John Amos Dudley had his assurances: he received orders to join a heavy cruiser in the Aleutian Islands, and Rainey was carrying his child. In June, three days before he was to ship out, he sailed in a rented skiff toward Block Island, alone, with fishing gear borrowed from Rainey's father. Weeks later, when the postcard had come, Dr. Roth had quietly paid the owner of the skiff and purchased new fishing tackle. Rainey, at three and a half months, had miscarried the child she had been so certain was a son. She understood that the man to whom she had promised herself was a coward. Beyond that, however, "the spirit that moved him" eluded her.

It was a chilly, overcast morning, and she was standing with her back to the heater, pasting handlettered labels on bottles of chive blossom vinegar, when Franklin Alfino returned. She did not hear him approach until he opened the door, setting her glass wind chimes clashing.

"Good heavens!" A handful of bright paper squares flew from her hands and floated to the floor.

The detective squatted awkwardly and began to gather up the scattered labels. "Scare you? Sorry."

"Startle a body out of her wits," Rainey muttered.

Alfino straightened up and gave her a mildly reproving look.

"Don't mind me," she said.

"Get up on the wrong side of the bed?"

"It's getting up that matters." She tried to sound businesslike. "Have you something to report . . . or do you just happen to be 'in my neck of the woods' again?"

"I've found him."

"Where?"

"I don't know how to say this tactfully."

"Never mind that. Where is he?"

"In New Bedford. In a cemetery."

Rainey Roth stared at Franklin Alfino. Her eyes, glistening with anger, were fiercely blue. "He's dead?"

"Almost 15 years. I'm sorry . . . "

Her lips flattened out in a hard, straight line.

"Maybe it's just as well," Alfino said uncertainly.

Rainey replied slowly, in a choked voice, "It simply is not . . . acceptable." She started to get up. Then, without warning, her mouth framing a small silent "o" of distress, she slumped to the floor in a dead faint.

245

Rainey came to like a person taking charge of a small emergency. "Don't fuss. I'm fine." When she sat up, too quickly, the color drained from her face. She dropped back against the soft cushions upon which Franklin Alfino had placed her. "I'm perfectly all right."

The detective wrapped the soiled sleeves of his raincoat around her shoulders. "Now just take it easy for a few minutes."

"I never faint . . . must be coming down with something."

"A shock. Want some water?"

"What happened to him?"

"We'll talk about that later."

"We'll talk about it now, Mr. Alfino."

"You ought to — "

"Now," she repeated.

Alfino sighed. "Seems he drank himself to death. Put in a state institution in '65, died within a year. He was buried there. No living relatives, he told them."

Miss Rainey Roth closed her eyes, nodding weakly.

"You sure you're all right?"

"He never even looked me in the eye." She turned her face to the rough, stern sofa back, and the detective realized that she was weeping.

"It's finished," he said softly. "You're rid of him."

"No," she whispered. "I am not."

The following week, Rainey sent a sizable check to Franklin R. Alfino, Private Investigator, for services rendered. Her feet were on the ground, her unfortunate past dead and buried. She tried to summon up satisfaction over the loose ends snipped from her life, and she kept about her work. In her herb garden, only the rue — that bitter shrub symbolizing repentance and said to restore second sight — remained green. She cut it back, pausing to bruise a handful of leaves and rub their oil on her forehead, for her head often ached.

Something had come over Rainey Roth of Wyoming, Rhode Island. Mary Alice Potter, the town librarian, marked the change. Rainey looked well enough, but her step seemed slightly less determined, her shoulders less straight. When she addressed the Friends of the Library, her ideas did not seem quite so "definite," Mary Alice said. The lines in her face were deeper yet softer, as if sorrow had won a victory over disapproval.

In short, Miss Rainey Roth had been widowed.

The first Sunday of Advent was bitingly cold. A furious wind lashed the last leaves from the trees and brought small branches down with them. Wearing a black gabardine coat which had hung in the back of her closet for a dozen years, Rainey drove to New Bedford.

She had called Franklin Alfino the day before for directions to the hospital. At first he had refused to give them to her.

"What do you want to do that for?" he said. "Let the past stay buried."

"This is *my* concern," Rainey told him.

"Mine, too.'"

"Why should you make it your business?"

"Like I told you, good lady, some things still interest me."

In the end, however, Alfino had given the directions and even offered to accompany her. Rainey had turned him down with unaccustomed gentleness. "I must do this myself. It's between me and — "

"Your husband," he said. "I understand." He sounded sad and old.

The state hospital was located to the west of the city, several miles off a straight, little-used highway. The cemetery, Alfino had told her, was to the left of the main gate, behind a grove of pines.

There were no other visitors in the graveyard, a small square tract of land monotonous with rows of plain markers. Rainey had no trouble finding the plot she wanted. It was identified by a gray granite slab the size of a dress box: J.A. Dudley, 1917–1966.

Wind tore through the trees. There was faint music from a nearby hospital building, but it could be heard only when the wind paused. Rainey stood beside the grave of her late husband, studying the two lines of letters and numbers meant to memorialize him, trying to recall his face.

But even now, John Amos Dudley refused to look her in the eye. The face of the young lieutenant commander was darkly tarnished and dim, and the 49-year-old drunkard buried here was unimaginable to her. Only a dazzling white sleeve and the color of the sky over Montauk came back to her. Rainey waited. Behind the wind she thought she detected a waltz. But even as she listened, she knew she was making it up . . . as deftly as she had made up the contentment of her life.

When the breeze abated, the music made itself plain. A march — John Philip Sousa, if she wasn't mistaken. The false heartiness of parades and toy soldiers. Rainey straightened her shoulders and gave a little shake of her head. Then she opened her handbag to remove a small pouch of unbleached muslin.

The dried herbs, mixed that morning, were comfortably rough and

247

familiar to her fingers. She shook them from the sack, cupping them in the palm of her right hand. Then, when the wind picked up again, she tossed the handful of earth-tone bits and pieces into the swells of air. They flew from her hand and seemed to rise over her head before they dropped unevenly upon the final resting place of her estranged and long-gone husband:

> Rosemary for remembrance . . .
> Thyme for courage . . .
> And rue, the herb of grace.

The Odor of Fish

•

T HE WHARF IS GONE now, charred to the water line. All that
remains are the stumps of a few pilings, smooth-worn and black
as the heads of seals, and the shells of some dories grown up in
brush so thick you have to know where to look to find them. There's a fish
cooperative where the packing plant stood — a low, whitewashed building
with several long ramps — that already looks ancient, though it can't be
more than a dozen years old; and the plant-owned houses, once as
stooped and gray as rheumatic old women, are now privately owned and
restored.

I don't get up that way much anymore, to Port Clyde Harbor where I
grew up. My parents are gone now, too. My father, just before he died,
worked up the coast in Warren for a company that built dragging nets,
while my mother, her hands knotted from years of work in the fish-
packing houses, spent her time at home knitting bait bags and lobster-trap
heads she sold to the local lobstermen. I live in Boston now, where I write
for a newspaper, and Sharrie, my sister, is a housewife in Illinois — both of
us far from the village in Maine. It's been 30-odd years since I was a boy
and since she worked her first summer in the fish-packing plant.

In those days my father, a tough, bitter man who didn't own his boat,
ran a trawler for the port. He'd be miles "outside" — the word then used
for the sea beyond our harbor — long before the whistle, a shrieking blast,
called the villagers to work at 6:30. At the whistle, my mother — a hale

woman with blue eyes and hair the color of beach sand — would bind her fingers with sticky, gray protective tape, while my sister tried to vomit so she wouldn't have to go in that day. In the dim light of the bathroom in the house we rented, I can see her still: her narrow shoulders hunched over the toilet bowl, her face pale as straw. My mother had cut Sharrie's red hair as short as mine so it wouldn't be in her way when she packed, and it curled around her ears and against the nape of her neck.

She was 16 that summer, when packers were either women or teen-agers, and when workdays could be 12 to 16 hours long, depending on the load of the carrier. Some held 2,000 bushels of fish, and packers worked until they were gone, often dragging from the packing rooms at nine or ten o'clock — no overtime, no bonus, and another carrier to unload the next morning. Since the fish were perishable, labor laws didn't apply.

Every morning but Sunday, packers waited in the half-dark packing rooms between long rows of rusting tables until the fish were pumped to conveyors. Then, on a shout from the overseer, they took their places. The conveyor belts keened in distress; 200 pairs of scissors clacked. The pumps chattered and whined over the sound of the grinding wheels where scissors-blades were sharpened, over the full-voiced yells of the workers as they tried to talk above the din. They stood all day at the waist-high tables. The woman nearest the conveyor, the scooper, slid her arm inside a rubber-lipped shunt and pulled down herring or sardines — occasionally an eel or a jellyfish — stiff with rigor mortis, preserved with salt. The vapor burned her eyes. Her partner, the woman opposite, picked cans from a conveyor belt above eye level, unable to see the ragged edges as she reached for them. Her hands were marked with tiny cuts that stung, then itched, when the salt seeped into them.

Besides scooping or picking cans, each packer scissored heads and tails and packed the fish belly up, five per can, not too full or slack. For a case of a hundred cans, she received fifty-five cents. She earned minimum wage, $1.05 at the time, or she lost her job. A good packer like my mother could earn $2.20 an hour. She got her whole body into a rhythm, didn't talk except to scream for more cans from supply, never looked up or away. But Sharrie could not make minimum wage, even with my mother and friends helping out now and then. She studied each fish, watched the clock. At her turn to be the scooper, she cried, clenching the sleeve of her Banlon sweater so the fish wouldn't touch her skin. When she walked home through the streets lit by window lamps — shuffled, really, as though she were still on the slippery floor of the packing room — the coral-pink sweater sleeve hung to her knees.

250

To me she seemed silly. I was 10 that summer, yet to know the frustrations of breakdowns or late carriers — dead time for which there was no pay — yet to learn of layoffs when fishing was poor. I spent my days crabbing with Jacky Wallace or listening to the talk of the old men on the wharf. Two generations separated many of them from my father, who called them idlers. He had no time for Sharrie's queasy stomach or for the old men's stories I found so wonderful — about the Coffin family who invented doughnuts that turned themselves in the cooking fat and jumped out when they were done, about the man who fashioned a curved rifle barrel so efficient that when he shot from his door he had to pull his head in quick to escape the bullet whizzing around the house.

The wharf, which stood down the harbor from the fish-packing plant, was a place full of wood smell and tar smell. It seemed to me time had stopped there, or at the very least had paused. The afternoon sun warmed your back and your neck and the planks at your feet, and a breeze often blew from the harbor. Though the old men still worked — and worked hard, to be sure, building lobster pots from red oak, painting marker buoys, and repairing hogshead bait barrels — they found time to swap yarns about the days before engines when lobstermen hauled their traps by hand and fished from Friendship sloops. They spoke their own language — a clear day, the ocean smooth as glass, they called a "grandmother's day"; rain with wind and chop, "some buggerish out there." Sometimes they argued the best way to cook sea-moss pudding.

Lester Eckstrom was the oldest, the senior member of the wharf, and when he spoke the others gave serious ear, but often grinned and wisecracked, too. "Was out in a dory," Eckstrom might say. "First thing I hauled up a pot and this great big lobster was hanging on it, come up and bit that boat in two." Somebody, maybe Stilly Orcutt, would finish the tale: "Lester jumped in the stern, you know, and sculled that half to shore!" And someone else might holler over from his workbench, "By gol he's here to tell about it!"

He was white haired, a slightly built man, and he could walk at a pace that made me gasp. He gave every corner and field its own peculiar name and history — here an Indian massacre; there a witch was tried and hanged; no one lives in the Baum house because footsteps are heard there at night. He could point to pocks in the shore dug by hunters of pirate treasure, and to ledges where ships had sunk.

"Did you ever *see* a pirate?" I once asked, as I tagged along after him.

He stopped and turned to look at me, narrowing his eyes. "Pirates," he said, "and plenty of them."

I thought it over as we walked. "What about a ghost?"

"Yes, sir, and ghosts," he said, and I took him at his word. With its mists and fog and black water at night, the Maine coast seemed a likely place for such things.

In his top vest pocket Eckstrom carried sharks' teeth turned to stone by the sea. Some were triangular, the size of his fingernail, others heart shaped and as large as the first joint of his thumb. All were polished by the tides, were cool and surprisingly heavy. I watched him search for the teeth in tide pools, bending every few steps to finger the sand, hunkering down on rocks, and sometimes he'd weigh a stone in his hands, turn it this way and that like a jeweler with a gem. He sold the teeth to a man in Martinsville who set them into bracelets, necklaces, and ashtrays, marketed for sale in Old Orchard Beach.

He knew the species of his fossils, Blue Shark or Porbeagle, and he liked to explain how the seas dissolved the original tooth, leaving minerals in its size and shape. Certain times were best for finding fossils: after a northeaster when the slate-gray ocean churned up spars, wooden kegs and crates, strips of linoleum, every kind of fish; and with the extreme tides of the new and old moons. I learned to listen for trawler warnings on the radio, secretly glad when my father cursed the weather and the loss of a fishing day, and I learned the cycles of the moon. My collection of teeth numbered 20 or so, though some were broken, and I kept them in an empty peanut butter tub. When I showed them to Lester Eckstrom, he grinned. One of his own teeth was capped with gold.

Most nights after supper I'd take my sharks' teeth from the peanut butter tub and spread them over the kitchen table, organizing them by size or by color — some glossy black, others grayish-white. My mother, when she had washed and dried the dishes, would sit on one of the kitchen chairs beside the front door jamb, where, screwed into the molding, there was a brass hook for knitting bait bags and lobster-trap heads. These she made from sisal twine, stitching with a wooden needle she'd carved herself, knotting and burning the twine ends so quickly it was hard to see how she did it. Near her in the lamplight, Sharrie would read romance novels she'd borrowed from the school library, always so absorbed by the books you'd have to shout before she'd hear you — it made my father furious. He'd sit in his armchair by the radio, listening to the Coast Guard, the night conversations of other fishermen, or just the static of the citizen's band, and he'd sip from a mug of tea.

He wasn't especially tall, maybe five-foot-six, though in my memory, no doubt incorrect, he filled two-thirds of the bed he shared with my mother. His shoulders and arms were thick; I once bragged that he'd lifted a barrel full of fish cuttings from his boat to the wharf (most of the fishermen winched them up), though I'm sure I never saw him perform the feat. He had run his boat aground — the boat that had belonged to his father — when he'd missed the entrance to the harbor in a storm.

He was, as I've said, a bitter man.

The last week in July had been one of those still, hot weeks when tensions between people get as heavy as the air. Fishing had fallen off. My father complained nightly: 20 draggers in a mile square, draggers up from the Carolinas and down from New Brunswick. Carriers, when they came in, sat high in the water, half-loaded, watermarks dry; days were lost in dead time at the packing plant.

I sat at the kitchen table, counting and arranging my sharks' teeth, feeling the coolness of them on my fingertips. My mother knitted by the door, trying to catch what breeze there was, while Sharrie lay on the rug propped on her elbows over a book. My father sat in his armchair. He cursed suddenly, angered by something he'd heard on the radio, and I turned to see him hit the switch with the heel of his hand. My mother turned, too, with a look of quiet apprehension, her needle poised above her lap. She watched as he sat forward and ran his fingers through his dark brown hair. Then, as he eased back, she resumed her knitting. A little later he got up and lumbered out to the porch, where I could hear him chafing the sole of his boot on the pine planks. When he came back in, letting the screen door slam behind him, he stood beside my mother, thumbs in his pants waist.

"About time for bed then, ain't it?" he said.

My mother looked surprised — it was early yet, even for a family who'd be up before light. But she lifted her knitting from the hook on the jamb, stood, and placed the twine and needle on her seat. I gathered up my sharks' teeth, snapped the lid on the peanut butter tub, and behind me felt silence. I slid from the chair. My father stood over my sister, scowling, shaking his head, his hands fisted. My mother quickly knelt and touched her shoulder. Sharrie glanced up like someone startled from a dream and, seeing my father, flinched.

The next morning I was wakened by the smell of dead fish. In the dim light I could taste it; waves of it would be rising from the carrier holds like steam. In the kitchen I sat at the table while my mother fried eggs, her fingers already bound. My father had gone. When the whistle blew, she called Sharrie from the bottom of the stairs, the spatula in her hand. My sister didn't answer, but soon I heard her step on the stairs, and she dragged into the room.

"Mama, the smell," she said. She lowered herself into the chair beside me.

My mother didn't look from the pan on the stove. She turned, slid two eggs onto Sharrie's plate, and dunked the pan in the sink where it hissed. Sharrie cut the eggs into triangles and pushed them with her fork in the runny yolk.

"Tape's on the stool when you're through," my mother said. At the counter she spooned jelly onto a slice of white bread and placed another on top. She wrapped the sandwich in waxed paper and dropped it into a bag.

Sharrie's fork clinked to the table. She held her head in her hands and whined, her red bangs hanging over her plate.

"Don't forget the dishes," my mother said to me, and swung around with the lunch sack. "I'll wait on the porch." She pushed open the door.

Sharrie sat still, staring at the tabletop. Then she skidded back her chair and picked up the tape.

"Sissy," I whispered.

She spun to face me, her blue eyes gleaming. As she went out she let the screen door slam.

I washed and stacked the breakfast dishes and took out my tub of sharks' teeth. I was about to lay my fossils on the table when Jacky hollered in. A freckled boy, his skin covered with dust, he stood on the porch with a broken fish-pole, his long-handled net, and a bucket of fish heads he'd freshened in the sun.

Passed only by a bus hauling commuters to the plant, we hiked half a mile to a backwater bridge. There, with the bait tied to a string at the end of the pole, Jacky lured the crabs to the surface, where I slipped the net under their swimming legs and hoisted them, pinching, into the air. By noon, as the water beneath the bridge became a stream trickling through black mud, we left our sport.

At home I fixed a sandwich and stuffed it down, jelly oozing between my fingers, then trotted through town toward the harbor. The roofs of the neighborhood sloped; the houses sat on rotting sills. Near the packing plant the sound of engines pumping fish from carriers — a low rumble punctuated by metal screeching against metal — shook the ground. I headed for an island where I had often followed Lester Eckstrom, walked the path to a cliff that jutted into the sea, and the noise and smell were gone. From the motionless crescent of his boat, a lobsterman checked his traps.

I climbed down rock to the stringy mounds of seaweed. The current swept into crags, water ferns washing back and forth. In my sneakers I stepped in, careful not to stir the sand. Stooping and pushing rocks with my toe, I searched the bottom, occasionally plunging my arms to pull up a stone.

In an hour I'd found nothing; in two, a pebble speckled red that I folded into a handkerchief. The tide was rising and the sun shone hot through the haze. My T-shirt stuck to my back. On hands and knees I crawled over the seaweed, stood to scale the rocks. And there at my feet, as if it had meant to bite the shore, I saw the tooth — a wedge of gray stone half the size of my fist.

I weighed it, first in one hand, then in the other. I held it between my thumb and forefinger and pressed it into my dungarees, wincing as I imagined it biting through my leg. I opened the handkerchief, placed the tooth carefully on top of the pebble, and folded the handkerchief again. I pushed it deep into my pocket and ran for the wharf.

Stilly Orcutt was there alone. He sat on a bucket in a flannel shirt, bent over a smoldering cigarette. Beyond him, on the water, a dory rocked at its mooring.

"Eckstrom!" I yelled, so excited and out of breath I couldn't think of what else to say.

Stilly, a bald, round-shouldered man, lifted his head and regarded me. "Ain't seen him," he said.

I turned and headed for town.

The boardinghouse was a three-story building with a mansard roof. On a bench set against its peeling clapboards sat the men my father called idlers — Griffin Alberts, Harley Maling, and others who lived there. They were quiet. One picked his tooth with a nail; another spat brown saliva to a dark spot in the dirt. Away from the wharf they'd lost their air of consequence.

Standing to one side of them, I asked for Eckstrom. A younger man, large and red faced, motioned to the doorless threshold. "Second floor," he said. "Two B."

I edged past them.

The stairwell led to a narrow hallway where a shaded window cast yellow light onto two doors along the far wall. I saw that neither bore numbers or letters, and a vague feeling of dread passed over me; I chose the left. Stacks of newspapers lay beside it, a shopping bag crammed with empty soup cans. I knocked softly. A swarm of gnats flitted from the bag. I knocked again, and waited. Nothing.

I made my way downstairs, into the sunlight, where I was startled by the high voice of the red-faced man: "Find him?"

I touched the handkerchief in my pocket. I meant to go home, but turned and shook my head.

Hands on his knees, he heaved himself up and yanked out a key chain. He motioned me to follow. We moved slowly up the stairs as he paused for breath on each step. At the door he banged and then tried the knob — open. Inside, a rubber boot stood upright on the broad floor planks near a clothes tree layered with khakis and flannels. Beyond, there was a small table littered with a bowl and plate, a can opener and spoons. In one corner a cot lay thick with blankets.

The man lumbered forward, dust spinning in slow motes behind him in the yellow light. He leaned over the cot. "Hey," he said, and prodded the blankets. "Eckstrom!" he said, prodding again. And then he straightened as if he'd been slapped.

I stood for a moment, confused. The man turned, gesturing with his hands as if to apologize, and through the heat it came in on me, an odor like fish. I stepped backward and ran from the room.

That night the heat had not let up. Fishing had improved — "turned itself around," as my father put it — though he seemed not much happier than the night before. We ate silently, the four of us, until my mother felt my forehead to see whether I was well: I could not finish my supper.

"Don't you get like your sister," my father said. He stared at Sharrie as he chewed. She sat still, head down, hands hidden beneath the table; she had eaten only a biscuit and some apple sauce. I said nothing, watching the muscles of my father's jaw work a bite of Spam.

Later I sat in my room, the peanut butter tub — the large tooth inside — unopened in the glow of the lamp. My mother had sent me early to bed. Downstairs, she must've been knitting at the door, her chair faced into the night, while Sharrie lay beside her, lost in a book. My father would have been seated in his chair, arms squared, or maybe cupping a mug of tea in his hands. I remember a murmur of voices, then quiet. All at once, over the static of the radio: "I'd be happy I *had* the job . . ." followed by Sharrie's quick step on the stairs, ". . . and a roof over my head!" he shouted after her. His voice rang, menacing, up the stairwell.

Sharrie's sobs came through the wall — her room, next to mine. The radio clicked off, my father said something to my mother, and the back door slammed. Slowly, quiet returned to the house, settling in like fog. Without knowing why, I left my room and crept through the hall. I found my sister sprawled on the bed.

256

"Sharrie?" I stood beside her. She lay still. "Sharrie?"

She rolled to her side. "What do you want?"

I stood by the bed, unable to answer. "I don't know," I said, and the tears started suddenly down my face.

She sat up, staring, and then she put her arms around me. She rocked me and smoothed my hair. I remember her breath on the top of my head. And in the dark, against my neck, I felt the damp sleeve of her sweater rolled tightly above her elbow.

At Flood's End

•

BY IAN MACMILLAN

THIS BAD WEATHER always reminds me of that time when Henderson's bridge was just a way of getting over the brook, and our road was dirt rather than macadam. Now, all newly painted with its shingle roof repaired, the bridge is a tourist attraction that stands next to a low sweep of cement over the brook, and our road is marked on the map as a major highway crossover. The only time in recent years that the brook ever rose and expanded into the proportions of a river was in 1958, back in the days when we cut cord and pulpwood and boiled maple sap for a living, and my grandfather Frank Hammond was still alive. He's been dead nearly 20 years, but a few people still remember him from the old days as the premier fiddler of the area.

During those weeks preceding the flood, only the very young and very old failed to be distracted by the heavy weather — the rippling little brook was suddenly a calm flow, no longer bouncing down the spherical rocks but expanding up its banks and almost smooth on its surface, muddy and swirling gently with little eddies and whirlpools. I was 25 and old enough to understand the danger this meant to any house on the brook banks. My younger brother Steve, whose life revolved around sports and girls, couldn't care less, especially that week, because he and Carol Parker, whose house sat at the outside of the bend in the brook 200 yards down from us, were going to a Friday night dance at the high school. It was a big occasion for them because the band was coming in from

Boston and was famous in the region. Carol sat all week in her room only 30 feet from that water and made herself a gown for the dance, and Steve spent most of his time in front of the bathroom mirror, bit by bit and day by day emptying a bottle of greasy white lotion onto his head, attempting to educate his rebellious hair into the proper backward sweep, with the forward and upstanding wave in front, James Dean style. You could smell him from two rooms away.

And then there was the old man. While my father and mother and I and Mr. and Mrs. Parker stood outside each day speculating on the swelling brook, he sat half-dozing in front of the television set watching daytime movies and waiting for sunset and his favorite shows — "Armstrong Theater," "Your Hit Parade," and "Colgate Comedy Hour." He would sit smoking handrolled cigarettes, depositing the ash on his pant leg and then rubbing it into the fabric with the heel of his hand, an old habit. He always went around with the gray streak on his left pant leg. He had long since misplaced his legendary fiddle up in the attic along with his Great War uniform and his old hunting rifles. We got the TV in 1954, and that was the last year he did anything. Before that he still split stovewood with our old radio blaring in the background, but the TV finally alienated him from the practical issues of the day, and if this was his way of going out to pasture, especially since he had made it comfortably into his eighties, then it was fine with us.

The Parkers were more vulnerable to the brook than we were. What worried Stu most was the new wing on his house, and as we talked, planning strategy in case the water came up any further, we did it either with the humming of Carol's sewing machine in the background, or up at our house, with the flat blaring of the TV and the occasional wafting of the smell of Steve's lotion from the windows. You could see his problem easily. The brook-turned-river swept in a gentle horseshoe past the corner of Parker's wing, slowly pulling chunks of sod into the water. If the brook stayed as it was, fine, but the conditions of early spring suggested to us that it wouldn't — the woods had huge pools of water everywhere and the mountain snow to the north still held in massive drifts, and it was raining more than usual. Further, as soon as the frost in the ground melted, the road quickly turned into a slowly deepening trough of muck, a mud so heavy and inert that it would become worse than snow and force us to go from car to truck to tractor in order to get out to buy groceries. By midweek we were already in the truck stage, meaning it was warming up too fast. The road didn't bother Steve and Carol at all, except for her fear that some of the chainsaw oil all over the truck might get on her dress.

259

That new wing meant a lot to Stu Parker. Like us, he scratched out a living just a hair to the good side of basic subsistence, and he couldn't afford repairs or replace footings or joists he feared the brook would suck away. He had awful visions of warped hardwood floors, stained planks. By the time the edge of the brook was only 15 feet from the corner and the soft rapping of the sewing machine, he was spending a lot of his time standing there watching it, sometimes in the rain and sometimes in the meager sun that poked through the overcast sky, looking like a flat, silver disc crossed by moving clouds. Once I walked to the edge where the sod was splitting away and felt the ground under me mush and sink. I jumped away and watched another piece of his lawn curl slowly into the brown water.

"See what I mean, Pete?" he said. "It's underground, like the road, just like a sponge. Anytime now the footings sink."

"What about moving some rocks and making a kind of dam? Kind of shore things up around the footings?"

"Might work, might not." He pushed his cap back on his head. "Might's well try, though. I'm sure tired of just watching it."

My father's back was bad, so we decided not to ask him. "I'll get Steve."

Parker laughed. "Let him alone. He's not worth much now. If he leans over his hair'll tip him down on his face."

"Hah. Yeah, he is a little top-heavy these days."

We built a little protective nape around the base of the wing with parts of a fieldstone wall buried in bramble on the woods side of his house. That was Thursday afternoon, and it rained that night and half of Friday morning, the day of Steve and Carol's dance. Steve was into his second bottle of lotion and the James Dean sweep was up there above his forehead like a big hood ornament. He stood and growled with frustration at the few disobedient cowlicks behind that oozing sweep, his arms exhausted, so that he would periodically let them flap limply against his sides.

I spent the day helping Stu Parker — the brook was up another foot, and shallow water lapped at the rock nape of the new footings. Around midday we began seeing objects in the water — planks, logs, predictable things. But then the unpredictable came by — first, Ball canning jars of tomatoes bobbed along in a line, their covers up, dancing in the eddies. Then came a basketball, a sawhorse, and a doghouse. Parker kept looking from the brook to the wing, thinking.

"See, you go down a little flight of stairs to get in there," he said. "Two steps. I should have built on the up side."

"Hey, what's that?"

"Quilt, looks like." It was, rolling to the surface and then sweeping under, looking like the back of a huge, tattered fish.

"Must be worse upstream," he said. "What about the bridge?"

"Nah — good six, seven feet above the water."

Then we heard the sewing machine again and Carol humming while putting on the finishing touches. Inside of an hour, blissfully oblivious to the brown, sweeping water, she emerged from the house, and I knew what all the elaborate preparations were for. "Hey," I whispered, "is that — "

Parker looked, then went a little gape-mouthed. "God almighty," he said. She wouldn't look at anybody. Instead she gazed around with haughty nonchalance, holding the paper bag where her heels were. She now wore drab green hunting boots.

Then my father came up with the truck. Steve got out all done up, with that sweep finally in place and gleaming. They looked completely out of place, as if they had stepped out of a magazine ad, and climbing daintily into the rusted, green-cabbed International flatbed, she looked even more out of place. They left us to our problem, their tires hissing in the mud and flicking bits of it back at us. We were still scratching our chins and watching more boards and barrels and tree limbs going by when my father came back, half-running, his hand on his side as if to hold his back in place. He looked a little white.

"Stuck," he wheezed, going toward our house. A little later he went off on the Farmall, bouncing over the ruts, standing up before the wheel to cushion the shocks.

"She's going to get awfully dirty standing on the drawbar," I said.

Parker shook his head. "Look at it, it's up another two, three inches."

"Listen, if they don't make that bus there'll be all kinds of trouble. I better help."

We hadn't bothered to check the road because of our concern for the brook, and as soon as I saw it, trudging along with the muck sucking at my boots, I knew that the kids didn't have a chance in the world. The truck was in over its axles, and my father tried loosening it from the mud, driving the tractor on the edge of the road, one back tire up by the barbwire fence and the other in the deep remains of tire trenches. He spun the back wheels, creating around them sprays of flying mud, and the chain attached to the truck remained slack.

Carol stood on a firm hummock clutching the bag of shoes so that her knuckles were white, and she looked off toward the hard road, her face held in an expression of fearful desire. Steve danced around the truck

261

yelling instructions to my father. When he tried to back up, the close-set tires in front slid down into the little drainage ditch at the road's edge. Once those little tires with the engine's full weight on them got stuck, I knew we wouldn't get even the tractor out. When he turned off the motor and got down shaking his head in disgust, I heard Carol say, "It's three miles. That's what it is — the hard road's just three miles."

"We can walk," Steve said, "hitchhike maybe. Maybe the bus is late."

"Ma'll never let me. I know it. She won't."

"Listen," I said, "let's run on back and see. I'll call into town, maybe get somebody to help, give you a ride."

"Ma'll never let me. Besides the phones don't work. Least they didn't before."

"Let's find out. C'mon."

We never got to help them out. She was right about the phones. They'd probably been dead all day. It was getting dark, the brook had risen more, and now a current was working against our protective nape around the foundation of the wing. You could see the curl and hump of running water against the base of the corner of the room where Carol had made the dress, and 200 yards away upstream, I saw my grandfather standing on high ground watching the water working against our tool shed.

"Now that's still below the water table," Parker said. "Floor's still dry. How much pressure do you suppose is on there?"

I shrugged and found a long stick, and approaching the water along the wall, I paused, shrugged again and figured my feet would be getting wet anyway, and waded toward the moving water. I held the stick and let its tip sink into the curl of current coming off the corner. I couldn't hold the stick in it. "Wouldn't guess it, but it's strong — here."

Parker tried, then shook his head. "Too much," he said. "Comes up a little more and the house'll move, floor'll get all wet." He turned. "Hey, let's get the rug out of — "

No one listened. Carol pleaded with her mother for permission to go, and Steve interceded with promises to make sure everything was okay. But Mrs. Parker wouldn't change her mind. Glancing fearfully at the water now fanning off the corner of the wing, she said that she could not permit them to go hitchhike to a dance 10 miles away and she was sorry it turned out this way. Carol folded her arms and glared at her.

We saw my grandfather coming down along the brook, hunched a little and working along on unsteady legs, which bowed like a wishbone.

"Look there," I said, "real life got Grampa away from the TV."

When he got near us, he seemed to disregard the brook and looked at

Carol and Steve. "What are you kids doing here?"

"Road's gone," Steve said, flapping his hands up and down against his thighs. "All mush."

"You ought to be walking right now," Grampa said. "My lord, she is pretty."

She didn't hear. She looked off in the direction of the hard road.

"Hey, you fellows got time to take these kids?"

"Road's worst I've ever seen it," I said, and the look he gave me made that explanation seem feeble. Grampa then looked with thoughtful sympathy at Carol and scratched his chin. A little later, while we worked at diverting the current away from the house corner in the light of the single, powerful bulb of Parker's spotlight hanging out Carol's window, we saw her again over by the front door of the house, looking at a little watch she wore. Steve had already changed back into his work clothes, the only remaining proof of his earlier intention being the gleaming sweep of hair still held in place, but she still wore the dress, still had the bag with her heels inside nearby. Steve went to talk to her, pat her shoulder. It's funny how things like this happen, but I'm sure she was never really convinced that she wouldn't go. When she knew it was eight and looked off into the blackness, almost seeming to hear that band start off, she turned and ran crying into the house. We heard her door slam a second later, and Steve came back looking a little hangdog in the harsh light.

"That road," he said miserably. "It's all that road."

"Poor kid," I said. Parker wasn't listening.

"It's up more," he said. "It's coming up faster now."

That was the last anything was said about the dance. An hour later we lost our tool shed, just managing to get the stuff out of it before it groaned, squeaked, and folded slowly into the water. That was only the beginning. The current against Parker's wing increased, and each one of our attempts to shore it up against the water, wedging two-by-fours against the side away from the current, piling rocks in the water to try to cut it off, was gradually swept away. We would climb out of the water, soaked now to our waists and cold, and plan something else. Around one o'clock in the morning, Carol poked her head out the window next to the light so that her giant profile blackened one side of the wall, and called, "A rumble! I feel a rumble in the floor, like moving! It feels like being on a train!" Splattering water on the smooth, hardwood floor, we moved out her bed, desk, books, and portable sewing machine, leaving behind the machine's table, an ancient, wrought-iron underframe from one of those old machines like my mother's, with the foot pedal, the kind that kids fool with

263

and pay for like I did, getting the flywheel going and then accidentally putting my foot under the working pedal and banging my toes so hard that the whole table would jump.

You could feel a vibration of moving water in the floor and just hear a funny sigh from the structure itself, like the almost soundless tension you sense just before a tree begins to snap inside at the beginning of falling. The water was sweeping under the house and up against the floor. We rushed out to continue to pile rocks and put up braces in the hip-deep water. Only two of us worked there, because up at our house my father and Steve worked trying to save our outbuildings and their contents. After the tool shed went, we lost an old hay-loader, five cords of cured stovewood, half of our backyard, and an old outhouse.

Parker would not be so lucky. Just before dawn, in water rib-high but blocked from the current by the house and not moving fast enough to pull us in, we heard an unmistakable sound in the wing, the screeching sound of nails being pulled out of wood. Although we could not at first see any movement, we waded out as quickly as we could, just before the house began to cleave, so that the new wing opened into the water like half of a suitcase being opened while sitting on one edge. Mrs. Parker had the presence of mind to run in and get the light out of the window and turn off the electricity before the wing went and the wires would hit the water, and in the pre-dawn blackness we stood dripping on the muddy lawn and watched the house open, the new wing slowly being upended by the water and then folding away into it with that sound of screeching nails and the groaning of wood bent to the point of splitting. As for the old house, it stayed where it had been for the past hundred years, except that now it had a hole where half of the old back wall had been, and inside you could see the dim shape of the dining room table with the chairs neatly placed around it. In all Parker had lost a hallway, stairs, one bedroom, and one bathroom. We would find later, after the stream went down, that the only thing that survived was that heavy old sewing-machine base of Carol's.

When it was clear that the wing was gone down the stream, Parker stood there shivering and said, "That's it."

"Hey," I said, "why not go inside and get some dry clothes on and come on up and have a little breakfast?"

He snorted and went into the house.

I went up to our place to check out the damage and change. The brook swept by in the beginning light of Saturday, still carrying in it the odd objects from upstream. Down below somewhere, I figured, people would see chunks of our outbuildings and Parker's wing sliding by, would pull in free stovewood. We were all exhausted from being up all night, but my mother set to cooking sausages and pancakes, and Steve and I went out to see what else we had lost. All in all we did much better than the Parkers. Just as we saw them coming up along the brook toward our house, my father came out. "Where's Grampa?" he asked.

The simple question gathered all sorts of momentum in a short time. By the time the Parkers had arrived and were milling around out back looking at the spaces where our outbuildings had been, Steve and I were running around yelling his name, both of us convinced that he had washed down the brook too. The scare lasted only a short time. Steve saw a light in the attic window and a shadow moving across it. "What's he doing up there?"

"Beats me — at least he's safe."

Steve went to investigate, and I went to the Parkers'.

"C'mon inside, get some coffee."

They were all sullen and tired-looking. You could tell that Carol had been crying a lot. We stood around in the kitchen waiting for the coffee to perk and talking about replacing what was lost. Parker continued to respond to ideas with hopeless snorts. Carol disappeared to find Steve, leaving us to our conversation.

As bad times go, or tragedies if you want to call it that, this one wasn't much after all. In a year Parker would have another wing built, on the up side of his house this time. Worse times had happened before, and worse ones would happen after. In six years Steve would be killed in Southeast Asia, and a couple after that my father would die. The macadam road would cover the dirt, and that beige sweep of cement would retire the covered bridge and turn it into a tourist attraction. More children would be born, some my own and some Carol's somewhere else in the state. Now it's my mother who dozes before the TV set.

But the end of the misery caused by this flood happened while we stood in the kitchen talking about replacing what was lost. At first we thought somebody turned the radio on, but the sound was too authentic, too close. I went and looked out toward the front of the house, and there sat Grampa with his fiddle playing one of those mournful but beautiful waltzes, while Steve and Carol, out there in the mud of the front lawn, danced to it, laughing at their clumsiness at the old-fashioned step. I hadn't heard the fiddle in 15 years, and the Parkers were brought out of their slump when they heard it, and came to watch, amazed that the old man's fingers were so limber. It was like he'd been practicing in secret every day since he misplaced the fiddle. He finished the waltz, and the kids

265

stood and waited in the copper light of dawn for him to begin the next. He pursed his lips with a look of studious concentration and addressed the strings again, setting the kids to dancing.

We all went out. On the way I stopped at the glass case in the dining room and collected some glasses and a bottle of apple wine. I set the tray on the wicker table on the front porch and poured.

Grampa turned and looked, smacked his lips, limbered his fingers along the strings. "Wine in the morning?" my mother said.

Grampa thought. "It's after six," he finally said, and we all laughed at that, and passed the wine around, and waited for him to go on with his playing. And out there on the muddy lawn the kids stood posed for their formal waltz, almost silhouettes in that rich morning light, their shadows a mile long, clasped hands out, waiting while Grampa lowered his eyebrows and laid his bow on the strings.

A Visit from …

•

BY KATHLEEN LEVERICH

I T IS NOT TRUE THAT he always wears a red suit and drives a team of reindeer. And it is ridiculous to say that he lives at the North Pole. He must be like the wind, like the grass on the ground; he must be everywhere and everywhere be inconspicuous, unremarked. The job requires him to keep a close eye on each one of us, but secretly, so that we don't suspect. He must contribute that sense of security to a place, so that we all relax and are ourselves in his presence, but ineffably, so that no one guesses the reason *why* we can relax: his presence.

Never believe that he enters your life by way of grubby chimneys and cold hearths. That you need do nothing but refrain from lighting a cozy fire, and he will come. That leaving a few stale graham crackers and milk, or even a shot of whiskey and chopped carrot sticks for the reindeer will be enough to attract him. There is more involved than that.

He hates snacks and never drinks alone. He eats large meals of local fare in whatever little village or urban neighborhood he finds himself as mealtime approaches. You can spot him at the crowded table where laughter is robust and conversation intimate, but not self-consciously so. He drinks house wines, beer, and sometimes aquavit — but this is only when it has just finished snowing and the sky is crystal clear. He drinks aquavit and then he goes skating on the river that extends forever.

You can watch him growing smaller and smaller, moving toward the

267

horizon. You wonder, will he ever come back? You grow doubtful, then lonely, then very, very frightened.

Night falls and there is still no sign of him. Probably he has found a more beautiful, a more interesting town, far down the river.

A nasty voice begins to whisper of the dark.

Just then, the door opens. It is he.

This is one time when the overdone remarks about his red cheeks and nose are justified. And his laughter. His laughter. You hear it and you forget your doubts and loneliness; you remember your fright. You run to him and bury your head in his chest. He hugs you.

Later when he smokes his pipe — yes, that part is true, too — and you all gather around his knees like cats and dogs, he will pet you and calm your fears. You will be devoted to him.

This is how it is when you know him, when he reveals himself and you recognize him. That used to happen often, but have you noticed? Such times have grown rarer and rarer as you've grown older.

Maybe it's a game, you think, and he is making it more difficult each year. Perhaps he is simply growing old and tired. Or maybe he isn't as amusing and powerful as you thought when you were younger. Children are easily impressed, after all.

Have you noticed that the presents under the tree are not wonderful anymore? You know what they are before you unwrap them; you can tell by the shapes, because you get only things you've asked for. Nothing else.

Where's his imagination, that used to stun with the fulfillment of unutterable yearnings? A phial of water from the spring at Delphi. An incantation against demonic possession from Swabian gypsies. A Sherpa child's doll that moves in its mind in the Himalayas. You get nothing, these days, but what you've asked for. And what wonders can *you* conceive of, these days?

Telephoto lenses and magazine subscriptions. I closed my eyes as I answered my own question, one snowless mid-December evening. Just then my wife came in, noticeably breathless.

"Write down," she said, "what you'd like for Christmas if you could have *things not of this world*. Make a list, and I will, too," she said. There was a glow in her cheeks, and she was half-whispering. She might have been suggesting some daring thing we should do before our parents came home.

Telephoto lenses and magazine subscriptions. Not even new magazines; she'd just renewed last year's.

"What's the point of that?" I said. Her excitement made me angry.

She looked frightened and went away to baste the roast. I sat at my desk and looked at the empty hearth. I fiddled with a pencil, and doodling, wrote, "What I Want for Christmas" on the top of a sheet of notepaper.

Things not of this world . . .

"A real Santa Claus," I wrote.

"The Collinses have invited us for drinks tomorrow at six." My wife was carrying holly and the crèche figures over to the coffee table. I crumpled the sheet of paper and threw it into the wastebasket.

"Fine," I said.

It never snows anymore.

I went to bed that night feeling hollow. Maybe that's just what he wanted. Maybe it's a game, and he empties us out to fill us up. I lay awake that night and watched the moon rise over the dead lawn. I thought about Christmases when I was a child. I thought of my mother saying to me, "Don't peek in the closet." I had been good; I hadn't peeked inside the boxes, only gazed for long, stolen moments at the presents, stacked on the shelves. Now, as I closed my eyes, I saw my mother. She was as old as she'd been when she died, and she spoke in that short complaining voice, "Where was my closet? Where were my surprises? Did you ever think that I might have inexpressible yearnings, too?"

The next day passed as a dream. I couldn't get my mother's words out of my head. I found myself pacing my office — a thing I never do. My secretary eyed me strangely. Finally lunchtime came. I ducked the crowd from the legal department and went out alone. I had no idea where I was going.

I walked away from the part of town I know. The blocks grew darker and emptier. The wind blew litter along the gutter. It was three days before Christmas, and the sky was threatening rain. It was 45 degrees. Rain.

I passed a door with a cat's-paw decal on the door. A shoemaker. I passed a grocery with stacks of canned garbanzo beans in the window. I passed a door with red curtains covering the top half and a poster paint picture opaquing the bottom. It was a picture of Santa Claus in a sleigh, driving a team of reindeer.

I walked carefully to the end of the block. I argued with myself on the corner for a few moments, then went back.

No one answered when I knocked. I tried the door. It opened. I looked around for someone to accuse me, for someone to stop me. The block was empty, except for people crossing the avenues at either end. I pushed the door farther open and went in.

There was a counter with two dilapidated desks behind it. One had a

269

phone, a blotter, and a pencil holder on it. The other had a typewriter. A bulletin board was tacked all over with what looked like order forms and bills of lading. There were "In/Out" boxes on the counter; both were full, but the "In" box was overflowing.

No one was there. I called out, "Hello" and "Excuse me" and "Can anybody help me?" but no one answered.

The telephone rang and nobody came. I stood waiting. The phone kept ringing. Finally I let out a "Damn it" and went over to answer it myself.

"Walter?" the voice said.

"Who is this?" I asked. My palms were sweating.

"This is Santa Claus, Walter."

Somebody had come into the back room and was shaking bells. There was music, too. I could hear it beginning very faintly at first, but getting louder.

Those clowns from the office —

"You came here strictly on your own, Walter. Remember?"

The voice was familiar. A smell like a bakery or a kitchen at Christmas hit me, and I thought I was going to pass out.

"I've come to town, Walter. I'm very close to you, so you'd better watch out."

I ran out of the little office without putting the phone back on the hook.

The following three days and nights were the worst I'd ever spent. I was afraid all the time. Afraid to be alone, but distracted in company and afraid people might see that I was distracted, frightened — and frightening. I kept hearing the voice on the phone in that little office.

On Christmas Eve while my wife was trimming the tree, I put on my coat and walked out. She called down the hall after me, first angry, then crying. I didn't look back.

I took a taxi downtown, but had it drop me two blocks from the spot, in front of a bar. I thought of going in for a drink, but just looking through the window, through the spray-on snow and tinsel, just seeing the dark figures huddled around the bar in the dim light from the overhead television, stopped me.

I walked down the block. It was windy and, again, felt like rain. It could have been an April evening, except for the occasional holly wreath and burst of canned caroling.

There was a muffled light behind the door. It made the red curtain and the painted Santa Claus glow faintly.

270

I hesitated with my hand on the latch.

I thought of Nat King Cole on the stereo and a fire burning on the hearth. I thought about mixing one big drink and then calling the neighbors in for another. I thought about dimming all the lights, except the ones on the tree, about putting my arms around my wife's neck and pulling her to me. About making love, slightly drunk, and falling into a dreamless, satisfied sleep. In the morning everything would be all right; the worst would be over. Christmas would be almost over; only the predictable presents to unwrap.

My hand tightened on the latch. I pressed it and pushed in.

There was a suit, boots, a hat, and a pipe lying neatly on the swivel chair behind the desk with the typewriter on it. On top of the typewriter was an envelope addressed to me, "Walter."

I put on the suit. It felt extremely comfortable, which surprised me, since I have never felt comfortable in red. My wife bought me a red sport coat one Christmas, and it's still hanging in the closet with the tags on it.

The boots were a perfect fit and didn't cramp my feet or make them hot, as I'd expected they would.

Could I get away with a pipe? I'd always avoided pipes on the theory that I'd look affected smoking one. I put this funny old meerschaum in my mouth and looked around for a mirror. There was one over the water cooler. No hint of affectation at all; it looked like part of my face. But the mass of white hair and the beard were partly responsible. I couldn't have gotten away with it before, but now that I had them . . . all perfectly in character.

Somewhere a church clock chimed.

Eight o'clock. I didn't have all night, I reminded myself. I went back to the desk with the typewriter and picked up the envelope. I heard bells, again in the back room, singing and, this time, tapping, like hooves. They sounded restless.

I pulled my spectacles from my pocket, settled them on my nose, and tore open the envelope.

A million letters tumbled out.

"Dear Santa," written in crayon.

"Dear Santa," in pencil.

It is not true that he always wears a red suit and drives a team of reindeer.

"Dear Santa, Are you coming to my house?"

Little girl, I am your house.

And it is ridiculous to say that he lives at the North Pole.

271

"Dear Santa, What is your real name?"

My real name is Santa, little boy, but people call me Walter and Ann and William and Irene . . .

The job requires him to keep a close eye on each one of us, but secretly, so that we don't suspect.

"Dear Santa, Can you see me? Can you see me when the lights are out and I'm lying alone in the dark?"

You are never alone in the dark.

I am like the wind, little girl. I am like the grass on the ground, little boy. I am in the next room, always. I am at the window, always.

Listen. I am very close.